Vivacity

ELODIE HART

Remember,
We may be messy.
But it doesn't mean we're broken.
Far from it.

Please note that this book contains lengthy discussions of intergenerational trauma, narcissistic parenting, emotional abuse of a child, and therapy. In particular, I use the framework of IFS (Internal Family Systems) and some Inner Child work to help Ethan plumb the depths of his trauma.

I've taken several liberties, most notably that Ethan's therapeutic progress is extremely accelerated! I've done this to avoid having the book be an extra 500 pages long and to keep the story on track, but I'm highly aware that a man as closed off as Ethan would likely have taken many more sessions to open up to his therapist.

The entire manuscript has been read and assessed by a clinical therapist specialising in trauma, and the IFS therapy sessions have also been read and assessed by a highly experienced IFS practitioner and teacher. Any inaccuracies are mine alone.

In terms of sexual content, this book explores light BDSM and exhibitionism. As with the other Seraph books, it is a fantastical exploration of sex work as a kink and in no way attempts to tackle the very real dangers and indignities of sex work in the real world.

I hope you enjoy Soph and Ethan's love story.

Elodie x

(OR: HOW TO PSYCHOANALYSE EVERYONE YOU MEET)

Darling readers, welcome to my favourite party trick!

The Enneagram is an ancient personality system that maps out nine core motivations driving human behaviour. Think of it as a personality framework with deep psychological research behind it—incredibly useful for understanding why your boss is such a controlling nightmare (spoiler: he's probably an Eight like mine).

The Nine Types:

One - The Perfectionist: Everything has a place, and that place is exactly where they say it should be. Lovely people, but exhausting dinner companions who will rearrange your cutlery.

Two - The Helper: Will give you the shirt off their back, then passive-aggressively remind you about it for the next decade. Martyrdom is their love language.

Three - The Achiever: Workaholics who've turned ambition into an art form. Success is their drug of choice, and they'll work themselves into the ground looking effortlessly perfect while doing it. Think most of my fellow seraphim. (Hiiii, Athena!)

Four - The Individualist: Tortured artists who feel everything deeply and make that everybody's problem. Beautiful, dramatic, and convinced no one understands their unique suffering.

Five - The Investigator: Intellectual introverts who retreat into their minds to observe the world from a safe distance. They'd rather understand humanity than actually have to experience it.

Six - The Loyalist: Anxious sweethearts who simultaneously crave security and suspect everyone of plotting against them. Overthinking is their Olympic sport.

Seven - The Enthusiast: That's me! We're the fun ones who turn everything into an adventure because sitting still with uncomfortable feelings is absolutely not happening.

Eight - The Protector: Natural-born leaders who bulldoze through life demanding control. Terrifying in business, magnificent in bed. Looking at you, Ethan.

Nine - The Peacemaker: Lovely, accommodating souls who will agree with everyone to avoid conflict, then wonder why they're invisible. Masters of procrastination and Netflix binges.

Now you're armed and dangerous. Use this knowledge wisely!

XOXO,
Sophia

CHAPTER 1

Ethan

From afar, she is entirely perfect.

Plenty of things are, in fairness.

People.

Relationships.

Lives.

Not much stands up to close scrutiny, though. Most things that look flawless from a distance are, in fact, ugly, stained, with flaws so deep they act like gangrene. Like rot.

And even if she is perfect, she's deep in animated conversation with my former executive assistant, Talia, who's probably telling her at this moment that *I* am like gangrene, so there's that.

'What do you think?' asks the woman by my side, who has undoubtedly earned every penny of her commission from me recently. Having had three executive assistants walk out on me this past year, I've tasked Camille with finding me a fourth. I'm sure she'd cheerfully wring my neck if she wasn't so consummately professional.

'I'd like to meet her.'

I won't give Camille any more than that. In her role as

CEO of the elite agency Seraph, she's as skilled at finding the perfect candidate as any MI5 recruiter, so she doesn't need me to spoon-feed her.

She doesn't need to know that there's one word I'd ascribe to the woman I'm watching across the roof terrace, or that that word is *lush.*

She is lush. She's a fucking rainforest, all curves and hair and eyes, in a way that's unapologetic to the point of being almost indecent. She's not sleek and lean like Talia, or Talia's two predecessors, or my ex-wife, come to that. She's abundant, and perhaps that's what I need. Perhaps I need someone so all-consuming that they drown out the emptiness simply by virtue of their presence. Their sheer, glorious physicality.

'That can be arranged,' Camille murmurs. She lays a hand lightly, fleetingly on the sleeve of my jacket. 'Give me a moment.'

I watch her walk across the buzzing roof terrace of my hotel towards the woman who's captured my attention.

Sophia.

It's a lyrical, exotic name, and it strikes me as perfect for that little temptress. I already know she's thirty-two years old, Greek, a member of the prominent Petrakis family, and that she's been working for another Greek shipping tycoon for the past few years, Thaddeus Karavitis.

While the sensitive nature of the Seraph EAs' roles usually necessitates NDAs—these beautiful, highly educated women are paid handsomely to fuck us on demand as well as run our corporate lives—Sophia and Karavitis have been unashamedly public. Never mind that he's well into his sixties and in possession of a wife and four grown-up children.

It's just lucky for me that he's apparently retiring from both shipping and philandering.

Also lucky for me is that, while Talia or any of my other former Seraph EAs will likely provide Sophia with the most devastating character assassination of me as a boss, they can't in good conscience complain that I short-changed them on the other key element of our relationships.

Because I am very, *very* good at fucking.

I sip my champagne as Camille kisses the other two women on both cheeks. There's a discreet incline of her dark head in my direction that has Sophia locking eyes with me across the crowded space. Talia's probably looking, too, but I have no time for her anymore. I don't know Sophia, but, given the shit Talia's presumably talking about me, I would have expected her look to convey something ranging from wariness to open hostility.

I spot neither.

Instead, her mouth twists.

She's amused, possibly triumphant, at my having summoned her. I'm not sure, although I *am* sure that it's precisely the kind of look that would get her a resounding slap on that lovely round bottom if she was in my employ. While I find a lack of respect distasteful, restoring that respect is very much to my taste.

I stand, impassive, as she and Camille make their way over to me. She's in an electric blue body-con dress that I know from past experience is Hervé Léger. While my ex-wife had them in every shade of beige and used them, as far as I could see, to make herself as small and appropriate and invisible as possible, Sophia appears to be aiming for the exact opposite.

Objective smashed.

Tits. Hips. Legs. Her cleavage is a sumptuous ravine men likely don't survive, though there would be worse ways to go, surely. She doesn't walk so much as sashay, and I swear my fellow guests part for her. She's a goddess. It's as if the Aegean Sea took one look at Sophia Vergara, said *oh, please,* and spat out its very own bombshell upon its shores.

Her eyes stay fixed on mine as she approaches, and I'm

oblivious to Camille's chic austerity beside her. That same smile, private yet triumphant, is playing on her brightly painted mouth, and I have the uncomfortable impression of having played right into her hands by summoning her over.

Truly, I'd rather she thought I was monstrous than the remotest bit predictable. It's that revelation that has me pushing back my shoulders and widening my stance.

This is my fucking hotel, and I'm no one's foregone conclusion.

The two women stop in front of me, and I feign impassiveness as Sophia openly checks me out. I'm not sure why that irks me—after all, if I'm assessing her for her carnal potential, then it makes sense that she'd want to assess me, too.

Perhaps it's that I prefer more awe and less cockiness on a woman's face when she does.

'Mr Kingsley, meet Sophia Petrakis,' Camille murmurs.

I don't tear my eyes away from Sophia. 'Thanks. I'll take it from here.'

As she slinks off, no doubt to broker another lucrative deal between one of my business associates and one of her seraphim, Sophia extends her hand.

'Charmed, Mr Kingsley.' Her accent is cut glass, but there's a sarcastic inflection I don't much care for.

I take her hand—slim, warm, soft—and shake. 'It's Ethan. How do you do.'

Observing her from less than a metre away is quite the experience, and it serves to underscore my first impression: that this woman is indeed lush. Her skin is tanned an even olive; her coral-coloured mouth is ripe; her brown eyes are huge and thick-lashed and half-hidden under a very long, very feathery fringe, the effect of which is alluring and coquettish and all sorts of other things that randomly chopped segments of hair have no business being.

At least it's keeping my gaze off her tits.

For now.

'Beautiful hotel, Ethan,' she says, breaking eye contact to glance at the stunning roof terrace with its waterfalls and ancient potted olive trees and panoramic views sweeping from the Houses of Parliament to the London Eye and beyond.

'Thank you.'

'I hear you've been on quite the tear with assistants this year,' she muses, toying with the cocktail stick in her martini. She holds it up to her lovely mouth and sucks an olive off the end, looking back up at me through those eyelashes and that hair. She's watching for my reaction—though whether that's to her provocative comment or her little oral teaser, I'm unclear.

'It's unfortunate.' I slide my free hand into my pocket. 'None of them were the right fit.' I linger on the *double entendre* of that final word.

There's a flash of something in her dark eyes as she swallows the olive. She strikes me as the type of woman who takes everything as a challenge. 'Is that a fact?'

'None of them had what it took to succeed as my EA.'

'Which is... what, exactly? Masochistic tendencies? A teflon coating? Wait—a degradation kink?'

So Talia has dished the dirt. 'Resilience. Backbone.'

'Right. Of course. I'm sure it was *they* who were lacking.'

If there's a happy medium between the seraphim who behave like a wet ladies' blouse at the slightest sign of pressure and those who are snarky little smart arses, then Camille hasn't done me the courtesy of serving those Goldilocks candidates up to me yet. It's only my dentist's voice in my head that stops me from grinding my teeth in frustration.

'I need someone who's unbreakable. Anything else is a spectacular waste of my time.'

This woman is not destined to play poker in her lifetime. The distaste on her face is palpable.

'Funny. From what I've heard, I'd have thought you'd enjoy breaking people. Or at least breaking them in.'

'I enjoy showing them who's boss. But I need them whole and fully functional for my purposes.'

'No time for broken things,' she muses. 'Got it. You know, you really should be more careful what you wish for.'

I narrow my eyes at her. What the fuck is that supposed to mean?

CHAPTER 2

Sophia

My toxic trait is that I psychoanalyse everyone I meet. Before someone has finished shaking my hand, I've mapped them on a mega-matrix of Enneagram-meets-IFS-meets-Meyers-Briggs-meets-Clifton-Strengths-meets-attachment-style-meets-dominant-nervous-system-state. It's annoying and presumptuous and, God help me, I fucking love my psychoanalytical crack. I suspect it's more a product of my personality than my psychology degree.

The upshot of my private party piece is that it gives me, I think, more insight and therefore more compassion than your average Joe when it comes to my fellow humans.

I fervently believe that the majority of us are trudging through life buried under the weight of two core fears:

I am not enough.

This situation is not safe.

In fact, I'd go so far as to say that these two can explain ninety-nine percent of human behaviour. I didn't say they *excuse* it, but they definitely help me to look beyond most jackassery and see the scared child beneath it.

But.

But.

Sometimes it's really, *really* hard to believe that someone isn't just a raging arsehole. Case in point: Mr Ethan Kingsley, to be henceforth known as *Eight*. Because my instincts tell me this guy is an Enneagram Eight; I'd put money on it. If Pixar decided to put an Enneagram spin on *Inside Out* next time, he'd make a fantastic Eight: The Protector, which is a more constructive take on the effective but harmful *control freak* concept.

An internet search might suggest he's a Three—The Achiever—but having met the man, I now know that's not true. I suspect this position as CEO of Kingsley Hotels, the empire his father famously built from one corporate hotel in Canary Wharf, is less about external validation for him and more about control. When I complimented this roof terrace a moment ago, there wasn't a hint of pleasure in his thanks. If anything, it was an awkward acknowledgement of the truth— that this place is objectively gorgeous.

We're all here tonight to celebrate the opening of his fifth London hotel. The party is filled with celebrities and super-models and high rollers, and I'm getting zero "basking" vibes from him. Whatever this guy gets off on, he's most definitely not high on achievement right now.

I consider him as I return his verbal shot across the net with an easy backhand. My brain is mapping him on an enormous mental whiteboard right as my eyes—and other body parts—are indulging in a leisurely perusal of the fan-fucking-tastic physical package shielding what is presumably a walking ball of unresolved trauma.

His light brown hair is perfectly styled and raked off his face. He's broad in the shoulders and lean everywhere—face, body—and wears his immaculate custom suit far too well. My friend Marlowe, who enjoyed a threesome with him and her now-boyfriend this summer, wasn't lying about the hotness factor.

But it's the pale grey eyes that are the most arresting. They're intense, insightful, and cold as fuck. I wonder what they do when he's close to coming. I wonder if they burn, or if they become mere opalescent rings, swallowed up by a ravenous void of pupil.

I wouldn't mind finding out.

His overall leanness may remind me of a predator—a panther, maybe—and his tightly wound energy is totally giving hyper-function. I bet this dude needs a truckload of orgasms to numb him out of his default nervous system state of sympathetic.

And it would definitely be a case of *sex as anaesthesia* for him. A quick fuck over his desk to momentarily obliterate the fear, the noise. No co-regulation through intimacy for this guy.

It's confirmed. This lovely specimen is my toxic trait's wet dream and possibly my lady parts' wet dream too, both of which point to encouraging silver linings given the dominant *raging arsehole* factor we're dealing with here.

So he wants full control, and he wants his assistants—and everyone else—to know exactly who's boss at all times, but what I'm hearing is if someone can't hack his Eight-ness at full-throttle then he'll ditch them, because broken people are far too real and vulnerable and confronting for him to handle.

What a keeper.

He broke Talia. He broke the two Seraph assistants who came before her. He probably broke his ex-wife. And, once he'd ruined them, he didn't want his broken toys anymore.

I'm pretty sure Taylor Swift wrote a song about that.

But he should heed my warning just now.

He really should be careful what he wishes for, because I am so emotionally healthy, so wonderfully robust, that I can take anything this controlling dickhead throws at me and then some. The problem with him seeking out someone unbreakable, someone who's done the work on herself and is secure within, is that she'll take none of his dominant bullshit in the workplace. And I'm not sure this guy is ready for how it feels when someone pushes back.

My only consolations are that he looks like *that* and that, in the bedroom at least, our needs will be compatible. He can dominate me all night long. He can dominate me until the cows come home and all his burdened, exhausted, controlling bodyguard parts can breathe a sated sigh of relief and lay down their weary heads. Because I am a whore for that shit.

Literally.

I am *literally* a whore for that shit.

It's the best part of the job.

~

'No time for broken things,' I muse now. 'Got it. You know, you really should be more careful what you wish for.'

He narrows his eyes at me. 'Meaning?'

'Meaning that most people don't enjoy being treated like shit. Unless they're an actual sub, which is probably the route you should go down if you want a rewarding relationship with someone who'll actually, willingly, submit to you with no issues.'

'I'm not a dom.'

I roll my eyes. 'Of course you aren't. Look. Talia didn't exactly paint a rosy picture of you. Not that it scared me off, but if you think you have tonnes of options among the seraphim right now, you're wrong. I'm willing to sit down with you properly and interview if you want me to. I'm seriously good at what I do—*all* parts of it—and I know I can deliver.

'But I don't take any shit from my bosses, and I'm not prepared to suffer because you don't understand or won't accept what particular kind of power dynamic you need outside of the bedroom. I won't play the stupid fucking power games you indulged in with Talia or any of the others to get— to feel in control. Do I make myself clear?'

I stumbled there at the end. I was going to say *to get your kicks*, but I have enough knowledge of the crazy, miraculous universe that is the human nervous system to understand that control for him is likely to be less about his kicks—or kinks— and more about his need for safety. When he's in control, he feels safe. When he's not, he probably feels existentially endangered. However complex Talia tells me he is, it's probably as simple as that.

Still, it's not like I minced my words. He deserves the *caveat emptor* speech if he's thinking of dipping his toe into the warm waters of the Sophia Petrakis ocean.

Maybe I'm mixing my metaphors. Maybe that speech was a shark warning.

He opens his mouth to reply. It's a lovely mouth, plushly at odds with the austere, repressed vibe that the rest of him is rocking, and I can't help but imagine how soft and supple it would feel between my legs. Mmm.

Except whatever retort he's about to serve up is interrupted by a server approaching us with a tray of what looks like delicious chicken satay mini skewers. I grab one, but Ethan stiffens and fixes him with a glare whose icy blast could freeze hell over. 'No used sticks on the tray,' he snaps. 'This is basic stuff.'

I observe this micro-interaction with the same fascination David Attenborough would glean from watching two ants shagging (if ants do, indeed, shag). One of the subtypes of all Enneagrams is the Social subtype, and I have a feeling our Ethan is *not* a Social Eight. His Type Eight may be known as

The Protector, but this dude is not leading for connection or communal responsibility. Nope. I suspect he's leading purely for control. Which means if one skewer-shaped cog in his predictable, seamless machine malfunctions, then Ethan, god bless him, believes that chaos will reign.

His form of management is probably fantastic if you're a hotel guest. Not a single patron will suffer from misplaced skewers or missing mini-shampoos or a lack of hospital corners on his beds. Every detail in a Kingsley hotel will be just so.

It's just probably less conducive to healthy functioning, you know, as a human being.

When the poor server has scurried away, tail between his legs, Ethan turns back to me. I'm wondering how he's going to respond to the little preemptive bollocking I just gave him when he surprises me.

'Come downstairs with me after my speech and we can make sure we're compatible *in* the bedroom first. You can help me take one of our new suites for a test run.'

So *that's* what he took away. Oh boy. I smile sweetly at him. 'It's adorable that you think I'd give the goods away for free. Nobody likes a tight-arse, Ethan.'

His eyes drift to my cleavage, which is in fighting form tonight. I could probably have smuggled a full-size revolver or a household pet in here between my boobs and no one would have been the wiser.

'On the contrary.' He drags his gaze back up to my face with apparent difficulty. 'I very much enjoy a tight arse.'

I reward his nerdy little anal pun with a genuine smile, and his face softens a little at the sight of it. He really is very fucking fine.

'You'd have to pay for that, too.' My voice has gone all husky, dammit. I know far too many women who've had the pleasure of being fucked by this man, which is to say I'm under no illusion that this part of the job would be anything other than a total fiesta. 'Look, if you want to do this, we do it by the book, okay? Give Camille a call. I'm in Greece next week for my leaving bash, then I'm back in London and we can set something up. Thank you for a lovely party.' I go to turn away and find Talia for a juicy post-mortem, but he takes a hurried step forward.

'Wait.' He grabs my wrist, his warm fingers encircling it in a grip that's obnoxiously entitled, and I'm pretty sure my thong grows a little damp spot. 'I want first dibs on you.'

My face heats—not, unfortunately, with anger. 'I'm not an auction prize, Ethan.'

'No. But you are a prize.'

I swallow. I don't even know why he's pursuing this, unless it's to prove a point. It's not like we'd be a good fit, personality-wise. 'It's not a case of first come, first served. I've been in the same role for four years. I'm going to take my time evaluating my options. You'll have to sell the job to me.'

He stands perfectly still, perfectly firm. The man has gravitas seeping out of his pores. He radiates quiet authority, which is by far the sexiest kind.

'Believe me,' he murmurs, 'I'll sell the job to you. Just you wait.'

CHAPTER 3

Sophia

It feels great to be back in London, as long as I can ignore the intense sense of foreboding I feel at the prospect of being cold for an entire winter. It's not like London is North Dakota, but it's not Athens, either. Or Montenegro. Or Monte Carlo. And, given I've been based between those three spots for the past few years, a bleak British winter with no actual daylight isn't something I relish.

I'm a creature of the sun, designed to frolic on balmy beaches and sprawl topless on the sun-drenched decks of superyachts in the Med.

I don't like coats.

I don't even like cardigans.

That said, it's been such a mild October as we approach Halloween that the trees have barely started to turn, and I muse that London is looking as pretty as it always has.

I haven't lived here properly in years. Camille, that scheming little Chanel-clad pimp, infiltrated a Google mixer and snapped me up when I was finishing up my MBA at Stanford, and I moved straight to Athens and into the bed of one of the most powerful men in Greece.

Before Palo Alto, I was mainly based here, working in the Hospitality and Leisure sector team in Morgan Stanley's Investment Banking Division. I had three years at Cambridge but attended school here: St Paul's Girls' School, to be exact. While my family is based mainly in Athens, my parents educated us all in London, a hoard of nannies and housekeepers filling in the gaps when the rigours of the British academic calendar threatened to curtail their international jet-setting.

London, therefore, is as close to a home as I've ever had, and I bloody love it. It may be a commercial powerhouse, but it's also a hedonistic playground for the entitled offspring of Europe's richest families, and, as such, both sides of my personality feel entirely at home here. I can flip between the all-nighters that involve thousand-line spreadsheets just as easily as the ones that involve fabulous cocktails and endless sweaty bodies.

It's perfect, really.

As soon as I started to wrap things up with Thad, my former boss, I got a broker to secure me a new London pad. With my six-figure-a-month Seraph salary and a trust fund that some may argue is obscene, I'm hardly short of options, but I settled for a gorgeous little rental on Walton Street in South Ken. It's petite and achingly chic, the prettiest little pale lilac dollhouse whose gnarly wisteria vines bode well for spring, and, most importantly, it's squarely in my old stomping ground and primely located for excellent socialising.

One must start as one means to go on, right?

So I've gathered together a few girlfriends for a little soirée. Nothing too crazy—it is a Tuesday, after all. Just some good drinks, and good food, and good gossip. But I've done enough work on myself to be self-aware, and as a Seven Enneagram, I know I need this buzz around me. Friends. Joy. Connection. Intellectual stimulation. I need a full life.

We've convened at a lovely little seafood place around the corner from my new pad on charming Draycott Avenue, and I'm gratified to remember that, in this part of town, Tuesday nights are just as buzzing as Friday nights. I've organised a table in a cosy alcove at the back of the restaurant so we can have a good catch-up.

The girls troop in, bang on time. (One of the perks of having relentlessly Type A friends is that they're all madly punctual.) My absolute favourite former seraph, Athena, is, *quelle surprise*, the first to arrive, with her BFF Marlowe in tow. I fell hard and fast for Marlowe this year, even if her tenure as a Seraph was only a matter of weeks, thanks to her gorgeous boss Brendan falling even harder and faster than I did for her and her daughter, Tabs. Athena went exactly the same way, shacking up with Brendan's brother, Gabe. Think of a sinfully hot former priest who is now a billionaire, and you'll get close to the gorgeousness of Gabe.

Then, bringing up the rear is one of my closest friends from school and uni, Lotta Duffy.

'Okay, so. Context.' I clasp my hands together once everyone is seated. One of the things I adore is bringing my favourite people from various aspects of my life together in the knowledge that they will enjoy and appreciate each other almost as much as I do. For that to happen speedily, I find that context is required. It's as if my mind is a constant connection-making machine, and I can't hold those connections in. I take a breath.

'Athena and I were seraphim together until she fell in love with her boss, Gabe,' I tell Lotta. 'Marlowe and Athena met at Cheltenham Ladies and have been BFFs for years. Marls was a seraph briefly this summer but is basically way less of a tart than me and Athena.'

There's a guffaw from Lotta at this. Marlowe looks morti-fied, even though I have her and Athena's express permission to out them as former seraphim. 'Oh—and Marlowe is in the process of preparing to record an album with Santi.'

Marlowe and Lotta both react with the surprise I've expected, and I beam. Why is it such a dopamine hit when your random friends find common ground?

'You know Santi?' Marlowe asks Lotta, shrugging off her embarrassment at having been outed as a high-class hooker. The Santi she's referring to is the world-famous tenor and billionaire owner of the Vale Music classical record label, Santiago Vale.

'I more than know him. He owes his entire future happiness to me,' Lotta declares with her trademark lack of humility. 'I hooked him up with his wife, Sabrina. She was my parents' chef before I got her that gig with the Vales. And the rest is history.'

'And you're neighbours,' I point out. Lotta runs a fancy-as-hell property development company called Elgin with her brother, and Santi owns one of their penthouses.

'And we're neighbours, when I'm in London. He's a good guy. So you're recording with him? That's a seriously big deal. Congratulations!'

'I'm still pinching myself,' Marlowe confesses, and I grin at her. Boy, has this woman been through the mill this summer. Her little girl, Tabby, had to have a pulmonary heart valve transplant, and there were complications, and the whole thing got pretty hairy, if you ask me. Happily, all the drama made Brendan pull his finger out of his arse and realise what she meant to him, and now they're properly together.

It makes me emotional when I think of it. It's hard to imagine anyone deserving a happy ever after more than Marls. And the idea that she and her best friend will almost certainly end up as sisters-in-law is too adorable to even process.

We get the wine flowing and cover off Athena's recent

engagement to Gabe in Greece and Marlowe's upcoming album.

'How was the leaving party?' Athena asks.

'It was fabulous.' I smile and pause for effect, because who am I kidding? This is *my* soirée. My friends have gathered here to celebrate my return to London. 'Thad organised a full-on Greek orgy for me.'

Right on cue, Marlowe, who still has moments of prudishness, chokes on her wine. Athena shoots her an alarmed look before slapping her on the back.

'That cough sounded very slut-shaming,' I tell her.

'Sorry,' she croaks. 'Just—warn a girl, will you? Jesus.'

'Sounds excellent, if a bit on the nose for you and Thad,' Athena pronounces, biting down on a smile and shaking her head ruefully.

'Clichés are clichés for a reason.' I raise my glass. 'Because they work.'

'I'm sure I'll regret this,' Lotta says, 'but tell us all about it.'

I smile dreamily, allowing my mind to drift back to my final hedonistic night in Mykonos. The Aleomandra peninsula stretched ahead of us as the sun fell on Thad's spectacular, sprawling villa, the lush gardens alive with revellers and, later, the vast infinity pool heaving with naked bodies.

It was pretty effing special.

'I'll tell you if you promise to set aside your British prudishness for a moment and open your minds. Athena, I'm not talking to you,' I add. Athena may look like an English rose, but the woman loves sex every bit as much as I do. More, possibly.

'Fine,' Marlowe says through gritted teeth.

'Divulge,' Lotta demands. 'I feel a Greek holiday coming on already.'

'Well, it was a traditional celebration of Dionysus.'

Marlowe frowns. 'Dionysus?'

'The Greek version of Bacchus,' Athena, our resident Classics scholar, tells her without missing a beat. 'Greek Jesus, more like, because he died and was reborn, a fact the Greeks celebrate with a giant phallus.'

'Of course they do,' Marlowe mutters.

'And was there a giant phallus at the party?' Lotta wonders aloud.

'There were many giant phalluses.' I smile happily.

'*Phalli*, if you're declining the noun in Latin.' This from Athena. Naturally.

'Oh, bore off. Yes, there was a huge big dick bringing up the rear, and torchbearers at sunset, and wine and fruit bearers, and musicians, and a lot of naked people wearing only masks.'

'And you...' Lotta prompts, waving her hands around, clearly hoping for something more salacious.

'And I was naked, too. We got very drunk and I fucked lots of guys. At one point I was lying at the very edge of the pool, and the water was lapping over me, and the sky was the most incredible coral pink, and all these hot European guys were just tending to me at the same time, you know, and I think it was the best moment of my life.'

I sigh at the memory. It really was perfect. I felt like I could float away on all that sensory pleasure as the sun commanded the sky and those guys commanded my body.

Athena snorts. 'Lucky bitch.'

I laugh, and the memory shatters. Marlowe looks like she's trying gamely to process this information while Lotta grins wickedly.

'Fuck, that's hot,' she says. She toys with her wine glass. 'Maybe I can get Aide to role-play that.'

'It might be a nice change from whatever you two get up to,' I deadpan. 'I can see Aide in a fig leaf.'

Lotta's husband, Aide Duffy, is a reluctant tech mogul and all-round good guy. He's also hot as fuck in a seriously brawny way. He likes his manual labour, and it shows. I imagine a fig leaf would be a good look on him.

~

'So it sounds like Soph is the only one who's not banging a billionaire at this moment in time,' Lotta says later.

'It was time for Thad to hang up his Speedo thong and start acting his age,' I say. 'Anyway, I might be banging another billionaire soon. I have a job interview tomorrow, so I'd better go easy on the wine tonight.'

'Anyone we know?' Lotta asks. 'Or are we not allowed to say?'

I hesitate. Seraph's NDAs exclude only fellow seraphim, allowing us to talk amongst ourselves about our roles. Camille believes it's important for us to be able to seek advice and support within the agency when we're in these intense and often confronting roles. Obviously, that technically excludes all three of these ladies, but if I get this job, it won't be any secret that I'm working for Ethan. It's merely the 'full service' aspect of my role that will be confidential.

Given two of my friends are former seraphim and the other has an actual Cambridge degree and knows I'm a seraph, I doubt any of them will struggle to put two and two together.

'Ethan Kingsley,' I say, my gaze darting discreetly to Marlowe. 'As in, Kingsley Hotels.' Brendan definitely strong-armed her into that threesome with Ethan when Brendan was in his Dickhead in Denial Era, and I suspect it's still an uncomfortable memory for her. Sure enough, she grimaces discreetly and Athena pats her on the arm.

Lotta sucks in a breath. 'Oh boy. Sleeping with the enemy. Nora and Theo will have a field day with this one.'

One of our closest uni friends, Nora, married another of our mates, Theo Montague, whose family's eponymous hotel group is Kingsley Hotel's biggest competitor. The Kingsley-Montague rivalry is well-known gossip in both business and social circles.

'I'm definitely going to pump the Montagues for dirt if I get the job,' I say. Theo's older brother Miles is the company CEO, their father the chairman.

'Makes sense,' Lotta says. 'But from what I've heard, Ethan's pretty obnoxious, just like his old man. Have you met him yet?'

'Briefly, at the opening of his Westminster hotel a couple of weeks ago.' I cock my head, considering. 'Obnoxious is definitely a fair adjective, as far as first impressions go, anyway. He's having major problems holding onto executive assistants.'

'Because he's an entitled arsehole?' Lotta guesses.

'Possibly.' I screw up my face. 'I think he has control issues that get people's backs up, funnily enough. He likes everyone to know who's boss.'

'And he wants to interview you?' Athena jokes. 'Poor guy's going to find out who's boss pretty quickly.'

'Exactly. His last executive assistant is very sweet, but she couldn't really hack him being a grumpy, bossy wanker the whole time. Is that fair?' I ask Marlowe and Athena, who know Talia.

'Sure,' Athena says. 'I mean, who wants to be terrorised at work all day long? But I have no doubt you can handle him, babe.'

'But is he hot?' Lotta, damn her, wants to know.

I turn to Marlowe, who gives me a little shake of her head. She absolutely does not want to field this one, so I ponder how to answer.

There's no doubt he affected me. No doubt at all. He's physically gorgeous, but it's his alpha demeanour that gets me hot under the collar. He may not have been basking in the achievement of his latest glittering hotel that evening, but when he got up to speak, he commanded the entire fucking terrace, and I mean effortlessly. He radiated power without lifting a finger. He had the audience rapt. And that kind of Big Dick Energy is the kind I can very much get on board with.

'He's really hot in a way that's icy and controlling, but in a hanging-on-by-a-thread kind of way, you know? I bet if you could get him to snap, you'd be walking funny for a week.'

My skin heats slightly at the thought. At the memory of him grabbing my wrist.

Wait. I want first dibs on you.

So entitled... and yet almost panicked. Like he wanted to lock me down, there and then, before anyone else had a chance. It wasn't unsexy.

Not by a long shot.

Athena settles back in her chair.

'Well, darling, if anyone can get the guy to snap, my money's on you. Every time.'

CHAPTER 4

Ethan

My father points at the Reuters dashboard on one of my desktop monitors.

'You know this makes sense, *and* you know it makes more sense now than it's ever done.'

I don't need to glance at the flashing green and red list of hotel stocks globally to know he's right, just as I don't need our bankers to tell me that the government would have no issue with this deal going ahead. Dad and his golfing, Scotch-drinking, cigar-puffing cronies have any potential monopoly issues tied up. And, given the pummelling The Montague Group's stock has taken over the past few days, this is the perfect time for us to move in for the kill.

The only thing that's *unclear*, in fact, is why this leaves quite such a sour taste in my mouth.

Late last week, it was announced that work on not one but two of our largest British competitor's new London flagships had suffered "indefinite" delays due to withheld planning permission. The news spooked investors, and their stock is currently off by as much as ten percent. While I don't expect the sell-off to continue, it's looking cheaper than it has for quite some time.

At first glance, the Montague and Kingsley hotel groups have a lot in common. Both are now run by the sons of the men who founded them. Both are considered standouts among their peers. And both have remained independent, despite the huge conglomerates—Hilton, Marriott, and IHG—sniffing around them.

But our differences, no matter how well concealed to everyone but us, divide us more than our similarities unite us. It's not just that the Montagues have increasingly pursued the family and leisure markets while we've doubled down on being the hotel of choice for discerning corporates. It's that the current CEO, Miles Montague, and his father Charles, who was at the helm previously, are thoroughly decent men who, as far as I can see, run their business with integrity, while Richard Kingsley wouldn't know integrity if it whipped out its dick and pissed all over his face.

That said, I'm a businessman. I'm the CEO of a listed company, and, to that end, my fiduciary duties are extremely clear. My primary objective is to create value for our shareholders, and boy, would this deal be value-creating. While The Montague Group may be suffering a setback, it's structurally better positioned than we are. Leisure travel recovered far better after the pandemic than business travel. Zoom has removed the need for a large proportion of meetings to happen face to face, but it will never remove the need for people to take holidays.

Their hotel assets are incredible, especially their flagship hotel in Knightsbridge, near Hyde Park Corner. That gorgeous Victorian *grande dame* gives me a hard-on every time I drive past it. And, in a genius move that I'm ashamed to say I didn't see coming, they formed a joint venture with the idyllic rural resort Sorrel Farm and have been rolling out new locations with great success.

In this, I'm my father's son.

Because *I want it.*

I want it all.

And what the Kingsley men want, we get, even if our motives are different. Dad wants the glory. The coup. The blood. He wants to lord it over his old rival, Charles Montague, conveniently ignoring that they were once on the same side when they rowed for Cambridge.

But I want the clout. The control. The jurisdiction over such a huge swathe of the industry that I can be assured my voice will be heard. By taking out a similar-sized player and bulking ourselves up so magnificently, I can assure Kingsley Hotels its autonomy for years longer. I can ensure we remain a force to be reckoned with. A whale—or should I say *shark*—rather than a minnow.

'You want me to set up a meeting with Miles Montague.' It's not a question.

He leans forward. *Shark* is right. It's like he can already taste the blood of his prey.

'As soon as possible. Go in gently. You know how to play it.'

I do. In this game of chess we're playing, the Kingsley board has planned for this day for a long, long time. Our bankers at Loeb drew up a detailed proposal for a takeover of The Montague Group years ago, and they keep the numbers up to date. We know how this deal could look. We know how much money we'd need to raise from our debt and equity investors. And we know exactly what their appetite would be for an acquisition like this. In a word: large.

Our investors would support us.

The market would reward us.

We just need the Montagues to agree to sit down with us.

Because what my father didn't have to say is that there's an easy way and a hard way for them to roll over. We can hash out a friendly acquisition between us and jointly pitch it to our investors and to the market more generally.

Or they can dig their heels in, and we go full hostile, buying out their stock in the open market and in blocks from their key shareholders until we have a majority stake. That route could not only get expensive for us pretty quickly, as all that buying drives their share price up and up and up, but it robs them of a lot of autonomy in the deal. When a predator moves in, the prey is usually fucked.

No, a friendly takeover is cheaper and easier for the acquirer and more pleasant for the target. It offers the Montagues a way to preserve the best of their culture. Their legacy. It's the sensible solution.

I'm just not convinced that they'll see sense, even when their backs are to the wall and we have them by the balls.

As soon as I've got rid of Dad to his token office along the corridor, where he'll preen for an hour before going out to lunch for the afternoon, I turn my attention to getting hold of Miles Montague. There may be no great love lost between us, but there's a grudging respect—at my end, at least—and we run in the same circles. We even play in the same golf tournaments on occasion, though he's far less active on the social circuit since marrying his indecently attractive second wife and former nanny.

In any case, we have each other's mobile phone numbers, and I stick my earbuds in so I can pace as I talk. I'll feel far more in control of the conversation that way—if he actually accepts my call, that is. He'd be stupid not to. He has to know why I'm calling, which makes him as obligated to take the call as he would be tempted to decline it.

Just as I'm pulling up his number, a WhatsApp comes in from my son, Jamie.

> Can u top up my tuck card

For fuck's sake. Fifteen grand a term after tax at one of the most elite schools in the country, and this is how they teach him to communicate. I'm bristling with nerves and apprehension, and I don't need an illiterate fourteen-year-old being needy right now. Before I can stop myself, I hit reply.

> Can u learn basic grammar and manners

I regret it as soon as I send it. It's infantile and generally dickish, and it's the last thing my already fraught relationship with my son needs.

He replies before I have a chance to delete the message.

> Dad please

I sigh.

> Sure. Give me a sec.

Even if this is his mother's job rather than mine. Still standing, I crouch over my keyboard and pull up Westminster School's parent portal, transferring a hundred quid. Hopefully that'll keep him in doughnuts and sausage rolls for a few weeks.

> Done.

K

One letter. How this kid is in the top set for English, I have no clue.

That small item of household admin covered off, I call Miles Montague. There's no point in hesitation or overthinking. I've been ready to make this call for five years, give or take.

He answers after three rings, and my pulse quickens. I leave the phone on the desk and jam my hands in my pockets, turning to face the window. Our headquarters on the Embankment are architecturally stunning, the executive suite as quietly luxurious as one would expect from a luxury hotel group. It's a sunny autumn day, and the view of the river never ceases to calm me. I feel like a king surveying his empire from up here.

An empire that's about to double in size.

'Ethan.' Montague's tone is clipped but not overtly hostile.

'Miles. How's tricks?'

'Can't complain. You?' His reply strikes me as unnecessarily stoic given that the shit's being kicked out of his share price, but maybe when his hot little wife slides down his body at night it makes matters like market capitalisation seem downright trivial.

'Good, good. How are Saoirse and the kids?' God, I hope I pronounced her name right.

'Everyone's well, thank God. And Jamie?'

'He's...' *Emotionally distant. Unreadable. Seemingly indifferent to me.* 'Fine, thanks. Look, I'm sorry about the planning curveball. I don't know what those pen-pushers over at the Planning Department are smoking. It's beyond irrational.'

He blows out a breath. 'I appreciate it. Yeah, it's never good to feel like your hands are tied.'

It's certainly not, mate. Remember that. Hold onto how much you dislike that feeling of powerlessness.

'Damn right it's not. Look, we'd love to help you turn things around. Do you think you and I could sit down for a drink and a chat in the next day or two?'

He hesitates, and I have the impression he's choosing his words carefully. 'I'm not interested in what strings Richard thinks he can pull with the council. It's not how we do business.'

I ignore his wholly accurate character assassination of my father. I also ignore the tiny, fleeting, and most unwelcome suspicion that rises up that Dad and his "string pulling" could have had any impact whatsoever on Westminster City Council's decision to kibosh both Montague projects. Even Richard Kingsley wouldn't stoop that low to engineer a favourable acquisition price.

'That's not what I'm offering, and you know it. It's time, mate. Time for us both to stop plodding along on parallel lines and at least consider joining forces. Think of the—think of the scale we could command.'

I almost said *think of the costs we could cut*, but that is categorically not the way to go. No proud business owner wants to consider that an acquirer, no matter how friendly, would swoop in and axe a ton of extraneous people. Even if that side of the equation is one of the most attractive parts of the deal. HR, payroll, finance, marketing: all areas we could cut back to the bone.

This time his pause speaks volumes.

'Ethan. I'm only going to say this once. We're not for sale.'

'That's not your call, and you know it. That's your shareholders' call. Believe me, you want to sit down with me so we can discuss this like adults. It's not black and white, and it doesn't have to be an end. It could be an amazing new beginning for both of us.'

'I'm not interested in discussions with competitors who circle like vultures the second we hit a stumbling block.'

'You should be,' I spit out. 'You know damn well we can do this the easy way or the hard way.' I'm losing my hold on the conversation now, showing my true colours. I may as well have bared my teeth at him. Shit. I'm not sure how the hell this discussion is unravelling so quickly.

'Listen very, very carefully, Kingsley.' A pause. 'You and your corrupt father can go fuck yourselves.'

And with that, he ends the call.

I spin around, tugging my earbuds out and throwing them on the desk. Fuuuuck! He's holding a losing hand, and he fucking well knows it, and he's refusing to play ball, refusing to engage with me on a professional level, despite it being his clear fiduciary duty to do so. Stupid fucking incompetent arsehole. There is *nothing* that pisses me off more than dickheads who don't understand when they are powerless and won't respect when I am power*ful*. I hold every fucking ace here, and he won't do me the courtesy of even acknowledging it.

I pick up my phone and throw it on the floor, and when that fails to make me feel one iota better, I take the great pile of research reports that the various banks have compiled on our sector recently and sweep them off the desk. They land on the carpet with a flurry of dull thuds. They can damn well stay there.

Still fuming, I stride across my huge office to the recessed bar in one wall. Decanter. Tumbler. Three, four fingers of scotch, sloshed inelegantly in. Done. I knock the entire thing back, and for a single blissful moment, the burn in my throat, in my sinuses, consumes everything else.

The whisky floods my bloodstream, but it's not enough. I'm looking around for something else I can throw, some other outlet for this useless fury, this impotent frustration, when there's a knock at my office door. It opens, and Alexis, our receptionist, peers timidly around it.

'Mr Kingsley? Ms Petrakis is here for her interview.'

CHAPTER 5

Ethan

Christ Almighty.

In the midst of this Montague drama, I'd forgotten I was due to interview Sophia.

'Give me five minutes,' I bark, and she nods and swiftly makes herself scarce. I slam the whiskey tumbler down on the marble bar as hard as I dare before dragging my hand over my face. God knows, I need a decent new EA yesterday, and I most certainly need one if I'm to wage war against the Montagues. I blow out a long, steady breath before sucking in more oxygen.

I know myself well. Within moments, my heated flare-up will have settled into an icy rage, an emotional state with which I'm far more familiar and in which I'm far more highly functioning. I tap out a message on my phone to Miles.

> You know as well as I do that you're obligated to take this expression of interest to your board. I'll confirm said interest in writing by the end of the day.

This is why we have boards of directors: so maverick CEOs

can't reject advantageous deals just because their noses are out of joint and their egos are feeling bruised.

I hit send and rake my hand through my hair. I've had the last word—for now—which affords me a modicum of mental capacity to allocate to my upcoming interview. I may be far from my most charming, but perhaps it's a good thing that she sees me like this. I need someone tough this time around. If the shit's about to hit the fan, I need someone with mettle. Something my instincts tell me Ms Petrakis has in abundance. I pick up the CV that my PA, Topher, left on my desk. I'd better reacquaint myself with her non-physical assets before I summon her in for a grilling.

SHE'S in a red dress that manages to be both professionally beyond reproach and a glorious reminder of why I've been so intent on getting her to interview with me. It's knee-length and fitted—*very* fitted—and made of tweed, with gold buttons down the front and adorning the little pockets. Short sleeves. Smooth olive arms and legs on full view. And it looks like it opens the whole way down like a coat.

God help me.

She's a knockout, her long, dark hair pulled back into a bouncy ponytail and her full lips painted fire-engine red. I'm struck once again by the huge brown doe eyes and that seductive fringe.

She really is a classic Mediterranean bombshell. Looks like she topped up that tan of hers on her trip to Greece. I suppose it's still pretty warm over there at this time of year.

'Thanks for coming,' I tell her before giving Alexis a curt nod of dismissal. I shake Sophia's hand. 'Did you, er—did you have a good trip?'

She frowns. 'You okay?'

'I'm about to get thrown into a hell of a work crisis, so not really,' I say tersely.

'Oh dear. Should we do this another time?'

She smells incredible. Her scent is heady and floral, and it's messing with my head. My gaze flickers down from the look of genuine concern on her face to the faintest shadow of her cleavage where her top few buttons are undone. Once again, she's walking the line of professional and intoxicating far too skilfully.

'You're good. Let's crack on.'

I spot the haphazard pile of angrily flung research reports lying on the carpet at the same time as she does, their mess such a blot on my perfectly minimalist surroundings that it makes my skin crawl.

Shit.

To her credit, she doesn't react.

'Have a seat,' I bark, my tone making it sound more like an order than an offer. She drops elegantly into the seat I've pointed at, and I round the desk, sidestepping the evidence of my tantrum and shoving my hands in my pockets. A glance at my phone tells me Montague hasn't replied to my WhatsApp yet, insolent fucker. I turn it face down.

'So. You're back in London and available to work.'

'Yes and yes.' She folds her hands in her lap.

'Have you interviewed with anyone else?'

'I don't feel the need to disclose that at this moment,' she says evenly.

I glare at her, and she gazes back at me. I took the first slot Camille offered me, but that doesn't mean she didn't offer another party an earlier slot.

'I told you I wanted first dibs,' I say, conscious that I sound even to my own ears like a mutinous child.

She cocks her head. 'Yes, you did.'

We stare at each other. She licks her lips, and I don't think it's intentional, but it's alluring as hell. Her failure to engage is pissing me off. She's neither affronted nor cowed. Just... tolerant.

I huff out a breath and begin to pace back and forth behind my desk. 'I see you have experience with the hotel sector.'

'As a banker, yes. I've never worked in the industry, but I've spent a lot of time with the managements of publicly listed hotel groups, and I'm familiar with the financial models, too.'

It's helpful, but it's not fucking interesting. I stare at her bare, tanned legs, demurely crossed. I don't give a flying fuck about her experience—I already know she's an academic rock-star and vastly overqualified to be anyone's assistant, executive or otherwise. Just as I already know what she looks like naked, thanks to the titillating thirty minutes I spent at the Seraph offices last week, viewing her portfolio while she was in Greece.

Her professional experience: as blue-chip as they come. Cambridge undergrad. Morgan Stanley. Stanford MBA. Karavitis Shipping. There are no red flags there, not in the slightest.

The so-called "intimate reviews", a Seraph staple whereby former employers anonymously rate the fuckability of their assistants—for want of a better word—were gushing. As far as I know, she's only worked for one man since joining Seraph, and the idea of a paunchy, egotistical pensioner like Thaddeus Karavitis lauding Sophia as *kinky and responsive and always up for pushing boundaries* makes me feel violated and resentful in equal measure.

But it was the intimate images I went there to see. It was their lure that drew me into the City like a moth to a flame. Seraph won't risk sharing these images digitally, you see. Prospective employers must go to them, where we're left alone with a large-screen Mac and a box of tissues.

Sophia in sheer black mesh underwear.

Sophia topless, her spectacular tits hanging heavily, their dark nipples and even colour the confirmation I didn't need that she enjoys her topless sunbathing.

And—the *pièce de résistance*—Sophia sitting on a high stool, completely, wonderfully naked, hair loose and knees wide, one hand cupping her breast and the other holding her cunt open for inspection as she stared at the camera with what looked like a challenge in those huge dark eyes.

I've had three Seraph PAs already. This is well-trodden ground for me. When I viewed Talia's portfolio and those of the two women before her I did it in a distant, appraising way. They were hot. More than hot. Stunning. Lean and sexy and perfectly groomed, and I was into it.

When I viewed Sophia's portfolio, when I saw for myself the sheer *decadence* of what I knew she was hiding under that blue dress at my launch party, I felt like I was inserting a syringe full of heroin into my vein and slowly pressing that stopper down, down, down.

Last week was the first time I've cared to empty myself into a wad of Seraph tissues. And, like an addict, I've been cranky and antsy and out of sorts since.

So no. I don't care about her knowledge of the fucking hospitality sector. What I'd *really* like to know is how she'd react if I told her exactly how I'd like her to uncross those long, tanned legs and show me the goods.

Because the only thing that matters here, the only thing that affects the likelihood of my hiring this woman for this role, is her ability to set aside her natural inclination to disrespect me at every turn and submit to my desires in the way that I so keenly need.

CHAPTER 6

Sophia

This man is distracted as hell.

He's acting like it's a gigantic headache to have to ask me these perfunctory but relevant interview questions, like I'm putting him out by even being here. It seems he's forgotten his insistence on "first dibs", which, it irks me to admit, I've given him.

Not that he needs to know that.

As he paces back and forth, he fires questions at me that I lob back easily while my head turns to and fro like I'm at Wimbledon. Finally he stops and grips the back of his chair so tightly his knuckles turn instantly white.

'You're obviously qualified,' he snaps. 'Frankly, the only thing I'm concerned about if I hire you is your attitude.'

'What a coincidence. The only thing I'm concerned about if you hire me is *your* attitude.'

That gives him pause. 'Excuse me?'

'Look. We both know I'm well qualified to do this job. We both know I've got the relevant expertise and skills. And, while I have no concerns at all about being able to handle all the steaming piles of shitty personality defects you serve me up every day, the question I'm asking myself is whether I *want* to. Whether you'll make it worth my while. Because, honestly, I can go somewhere else tomorrow and work for someone who doesn't have his head up his arse and treats his EAs with the basic human decency they deserve.'

I primly uncross and recross my legs, and he tracks the movement. Of course he does. He's been staring at them for the past twenty minutes. He opens his mouth to speak, but I shake my head.

'Nope. I'm not done. Nothing you've said or done since I've walked in here has dissuaded me from what I've already inferred from Talia's take on you, which was very diplomatic, by the way: that you'd be a gigantic pain in the arse to have as a boss.

'Your attitude stinks. I've done you the courtesy of coming in to see you as soon as I can, which is what you basically *demanded* when we met, and you're acting like I'm wasting your time. If you think this interview doesn't work both ways then you're sorely mistaken, pal, because I have far more options right now than you do, and I'm sure Camille's told you as much.'

He glares at me as if my very existence is the height of effrontery, and I couldn't care less. I extend my hand in front of me and pretend to admire my immaculate red nails.

'Can you please explain to me why Camille can't find me an EA who's prepared to do exactly what I ask without either running off to the loos in tears or being unacceptably impertinent?'

I sigh and close my eyes for a moment, seeking inner strength. It would be lovely if he could show just a *soupçon* of self-awareness. 'I already did, last time we met. That kind of woman is called a submissive, remember, and you should really consider hiring someone like that.'

I open my eyes and fix them on him. Just like that, I'm

uncomfortably reminded that, no matter how allergic I am to his particular brand of people management, I am definitely not allergic to the sight of his body or, alas, his face. He looks even more fine in daylight, and all this pacing is giving me an excellent opportunity to enjoy his leanly athletic physique, the broad shoulders flexing against the crisp white cotton of his shirt and, of course, the deliciously toned arse in those expertly tailored dark grey trousers.

Even worse, no matter how much I despise myself for it, my pussy is loving his obnoxious power plays just as much as the rest of me is hating it.

If this entitled douche wants his very own sub, all he has to do is look up my dress.

He gives a little shake of his head, like my opinions are too ridiculous to give oxygen to. 'Look. I'm not asking for much, just someone who can stay professional, rational and respect-ful. Is that such a stretch?'

I lean forward. 'Same, bruh. Like I said, this needs to work both ways. You may be paying my salary if I work for you, but this will work much better as a partnership than a permanent stand-off. Am I right?'

Okay. Perhaps bruh-ing a potential employer was excessive, even for me. But if I blow this, I don't give a crap.

He sighs, and I think maybe I've hit a nerve. 'Look.' It seems he's the kind of guy who prefaces every law he lays down with *look*. 'It's been a rough day. I'm under a lot of stress.'

'Yes, and you mentioned you're *about to get thrown into* a work crisis, so clearly things will get far worse before they get better.'

He glares at me.

'Look.' *Two can play that game, mister.* 'I don't want or intend to add to your stress. On the contrary, a large part of my role would be helping you manage it.' I pause to let that reminder sink in. 'But I also won't be your punching bag. I have far too much self-respect for that. Do I make myself clear?'

'Crystal,' he mutters, but he's looking like he sees me a little more fully. Like I'm an actual participant in this conversation rather than just an audience member of the Ethan Kingsley show.

He strolls back around the desk and motions for me to push my chair back, which I do. With his arse resting on the front of his desk, he towers over me and crosses his arms over his chest. I don't hate it. 'Tell me this, at least. Are you this much of a pain in the arse in bed?'

'God, no. You can be as bossy as you like in bed. I lap that shit up.'

A little huff of what I think is amusement leaves his mouth, and his face softens slightly. 'That's a major relief. Why don't you show me?'

People don't often take me by surprise, but my eyebrows wing up. 'Excuse me?'

'You heard me.'

Now, Seraph has a strict interviewing process, and for good reason. The first round is purely professional. If—and it's a big if—both parties are happy that they're a good fit professionally and would like to move forward, the interviewer places twenty-five thousand pounds into Seraph's bank account.

The second round is usually a hotel dinner during which the sex stuff is discussed, after which we retire to a suite for the "audition". Make no mistake: the guy is auditioning just as much as the seraph is, and it's usually we who walk away after the first or second round. Either way, if we fuck them, we get all the money. It's a proven way to ensure that no one tries to work his way through the seraphim during the audition rounds without paying handsomely for the privilege.

'You want to skip the dinner and just roll straight into the audition?'

Another hint of amusement. 'I didn't realise you were such a stickler for process.'

'I'm a stickler for my wellbeing.'

He shrugs. 'The money is already in Seraph's account. By all means, call Camille and ask her. Unless it's not about the money.'

I look at him properly then, and I can't imagine there's anything in my expression that suggests I'm not shamelessly up for this. Because the truth is that arguing is my absolute favourite form of foreplay, and having a dick-swinging competition with this dude has majorly given me the horn.

He's dysregulated and obviously not in control of his stress levels, which should be a red flag and is in fact a gigantic green one, because I want him to work it out on me. I'd rather he was like this, all wound up and in clear need of an outlet, than the coldly impassive man I met on that roof terrace.

I can definitely have some fun with this one.

He presses on. 'Look at it this way. You asked me if I could make it worth your while to work for me, and I'm telling you I can. Every fucking day. But I'd very much like to show you while I have the chance. Because we both know that if you walk out of here after this conversation is done, you won't sign up for the next round. What do you say?'

Oh my fucking God, he is so hot. In an instant, I understand where this guy's sexual power lies, what form his hold over me will take. It's simply this: he looks so disdainful, so utterly underwhelmed by everyone and everything, that when he acts like he really wants you, it's the most potent narcotic ever.

Supply and demand, baby. When someone withholds their regard so meanly, it's impossible to withstand the temptation to pry it from them.

Without a word, without breaking the beseeching, hungry gaze in those beautiful pale grey eyes of his, I lean forward and pull my phone out of my bag. I glance down for a second as I pull up Camille's name and hit dial. Once I have the phone to my ear, I settle back in my chair and gaze up at him.

She answers on the first ring.

'Sophia. All okay?'

'It's fine. I'm in the interview with Ethan and he wants to proceed to the audition round while I'm here.' Hopefully that's a classy way to tell my colleague that my potential future boss wants to bang me on his desk post-haste.

'Oh.' She falters. 'Are you sure everything's going well? Are you comfortable with this?'

'Yeah, I'm fine. Honestly.'

'Well, as long as you're happy and comfortable, you should go ahead. We've already received his funds.'

'That's all I needed to know. Thanks.'

I disconnect the call and drop the phone back into my handbag, luxuriating in the heat of Ethan's gaze, in the warmth of his rapt attention.

'So. How do you want me?'

CHAPTER 7

Sophia

His grip on the edge of his creepily minimalist desk turns white-knuckled as he surveys me, and I lounge back a little further in my chair. I know Eight here is going to want to call every shot, and I intend to let him have his way. Once I've wound him up a little, that is. Let's just say I have an inkling that pushing his buttons will make everything even hotter—for both of us. And he's far too uptight. It would be a shame not to have some fun with him.

Which is why I reach for the top button of my dress and slide it out of its buttonhole.

He pushes off the desk. Before I know it, he's towering over me, a strong hand wrapped around each of my wrists, holding them rigidly away from my dress as if I've been in danger of pressing a *detonate* button—which doesn't feel too far from the truth. I gaze up at him. He's fuming, and I don't hate it. His lovely mouth is pressed into a thin line.

'I call the shots. What part of that do you not understand?'

I smile at him. 'Just trying to help.'

'Well don't. Not without my authorisation.'

I shrug. 'Got it.'

He reluctantly releases me and collapses back against the desk. 'Do you have a safeword?' he barks. He resembles someone in the midst of a major sugar crash surveying a dessert buffet—like he doesn't know where to start. Like I'm breaking his brain.

'EBITDA,' I say sweetly. It has the desired effect of stopping him in his tracks.

He frowns. 'EBITDA, as in Earnings Before Interest, Tax, Depreciation and Amortisation?'

'That's the one.'

'Why on earth?'

'Because it's deliberately unsexy. It breaks the moment.'

'I don't know about that. I happen to think a figure that represents my company's underlying profitability, without all the noise of financial fees and accounting adjustments and intangibles, is actually pretty sexy.'

He says it with a straight face, and I reward his deadpan delivery with my biggest, most seductive smile. It's as if I've shot a stun gun between his eyes. He stares at me like he's never seen anything like it.

'I don't disagree. I may have to rethink it. Not that I've ever used my safeword,' I add, just to break his brain a little more.

'You've never safed out? Ever?'

'Nope. I can handle a lot.'

'I bet you can,' he drawls. He slaps the desk suddenly, aggressively, and it makes me jump. 'Now swap places with me and do exactly as I say. You hear me?'

With a little nod of acquiescence, I rise to my feet and pass him, my mostly bare arm brushing against the cotton of his shirt as I do. God, I love this state of anticipation, of putting myself wholly in the hands of a man I know will command me to perfection.

When I was doing my MBA, I fucked a guy on the Stanford swim team for a few months. He was the epitome of physical perfection—not a subcutaneous fat cell on his body —but the sex was *meh*. He was far too easygoing.

Then I prostituted myself for Thad, a belligerent arsehole older than my father, with skin beaten by decades of sun abuse to the colour and texture of walnuts and moobs for days, but he still made me lose my mind every time he ordered me about.

Bottom line: I'm a ho for an alpha guy.

A dominant personality will do it for me over a perfect body every time.

Happily for me, this dude looks as if he has both.

He settles in the chair like a man about to enjoy a private show, which is exactly what he is. I may have height on him in this position, but there's no doubt who's in control of this little scene.

'Now you can unbutton your dress, *slowly,* starting at the top.'

I do as he says, enjoying the brush of my fingers against my skin as I work my way slowly down the rest of the big gold-and-enamel buttons. Enjoying those arresting grey eyes riveted to my body. If I take this job, which, let's face it, I already know I will, we'll fuck hundreds of times. There's something almost sacred about uncovering myself for him for the first time, about preparing myself for him to profane me in whatever way he likes. It's the allure of the unknown that makes this feel so thrilling.

His eyes lock onto the black lace of my bra as I arch forward to undo the lower buttons. When the last one is undone, I straighten up and pause, the dress hanging open like a coat, my soft curves and black lace lingerie on partial display for him. I remain leaning against the desk, letting my hands rest on it too. He hasn't told me to take the dress off yet, and he's about to find out that I'm as pliant in a sexual context as I am feisty out of it.

'Stand up and take it off,' he orders me. His body is still, his gaze rapt.

I push myself off the desk and tug the dress off my shoulders, shimmying a little so it slides down my arms like a coat. He holds out a hand and I pass it to him, watching as he leans over and lays it reverently on the floor beside him. Appreciation for Chanel will always win him brownie points.

He straightens up and stills. Everyone loves having praise and compliments lavished on them, but anything he could say right now would surely appear trite compared to the enraptured expression on his face. His eyes wander over my body, taking a leisurely perusal of the generous curves of my hips and tits, the decadent lace of my lingerie, and my bare legs, still in their red heels. Finally, our eyes lock, and he swallows.

'Take off your bra.'

His voice is brusque. Husky. I reach behind me and unhook it. I know he's seen me naked. I know he's seen my portfolio, and I even know from Camille that he left a *lot* of tissues in the office bin for a man who didn't appear to be suffering from a cold. All of which is to say that, despite his history of hiring slim, sleek gym-bunnies from Seraph to date, I'm not worried that he'll find my body too much.

On the contrary, I want to know what it feels like to have him gorge himself stupid on it.

The office is cool, and his gaze is hot, and my exposed nipples react accordingly, growing taut and achy.

He grips the chrome arms of the chair much like he gripped the edge of the desk: *hard*. When he speaks, his voice is a rasp of barely controlled need. 'That's very, very good. Now turn around.'

That I can do. I smile seductively and push off the desk, turning around like he asked. His face must be level with my arse, and I know what he'll see. A scrap of black lace dissecting plump, tanned cheeks. No tan lines on this girl.

I can feel the scorch of his gaze on my bottom as surely as if his eyes were laser beams.

The chair creaks.

He's standing up.

I sense the air move as he steps closer.

When he speaks, his voice comes from right behind me.

'Now. Bend over. *Slowly*. I want to watch.'

While I didn't necessarily expect today's interview to take this turn, in this job you're always prepared for nakedness. In this job, the layers underneath the interview outfit are as important as the outfit itself.

So my lingerie is perfect. My skin is buffed and waxed and moisturised, my tan freshly topped up from a cheeky couple of days of naked sunbathing on Thad's super yacht before the party. In a nutshell, I'm primed and ready to give this guy a show.

I place both palms on his desk and slide them forward over the empty expanse of white as I hinge elegantly at the hips. I guess Eight's dislike of any type of clutter is conducive to spontaneous sex on junk-free surfaces. And this beautiful slab of smooth white marble looks like it can handle a good railing.

As can I, my friend. As can I.

I slide my hands forward until I'm bent right over and my boobs hit the cold stone. I can't help but feel a little like a sacrificial lamb. Eight's intake of breath is audibly sharp, but he still hasn't touched me. I suspect this man likes to exert as much control over himself as over everyone else.

I can't resist giving my bum a little wiggle. 'Well? I thought you had something to show me.'

Instantly, he's right up against me, his wool trousers brushing against my bare thighs and a very nice erection pressing against my pussy. He grabs my hips, his thumbs dragging over my arse cheeks.

'Your self-control is deplorable.' He sounds deeply disappointed in me.

'Self-control is overrated. And I don't have all day. Unless you're stalling because you're worried you won't be able to deliver?'

He pushes his hardness further against me, his strong fingers and thumbs kneading my bare skin. 'I have no concerns. And if you're going to work for me, you'll need to learn to shut up and take what you're given.'

Hell, yes. My head is turned sideways, one cheek is pressed to the coolness of his desk, arms cactused. So when I let my eyes flutter shut at this most delicious threat, I guess he sees it.

'You like that.'

Yes. 'Maybe.'

With my face like this, I can see his arm and not much more. He releases his grip on me and slides his fingers underneath the elasticated lace at the top of my thong. *'You like it.'*

He waits, and I sigh in defeat, because I have no interest in going up against Captain Edger in a self-control contest.

'Yes. I like it. But I'd like less conversation and more action even better. I'm not the only one who needs to learn to shut up.'

'Like I said. You'll take what you're given.' The strain is evident in his voice, and that's enough to shut me the hell up. A few seconds of meek silence on my part seem to do the trick, because he slides that thong over my arse and right down my legs, and my mind reels. It reels as much at the pleasure of having damp lace peeled away from my swollen flesh as at the knowledge that Eight is getting his first good look at my goods and his first real proof that, despite my backchat, I'm evidently more than ready to "take what I'm given".

I wonder what he thinks.

CHAPTER 8

Sophia

He doesn't give much away aside from a ragged exhale that I suspect he'd rather suppress. The man is not a gusher, but I kind of love these unwilling breadcrumbs of his.

He leaves my thong hanging around my ankles. 'Legs wider. Otherwise, don't move a muscle.'

I do as he says, sliding my feet further apart until the stretched thong bites at my ankles. It's a basic, tawdry form of restraint, and it feels great. Almost as great as being naked and bent over for a very powerful, fully dressed man who receives all his safety cues from his ability to control others.

'That's good,' he acknowledges gruffly, and then I hear the tear of foil. The sneaky little shagger must have had a condom in his pocket the entire time that he was sitting across from me and grilling me. I fucking adore that he was planning on jumping on me before I even showed up.

'Friendly reminder,' I say, my cheek and tits and stomach still plastered to his desk, 'but a lot rides on this for you. Pun intended. I really hope for your sake that you know how to use your dick well enough to compensate for your total lack of charm, because—*oooh fuuuck.*'

That last bit is unintentional but unavoidable, because he slides a couple of leisurely, entitled fingers between my legs, gliding over my clit and dragging backwards through my soaked flesh before pressing against my entrance lightly enough to be sheer torture.

'Clearly there's only one way to get you to shut the fuck up,' he muses, and then he's pulling his fingers away and replacing them with the wide, latex-covered head of his big fat dick, and pushing in. No warning. No preamble. His three-second fingering provided him with, I assume, ample evidence that I was aroused as fuck, and now we're off to the races.

I claw uselessly at the relentlessly smooth desk beneath me and brace myself as he grips one of my arse cheeks hard and guides himself in.

God, he really is big. Even without having had a peek at it, I can tell this is a lovely dick. I push back against him, taking him deeper, and all my flesh jiggles on the desk. He shunts forward, gaining a couple of inches, and we both groan.

My skin is already prickling with sweat. I blame the unmit-igated anticipation of getting a really good fucking from someone I don't know from Adam, from a man who's willing to pay an awful lot of money to have me at his beck and call every single weekday, although I'm slightly surprised he's gone straight in. This is supposed to be our chance to explore each other thoroughly, but he's barely touched me with his non-dick body parts.

He pushes home and stills for a moment, his cock buried deep inside my body and his wool trousers ticklish against my thighs. 'Fuck, yes,' he hisses before dragging himself out in a smooth glide that has my nerve endings singing.

And we're away, him quickly establishing a rhythm of vicious, feverish thrusts that light me up inside and me holding on for dear life as I take every glorious inch that he sees fit to give me. I wish I could see him, wish I had a clear view of his face. I've seen it work through a limited emotional range of dispassion, disapproval and hunger, but I haven't seen it when he's in the throes of getting exactly what he's been craving.

But it's hot, too, the relative anonymity of this age-old position, the privacy it affords him, at least. Being bent over his desk as he samples me, as he enjoys the spoils he's paid through the nose for, is a thing of staggering pleasure. And, because I have little visual stimulation aside from the view across the expanse of desk to palest grey linen-covered walls and black-and-white photographs of details from Kingsley's hotels spanning the twentieth century, I'm afforded a richer appreciation of other sensory marvels: the harsh rasp of his breath as he fucks me in the angriest way; the bite of marble against the tops of my thighs as the force of his drives shunts me forward over and over; the impossibly good ache so deep inside my body each time he bottoms out.

The pleasure is growing, and I know it's only partly physical, even if this man is conducting a masterclass in carnal pleasure. The dynamic itself is just as arousing: his demand that we do this here and now; his arrogant entitlement; his conscious failure to provide me with any foreplay. I'm not sure if it's dismissive or presumptuous; I'm unclear whether he knows he can perform well enough to sell this job without any warmup or whether he simply doesn't give a shit, because I'm here solely for his pleasure.

Honestly? Both are equally, obnoxiously, hot.

As he continues his barrage, my mind clears of thoughts and sensation takes over. I give myself over to the delirium of it, my consciousness shrinking to the truly excellent pounding he's giving my pussy.

'*Fuck*,' he grits out. 'So fucking good.' His next thrust

elicits a whimper of delight from me and a low groan from him. He drags his hands roughly up my sides and wedges them underneath me so he can cup my boobs before extracting one hand and slamming it down on his desk in front of my face. He's rolled up his sleeves, it seems. The sight of his leanly muscular forearm flexing under the weight of his drives is a far more gratifying sight than a photo of an Art Deco cocktail bar, that's for sure.

I bite down on my lip. Every exhale is a whimper now. It's an effort, but I wrap my fingers around his wrist, and he grunts with what sounds like approval.

'Harder.' I dig my nails in.

'Jesus.'

'Please, Ethan. So good. Fuck me harder.' I'm slurring now. My voice, even to my own ears, sounds pitiful, and I consider dimly that he should enjoy this. He should really fucking like watching me unravel beneath him. And he should absolutely get off on having me beg.

The sound he makes is positively anguished. He extricates his remaining hand from my boob and grabs my hip so hard I suspect he'll leave bruises.

'Told you I'd make it worth your while.' He accompanies his *I told you so* with a savage thrust. 'Told you you'd want to turn up and get railed every day. Fuck, this cunt is so greedy.'

'You're so fucking full of yourself,' I gasp, because I'm close. I'm so close that I'd be mortified at what a pushover I am if I wasn't so intent on seeing this orgasm through. Because he's right. When it comes to sexual pleasure, I'm basically Veruca Salt, and I am *this* close to stamping my stiletto heel into his shoe to spur him on.

'*Enough.*' He wrenches his wrist out of my grasp. 'Hands on the table.'

I comply, and in a turn I didn't see coming, he pins me to the table by *my* wrists. He's leaning forward now, and his breath is warm on my jaw, my neck, as he rams into me over and over. Fuck, he's bossy, and fuck, he's good at this, and fuck, backchat really gets him going. No stilettos needed—verbal spurs work a treat, it seems.

There's a real risk I drool on the table. I may spurt. It's a swamp down there. I'm so intensely turned on, and my entire body is on fire, and having Ethan Kingsley unleashed on my pussy—and by my pussy—is a fucking riot, as it happens.

Bloody hell. I could put up with a lot of shit if he gave me this kind of treatment every—

Oh my god. Oh my god. My climax hits me like a fucking forklift truck, slamming through my body and obliterating absolutely everything that is not white-hot pleasure. I splay out the fingers of my restrained hands and screw my eyes closed as I buck and buck beneath him, only vaguely aware of the unhinged shrieks that I think are coming from me.

But one sound does cut through the fog of ecstasy.

Ethan's voice, shot through with the pain of a man on the precipice of losing all control.

'Fuck—fuck—beautiful. *Beautiful*. Jesus Christ.'

He may have broken me, but it sounds like my greedy pussy and I have broken him, too. It's with a steady, desperate volley of thrusts that he fucks me through my orgasm before he vaults over the edge with a roar that's defeated and triumphant in equal measure. I soak it all up as I drift down from my high: him stilling inside me, impossibly huge, then rutting into me over and over. Done, he collapses on top of me, his breathing harsh and ragged, and drags his lips along my shoulder.

No notes.

Not a single note.

That was flawless, and I don't know whether to be smug as fuck or pissed off beyond all belief that he has the goods to back up the ego.

'Don't move,' he grunts in my ear before hauling himself off me. 'Just give me a second.'

There's a sting as he withdraws—I've taken a major pounding, after all—and he disappears to dispose of the condom. I assume that's an ensuite back there. I lie where I am, boneless and sated and woozy. Then he's back, sliding my thong up my legs and over my bottom before putting his arms under me and hauling me up. It's very much a practical move, but his movements are gentle when he turns me around and props me against the desk.

He takes a step back, crossing his arms over his chest. He's already put his dick away, and there's not a hair out of place. On his face is a self-satisfied smirk.

'You were absolutely gagging for that, weren't you?'

I narrow my eyes at him. I'm still almost naked, and I couldn't give a shit. Smug fuck. I mirror his position, crossing my arms below my most excellent boobs, a movement his eyes track. I blow an errant piece of hair out of my eyes. My legs are trembling from that earth-shattering orgasm, something I have no intention of disclosing to him. Somebody needs to take this guy down a peg or two, and that someone is me. I'll be damned if I let him see just how much that magical dick of his affected me.

'Look, *dickhead*,' I say, hating that my voice still sounds Marilyn-Monroe-levels of post-orgasmic, 'my last boss was sixty-five years old, so the bar is really fucking low.' I glare at him. 'Okay?'

That gets me my first proper smile of the day, and it's far more dazzling than I'm comfortable with. Crinkled eyes. White teeth. Dammit. He's indecently gorgeous, and it's a disaster.

He looks pointedly at my traitorous nipples, standing proudly to attention, before dragging his eyes up to my face. 'Whatever you say, sweetheart. So. When can you start?'

CHAPTER 9

Ethan

What my natural charm lacks in terms of its persuasive powers, I make up for with my dick. That works well for me when my target is a beautiful woman I'm trying to hire and less well when my target is a straight man I'm trying to shaft.

I can compare the extent of my sexual interaction with Sophia earlier to ordering a full banoffee pie and merely swiping one's forefinger through its cream. It was a taste, a shamefully inadequate way to sample her goods. Yet the sheer, indecent pleasure of it was just the balm I needed to embolden me for this evening's next steps against the Montagues. Not to mention, the satisfaction of having her accept my formal offer while still orgasm-drunk was real.

She starts on Monday.

At least I've closed one deal today.

And at least I know that, whatever fresh hell next week brings, I'll have the delights of her body to take the edge off it, even if I'll be enforcing a strict diet where she's concerned. The woman may be binge-worthy, but I am not a man who binges. I'm a man who exerts self-control in all things. I'd like to think so, at least.

After she'd left and I'd gathered my wits, I lost no time in instigating emergency mode with our banking and legal teams. With Loeb's help, I've drafted a preliminary letter to the Montague board, informing them of our intention to pursue a friendly takeover in good faith. We've kept the tone civil and high level, focusing on the impact the two groups could have as one enlarged party and only alluding in the most vague terms to 'economies of scale'. It's still not the right time to scare them off with talk of cost-cutting, and so the pitch document I'm attaching is very much a partial, look-what-we-can-achieve-together one.

This pitch has been sitting on our bankers' desktops for months now. I'm absorbed in reading it over for the millionth time when the door to my study opens without warning and my son Jamie pops his head around. I blink in surprise—I wasn't aware he was staying with me tonight. He's still in his school uniform, although it's a disgrace—sleeves rolled up and tie loose and shirt creased and a large blot of blue ink on the front.

'What are you doing here?'

He shuffles into the room, head bent. If fourteen-year-old boys are capable of any form of walking that doesn't involve shuffling, I haven't seen it. 'Mum's in Brussels.'

'Oh, that's right.' I vaguely recall that my ex-wife, Elena, mentioned a trip to Brussels this week, something that evaded me pretty much as soon as she spoke the words. As a translator for the UN, she travels more than I do.

'What's for dinner?'

I haven't the foggiest. I haven't registered until right this minute that I'm famished. 'Ask Davide to make you something. And say please.'

'He's gone home. So has Susan. Can I get Shake Shack?'

I glance at my phone. It's gone eight already. Shit. How the fuck did that happen?

'Have you done your homework?' I hedge. I only have leverage up until the point that I agree to Shake Shack.

He looks at the carpet. 'I did my biology.'

'And...?'

'I've still got maths.'

I hand him my phone. 'You can get a burger. No milkshake. Order me some sushi while you're at it. And get out of that filthy uniform and do your homework while it's en route. You hear me?'

'K. D'you want to watch *The Rookie?*'

'I can't tonight. I'm up to my eyeballs in work.'

We've been watching *The Rookie* together on occasion. He got into it at a friend's house, but now he only watches it when he's here with me. While I realise that watching television isn't the highest form of leisure activity, it's something we can do together: an easy way to hang out and bond over a common interest.

When you're in no way a positive role model for your teenage son, this kind of cop-out is worth its weight in gold. The only good I can do in his life is to provide for him and his mother, to ensure that they have the financial and physical security they need. Safe, comfortable home. Round-the-clock protection. And a household income that my divorce lawyer deemed borderline insane.

But of all the potential ominous forces in my son's life, the most potent is also the most insidious: the toxic, fucked-up legacy of the Kingsleys, where money and optics and glory come before all else. It stands to reason, therefore, that my ultimate role as a father is to hold Jamie at arm's length, to do everything in my power to protect him from infection. His mother has already been brave enough to take the first step, to cut ties with me and my family, to call time on her involvement and to take our son with her. And so it behoves me to walk the endless tightrope between perpetuating that and distancing myself from him so fully that he loathes me. It's a tightrope his warm, nurturing mother will never have to walk with him. She's all in, overtly so. She's Team Jamie, all the way, and I envy her for it just as much as I'm unspeakably grateful for it.

Which is to say that the occasional hour on the sofa, watching in quiet contentment as a group of professionals with impossible levels of altruism and integrity go about their jobs, is about as benign a use of time spent together as it gets. At least in these moments I can be sure that the Kingsley demons aren't actively at work, rotting his thoroughly decent character.

It's my own silent way of being Team Jamie, even if it looks to everyone else like a pitiful failure of parenting.

'We haven't watched it for ages,' he mutters.

'Yes, well, I have a million balls in the air, so you'll have to suck it up. Besides, you have homework to do.'

He doesn't comment, but it's only as he turns and shuffles away that I take in the dejected slump of his shoulders. There's bad posture, and there's defeat, and I suspect what I'm seeing in him is the latter. I'm acutely, painfully aware that there will come a time when he'll stop asking me to hang out at all, and I'll do better. I will. But right now, I have to put this fucking Montague offer to bed.

I BARELY REGISTER him dropping my sushi off a little later, or eating it, for that matter. We get the email out to all the registered Montague Group board members, blind copying our own board on the correspondence. About an hour after I've sent the emails, I get a text from Miles.

Covering all your bases, I see. Our stock
had a strange bounce in the last hour of
trading. Don't suppose you power-hungry
arseholes know anything about that.

A sickening blend of anger and moral outrage curdles in the pit of my stomach. I don't know which accusation bothers me more: that I've been building a stealth stake—buying their stock in the open market—while pretending to play nice, or that I'm launching this takeover bid because I'm on some kind of power trip.

Calling me power-hungry is frankly a lazy accusation and a clear sign that Montague doesn't know me at all. It's a sloppy leap from seeing someone leading the charge to assuming they're in it for the glory. Glory is overrated. It's not worth its price, which is visibility, and expectations, and vulnerability. You'll never see me court any of those things—especially the latter.

Control, on the other hand, is worth it every single time. When you're calling the shots, then, and only then, can you relax. I don't do this job for status. I do it to avoid being at anyone's mercy, to ensure that things get done properly and that the lights stay on.

Sometimes, it feels as though the wheels will come off this gilded chariot my father has passed onto me, that it will careen off into the night, dragging the thousands of people who depend on it along for the ride.

I suspect I'm as terrified of crashing the damn thing as I am resentful of being made to drive it in the first place. And if it goes off the rails, it'll be my name on the wreckage.

It's only when I finally stagger upstairs around eleven, brain hurting from the endless scenario analysis it's insisted on spitting forth all evening, that I get a chance to check in on Jamie. He's spreadeagled face down on his bed, fast asleep and fully clothed. He's had a huge growth spurt this year—he must be five eleven or close enough. His bedroom blinds are still up, ensuite bathroom light still glowing, and the room stinks of burgers. Beside his bed lies the debris of an abandoned Shake Shack delivery, including the milkshake I categorically forbade him from getting. Fuck's sake.

Teenage boys are pigs. Perhaps I should have discontinued the Kingsley family tradition of schooling us at Westminster School and opted instead for a boarding school. It might have knocked some basic self-discipline into him.

I gather up the various grease-streaked cardboard receptacles and place them by his bedroom door before lowering the blinds and turning off the bathroom light. I manage, with some difficulty, to extract the tangled duvet cover from beneath his prone body and cover him with it.

He stirs slightly, his face in profile and mouth slightly ajar, and a rush of love rips through my body, so great it almost brings me to my knees. I place a hand on his head and let it pass lightly over his mop of light brown hair. I can still see his two-year-old self in his sleeping face.

When he was tiny, the terror of keeping him alive may have been a visceral thing, but it was also straightforward.

The terror of fucking him up is, in many ways, far more suffocating.

Unbidden, the words his headmaster spoke at the last parents' event come to mind.

Parenting a teenager is tough. In many ways, they need far less physical care than we've been used to giving them during their younger years. But it's when they withdraw the most that they require the most emotional care.

Reluctantly, I remove my hand lest I wake him and instead pull the duvet further up over his shoulders. At least when he's asleep my brand of care won't threaten to destroy the very essence of who he is.

CHAPTER 10

Sophia

My new workplace may be soulless, but I have to admit it has a certain stark beauty: the benefit of joining a hotel empire known for its sleek, minimalist aesthetics.

The secret to successful minimalism, of course, lies in the quality of the fixtures and furnishings. Take that lovely, obliging slab of marble upon which my new boss railed me last week. I suspect no expense was spared in procuring that. I suspect a thousand slabs of Italian marble were inspected before Ethan's designer pronounced that one just right for her exacting client.

It's the same with everything else in this cavernous office suite. My office is next to Ethan's with a convenient interconnecting door. The white bookshelves are empty, something I intend to change quickly, and the sculptural glass-topped desk has been buffed to an inch of its life. No grimy fingerprints here. It's empty aside from a sleek monitor, wireless keyboard, and phone console: all top of the range.

Everything is perfectly tasteful, frightfully expensive, and utterly bland. The only flash of interest, of colour, in this place will come from *moi*.

No problems there.

It makes me all the gladder that I've chosen to wear my new Roksanda dress. It's a ruthlessly tailored confection of candy pink with a red-lined cape thingy. Never let it be said that I'm a believer in understatement.

My day is off to a good start. I nailed Connections on the Tube with zero errors and smugly sent my results through to Athena, my Connections nemesis. That she made an error—it looks like she fell for the red herring—has made my morning all the sweeter. We may be besties, but we're disgustingly competitive with each other on an intellectual front, and I wouldn't have it any other way. In any case, it's a nice win with which to start my first day on the job, and it feels auspicious.

When I sashay through the connecting door to greet my new lord and master, he looks every inch the king of the underworld. Hades himself had more flair than this guy. Today he's in a palest grey shirt and dark grey trousers. Not a speck of colour. Not a hair out of place. And, much as it pains me to admit it, he pulls off the exact same design rule as his office does: when everything is this high calibre, there's no need for details or distractions.

Because he's fucking perfect, even if he's positively vibrating with stress.

'Good. You're here. Shut the door so we can get the most important thing out of the way first.'

Fun fact. When Camille polled the seraphim recently, she found that every single one of us had some sort of sexual encounter with our new bosses before lunch on the first day of our employment. These billionaires are as hungry for sex as they are for money and power, it seems.

And I'm so up for it. I'm so up for being his sexy stress ball.

He strides towards me, hands in his pockets, gaze fixed longingly on my mouth, and I allow myself to drink in his austere beauty. He's all eyes and jaw and cheekbones, hair combed carefully off his face and his shirt collar, with its single undone button, the perfect frame for his Adam's apple and the hollow below. His shirt is tailored so perfectly to his torso that it makes me think this guy never allows his weight to deviate by so much as a pound. He probably monitors it with the laser focus of a jockey or a boxer.

The certain knowledge that getting naked with him is in my near future is an anticipatory pleasure so great it takes my breath away.

I'm smiling at him when he stops abruptly in front of me and gestures at the seat in front of his desk—the one he occupied as he watched me strip.

'Have a seat.'

It's definitely not a request. Okay then. Even by his standards, he seems extra pissy this morning, and I wonder what's crawled up his arse over the weekend.

I head over and sink into the chair, crossing my legs alluringly. Ethan doesn't go around to his side, instead standing next to me and turning the huge monitor so I have a clear view of it. There's a Zoom call live with several suits, all at their desks.

What the fuck? I didn't have Ethan down as an exhibitionist, but if he wants to fuck me over his desk while his pals watch, I'm game.

Ethan unmutes us and hinges forward, planting his palms on the marble. 'Thanks for holding. I'm with my new executive assistant, Sophia Petrakis. Sophia, these gentlemen are from our banking team at Loeb. We're in the early stages of a large transaction, and I need to get you wall-crossed asap.'

My years in investment banking have familiarised me with the intricacies of M&A and of the wall-crossing process. With any merger or acquisition or other material transaction, especially one involving companies whose stocks are publicly traded, strict Chinese walls must exist to separate those with the knowledge of market-sensitive information from those who buy and sell stocks. So when someone is brought over the wall—i.e. given access to this private information—it has to be rigorously documented.

Even as my pussy mourns this delay of sexy times, my business brain kicks into gear at the promise of being let in on a juicy secret. Was this the "work crisis" he alluded to last week in our interview?

I lean forward and address the guys on the screens. I swear one of them is staring straight at my tits. 'So what's the transaction?'

Ethan answers for them, and I crane my neck to look up at him. So near and yet so far... from being railed. 'Last week, we proposed a friendly takeover to the board of The Montague Group following its recent share price weakness.'

My eyebrows shoot up in surprise. I haven't seen Theo or his brother since I've been back, but the devastating planning setbacks they're suffering have been all over the financial press. 'Got it.'

He continues curtly. 'They spent this weekend holed up in talks, and they let us know late last night that they've rejected our proposal outright... so now we go full hostile.'

I sit back in my chair.

Holy *shit*.

Miles Montague must be spitting fire. The Montagues do *not* hold the Kingsleys in high regard.

'But you won't announce it yet,' I hazard as I process this information. 'Not until you hit the threshold.'

The UK's financial regulator, the FCA, allows companies to build a stake in another company of up to three percent before triggering the requirement to disclose this publicly. The second the market gets wind of an acquisition, hedge funds and risk arbitrage funds will go crazy, shovelling up the target's stock as a bet that the buyer will have to pay an even higher price and they'll lock in a profit. So it stands to reason that the more stock the Kingsleys can accumulate on the quiet before that happens, the better—and cheaper—for them.

He nods curtly. 'Precisely.'

'We're already at nought-point-four percent as of the close on Friday,' one of the bankers announces with a self-satisfied smirk. 'And our traders will continue to maintain a decent share of the trading volume over the next couple of days, so—'

'Hang on.' Ethan's voice is quiet, but, beside me, his entire body has gone ominously still. Stiff. 'Who authorised them to start buying?'

'Richard sent through the instructions on Thursday,' the banker says, the smirk instantly replaced with a nervous frown.

'Of course. Keep me posted as you buy. I want updates twice a day. Now, let's get this wall-crossing submitted.'

I turn my attention to the iPad lying on the desk in front of me and sign the document electronically. Loeb's Compliance department now has a record of when I gained access to this privileged and highly sensitive information.

As soon as the call concludes, Ethan pushes off the desk and rounds it, sinking into his own chair. He hits a button on his console. 'Topher. Ask my father to come in right away, would you?'

I survey him from across the desk. He's grabbed the arms of his chair and is white-knuckling them, his jaw working.

'There'd be a lot of cost efficiencies to come out of a deal like that,' I muse aloud, not taking my eyes off him.

'One of the many reasons they've rejected our advances, I'll warrant,' he says shortly. It makes sense. The Montagues have a widespread reputation in the industry for treating their people like family. They can't possibly want the Kingsleys wading in and giving thousands of employees the axe.

'Do you think the rejection was a knee-jerk reaction? Because no matter how much they hate the idea of you acquiring them, it would make a lot of sense.'

His tone is even. 'If it is, then they're guilty of putting their own interests above their shareholders. But no matter. We approached them in good faith, and they've insisted on doing things the hard way. Now the market gets to decide.'

I screw up my face, trying to remember the Montague ownership structure. 'How much does the family still own?'

'Thirty-eight percent.'

'Yikes.' Yikes is right. Shares equal votes. If the family only controls around a third of the voting rights, then the Montagues have no power over whether the Kingsleys can acquire them. Like Ethan says, every shareholder will get to decide for himself or herself.

Obviously, when you give up your majority stake in what was once a family-owned company, you also give up your autonomy in exchange for the money your new shareholders give you, but it must still rankle *badly*. For the Montagues, that is. Something tells me that acquiring them isn't a new idea for the Kingsleys.

Ethan doesn't comment. Instead, his eyes flicker to the door and his stress levels appear to ramp up a notch, if that's possible. On instinct, I turn around in my seat and am confronted with the Sexy Daddy Ghost of Christmas Future. Oh sirree—these Kingsley men age *well*. Richard Kingsley is a total SILF (Senior I'd Like to Fuck). He's probably pushing seventy, but boy, has he still got it.

While I think about it, the ageing-well proof is yet another silver lining around the cloud of Ethan's Raging Arsehole factor that seemed so indisputable when I first met him.

'And who is this?' Ethan Senior positively purrs, advancing into the room. On second thoughts, he looks entirely too self-satisfied. And is a three-piece suit really necessary? Nobody in this country wears three-piece suits anymore unless they're at a wedding—or Ascot. And even then, it's morning suits all the way. A three-piece pinstripe suit in one's place of work seems gratuitous. Aggressively so.

'This is Sophia Petrakis, my new EA. Sophia—my father, Richard Kingsley.' Ethan grunts out the introduction reluctantly. I sense he resents having social niceties interrupt the beef he clearly has with Daddy Dearest, who's apparently been moving the hostile bid along without notifying his son, who's the fucking CEO. Tut, tut.

'Charmed, dear.' Richard stops in front of me and holds out his hand as I stand and shake it. I don't miss the naked appreciation of my appearance in his eyes.

'How do you do.' I don't give him more. I'll take my cues from my boss, and right now I see no reason to pander to Richard.

'She's wall-crossed. And you've been buying stock. Since *Thursday*.'

I sink back into my chair, angling it for a full view of both men as Ethan glares daggers at his father across his desk.

'Someone had to get in front of this, and it was clear you weren't going to.' Richard slides his hands into the pockets of his suit trousers, looking entirely too smug. 'I could have told you we'd end up going hostile.'

'It wasn't your role to make that call. I'm the CEO. I'm leading this transaction.'

'I'm still the Chairman of the Board and the founder of this company.'

'I was negotiating in good faith. Miles called this—he accused me of buying up their shares in the open market. Jesus Christ.'

Ethan is shaking now, with ill-disguised fury and what looks like genuine distress. My first, private reaction upon hearing about the deal was pity for the Montagues. Ethan may come across as an aggressive bastard who has no qualms about going after what he wants, but this enlightening little exchange suggests he has integrity and scruples, at the very least.

He may want a fight, but it sounds like he wants a fair fight.

Unlike his darling papa.

Richard's voice stays perfectly charming, perfectly even—for my benefit, I suspect. 'This may be a rare opportunity to acquire our most complementary competitor, but that doesn't mean I want to pay any price. *Not* buying up stock as soon as we approached them is nothing short of naïve, my boy. I for one intend this deal to go smoothly. We want to show the market—and the Montagues—that they're dealing with professionals. We get this done, and we're far less susceptible as a target. Far less. I didn't build this empire to see us taken out and have some ghastly Americans put their name on the door.'

Bingo. If Ethan's an Eight Enneagram, I suspect his father's a raging Three. I mean, I've only spent a minute with the man, but I'd put money on it. Three—AKA The Achiever, or sometimes The Performer. Both fit. Everything about this guy seems performative. He builds and he builds, and as his empire swells, so does his ego.

Like I said, I'd put money on it.

Most of the seraphim are Threes, actually, with my darling Athena the most Three-ish Three I know: Driven. Outward-looking. Image-conscious. But while many of my girls seek their worth through validation and recognition, they're at the healthier, more well-adjusted end of the spectrum.

And as for this dude?

Hmm.

He's looking more and more like the kind of Three who'd

run his own son over with a bus to get what he wants. Threes can't help looking to others, but I suspect this guy is all image and no substance—an impressive shell that's entirely hollow.

Fascinating.

And pretty shitty for Ethan, if my instincts are right.

CHAPTER 11

Ethan

I'm still shaking when I usher Dad out the door: shaking not just with anger, but with that ridiculous, primal kind of fear that comes from a long history of cautionary tales. In my younger years, going up against my father never went well for me—or for anyone. I may be a grown man and the elected leader of this company, but it seems my body still hasn't got the memo, and it fucking kills me. Whenever I confront him, which I only do when I'm forced to, it's as if there's a ten-year-old version of me cowering in a corner, waiting for him to punish me by withholding his love and attention, by freezing me out.

But I'm not out in the cold anymore. I'm forty-one years of age, and I despise the physical signs of weakness that wash over me every time we have an altercation. We're both grown men, and he's no longer my keeper, and even if he gives me the classic silent treatment, I shouldn't care. I'm in control of my world and my relationships and this company, and that doesn't change just because Dad chooses to blindside me with the occasional dick move.

He'll be furious that I called him out in front of Sophia.

Absolutely furious. The uglier his soul grows, the more intent he becomes on maintaining his pristine image of urbane, benign businessman—the gracious patriarch. He's a walking, talking portrait of Dorian Gray.

A smiling assassin.

'So your dad's a piece of work, then,' Sophia offers, tilting her head to one side as I shut the door behind me. If she notices me locking it, she doesn't mention it.

'My father can go fuck himself.' I walk back to her and grab the iPad. I notice dispassionately that my hand is still shaking. 'Now, I need you up to speed on the details of the transaction as soon as possible. Here's a more detailed version of the deck we sent to the Montague board. Go sit at your desk and look it over.'

'Of course.' She takes the device and stands, and I catch a fleeting, quizzical look from her as we stand face to face.

She's wondering, no doubt, why I don't just bend her over my desk again and vent my obvious rage out on her. But we're going to do this my way. My way will be better for her, and better for me, because I need something very particular in this moment.

If I have tried to forget, over the past few days, that Sophia is a beauty for the ages, then God help me, I'm under no illusions now. Her presence is enough to remind me that hiring her was greedy, greedy, greedy.

And greed is something I simply don't do.

That's firmly my father's domain.

I indulge, certainly, but in carefully prescribed moderation, and hiring this woman is like ordering a foot-high stack of syrupy pancakes when I'm used to plain egg white and spinach omelettes. (It's not a bad analogy, except that I do allow a single yolk in my breakfast omelette in acknowledgement of its nutritional value.)

She's as lush as I remember, her eyes as dark and lips as

pillowy and hair as silken as I knew them to be. And don't get me started on this body of hers. She may have dressed it in some gratuitously colourful, high-fashion contraption today, but I know what it looks like naked, how golden and soft and sumptuous, a body a man as tightly wound as I am could find solace in for days and days.

Which is why I maintain that hiring her was greedy. I need a tight pussy and a wet mouth to chip away at my stress in a manageable fashion. On that particular front, my sleek, desirable, eager-to-please former assistants have done perfectly well. I do not need every single other enticement that Miss Petrakis has to offer, and I'm frankly disgusted with myself that I've been so weak-willed as to pursue this thing with her.

Still, the greater the temptation, the greater the self-control needed to withstand it. If nothing else, she'll make for a fine test of my mettle, every fucking weekday.

I give her a few minutes to settle herself at her desk, watching her through the open interconnecting door between our offices.

Her glass-topped desk is new.

And far from accidental.

We're about to test out its benefits.

~

SHE LOOKS up as I enter her office, and I take a moment to appreciate how fine she looks at her new desk, a jolt of beauty and colour amid the stark backdrop of pale grey walls and huge windows. She has the iPad in front of her and a large notepad beside it upon which she's making notes.

'As you were,' I say, crossing the room and making my way behind her chair. 'Don't let me disturb you.'

'Okay.' There's a note of doubt in her voice, like she's trying to figure out my game here, but she goes with it, casting her eyes back to the presentation. It's a far more detailed version of the deck we sent to the Montague board, complete with page after page of data around cost-cutting opportunities as well as the top-line synergies we proposed to them.

I stand behind her and glance over her shoulder at the presentation. She's looking at a page of pie charts detailing the market share the combined group would have by region and by category. It's only after noting this that I allow myself to still, to gaze down at the top of her dark head and admire the thick, glossy waves cascading over her shoulders. Her dress features a modest V-neck, but the shadow of her cleavage is visible from this angle, as are her knees and the bottoms of her thighs through the glass desk. It looks like she's wearing nude stockings.

This may just be my favourite thing: that heady moment of anticipation before I make a move. The certain knowledge that the shit-storms of work and life and fathers and sons can wait while I claw back the control I know I need to quiet my mind and restore my equilibrium.

I'd do well to remember that I need to submit to my own self-control just as much as I need this stunning woman to submit to me. Not for the first time, I wish I was one of those men capable of discarding that self-discipline and turning themselves over wholeheartedly to their basest urges. But I didn't get where I am, and I haven't survived where I am, by being weak-willed.

Finally, *finally*, I allow my hands to slide through Sophia's dark tresses.

SOPHIA

Ethan's fingers rake slowly, surely, through my hair, and I can't stop the pleased, soft breath that leaves my mouth at the sensation. Fuck, I hope he's come in here to pulverise me like the ultimate stress toy.

'Don't stop on my account.' It's less a request than an order, so I play along and keep reading, forcing myself to jot down the occasional figure on my pad. He rakes my hair back into a ponytail and winds it slowly around his wrist. When he pulls, the burn is delicious. And when he uses the rein he's fashioned to tug my head to one side, my pulse picks up, because he's leaning over, his mouth ghosting over my jaw, down my neck.

I try to turn my face so my mouth is closer to his. Surely, if I tempt him enough, he'll give in and kiss me? Fuck knows, I want this man to kiss me. I want him to thrust so deep inside my mouth with his tongue that it makes me moan. I want him to know how good my mouth feels, to spell out for him how fantastic I could make him feel if he let me wrap my lips around his cock.

But he's not having any of it.

'Stop it. Don't move. Keep reading.'

Jesus. I'm sweating a little already, trying not to pant like a bitch in heat. If Ethan needs to exert some control over me to regain his control overall after that little hissy fit from his dad, then I'm one hundred percent on board. Not to mention, he smells great. No cologne. I can't imagine he bothers with bells and whistles like cologne. Just clean, soapy, male skin. I hope he's enjoying my scent, too. I hope he spends the rest of the day unable to get my perfume out of his nostrils.

'I hope you're noting how complementary these businesses are outside of London,' he murmurs, his lips trailing down the side of my neck again. 'Their Sorrel Farm JV would give us so much reach in the rural leisure market.'

I am not noting that. I am, however, noting that my clit is thrumming wildly and my skin is on fire.

'There's a lot of overlap in London, though,' I say with difficulty.

'Doesn't matter. Target demographics are different. They're more tourist-focused, we're stronger in business travel.'

He straightens up, releasing my hair, and there's a pause before he slides his hands over my shoulders and down my front until they're brushing my breasts. I make a strangled little sound at the back of my throat and stay stock still. I don't want to do anything to throw him off his mission, which is hopefully to play my body like a fucking violin. Silently, I beg him to ramp up his groping. My dress may be made from annoyingly robust fabric, but my bra is sheer mesh. I want all the sensation he can give me.

Sure enough, he starts to knead my breasts slowly, palms and then thumbs skating over my nipples in a way that's glorious and yet not remotely enough. While I daren't actually arch into his touch, I take a full breath, expanding my lungs enough to push my tits a little further against him, my nipples steely, needy little bullets.

'It's very hard to give a shit about my father when I have your tits in my hands, Sophia. It's very hard to give a shit about anything at all.'

'Tell me what I can do to make you feel better,' I say, my voice breathy.

'Sit still, and shut up, and keep reading, and do as I say. That's what you can do.' His voice is as stern as it is tense.

I'm about to be a fucking Girl Scout for this man.

Just wait until he sees how good I can be. For good measure, I turn the page to some lovely charts on the breakdown of the business hotel market. Fascinating. Just fascinating. I pretend to scour the page for information as the extremely hot, controlling billionaire behind me continues to play with my breasts, cupping and stroking and kneading, his fingers teasing and rubbing my nipples, which are winning against my dress fabric. And it feels so good. So, so good. My pussy is aching. Blazing. I can't squirm, but I can squeeze my thighs together, and I can secretly do my Kegels and try to find some relief that way, and I can—

'Stop that at once.'

I stop.

'What do you say?'

'Sorry, Mr Kingsley.' As if to underline my virtue, I scribble *twenty-six percent* down on my notepad.

He pinches my nipples through my dress, and I moan softly.

'Apparently, I'll have to teach you some self-control.'

'I'll enjoy every minute of being your pupil, Mr Kingsley.'

He blows out a ragged breath. He likes that. I bet he's hard as a rock.

'Keep reading.'

I flip to the next slide.

He bends over me and slides his hands down, down, down, until I can see them through the glass table, snagging on the hem of my dress. Behind me, his body is a wall of heat.

Yes yes yes!

'This isn't for you. You're just a body for me to enjoy. Don't let me interrupt you.'

Oh god, this is so hot. I give myself a gigantic silent round of applause for having had the foresight to lean the iPad vertically against my monitor rather than flat on the desk. My notepad is off to my right, meaning we both have a clear view of him tugging up the hem, up over the lace tops of my stockings and the little clips of my suspender belt, until he unearths my pink lace thong. (It's the exact same shade as my dress. I'm a details girl.)

'Open your legs. *Slowly*,' he barks, with as much warning in his voice as if he's asking an armed criminal to show him her hands. As I enthusiastically obey, he moves his hands around to the sides so he can ruck the hem of my dress up even further over my arse so it bands around my middle.

'Next page. Keep reading. *Out loud.*' He slides one hand beneath my legs and strokes a couple of fingers over my lace-clad pussy with maddeningly lightness as he releases my dress and sticks the other hand down the front of my dress and into my bra, his fingers finding and brushing softly over my nipple. It's utter, utter torture, having both his hands in exactly the right locations and yet refusing to touch me properly.

Desperately, I swipe and read. '*Cost Efficiencies and Economies of Scale.*'

'Go on.' His mouth is by my ear, his breath warm on my jaw, his fingers conducting some kind of diabolical warfare on my most erogenous zones. My nerve endings are screaming. He's setting me up to fail and undoubtedly loving every minute of it.

'Um, *Integration of Kingsley Hotels and The Montague Group will enable significant reduction in duplicated corporate functions.*'

'What a good girl.' Oh-so gently, he hooks a finger into the lace strip of my thong and pulls it aside, baring my molten pussy to the air. 'I bet you can get those legs even wider for me too, can't you?'

I practically pull a muscle with how quickly I spread 'em. 'Yes—I—'

'Look at that.' His voice is low and cajoling and vaguely patronising. 'Such a pretty cunt. It's just begging to be stroked. Keep reading.'

I'm sweating properly now. My clit is throbbing and

straining. I'm so hyperaware of *just* how close his hand is to where I'm vibrating for him. I'm his slave, and he knows it, and I will do whatever I need to do to earn my reward.

'*Combined entity anticipates elimination of redundant positions across finance, human resources, legal, and procurement departments.*' My entire body is trembling with need. My voice is so shaky I can barely get the words out. And the sick bastard must like it, because he finally ups the ante, rolling my nipple around between his thumb and forefinger as he strokes two taut fingers down the slippery channel from my clit to my entrance and pushes them in, hard. The unadulterated pleasure of it has me lightheaded; the sight of his hand through the glass, moving between my legs is filthy. Nothing to see here— just me trying to do my job as my boss takes whatever he wants under my desk.

I'm not sure I've ever been so hyper-aware as I am in this moment.

'*Fuck*. Keep going.'

'*Conservative estimates project three hundred and fifty to four hundred administrative role reductions within*—oh my god.'

He halts. Stops rolling my nipple. Withdraws his fingers from my soaking pussy.

'Wait. No—sorry—*within eighteen months of completion, representing approximately eighteen to twenty-four million pounds in annual savings.*'

He pinches my nipple hard and fucks me deep and slow with his fingers, the tendons in his hand flexing tantalisingly through the glass as he does. And finally, finally, finds my clit with his thumb and begins to circle it. God, that's a really, really excellent rhythm.

It's so much to focus on—his grip on my nipple, and staying perfectly still for him, and the burn of his fingers as he fucks me, and making sense of this dry finance mumbo-jumbo, and that rough drag of his thumb around and around my clit. I shudder with the effort needed not to lose control right now and gush all over his fingers like a burst water main.

'What else?'

'What else, uh… *Technology Infrastructure Rationalisation. Migration to unified Kingsley property management systems will eliminate dual-platform maintenance costs,* shit, *and enable staff reductions across IT support functions.*'

'I don't think we really included the word *shit* in our deck, did we?' Ethan says primly, fingers and thumbs stilling on my flesh.

Fuck. 'No, I'm sorry, I'm—no.'

I'm barely holding it together. My body is vibrating as if I'm sitting through a spin cycle on a washing machine, and sweat is trickling between my breasts.

'Just read the rest of this paragraph like a very good girl,' he says in a kindly tone, 'and then I'll let you come.'

I can do this. I can. He's finally shown me where the finish line is, and I'm so close. I really am. I grit my teeth and blink to focus my lust-blurred vision.

'*The estimated timeline to integrate the Kingsley legacy reservations system on a group-wide basis is twelve to fifteen months.*' I swallow hard. '*Eliminating forty to fifty technology roles across both organisations.*'

'That was *very* good.' He brushes his thumb over my slick clit, and I tremble. 'Now, let's see just how beautifully you can come for me.'

Finally. I let my eyes drift closed as he stays bent over me. He ramps up his ministrations, squeezing my nipple punishingly and pistoning into my pussy with his fingers, that thumb of his working my clit like a champ.

The heat where he's touching my body is extraordinary, the pleasure breathtaking. He's breathing heavily against my ear, as if this is affecting him as much as it is me, and I woozily congratulate myself on having taken up the role as Eight's official stress ball. Rather, my body is his stress ball, my clit and my breasts there to soothe him and numb him... and boy is it working out well for me.

'God,' I say, my voice shuddery, and he huffs, pleased.

'That's it. That's it. Show me.'

Of course he wants to undo me. However powerless he may have felt back there, he needs to feel just as powerful here, with me. If he needs a woman to fall apart in spectacular style in order to reclaim his sense of control, then he's picked the right girl.

I need his fingers dragging through my flesh. Need his voice in my ear telling me how very well I'm doing. Need to cede all my agency to this beautiful, difficult, enigmatic man towering over me as he does wicked things to my body.

'Omigod omigod omigod.' That molten feeling has spread through every inch of me. My nerve endings are tingling and dancing. Crimson and orange and magenta dance across my eyelids. I'm going to come. I arch my back and shove my pussy against his hand and take everything he has to give me, the pleasure cascading over me in beautiful, brilliant washes as my orgasm slams into me over and over and over.

Ethan's teeth drag along my jawline. 'So beautiful. Jesus, so beautiful.' His voice is a rasp.

I ride out my climax, my entire body convulsing in my chair. Slowly, slowly, the waves ebb away, and I let my eyes drift open. The sight of his big, masculine hand clamped between my legs, my pink thong stretched tautly to one side, is filthily decadent.

Dreamily, I turn my head so that his lips skate closer along my jaw to mine.

But there's no kiss.

Instead, he whispers in the fevered tone of a man driven to the brink of his control, 'My turn now.'

CHAPTER 12

Sophia

He extricates his hands from my body and steps away from me, swivelling my chair around so I'm facing him. My dress is still rucked up around my middle, my thong askew and digging into my swollen flesh. God knows what my face looks like. My pupils are probably the size of saucers.

Just like his.

Because he may have roughed me up good and proper, but he too looks like he's already gone a few rounds. A few locks of his sleek brown hair hang loosely, sexily, over his eyes, which are, in a word, wild. He's breathing hard, and it would be remiss of me not to mention the actual, literal elephant in the room: that monster erection.

He glances down at the spoils of his handiwork between my legs and groans raggedly. I suppose this is a far better view than he had when he was touching me over my shoulders. 'Undo my belt and unzip me. *Carefully.*'

'Yes, Mr Kingsley.' That boner of his probably feels like an unexploded grenade—lethal, and mere seconds away from unleashing havoc. I can't wait to get my hands on it. It may have been inside my body last week, but I'm dying for an actual peek.

As directed, I unbuckle his belt and make easy work of his trouser fastenings without taking my eyes off him. I'm hyper-aware of every perfect nuance of our current situation. This beautiful, powerful man is paying me to suck him off in the icy splendour of his office. I bet every woman outside of this door would kill to get her talons into Ethan Kingsley—even *with* his dubious personality. And not only has he chosen me, but he's paying through the nose for the privilege.

Oh, and he's seconds away from detonating at the singular experience that is the Sophia Petrakis Blow Job™. (I really should trademark it properly.)

I push up his shirttails, and there it is: a beast of a dick peeking out of the waistband of his black boxer briefs. When I pull them away from his skin, the unruly beast rears up like a stallion, a perfect little pearl of precum beading at the tip. I feel like I should shout *woah!* like I'm on Yellowstone (I do not.)

But it's gorgeous. Oh, dear Lord above, is it gorgeous. Long, thick, and as sleek and powerful-looking as its owner. No wonder it got me from nought to sixty in about three seconds last week.

I shove his boxer briefs down to mid-thigh and wrap my fingers around it.

'Listen very carefully,' Ethan grits out, with the intensity I'd personally reserve for talking someone through how to defuse a bomb. 'I want you to do everything I say.'

'Really, I've got this,' I say, but he shakes his head, annoyed.

'No. I want this my way.'

I'm being dim. This isn't about whether my technique is up to scratch. Of course it's not. Blow jobs are the ABC of the Seraph service offering.

No, this is about control. It's about Ethan being able to

make a woman suck his dick in exactly the way he wants. It's about him knowing he can call every single shot.

'Whatever you want.' I lick my lips, and he blows out a breath. His dick is so hot, so hard, in my hand.

'Okay. Lean forward, but don't put your mouth on me. Yet.'

I'm still sitting, Ethan standing between my legs. I do as he asks, leaning forward and opening my mouth when it's just a couple of inches away from his lovely, weeping crown.

He shoves one hand through my hair, as if to hold me in place, and presses the thumb of his other hand into the centre of my lower lip. I've been told by many men that I have a mouth made for fellatio, and the expression on Ethan's face suggests he's reached the same conclusion. Honestly, the poor guy looks more stricken than aroused.

I sit there patiently, the picture of dishevelled, wanton possibility, gazing up at him. I can feel him pulsing in my grip, can feel just how badly he needs this release. What I don't know is whether he's trying to control me or himself.

Finally, he removes his thumb and uses the hand entangled in my hair to pull my face closer. 'Lick it. Just the slit. Very, very softly.'

I do exactly as he asks, running my tongue up his slit and through the precum, and he emits an unholy groan.

'Good. That's perfect. Again.'

Obviously, I oblige, but I'm fascinated by his insistence on holding back. I don't think I've ever seen anyone edge themselves quite so spectacularly.

'Now run your tongue around the tip. *Not* your lips—just your tongue.'

What's actually on the tip of said tongue is the strong impulse to remind Ethan that no one likes a back-seat driver, especially when they're giving head, but I refrain. He's not the only one with admirable self-control, it seems. If this guy wants to pay through the nose to micro-manage me and torture himself into the bargain, who am I to refuse?

(Also, it would be a lie to say I'm not totally loving the effect this is having on him. It's a *lot* of fun, watching him gradually lose his mind through sheer pleasure.)

I stick out my tongue and run it delicately around his clean, delicious-tasting crown, keeping my mouth open and my lips away from his dick. God forbid I should overstimulate him. With an effort, I tip my head up so I can check him out through my eyelashes. He's staring down at me with a level of admiration I'm not sure I've earned yet.

I wish I could take matters into my own hands. By *matters*, I mainly mean his arse. And his stomach. I'm bloody dying for a peek. This man has maintained Victorian levels of prudishness so far with regard to getting his kit off. I want to dig my nails into his arse cheeks and squeeze as I demonstrate how well I can deep-throat him. I want to shove up these pesky shirt tails and drag my hand over his stomach and enjoy all that hair and those abs.

He's such a spoilsport.

'Now with your lips,' he commands me, and I waste no time in wetting my lips and closing my mouth around him so I can suck, just a little. The noise he makes has me wanting to go off-script. Maybe I can take control, just a little, while making him think it's his call? If I act desperate enough for his dick, maybe he'll allow me more of it. Any guy who claims not to like cock worship is a bare-faced liar.

With my lips a plush seal around his crown, I lick him slowly, sensually. I want this experience to be the height of decadence for him. Of indulgence. I'm not sure he knows much about the concept. I suspect Seraph is less about self-indulgence and ego and more about sheer maintenance, much like a PT or a daily supplement regime.

Pop some vitamins, work out, have an orgasm.

Rinse and repeat.

He's shuddering against my hand and mouth, and the thought occurs to me that maybe he's trying to hold off for the sake of his image. Maybe he feels the need to last longer than thirty seconds on my first day. Or maybe he's trying to maximise his investment—but if that was the case, surely he'd have me naked in one of the many bedrooms in his hotel building a single block away?

God only knows.

I pop off for a sec and lower my lids to half-mast. 'Please let me take you deeper,' I beg in my throatiest, most porno voice. 'I need you to fuck my mouth so badly.'

He gazes down at me, conflict written all over his gorgeous face. I bet he's thinking about puppy training. *If we give in straight away, we'll create a monster. Better to show them who's boss.* I need to flip the script, make him realise that control here should look like taking action, not holding back.

'I want you to use me,' I continue. 'Please, Ethan. I want you to show me what it's like when you do what you like with me.'

Really, I'm just messing with him. But it's for his own good. He may think he's already doing what he likes with me, but I can't see there's anything enjoyable about this for him. His balls must be fucking agony. No, he's doing with me what he thinks he should.

He thinks he should hold back, show us both how disciplined he is, how in control of even the most intense situation he is, when really he should let rip.

Ideally, down my throat.

His fingers flex restlessly in my hair. He doesn't answer with words but slides both hands forward so they're gripping my jaw and thrusts, filling me up. As a pro, I've anticipated this. I accommodate him as best I can, but bloody hell, is he big. He tastes lovely, and I make a noise of appreciation that should also tell him I'm good. When he hits the back of my throat and my lips meet my knuckles, I stiffen a little, and he moans, low and pained.

'Fucking hell.'

I can't speak, for obvious reasons, so I can't tell him to fuck my mouth properly, but it seems his dick is able to advocate for itself, because as soon as he recovers he's pushing out and slamming back in.

Finally. Finally I can show him what he's capable of, why this deserves a trademark.

Ethan restrained and repressed was sexy; Ethan on the brink was hot; Ethan unleashed is dazzling. He's all animalistic moans and feverish thrusts, his hands holding my jaw in place for dear life.

I take the initiative to give him every single part of the Sophia Petrakis experience, removing my hand from its grip to take him deeper, fondling his balls, grabbing that tight, toned arse *(delicious)* and scrabbling under his shirt to claw at his stomach, which is every bit as taut and alluring as I've suspected, and I want *more*. More of him. More of this.

He doesn't last, of course. He can't possibly. He was about to blow his load before he let me anywhere near his dick. I'm sucking and licking and groping and moaning, and it's wet and messy and punishing and arousing as fuck. Working on the basis that Ethan's not about to dole out any more orgasms, I may have to get myself off in the loos after this. I feel him swell up in my mouth and quickly wrap my fingers around his base again as I reach for his balls with my other hand. In his far-gone state, he seems to have forgotten all about his desire to call the shots. He's basically given me free rein, and I'm damn well exploiting it in every way I can.

'*Fuck.*' He's practically shouting now, his voice all strangled and sexy. I wriggle in my chair, but it has no impact with my legs spread like this. 'Fuck. *Jesus!*'

And it's with that glorious curse that the man who is his own worst enemy allows himself to finally, finally come. He erupts into my mouth, rope after rope of hot, thick cum hitting the back of my throat. I suck him through it, swallowing around him with difficulty as he's coming down, a stunt that has him practically shooting through the ceiling.

When I'm content that he's done, I slide off him and lick him clean, my head tilted to one side in a way I know gives him an excellent view of my tongue lapping at his dick.

He looks shell-shocked. Devastated. Completely and utterly wrecked. And, honestly, I feel pretty fucking smug. Horny, but smug.

I release him from my grip and tuck him back in in silence. I don't want to burst his post-orgasmic bubble. But as I'm fastening his trousers, he wrenches himself away.

'I'll do it.' He nods at me, and it's way more dismissive than appreciative. Disgusted, even, though whether he's more disgusted with me or with himself, I'm unclear. 'Go clean yourself up and get back to work.'

Ahh. The textbook move. One step forward and two steps backwards. A moment of vulnerability, and now he's building those walls again.

I allow myself to enjoy the fine sight of his backside as he strides back into his office and slams the interconnecting door behind him.

What a glorious, fucked-up arsehole.

CHAPTER 13

Sophia

THE SERAPHIM

ATHENA:

Well??? How did the first day go @Sophia?

BREE:

I swear someone needs to give this girl the memo that she's no longer a Seraph

ATHENA:

I'd like to see you try, bitch

MARLOWE:

Um, does that mean I should leave the chat too?

BREE:

No way. We really like you

ATHENA:

I won't forget that.

TALIA:

Come on, babes. Put us out of our misery.
How was it??? If he didn't make you 💀,
you should take that as a win

CAMILLE:

Hope it all went smoothly. Please check in
when you can.

ME:

Hey, hey. Sorry. Yeah, all good. @Talia you
were right, he's a piece of work

Dude needs to touch some grass

But no tears

I'd like to see him try

ATHENA:

Did you get much 🌭🌭🌭?

ME:

One excellent ✨✨✨

He made me read some really dry report
out loud at my desk while he got me off

It was truly fabulous 💀

Then I returned the favour 👄🌭💦

> He fucking loved it

BREE:

Nice 😥

CAMILLE:

I'm so pleased it all went well. Well done.

ATHENA:

Excellent work 👏👏👏

MARLOWE:

Sounds 🔥. Any fucking?

BREE:

Look at you!! Who is this insatiable ho?

MARLOWE:

😳😳😳😳😳😳😳😳😳😳

ME:

> No fucking

> Honestly, he has epic self control

> It's going to be sooooo much fun watching him wrestle it like an alligator every day 😄

TALIA:

😥 It's the only thing I miss

Fuck he's hot

Well done for getting it all in your mouth - no mean feat

ME:

He really is

Thanks for the sloppy seconds!

And yeah. It was a proper mouthful

Why is the self-control thing so hot???

BREE:

Anything that involves bringing a man unwillingly to his knees is hot

ATHENA:

Amen sister

CHAPTER 14

Sophia

My first week of being Ethan Kingsley's EA with benefits proceeds in a pretty linear fashion. In between countless meetings with his strategy team around the transaction, Ethan uses me in a ridiculously restrained, tightly rationed way: quick BJs and gratifying but too-short fucks on his desk, basically.

It feels as though he needs my orgasms as much as he needs some of his own. I suspect they represent wins for him, reminders that my satisfaction is within his control. All of which is great for him, but he still hasn't kissed me, and I still haven't seen the guy naked, and the latter in particular is *seriously* pissing me off.

I sit down with Topher, his long-time PA, who is as nerdily impressive as he is impressively nerdy. He has an MBA from London Business School and is more than qualified to be Ethan's EA, except for the fact that he's lacking a vagina. I like him instantly. He's probably mid-thirties, married with three young kids. I get the distinct impression that he finds dealing with Ethan's anal retentiveness and hissy fits to be a welcome reprieve from life with a triumvirate of rug rats and is delighted to put in whatever hours are needed.

I feel for his poor wife.

Most interestingly, Topher's worked for Ethan for nine years, a datapoint I file away for when I need it. The things this man could tell me if he wanted to. I definitely need to coax him out for a strong drink at some point. It shouldn't be difficult, given his apparent aversion to being home for bath time.

I also enrol at the epic gym in Kingsley HQ's basement. It's sleek, minimalist—shocker—and extremely well kitted out with everything from a wall of Theraguns to an IV station. Best of all? I hire myself a PT. Caio hails from Rio. He's drop-dead gorgeous, moonlights as a dancer, and promises to be very entertaining. I like my workouts, but you've got to keep things fun, you know? I can't maintain glutes like these babies through willpower alone.

By Friday, I have a pretty good idea of the lay of the land. I meet most of the rest of the executive suite, all of whom seem proficient, decent, and less wankerish than Ethan's dad, who I steer well clear of. He absolutely strikes me as the kind of guy who builds allies and weaponises those allegiances when he needs to. I'm Team Ethan, and I'm not about to give Richard any ammunition.

My initial instincts about Ethan were correct. This guy most definitely isn't a Social Eight. It strikes me that he takes little interest in his vast network of employees. Everyone seems well looked after, but it's probably because he feels obligated and, I'd hazard, because he knows that people who are well looked after are less likely to act up and cause headaches. This guy does things by the book.

The biggest event of my first week is that as of the market close on Thursday—last night—we've hit the three percent threshold of ownership in Montague stock, meaning Kingsley

Hotels has triggered the need to disclose its stake to the market.

I have to say, the way Ethan and his strategy team have handled it is *chef's kiss*. At this point, they're not required to disclose anything about their intentions. All they need to do is notify the market of their stake as a statement of fact.

And that's exactly what they do.

The disclosure they released after the market close was short and dry and deliberately anti-inflammatory. *Kingsley Hotels has acquired a three-point-one-percent stake in The Montague Group. The investment represents a strategic holding in a well-managed fellow hospitality company. Yada yada yada.*

Obviously, this hasn't stopped the market from reacting for a second. It's ten o'clock on Friday, two hours after the FTSE opened, and already The Montague Group stock is trading up nine percent on speculation that it's in play. The hedge funds and risk arbitrage funds are circling, hoping to make a quick buck on a quick bet, and with every percentage point the share price ticks up, Ethan looks like he's about to have a coronary. The spreadsheet that's permanently open on his desk shows the acquisition getting more and more expensive for the Kingsleys. The more the Montague share price rises, the more of a premium price the Kingsleys will have to offer to placate shareholders. To make matters worse, it looks like plenty of hedge funds are placing their bets by buying the target and selling the acquirer.

Still, there's no way to avoid market speculation. This is how the game is played. It's all standard practice. The beauty of the way Ethan's approaching it, in my opinion, is that he currently controls the narrative. The plan. The Montague board may know exactly what's coming, but the market can't know for sure. And if he wants to reverse course and pull out of this deal at any point, the market will be none the wiser.

The three percent stake disclosure is more of a warning shot across the bow than an overt declaration of war, and it leaves most of the cards in Ethan's hands.

Played like a true Eight.

Swoon.

~

WHAT FOLLOWS IS a brutal text exchange with my friend Nora Montague, who's all too aware of my brand-new position.

NORA:

3% stake?????? HOLY FUCKING SHIT.

Can't discuss it, obviously

Is Theo spitting fire?

He's throwing his toys very, very loudly. But he said Miles is fucking furious

We saw him last week and there was a lot of angry whispering between the boys

Now I know why

Your boss is a dick. Why can't he leave them alone? Fucking predator

You and I both know that's not how equity markets work, babes

The only thing that matters is creating shareholder value

You're assuming I actually know, or want to know, anything about how equity markets work

Did you know before you joined?

No! Of course not! But I got wall-crossed AKA totally blindsided about 3 mins into my 1st day on Monday

Brutal 💀

It's inevitable I'll end up in a meeting with your in-laws at some point. Pls tell them I'm not the enemy!!!

Obvs

They wouldn't think that anyway

Let's try to stay out of it as much as possible, huh?

Stay out of what? I have no idea what you're talking about x

That's my girl xxxx

CHAPTER 15

Sophia

I t's nine on Saturday morning when I show up on Ethan's very nice doorstep in Notting Hill. He has an enormous pad on Elgin Crescent, just a couple of hundred metres away from the development my pal Lotta's company built. It's a shame they don't know each other, but Notting Hill's not exactly the kind of place where you knock on someone's door to borrow a cup of sugar, and I'm sure Ethan would find Lotta's vivacity levels even more distasteful than he seems to find mine.

Unlike Elgin, Lotta's modern, environmentally precocious baby, Ethan's home is a classic, white-stuccoed Georgian villa, all generous proportions and gorgeous features. The security detail on the gate lets me through with a smile and a nod— he's one of the guys Ethan has on rotation—and I advance down an immaculate sandstone path. It's flanked by a herring-bone border that divides it from the perfect front garden: tiny pure-white pebbles; discreet water feature; imported ancient olive tree for a spot of character. I wonder if Ethan has his housekeeping team polish the pebbles. I wouldn't put it past him.

He asked me yesterday if I'd be willing to come over and plough through some work today ahead of the meeting that the Montagues have finally agreed to next week.

'Only deal-related stuff,' he clarified swiftly. The seraphim have a strict office-hours policy for the sexy stuff. Rock-hard boundaries are critical in this career. Usually, we have a Monday-to-Friday policy full stop to ensure that we get the necessary distance from the rigours of the job, but at crunch times like this I would never play that card. Besides, I'm a former banker. Working all hours on a deal is in my blood and, if I'm honest, I love it. It's so much more fun than the boring day-to-day stuff.

A woman answers the front door. She's dressed all in black, her greying hair tied neatly back. The housekeeper, I assume. She smiles but doesn't make a move to introduce herself, so I do.

'Sophia.' I stick my hand out jauntily. 'I'm Ethan's new executive assistant.'

An executive assistant in fabulous burgundy-coloured leather leggings and a big black Moncler sweater, because it's far too cold for my liking, but hey-ho.

'I'm Susan.' She shakes my hand. 'I'll show you to his study.'

The house is like a very beautiful mausoleum, the hallway a chilling, if flawless, mix of white marble floors inlaid with black borders, white walls, and a couple of seriously inaccessible sculptures—again in white marble. A marble cantilevered staircase that I wouldn't want to let a toddler near. Total death trap. It's the polar—appropriate word—opposite of the kind of hallway you'd want to come home to after a walk on a freezing cold day.

Nothing about it surprises me, knowing its owner.

Susan leads me off to the left, down a white marble corridor. She knocks briskly on a white-painted panelled door and opens it without waiting for an answer. 'Miss Sophia here to see you,' she announces and leaves me with a little nod that looks a lot like *rather you than me.*

Ethan isn't at his desk but at the small, circular table to one side of the room, papers and a laptop scattered in front of him. To one side—Hallelujah—is a tray with a French press and a couple of coffee cups.

'Thanks for coming,' he says tiredly, gesturing to the chair beside him. 'Grab a seat.'

I survey him as I take my seat. He looks weary and inscrutable and gorgeous in a pale grey cashmere sweater, his hair a mess from where he's probably been taking his stress out on it. It's the strangest thing. I've been intimate with him in a number of ways—very intimate—and yet I feel like I don't know him at all yet, physically speaking. Still haven't felt his skin properly. He hasn't got me naked again since my interview. Hasn't gone down on me. He hasn't really let himself go to town on me at all.

I wonder if he will.

I wonder when he'll break.

'Help yourself to coffee.' He reaches out and draws the tray closer to us. 'So we have a date for the meeting. Montague messaged me last night. We're going in to present to their board on Tuesday.'

'Wow.' This is a turn-up for the books. 'That's not long.'

'Nope. And I want to make sure our numbers are bang on. The strategy team's sent over a load of data, but I want us to comb through it again. I don't want a single chink in our armour when we meet these guys. So ideally, we get the numbers finalised today. That gives our bankers and lawyers tomorrow and Monday to get themselves fully acquainted with the data.'

'Are they coming too?' I ask in surprise. For some reason, I assumed the initial meeting would be as close to a fireside chat as possible—a way for both parties to test the waters in a tentative way before things escalate.

Clearly, I was wrong.

'We need a united front, an indisputable show of strength. They need to know we mean business, and they all need a bloody good reminder that we're the bigger, stronger party here. From the way Montague bawled me out over our friendly offer, it seems I need to show him who's running this show.'

'Got it. Makes sense.' My tone is briskly supportive, but oh boy, is this guy armouring up. Brené Brown would have a *lot* to say about Eight's brand of armoured leadership. I wonder if sneaking a copy of *Dare to Lead* onto his desk would be an overstep?

WE WORK HARD UNTIL LUNCHTIME. Ethan is relentless when it comes to fine-tooth-combing through the numbers. As his stress levels ratchet up, so does his need to be on top of every single detail. I can't deny the data looks good. The cost synergies, banker speak for *job cuts*, are impressive.

Miles is going to hate them.

At one on the dot, a text comes through on Ethan's phone.

'Lunch.' He pushes his chair abruptly back from the table. 'Come on, let's eat.'

'You don't need to tell me twice.' I stand and stretch, not missing the hungry way his eyes rake over my sexy leather leggings. Honestly, why won't he just ravish me? Or ravage me? I'm not quite clear on the difference and I definitely don't care. I just want some Ethan Kingsley-branded throw-down.

I'm a confident woman, and I assume he's attracted to me, given his little *you're a prize* speech when we first met. But he's paying a fortune for my services and doing very fucking little with the goods, and it genuinely makes me doubt myself. Maybe he hired me as some kind of status symbol rather than acting from a deep physical desire? Maybe he has buyer's remorse. Maybe he's regretting opting for someone like me instead of the usual lean, teeny-tiny type of women he's gone for in the past? Beautiful, sleek Talia with her washboard stomach and boobs so small and neat that they require little more than a pretty little lace bralet?

I don't bloody know anymore.

'That's a very big sweater,' he observes as he rises.

'It's big because I'm cold.' I can't hide my grumpiness.

'Cold in here? You should have said.' He looks genuinely horrified.

Yes, cold in this beautiful, frigid mausoleum, oh king of the underworld.

I shrug. 'Cold generally. All the fucking time. I'd forgotten how much I dislike London weather.'

'Must make a change from the playgrounds of the Med.' His tone is distracted, though. He strides ahead, out of the room, my body temperature already forgotten as he likely grapples with whether to lead with IT or human "cost synergies" on Tuesday.

What I'm *not* expecting, as I follow Ethan through into a large kitchen that's sleekly industrial enough to belong in a Michelin-starred restaurant rather than a home, is to find a tow-headed mini-Ethan slumped at the central (grey marble, you guessed it) island.

I stop dead.

'Sophia, my son Jamie,' Ethan says disinterestedly. 'Jamie, this is my new executive assistant, Sophia.'

The kid looks up from his bowl of soup for a fraction of a second, interest levels in this introduction mirroring his father's. 'Hey.' It's more of a mutter than anything else.

'Hi, Jamie. Good to meet you.'

That doesn't get a response.

I'm a bit dumbfounded. Has he been here all morning? You could have fooled me. Ethan hasn't so much as glanced outside his study since I arrived at nine. The boy looks to be a young teenager—fourteen or fifteen, maybe? And my god is he *sweet*. He has his father's eyes, only brown, and the same lightish brown hair, albeit a lot messier. He's wearing an oversized Westminster School hoodie—must be a clever boy —but even so I can tell that he's still slight, all thin, gangly limbs.

Just wait until he discovers the gym and they'll be queuing up to cast him in some British version of *The Summer I Turned Pretty*. I'd put money on it.

I knew Ethan had a son, but he's mentioned him so rarely over the past week that I'd assumed he didn't see much of him.

'Do you live here?' I ask Jamie.

'It's Dad's weekend,' he mutters.

'He lives with his mum,' Ethan clarifies.

'Ah, I see.'

So Ethan gets Jamie, what, every other weekend? And he's holed up in his study with me and endless spreadsheets? I realise it's not every weekend that he's preparing for a ten-figure hostile takeover, but that's got to be shitty for both of them.

It's none of my business. At least that's what I tell myself. Still, I'll be fascinated to see the arctic Ethan Kingsley inter-acting as a father. I turn to the man operating the huge indus-trial hob.

'Hi! I'm Sophia. That smells amazing.'

He gives me a kind smile. He must be late fifties, with a round face and dark brown eyes. 'Davide. Ciao. And thank you. Would you like some?'

'I would absolutely love some, thanks.' It looks to be a

hearty minestrone—just the ticket for warming me up. Finally, something warm and comforting in this house.

Ethan has seated himself opposite Jamie at the island and is scrolling on his phone. I take a seat next to my boss.

'So, Jamie. Got any plans this weekend?'

He shrugs. 'Dunno. Can we go to the driving range later, Dad?'

'Afraid not.' Ethan doesn't look up from his phone. 'Far too much going on at work. Why don't you call one of your mates?'

'No one's around.'

'That's ridiculous. There are one hundred and fifty kids in your year group. I guarantee someone is "around".'

He misses his son's eye roll, but I don't. I get it. He wants some time with his dad, not dismissive, snarky rejection.

Davide sets a shallow soup bowl in front of me and Ethan. The liquid of the minestrone is thicker than the usual broth—it looks like he's blended the tomatoes and broth into a wonderful, velvety consistency. It's dotted with colourful diced vegetables and beans, but no pasta. Ethan doesn't eat gluten. When I asked him about it earlier this week, he said he wasn't allergic but avoids it given its inflammatory properties.

Seems pretty standard for Ethan, though I'm amazed no one's filled him in on the inflammatory properties of chronic stress and holding onto life with an iron fist.

Again, not my business.

I run my spoon slowly through my soup in an attempt to cool it down and try again with Jamie, who's clearly been here for a while. His soup is nearly finished. I'm sure a teenage boy doesn't want to make awkward conversation with his dad's random assistant, but Ethan's ignoring us both, and I can't sit here in this awful silence, especially as Davide has made himself scarce.

'So you're at Westminster, Jamie?'

'Yeah.'

'It's an incredible school. What year are you in?'

'Year ten.'

Fourteen going on fifteen sounds right, then. 'So you've just started your GCSEs then? How are they going?'

He shrugs. 'Fine.'

'Can I ask what options you're taking?'

If I'm pissing him off, he's doing an admirable job of hiding it. 'Um, Computer Science, Design Technology, Art and Geography.'

'Cool. Those sound fab. Want to go into the family business when you're done?'

His look of abject horror nearly makes me laugh. Luckily Ethan, who's replying to an email on his phone while eating, misses it. 'No. I want to work in animation.'

'Your science teacher hasn't come back to me,' Ethan says without looking up.

'It's fine, Dad. Just leave it.'

'I will not leave it. You should be in top set. We're nearly halfway through the term and they still haven't rectified the situation.'

'It's not a big deal.' Jamie's voice is quiet but firm. 'If I do well, they'll put me up at some point.'

'I want to make sure you're on the right path for Triple Science. I'll get Grandpa to put in a call.'

Ahh, I remember this from school. They'll steer some kids towards a triple science qualification, some towards double, depending on abilities. Though why he needs to do triple science if he wants a creative career is beyond me.

'He'll just embarrass me. He's so dramatic. It's not that deep.'

Ugh, so Richard must be a Westminster alum too. I can imagine him striding in there and throwing his weight around on a subject that's categorically none of his business.

Poor Jamie. I really hope his mother is lovely, because he hasn't exactly lucked out on the family of origin front, from what I can see.

'Are those your drawings, Jamie?' I ask him in a desperate attempt to rescue the conversation from the car crash it's becoming.

His gaze slides to me and back to his pad. 'Yeah.'

I cock my head and give him my best smile. 'Working on some animations?'

He wriggles uncomfortably and pulls his cuffs down over his hands. 'I mainly use Autodesk Maya for that, but I sketch out the ideas first by hand.'

'Any chance I can get a peek at what you're working on? I draw like a three-year-old. I'm always so in awe of people who can draw.'

'Sure.' He shrugs and leafs through the pad, folding back the top pages once he's found what he's looking for and sliding it across to me. 'I only do anime. I'm trying to get her right, but it's hard.'

I pick up the pad. The page is filled with stunning, delicate pencil sketches of a single anime character with huge eyes and a perky ponytail. He's depicted her face from various angles and with several expressions.

'These are exquisite,' I tell him. 'So amazing! You have such a talent. Ethan, have you seen these?'

I wave the pad at him excitedly. He glances up from his phone and studies the page for a moment. 'They're good. You need to pay more attention to proportion, though.' And with that, he resumes his emailing.

My blood runs cold. Honestly, I feel sick. How can he be so dismissive of his own son? So disinterested? How can he not possibly discern that what Jamie needs in this moment, having had his golfing request knocked down, is just a second of validation?

Surreptitiously, I look over at Jamie. His shoulders have slumped dejectedly, and he's grinding his teeth. I slide the pad back across to him.

'They're really gorgeous,' I say lamely.

He shrugs his acknowledgment in the most disinterested way possible. 'Thanks. Dad, can I be excused?'

'Yes. Put your bowl in the sink for Davide, please. And go find some way to entertain yourself. I'll see you at dinner.'

He slides off his stool, taking his bowl over to the sink. Then he's back for his pad and pencil and slinking away into whatever corner of this cold, lifeless house he holes up in when he's staying with his dad.

I sneak a sideways glance at Ethan.

I want to take him by his lovely broad shoulders and shake him.

I want to yell at him, to demand that he goes out there right now and suggests a trip to the driving range with his gorgeous boy, so tall and gangly and yet so clearly still a kid.

I'm giving myself a stern talking to, reminding myself that it's none of my business, when Ethan drags his hand down his face and shudders out a huge sigh.

'Fuck.'

He knows he's done badly. That's something, I suppose. And it gives me an opening to stick my nose into his business. I decide to couch it in *can I help* terms.

'Is there anything I can do so you can sneak off with him for a couple of hours?'

He shakes his head, once, curtly. 'Believe me, the last thing that boy needs is more time with me.'

I'm aghast. 'What on earth does that mean?'

'Exactly what I said. He's better off steering well clear.'

Okay.

This I cannot ignore.

It may be clear as day that Ethan has a lot of what some

might call *baggage* and I would call *unresolved trauma,* and it's also clear that his parenting style leaves a lot to be desired, but this is another level of dysfunction altogether. Ethan dismounts from his barstool, a sign that he sees this conversation as closed, but I'm having none of it.

The question is what to say. I could tell him home truths until I'm blue in the face, but the chances are he won't hear them. Not at a somatic level where he needs to viscerally understand them, anyway.

Besides, he might actually fire me if they're unwelcome and unpalatable enough.

I clear my throat. 'You can say things like that, but that's not you talking. It's a part of you that's very protective—and probably very fierce.'

He gives me a *who knew she was a nutter* look. 'I have absolutely no idea what you mean.'

'Look. I know he's your son and this is absolutely none of my business, but—'

'But I can't imagine that'll stop you.' He sounds weary. Weary but resigned, which is good, I suppose, because he's already come to terms with the fact that I'm getting stuck in.

'When we have... issues,' I say carefully, 'with... family members—parents, say—and those issues aren't resolved, we develop these protective parts inside of us—kind of like emotional bodyguards—that guard the vulnerable parts so that we don't have to feel pain. It's a very well-established therapeutic model.'

'Otherwise known as psychobabble.' He picks up both our bowls and puts them in the sink.

Of course that's his reaction. He knows I have an actual psychology degree from Cambridge, which should warrant a modicum of respect (even if IFS, the modality I'm referencing, lies outside the traditional therapeutic models that I studied), but whatever.

'I don't think that's fair. It's helped me a lot. But my point is that whatever part of you believes you need to stay away from Jamie to keep him safe is just that. A *part*. It looks to me like it's working very hard right now, but it doesn't have the whole picture—not even close. Because Jamie loves you, and he wants to spend time with you.'

'You know precisely nothing about my family, which gives you precisely zero right to wade in.' He strides out of the kitchen without looking at me. 'Stay out of my business and stick to your fucking job.'

CHAPTER 16

Ethan

Sophia's mere presence beside me in the car is enough to make me want to kick myself for not having fucked some part of her body before we left the office.

I'm tense as fuck, and she's irresistible: a veritable symphony of all the alluring things that make up a woman. On this dreary October day, she's in a cherry red dress that, as usual, skirts the line between professional and coquettish all too skilfully. It's long and silky, its pleated skirt billowing around her on the cream leather seat, and it matches the perfect red of her mouth. Her dark hair cascades down over her shoulders, shielding most of her face as she sends messages on her phone at lightning speed.

She's ignoring me, but she's ignoring me in her regular blithe, no-fucks-given kind of way. I'm simply not entertaining enough for her to bother with me. She's not withholding her attention in that pointed, fragile, defensive way that women do when they want you to understand just how fully you've pissed them off. Or offended them. Delete as appropriate.

A vivacious pain in the arse she may be, but at least Sophia doesn't hold grudges or throw her toys. If she disagrees, she says so. If she disapproves, she says so. While I maintain that I was fully justified in giving her a dressing-down at the weekend when she butted into my business with Jamie, she shrugged it off immediately. She didn't burst into tears or barricade herself in the loo, both of which are the kinds of bullshit stunts that Talia and my previous two Seraph assistants were well known for.

She just got on with it, and for that resilience I'm privately, but extremely, grateful.

And here she is in the back of my car, looking like a fantasy come to life, as I attempt to hold it the fuck together. It would be so easy to ruck up those long skirts and find her wet heat with my fingers, to have her slide onto my lap. I could bury my face in the decadent fragrance of her neck and be inside her in seconds.

Seconds.

But I need this edge, because it's my life force. I need to preserve this stress, this tension. I'm about to walk behind enemy lines, and the last thing I need is to be in a blissed-out, post-orgasmic haze.

I need every fucking advantage I have.

Sophia throws her phone into her ridiculously large bag. It's a Birkin. I should know. I bought several of them for my ex-wife.

'I should warn you, I'll know quite a few of the Montague party,' she says perkily. 'Just as long as you don't think I'm a spy.'

'You'd be terrible at corporate espionage.'

'I don't know. I could be one of those hookers who gets all the secrets out of the enemy the moment before they shoot their load. I wouldn't underestimate my feminine wiles.'

I roll my eyes, although the thought of Sophia fucking her way through enemy ranks makes me feel vaguely queasy.

'I know Miles and his brother, Theo,' she continues. 'And their parents, Charles and Laura. They're so lovely. I told you I was a bridesmaid at Theo and my friend Nora's wedding, I think.'

She did tell me. I grunt in response.

'And I know their Finance Director, Jonathan Holmes, too. We were all at Cambridge together—me, Theo, Nora, and Jonathan, that is. He's a good guy. He dated Nora for years and years. It's so funny—he's literally Theo's polar opposite. You'll see. Can't imagine what a boring shag he'd be— Jonathan, not Theo—but he was born to be an FD. Anyway, I told Theo to let them all know I was working for you. I didn't want it to be awkward when I walked in with the nasty Kingsleys. At least they don't know I'm actually *sleeping* with the enemy. That would be awkward as fuck.'

'I can't imagine they'll spend a moment thinking about it,' I retort when she finally pauses to draw breath. 'And this is a very important business meeting, not a soap opera. You'd do well to remember that.'

She turns and looks at me properly, her dark eyes flashing. She's truly magnificent. 'Here are a couple of life lessons for free, Ethan, because I know how much you enjoy them. One. If you think personal relationships don't matter, especially in situations like this, then you're a lot less smart than I thought you were. I wouldn't betray my friends for you, *ever*, but at the very least, you'd think that my knowing them would work to your advantage. And two, you're even more unbearable than usual when you haven't come. If you won't let me touch you before events like this, you should really consider beating one out in the shower first thing. It's the decent thing to do for everyone else's sake, after all.'

Her dark eyes drop to my crotch. Before I can react, she reaches over and places her hand over my dick. I can feel the warmth of her instantly, even through my trousers and boxers.

Lightning quick, I grab her wrist and hold her in place, my eyes boring into hers.

'I *want* to be unbearable. Did you think of that? I want every person around that table to understand the full force of what I'm bringing to this deal.'

We stare at each other, and my dick twitches beneath Sophia's warm hand. A couple of seconds pass like this. It's not like her to miss an opportunity for a quick retort.

'What are you thinking?' I demand.

She snags her bottom lip with her teeth before responding, her hand pressing more firmly against my dick.

'I'm thinking that the more objectionable you are, the more I want you to rail me. And I'm thinking that that makes me seriously question myself.'

From the unimpressed line her lips make when she's finished speaking, I know she's telling the truth.

SOPHIA WASN'T LYING about knowing half of the Montague delegation. What should be a tension-filled meeting between two parties who dislike and distrust each other threatens, for the first few moments after we file silently into the large oak-panelled boardroom, to become a family reunion of sorts.

I watch with deep unhappiness as she kisses Miles Montague, the man responsible for every headache I have currently, warmly on both cheeks. She then full-on accosts the cocky-looking guy next to him, who must surely be his brother, Theo. They rock from side to side as they hug, and he whispers something in her ear that has her throwing back her head and laughing. It's completely inappropriate for the occasion.

My father, who came in another car with our Finance

Director and Senior Counsel, mutters from behind me, 'She could be an asset.'

I don't turn around. 'No.'

Once Sophia has finished effusively greeting everyone, including the senior Montagues and their FD, the guy she deems to be "a boring shag", the rest of us make our introductions far more curtly. The Montagues may be cursing our very existence, but at the end of the day, we're all British. We shake hands and murmur *how do you do* and *good to see you again.*

Mistrust is etched into every line of Miles Montague's face, but his greeting is perfectly civil. His brother, on the other hand, shakes my hand a little too hard. Cocky little shit.

It's time to show these people who's in charge. We take our seats as a couple of assistants hand out coffee. We may be on Montague turf, every oak panel a reminder that they favour a classic look as clearly as we prefer minimalism, but this is our deal, and this is our meeting. The Montague Group is under siege, and its board damn well knows it.

'Thank you for hosting us,' I say. 'Firstly, I'd like to acknowledge that last week's disclosure to the market, and the friendly approach that preceded it, may be unwelcome to some of you.' It doesn't hurt to be gracious. It doesn't hurt to produce a semblance of empathy. 'After all, we're both relatively small, family-founded parties in a sea of aggressive and bloated acquirers. It could be us sitting in your seats just as easily.'

Charles Montague nods his brusque acknowledgment, if not his approval. He won't give anything away that easily.

'That said,' I continue, 'we find ourselves here, having acquired the requisite three percent and continued to amass a stake from there, attempting to find common ground on which to build a joint vision for our future. I'd be grateful if you'd spare me a few minutes to paint a picture of how I imagine that future to be.'

~

THERE'S something reassuring about the machinations of a hostile takeover, machinations that are firmly rooted in the Financial Conduct Authority's acquisition playbook. With the friendly offer, we had no control over the situation. Montague were free to call the shots, to ride roughshod over a proposal we'd spent years finessing.

But now that we're going hostile, the dynamic has shifted and, with that, the control. Assuming the mega-corporates—Hilton or IHG—don't try to waltz in and fight for our prize, we can control this deal. Not the price we pay, sure, but pretty much everything else. And, even as our presentation is met with increasing amounts of displeasure from the Montague Group board members around the table, I hold on tight to that knowledge.

'These cost-cutting measures are downright criminal!' Miles' father, Charles, spits out, staring at the appropriate page in the deck with what looks like utter disbelief. 'Almost all of these are human costs—these are *people* you're talking about slashing here. Employees who've given our family their undivided loyalty for years and years.'

'Loyalty never helped the bottom line,' my father says smoothly. 'And you know as well as we do that cost synergies like these are precisely what the market will be looking for, no matter who acquires you.'

'My father's correct. The thing to focus on here is the creation of shareholder value. That's what'll get this deal over the line. We may both have built family businesses, but those businesses stopped being family at some point in their growth. They had to. And when we both took the leap and listed publicly, we pledged to make the creation of shareholder value our top priority.'

'We will never not think of our employees as family, no

matter what size we are,' Miles interjects viciously, 'and I wholeheartedly disagree that loyalty is not good for the bottom line.'

I give him a shrug. I suspect it spells out exactly what I think. *Well, mate, that kind of approach is naïve at best and parochial at worst, and it's precisely why you're not fit to run a multi-billion-pound business.*

'This very substantial part of your pitch was notably absent in the first presentation you sent over,' Miles continues. 'I'd call that pretty fucking suspect.'

Under the table, I dig my thumbnail into the palm of my opposite hand.

Show nothing. Feel nothing. Win everything.

'I'd call it commercially prudent.'

We glare at each other.

'Let's be clear. We're going to fight this every step of the way. We intend to sit down with all of our major shareholders and appeal to each of them in turn.'

Dad scoffs. 'No financial institution is going to turn down the chance to create this kind of value. You may not like the cost-cutting scenarios, but the reason they're so aggressive is that our two companies have such significant synergies. There's not much anyone can say to that.'

Control the room or lose everything.

'Let *me* be clear.' I lean forward, addressing Miles and his father directly. 'We will also spend the week making ourselves available to your major shareholders and persuading them of the wisdom of this deal. At the end of the day, we already have a good deal of overlap between our shareholder registers. These investors are already established relationships for us, and I believe most of them will be willing to swap their Montague Group shares for Kingsley Hotels ones, especially when they see that we're not afraid of shying away from the tough actions necessary to create value for them. They'll compare that to your, shall we say, sentimental inefficiency, and they'll be in no doubt as to which horse to back in this race.'

I sit back in my chair and place my palms flat on the smooth walnut of our nemeses' boardroom table, willing my heart rate to slow. Contrary to the coldly impassive expression I have fixed on my face, confrontations make me extremely anxious. But I know that the more anxiety, the more terror I feel about taking actions like this, the more critical it is to show no chinks at all in my well-crafted armour.

Show nothing.

Feel nothing.

Win everything.

In my peripheral vision, Dad gives me an approving nod. He likes it when I bare my teeth, make a show of strength. He likes having an ally when he's bullying people. With my father, there are only ever two choices:

Stand with him, or stand against him.

Comply, or die.

And I'll choose survival every time.

CHAPTER 17

Sophia

Ethan is true to his word. As soon as the meeting is done, he sweeps me out of there and into his waiting car and wastes no time in getting on the phone with The Montague Group's largest shareholders.

'Get me their shareholder register as of last night,' he barks at me in the car and immediately puts calls through to the Chief Investment Officers of BlackRock and Legal & General, setting up urgent in-person meetings for tomorrow and Thursday.

I know this is a knee-jerk reaction to having come under fire in there. I can feel it is as surely as if he's admitted it in so many words. He's been confronted, his integrity attacked. He's feeling out of control, and what's the easiest way to regain a semblance of control?

Taking action.

What's unclear is whether *Ethan* knows that. Also unclear: why he's standing shoulder to shoulder with his father on this. From what little I know of Richard, this deal has him written all over it: egotistical empire-building and the total assumption of control over an old rival.

None of that says *Ethan* to me.

In fact, he's clinging to the numbers, the dreaded cost efficiencies, like they're a lifeline. He's deep in the reeds of this, mired in the process. I have no idea if he actually wants this.

On the ride back to Kingsley HQ, he gets hold of Vanguard, Credit Suisse, and Invesco, too. Once the top five shareholders have been secured, he collapses back against his seat and blows out a huge breath. He may be exhausted, but he's positively vibrating with nervous energy. I'd bet the cortisol is pumping around his body right now.

What is it about this man that I find so intoxicating? I may flatter myself that I can see beneath the veil where he's concerned, but I'm as much of a sucker as the next girl for Ethan Kingsley's particular type of armour. Maybe it's precisely because I can see the chinks that he's so attractive. I can appreciate every moment of his cold swagger and ruthless power plays while also being drawn to his vulnerability.

Vulnerability that's clear as day from where I'm sitting.

Vulnerability that it would kill him to reveal, even inadvertently. Especially inadvertently. And I don't use the word *kill* lightly. Eight here doesn't choose to command people or situations for kicks. He does it to survive. His fear of losing control is existential to him. And right now the only narrative he wants to hear is that he's got this entire shit show under control, when in truth, it's a fucking tinderbox.

I've only seen an acquisition get this nasty once, back when I was at Morgan Stanley. One Italian regional bank launched a hostile takeover of another, and holy fuck. It was like bloody *Romeo and Juliet* meets the Italian Wars of Religion. I thought blood would be shed, I honestly did.

But this one has the potential to get even nastier, even more personal and vicious and polarising, and we're only a few days in.

The beautiful, complex man beside me is breathing

raggedly and scrolling through his phone so quickly, so aggressively, that the little metal box is in danger of bursting into flames.

I make a decision and lay a hand on his thigh. God, his quad is like steel.

'Hey. Ethan. Take an hour for yourself, why don't you? Whatever you're feeling right now, take it out on me. That's what I'm here for.'

～

ETHAN

This deal is toxic.

My father is toxic.

Even the blood coursing hotly through my veins is toxic.

At least, that's how it feels in my body. My brain, however, is in another place.

You have full control of this situation.

That sentimental outburst from Miles' old man was frankly embarrassing. If only his shareholders could hear him speak like that about cost synergies that are any Finance Director's wet dream.

Emotion is the enemy of execution.

And the Montagues are about to find that out the hard way.

Still, I'm not stupid. There are so many moving parts to this transaction that any one of them could derail this deal. I talked a good game in there, but the palpable tension in every muscle in my body tells a different story.

And now the beautiful woman sitting next to me is emitting her siren's call, and her hand is warm and soft and suggestive on my thigh, and it's not helpful, it's really not, because this is the last fucking thing I have time for.

'I need to get to the rest of the shareholders before they do,' I grit out, my quad tensing up even further under her touch.

'You've already got the top five. Those guys control twelve, thirteen percent of the free float between them. Add in your stake and you've already got high teens wrapped up.'

She's right, of course. Our newly acquired stake, and the calls I've made just now, have put us in a strong position. Still, I need to keep acting, need to keep pushing forward, if I'm to stave off this creeping, chilling feeling of helplessness.

'It's not enough. I need more votes.'

'And you'll get them. But think of it from an efficiency standpoint. You're wired and drained. That meeting would have exhausted anyone. Take an hour to work it all out on me, and I promise you, you'll be operating at your absolute peak afterwards. Even better, get the bankers to put the calls in while you're "recharging your batteries". Let them set up the meetings. It's part of their bloody job, after all.'

I twist my body around so I can drink her in. It feels as though there's a vice around my poor, exhausted brain. I didn't sleep well at all last night. But she's a fucking mirage, a fertile oasis in a desert of vertiginous stakes and power games and dick-swinging. Her face is so close, her lips so full, dark eyes grazing over my face like she's waiting for me to admit that she can fulfil every single need I have in this moment. Her heady floral scent pervades my senses and fucks with my head, and somewhere, deep down, I know she's right. I know I'm good for nothing like this, running on empty.

This Seraph gig was supposed to be carefully managed, strictly prescribed titration: a drip-feed of timely releases, if you like. After all, my needs should be managed, not indulged.

And that's precisely what Sophia's three predecessors provided. The sexual side of my previous Seraph contracts ran perfectly, in fact, because those women met my needs without overly fuelling my appetites.

This woman is another story. Another story indeed. And that's why I have to be the one to apply the brakes when it comes to availing myself of her sinful body and wanton ways. The problem is that being the one to keep your foot on the brake the entire fucking time gets tiring pretty quickly.

And when you're already exhausted, the risk that your foot slips entirely and you go from nought to sixty before you're even conscious of having done so grows all too real. To beat this analogy to death, that's when you hit the guardrail at high speed and blow everything you've worked so hard for up in a flash of self-indulgent oversight.

But as I take her in, I can feel my foot slipping.

Perhaps I should take it off the brake altogether. My stress levels are through the roof, after all.

Perhaps my usual practice of careful titration is woefully inadequate for this crisis.

Perhaps what I need is to overdose. To binge on the carnal banquet that is Sophia fucking Petrakis for a few allocated hours until I'm numbed and sated, until the voices of Miles Montague and his father and my father have quietened in my head, and that toxic blood in my veins has turned to treacle, and I'm sex-drunk enough to enjoy the brief, phony sensation that all is good with the world, that this is all manageable.

My gaze lingers on Sophia's plush lips, and I drop my forehead to hers.

'You really should be more careful what you wish for.'

I could claim her mouth so easily, I really could, and I'm indecently proud of myself for resisting. It's a sign that I still have some semblance of control of myself if not much else. She's worked for me for over a week and I still haven't kissed her. Much like the miser who's too busy counting his money to spend it, I've arguably enjoyed looking at that mouth and knowing I have yet to plunder it.

'I'm not interested in being careful,' she murmurs so close to my face. 'I know what I'm doing, and I can handle it. I can handle you. So for fuck's sake, take whatever frustration and lack of agency you're feeling right now and unleash it all on me.' Her voice drops to a low purr. 'You have heroic levels of self-control, Ethan. You've made your point. It's time to show me who's boss.'

CHAPTER 18

Ethan

I've never pressed an intercom button so fast.

'Detour,' I bark at my driver, looking wildly out of the window to get my bearings. 'Take us to the Kingsley Westminster.' Our newest hotel—the one where we met—and also, critically, the closest to our current location.

Sophia withdraws her hand from my thigh and collapses back in her seat. When I look over, her smile is that of the cat that got the cream.

Not yet, sweetheart. But you're going to.

Let's just see if you can walk afterwards.

We sit in charged silence until the car pulls up under the porte-cochère and two valets promptly open our doors. I take Sophia by the hand and march her through the lobby, its cool serenity instantly soothing me. This really is a compelling new addition to our portfolio as well as a welcome reminder that we're very, *very* good at what we do here at Kingsley.

'Mr Kingsley!' the blonde at the reception desk exclaims when she spots me. 'Were we expecting you, sir?'

'Which suites are empty?' I demand, ignoring her question. It's none of her business. 'Is the Jubilee free?'

'I—um—yes, I believe it is. Give me a moment, please.' She glances from me to Sophia and down at her monitor. 'Yes, it is. Will you be requiring it?'

'Yes. Just for the afternoon.'

I couldn't make it clearer that I'm about to take Sophia up there for a quickie, but no matter. All I care about is getting this woman naked and on a bed, and ideally in the next two minutes. Now that I've decided to go down this road, the blinkers are on.

'Of course. Can I send up any—'

'Nope. Just the key card.' This gossip will be all over the break room by the end of the day, I'm sure, but I don't care. I hold out my hand, causing her to fumble as she activates the card.

When I have it in my hand, I waste no time in getting Sophia into the lift. As soon as we're alone, I walk her backwards until her back hits the wall. I put a hand out and close it over the front of her neck, my grip light but proprietary.

I stare down at her. I like my fingers around her neck. I like the way she's looking up at me, her cherry-red mouth parting as her tits heave under their silk.

'My God,' she says softly. 'You really are good at delayed gratification, aren't you?'

'I'm very good at it.'

Her lips curve up into a little smile. 'What are you going to do with me?'

I shrug. Now that I have her here, it's simple. 'Everything.'

'Don't make promises you can't keep, okay? It's not fair.'

'I would never.' As I hold her in place, I skim the fingertips of my opposite hand down the gauzy fabric of her sleeve. 'You are a very beautiful woman.'

Her face softens. My admission has pleased her, I think. How can that be? How can a woman who looks and acts like

Sophia does be in the slightest bit uncertain about my attraction to her?

'I was beginning to wonder if you'd noticed that I was a woman at all. You certainly haven't been getting your money's worth.'

My fingers drift over her bicep to her breast as if of their own accord, and she shivers as I graze her nipple.

'Believe me, I've noticed. You're far too beautiful to be safe. Hiring you was the most self-indulgent thing I've done in a very long time.'

'Until now. A whole afternoon of doing whatever you like to me.'

I frown as I flex the hand I'm using to collar her. 'We said an hour.'

She laughs. 'An hour won't be nearly enough.'

She's right. She's so fucking right. An hour won't even scratch the surface of what I want to do to her.

The lift comes to a halt, the doors opening on the top floor. There are only two penthouses up here, right below the roof terrace where I first met Sophia, and the Jubilee is the most desirable, with its breathtaking views of the Houses of Parliament and Westminster Bridge.

I'm under no illusions that Sophia is easily impressed. She was born into obscene wealth and has been gallivanting around the Med with Thaddeus Karavitis for the past few years, after all. Still, the soft gasp she makes as we enter the suite and the iconic view hits us is gratifying.

'Fuck, I love this city.' She makes a beeline for the bank of French doors leading out onto the terrace. 'Look at that! How the hell you got planning permission for this place, I will never understand.'

The answer to that is that my father greased palms while I committed to all kinds of extortionate conservation budgets for Westminster Cathedral. I love this city as much as Sophia does, love the sheer, unapologetic splendour of these majestic buildings that provide a home for our government.

But, right now, my eyes are fixed on one perfect sight—and it's *not* Big Ben. It's the spot of crimson in this sea of neutrals, the woman whose sensual curves make it impossible to look at anything else.

I slide my hands into my pockets as I take her in. 'Come here.'

~

SOPHIA

I turn away from the panorama to the man standing in the middle of this sumptuous suite.

Ethan Kingsley. Anally retentive billionaire CEO, emotionally inadequate father, probably badly traumatised son, and a beautiful, beautiful man. Finally, *finally,* I'm alone with him, properly alone, in a room that presumably has an actual bed—not that I've spotted the bedroom yet.

He's standing perfectly still, a commanding figure with his hands in his pockets, and he's watching me with precisely the level of ravenous need I've wanted from him for the past week.

I cross the thick white expanse of carpet, not stopping until I'm close enough for him to sling an arm around my waist and tug me flush against him. And then his other hand is gripping the back of my neck, and he's lowering his lovely, frowning face to mine, and *Jesus.* About bloody time.

His kiss is hard and hungry and unyielding. There's no easing into it. His lips may be supple, but they're relentless over mine, his tongue licking along the seam of my mouth, seeking access. I open for him immediately, and he plunges inside my mouth, fucking it with the kind of entitled assurance that makes me want his tongue between my legs *right now.*

Ethan hasn't just held back on me this past week. He's made me hold back on him, too. So if he's going to unleash himself, I'm damn well going to go for it. I slide one hand over his perfectly broad shoulder and clamp the other one to the back of his head, my fingers buried in his soft hair, so I can really kiss him back. And I do. I go for it, letting my lips slide against his and my tongue entangle with his, matching him beat for beat.

He groans a little inside my mouth, a sound so full of defeated delight that it has my pulse ratcheting up, and grabs my bottom, pulling me even closer. He's hardening already, and it toughens my resolve, because *I will get this man naked today if it kills me.*

'Dress. *Off,*' he says against my lips before kissing me again, and I immediately reach behind to get the top of my zip undone while simultaneously trying to keep my mouth glued to Ethan's.

I fail spectacularly.

'You do it.' I spin around and tug my hair over one shoulder, giving him access. Deftly, he pulls the zip all the way down before pressing his mouth to my shoulder and snagging the skin between his teeth. He doesn't stop there but kisses and licks a line towards my neck. I get the impression he wants to gorge on every single inch of my body today.

He turns me back around and pushes the top of my dress down so it's pooling around my waist, then he's gathering me up in another all-consuming kiss, his hands roaming everywhere: sliding over my back and tangling in my hair and grabbing my bottom. I allow myself to melt into the sensation of being devoured by him.

I called it during that first interview. The appeal of this

guy is that he is so disinterested, so disengaged, that when he really wants you, his focus feels chemically addictive. Like it's lighting you up from the inside. It's funny to think that he's already fucked various parts of me several times, yet all I want is to be naked on a bed with him. Vanilla as fuck, but there you go.

He holds my neck in a firm grip as he uses one hand to shove my dress down over my hips. As soon as it hits the ground, I step out of it. I'm in crimson lace underwear today—it's Dolce and Gabbana, like my dress—with a full suspender belt and nude stockings. Even I couldn't justify staying bare-legged any longer in this shitty weather.

He presses his forehead to mine and glances down my body, his hands going to my bare waist. 'Fuck me. I don't know where to fucking start.'

'We are starting,' I say sweetly but firmly, 'with you getting naked. I need it. You've been hiding yourself away all week, and I'm done waiting.'

That gets me a pained laugh. He straightens up and fixes me with his CEO Look. It's a sexier version of the look he gave Miles and Charles Montague earlier when they were pushing back on his proposed job cuts. He really is disgustingly hand-some. 'Let's not forget who's calling the shots here. Or paying your salary.'

'So tell me what to do, why don't you?'

His eyes linger on my breasts in their decadent Italian lace. 'Loosen my tie and take it off.'

'Yes, sir.' He'll see how good I can be, how obedient. I'll have him wanting to drag me off to one of his lovely hotels every single lunchtime.

I put his collar up and loosen the tie, taking it off over his head.

'Unbutton my shirt.'

Yesss. I get his collar open and begin to work my way down, keeping my eyes fixed on his face. *Kingsley* is a suitable name for him. He looks positively majestic as he stands here, in the middle of a penthouse within one of the crown jewels of his hotel empire. In his impeccable white shirt and habitual slate-grey trousers, Ethan Kingsley is a king among men. And while he's self-assured and arrogant in many ways, I somehow doubt he fully understands his own worth. There's no trace of smugness on his face as I undress him. Only intensity. He's practically vibrating with it.

A fine dusting of brown chest hair comes into view as I work on his shirt. He has beautiful skin—far fairer than yours truly, obviously, but still tinged with his summer tan. I tug hard, releasing his shirt tails, and make quick work of the remaining buttons so that the shirt is hanging loose, framing the lean body I knew was under there: the perfectly toned pecs and flat stomach of a man who sees his body as just another kingdom to conquer. The sight of that trail of hair disappearing into his trousers honestly makes me feel a little light-headed.

Ethan briskly opens his cufflinks and gets his shirt off, balling it up and chucking it on the ground. I take him in. Such lovely broad shoulders. Such perfect posture. His hair is falling over his eyes—a result of my handiwork while we were kissing. His grey eyes are almost all pupil now, and they're still fixed on me as he wages some kind of internal war, presumably with his self-control. The man is fine, fine, fine. He's definitely my reward for years of putting up with a wrinkled sexagenarian and his moobs.

'Undo my trousers,' he tells me, and it sounds like a dare.

I am *not* a girl to ever turn down a sexy dare.

With a couple of moves, I have his belt open and I'm tugging his trousers down carefully over his monster erection.

God, I hope he hits me really, *really* hard with his great big rhythm stick.

He bends to remove his shoes and socks, kicking off his trousers impatiently as he does. When he straightens up, he's wearing nothing but a pair of black boxer briefs, and my breath catches. Holy hell. We eye-fuck each other with all we have before he takes a step forward and reaches around me, unhooking my bra. It falls down my arms, the lace snagging against my rock-hard nipples as it goes.

I thought we'd come in here and tear each other's clothes off in ten seconds flat, but Ethan's brand of delayed gratification has its upsides; it really does. Because I am *gagging for it*. He hooks his thumbs into the sides of my red lace thong, which, because I'm a pro, is obviously sitting outside of my suspender belt. Squatting, he slides it down my legs with an icy focus that makes me shiver, his face level with my pussy.

He hasn't gone down on me yet, a fact I'm far too aware of. When I was texting with Talia this week about how I was getting on, I asked her about it, and she said he was excellent at it. That information was both reassuring and unhelpful. I really hope he feels like indulging today because I need Ethan Kingsley's face between my legs, like, yesterday.

I step out of my thong, and he stands. Even with my heels still on, he's towering above me.

'Get mine off.'

I smile at him and lick my lips. Yes *sir*.

He surveys me with interest. 'You really want this, don't you?' He's not goading me. If anything, his tone is interested. Curious.

'I really, *really* want this.' I get his waistband over his cock and it springs out. At least one part of his body knows how to express exuberance.

As soon as we get his boxers off, he crushes me to him, the full length of him pressed against me and his dick jerking between us, as he kisses me with a ferocity, a hunger, I haven't seen in him until now. Our hands are everywhere, and my head is spinning. Yeah, we've fucked before, but I cannot express how incredible having head-to-toe skin on skin with him is. The guy may give every appearance of being cold, but his skin is smooth and warm. *So bloody warm.*

I grab his arse and pull him closer so I can grind against him, and his dick responds by painting damp spots on my stomach. Now that he's naked, his gym regimen is all too clear. He's beautiful. *Beautiful.* Strong and lean and supple. He has the build of a natural athlete. I could compose a sonnet to the glutes contracting under my hand. Why is standing-up, naked, full-body groping so incredibly excellent?

Before I can answer my own question, he unglues himself from me with a ragged groan and jerks his head towards the open double doors to my left.

'Through there. I want you on that bed. We're doing this my way.'

He bends to pick his tie off the floor and procures a strip of condoms from his trouser pocket before he straightens and snags my hand. His gigantic boner leads our way like a jaunty lightsabre through the expanse of plush white carpet and platinum-coloured silk walls and sculptural light fittings to a bedroom that's kitted out in more of the same. If I was less horny I'd be fawning over the gorgeousness of the art and the quality of the fixtures, because this place is to die for. As it is, my only interest is getting on that massive white bed and spreading my legs as quickly as I can.

'Up,' Ethan commands. 'Heels off. Stockings stay on.' Nobody should be this comfortable barking orders when they're stark, bollock naked, but I love it. I kick my shoes off, getting one knee up on the high bed and then the other, and I crawl across its snowy expanse in only my stockings and suspender belt. I'm not above trying every trick in the book to get this guy to home in on my poor, needy pussy.

'Fucking hell,' he mutters, and I smirk to myself.

It's only then that I flip over and spread myself out for him like a banquet.

Let him have at me. And may we both survive this.

CHAPTER 19

Ethan

Sophia lies back for me on the huge bed, just as I've told her to, and I experience the most extreme sense of satisfaction. Vindication.

I recall that moment when Camille pointed her out to me across the crowded terrace upstairs. I wanted her then. I was intent on getting her, and I told her as much. I told her she was a prize.

And, sweet Lord, what a prize she is.

She was the bold choice rather than the easy one. Far too self-assured and nowhere near respectful enough, for one. I knew I'd have my hands full.

And the bounty of her body, the likes of which I've never allowed myself before. The sense of lushness, of excess, that I got from her as soon as I laid eyes on her is magnified a hundredfold as I climb onto the bed, marvelling at the stunning display she makes on the white sheets.

Like I said.

I knew I'd have my hands full.

I crawl over her, drinking her in. Her pink mouth is already bee-stung from my kisses, a fact that's immensely gratifying. Under that long fringe, her beautiful eyes are molten and watchful and expectant, but also peaceful. There's an assurance there. She knows as well as I do how good this will be.

'Arms up,' I say hoarsely. I may finally be giving her what she tells me she wants so badly, but we're doing this on my terms. And a little restraint will give me more agency.

She raises her arms languorously, crossing her wrists, and I marvel at the supple way her body moves on the bed as she does. Her abundance of hair is a dark, shiny halo around her, its tendrils everywhere. I slip the still-knotted tie over her wrists and tighten it with a tug before pushing her arms back so they're flat on the sheets above her head. As far as restraints go, this one is pretty vanilla, but I'm no Boy Scout, and I didn't exactly plan this.

'Where to start?' I murmur, gazing down her body. I haven't seen her naked since that fucking amazing interview, when she stripped for me on my desk, but that was the definition of a quick fuck.

This is the first time I'll get to really enjoy what I've paid for.

She lets out a breathy little moan, as though she's up for all of it, and I can't resist. I'll go to work on her in a minute—my frazzled brain really needs the win of knowing that I can command this woman if nothing else in my working day—but I'll allow myself just a moment of seeking solace in Sophia's astounding body.

I lower myself down on top of her, my dick trapped between us, my pecs pressing against her pillowy tits, and brace on one elbow as I claim her mouth. My kiss is hard and hungry, a clear foreshadowing of exactly how I intend to fuck her, and she writhes beneath me as she responds in kind. She may be pretending to submit to me, but god knows, this woman gives as good as she gets.

I use my free hand to enjoy her body. Really enjoy it. If it wasn't for the painful throbbing of my cock, the most pressing kind of ticking time-bomb, I could touch her all day long. I smooth my hand down her arm, shifting slightly so I can access the soft mass of one of her beautiful tits, rolling her nipple between my fingers and noting with pleasure how taut, how pinched, it already is, how intoxicating it feels to have her moan her encouragement into my mouth.

I move lower, my hand dipping into the lace-covered curve of her waist before skating over her hip, her arse. She slides a leg up, and I caress it. Fuck this. My body may be revelling in using her as the most sumptuous pillow, but I need to see more. Feel more. I push myself up so I'm crouching over her, my legs between hers, her body now fully accessible to me.

'A man could get lost in a body like this, Sophia.' I dip my head and allow myself a leisurely suck of the nipple I just played with, tugging it softly between my teeth and eliciting a sharp intake of breath from her. I release it and straighten up, looking her in the eye as I stroke over her stomach. It's not a tender move but an assessing one. She's all mine, and I intend to get to know every inch of her. I use my thumb to smear the spots of pre-cum I left across her skin. 'A man could get lost for days and days.'

She watches me avidly, lips parted. For once, it seems she's at a loss for words, and I like it a lot. I drag my hand lower. She has the tiniest, tidiest landing strip of dark hair. I brush over it and slide a couple of fingers between her legs. The flesh I find is so impossibly soft, so wet, that I let out an involuntary moan. How is it that every inch of her glorious body is so alluring? So welcoming?

I watch in fascination as my fingertips glide over her perfect pink cunt.

'Oh, god,' she moans.

'That feel good?'

'God, yes.'

'What do you want most in the world right now?' I ask, my tone as idle as the way I'm touching her.

'Your tongue on my clit,' she says immediately. 'And your fingers stretching me open. And then your big dick in my pussy.'

'Demanding little thing, aren't you?' But I can't deny I'm delighted by her answer. Out there in the world, there are endless people who don't know what's best for them and situations that can't be managed, while here in this room, on this bed, lies a beautiful, pliant woman whose needs I can meet in my sleep and who is prepared to submit, to *admit* that I know best—for now, at least.

It's the purest, cleanest, and most efficient way to get myself back on track. To blot out every single other shit-show beyond these four walls and restore my equilibrium.

It's time to give the lady what she wants.

I kneel. I crouch down. I push her legs wider, my palms imprinting themselves on her soft, tanned thighs. And when I have her spread precisely how I want, I lean right in. Run my nose and mouth along her skin, so slowly that her legs shake beneath my palms as I reach the spot where she wants me so badly.

'Shit, Ethan. *Please.*'

'We talked about this.' I kiss the crease at the very top of her thigh. 'We're doing this my way. This is for my pleasure, not yours.'

It's not true, of course, not in the slightest, but Sophia's predictable enough and stubborn enough to make reverse psychology a real joy. If she thinks I in any way resent her chasing her pleasure, she'll come like a fucking freight train.

I turn my head, my lips millimetres from her swollen clit. God, she's as beautiful down here as she is everywhere else: pink and silken and all mine to play with. To feast on.

'Now. Where was I?'

Her breath catches raggedly in her throat. Whether she's bracing herself for me to touch her or not touch her, I don't know. Either way, it's an entrancing sound.

'Keep your legs like this,' I order her, although I'm confident the heft of my shoulders will act as a wedge between them. I withdraw my hands and splay one across her stomach to hold her down as I use the other to part her labia as delicately as possible. I'm a mesmerised explorer pinning down a rare butterfly, even if my motives are less altruistic: I know she's aroused enough to find the lightness of my touch positively maddening.

Sure enough, she groans like a stroppy teenager, and I allow myself another private smile against her flesh.

Fortuitously for her, her scent is fucking up my senses far too much for me to hold off much longer. She's intoxicating, and I'm not a man operating at peak willpower. Not after that meeting.

I need my fix, even if I'm selfishly intent on drawing it out. I need to throw myself a bone here.

Proponents of mindfulness should offer up Sophia Petrakis and her beautiful cunt, because it's my whole world right now. Like a man stupefied, I allow myself my first taste.

CHAPTER 20

Sophia

Oh god.

Oh *god*.

Ethan licks a line up from my entrance before his perfect tongue circles my clit, and I might die from the pleasure of it. If that doesn't kill me, his low, hungry noise of approval will. My own noise of approval is more high-pitched, more desperate. I keep my legs spread and my arms stretched out above my head like the good girl I'm pretending to be, but I also absolutely thrust my pussy against his face like the brazen ho I actually am.

Why the fuck has he been withholding his tongue from me all week? It's clearly his second-best attribute, and I'm *not* talking about his personality. He circles my clit again, the slippery sensation telling me that I'm soaking down there. I moan out an involuntary *ah-ah-ah* sound and begin to pray.

Please god, let him be a generous lover and not a sadistic arsehole.

It seems there is a god, because he takes the fingers holding me open and shoves two of them inside me with a single hard thrust that would have me shooting off the bed if it wasn't for those fingers splayed firmly, possessively, over my stomach.

'Fuck, you're ridiculous,' he hums, his breath warm on my pussy. *'Ridiculous.'* (I am extremely confident from his tone that he means this as a compliment.) 'The question is, can you give me what I need?'

'Anything,' I say with a pathetically breathy gasp. It's not my coolest moment. 'What do you need?'

'I need you so fucking hot for this that you blot out every single thing that's happened today up until now. I want to destroy you, and then I want to fucking drown in you.' He pauses, his voice dropping to a whisper. 'I need a win today. Think you can manage that?'

Be still my heart.

My uptight, controlling, humourless boss confessing his vulnerabilities, and against my clit, at that?

He's already destroyed me.

He'll be drowning his dick in my dead, smutty corpse at this rate.

But he doesn't need my pity. Absolutely not. All he needs, in this moment, is to know that my greedy, greedy vagina and I have his back. He's treating me like a whore in the best way: he's paying for this, and he's asking me to give him what he needs. This isn't some random hookup. It's a transaction, and I'm about to prove to him that I'm worth every penny.

'You've got the right girl,' I promise. 'Try me.' I'm suddenly glad that he's tied me up in this token way. Otherwise, I wouldn't be able to resist reaching down and stroking his hair.

He clears his throat as if he's already embarrassed. 'Glad to hear it. Now *show me.*' And with that, he presses his mouth to my pussy, issuing what's probably the easiest demand of my entire career, because I'm physically incapable of *not* showing him.

Heat courses through my entire pelvic region like molten treacle as his tongue slides over me and his fingers lance me with a perfect sting, over and over. I raise my chin a little to catch a peek of the fine, fine sight of his head between my legs as he licks me, his hair tousled. He glances up, and the look he gives me through his eyelashes is so depraved, so feral, that it practically sends me over the edge. I let my head flop down and stretch my arms out above my head and focus on withstanding his sensory barrage.

My whimpers grow louder, and they seem to galvanise him. He ramps up his ministrations, twisting his fingers viciously inside me at the top of each thrust as he uses his supple lips and strong tongue to wreak total havoc on my clit.

It's too much. I'm incandescent, breathless with desire. My orgasm shimmers around my consciousness, a beautiful halo. I try to arch my back, but Ethan holds me down, forcing me to absorb every single ounce of this onslaught. My only outlet is my voice, and by god do I let rip.

'I can't—oh my god, Ethan. It's so—harder. Harder. Please. It's—god, just there, just there, I can't—'

The blessed man doubles down, lavishing my pussy with every ravenous lick, every suck I need, like he's eating me for breakfast, lunch and dinner. And as he does, the white-hot heat flooding my body ignites into something the intensity of which I can't name or understand, and I'm consumed, writhing and bucking and shaking as best I can as he licks me and finger-fucks me relentlessly through it all.

I pull my bound hands up and press the heels of my hands into my eye sockets as planets collide and stars combust behind my eyelids. I'm still crying out, I realise, but it's gibberish, utter nonsense. Gradually, I float down from my extraordinary climax. Ethan's touch has softened, and, right as my flesh grows too sensitised, he withdraws his mouth and fingers.

He crawls up my body, looking for all the world like a man on the brink of losing his sanity altogether, and crouches over me on all fours. I stare up at him, stunned, as he reaches for the strip of condoms.

'I'll take that,' he says, 'as win number one.'

~

ETHAN

I've seen Sophia post-orgasm before, of course. The sight of her when I peeled her off my desk after her interview is a memory I've jerked off to with particular pleasure.

But seeing her like this, her beautiful body sprawled beneath me in a semi-restrained, sex-drunk, sated heap, is... affecting, on a whole other level.

Out there somewhere, my father and the Montagues are presumably engaged in mud-slinging and war games and brinksmanship, and I should probably care.

While in here, Sophia stares up at me with glazed eyes, her breathing ragged, her tits heaving. She looks at me as though I'm her god, as though I'm some kind of miracle worker, when, really, it's she who's the alchemist. It's she who's slowly transforming the poison that's been coursing through my veins all day into honey.

I rear up onto my knees between her legs, tearing a condom off the strip and ripping open the foil. She watches me pinch the condom and roll it over my impossibly hard, impossibly painful dick. I, in turn, take her in. She's still so tanned. Such a vision against these white sheets. Those lashes. Those *eyes*. All that dark, glossy hair. She's undoubtedly a siren, and her call is fucking deafening, and if I crash against the rocks and perish, it will all have been worthwhile.

'Time for win number two,' I tell her. I want her like this

for now, bound and supine and at my mercy. I want to lower myself down on top of her and blot everything else out and consume her the way she's just consumed me.

Her mouth makes a little *O*. Her gorgeous face is still dazed. And I can wait no longer to plunge inside her and let myself drown.

I'm a lucky man, I suppose. Since my wife did the only feasible thing she could do and ran for the hills, taking Jamie with her, I've been able to subjugate any sense of responsibility I feel for other people's happiness and wellbeing. That's a good thing when your mere presence is usually the antidote to their happiness *or* wellbeing. And the bonus is that, rather than go through the motions of dating in order to get laid, I can employ spectacular women to take care of my needs.

My need right now is a hard fuck, a fuck punishing enough to obliterate all my problems, and I have faith that my newest and most alluring employee will give me just that. After all, she served me up her own utter destruction with aplomb, just as I instructed her.

I don't take my eyes off her as I brace on one elbow and feed her my dick. Beneath me, she moves to accommodate me as best she can. Sophia's no blushing ingenue, and she's wet as fuck, but it's still a tight fit. Sweat pricks my skin as I endeavour to ram home without losing it.

She truly is a sight to behold. The way she's blinking up at me from under that feathery fringe is so seductive. Her legs are still drawn up, her soft inner thighs the most heavenly cradle for my body. In my world of self-denial and self-control and, probably, self-sabotage, she is an oasis of carnal abundance, and I'm about to gorge myself stupid.

As I sink deeper, I can't resist: I lower my mouth to hers so I can fill her up at both ends. I want her to taste her own honeyed sweetness on my lips. My tongue toys with hers as I give another thrust and bottom out in her. Jesus Christ. I really need to find a way to get this woman bare so there's no barrier between my starving dick and her glorious inner walls as I drag my way in and out of her.

But even so, it's heavenly in here. I hold still and kiss her harder. I want her to feel it too, feel how perfectly we fit.

With the hand not holding my weight, I grab her arse. It's so fucking round and plump against my palm. I dig my fingers in, finding purchase in her smooth skin so I can ensure I maintain deadly focus once I start to move.

And I really do mean deadly.

Still kissing her, I slide out and plunge brutally back in. The moan she makes in my mouth tells me she feels the vicious beauty of it as much as I do.

I'm moving inside her properly now, with long, fevered thrusts that have my poor dick on fire. I can't take my eyes off her. I watch for every flicker of pleasure over her stunning face as I drive home, over and over.

She's watching me too.

I knew the moment I saw her that she was a knockout. But there's nothing quite like having your own arousal reflected in her eyes to understand that she's far, far more than that.

She brings her bound hands up and over us, smoothing them down my back and then up again so she can stroke my neck. It's an act of defiance I shouldn't tolerate, but it feels so good.

''Even when you're being fucked you're a disobedient little thing,' I growl.

She looks anything but contrite. 'Can't help it. I want to touch you.'

'Fuck. Take it off.'

She shrugs off the cursory cuff and cups my neck, pulling my head down for a hard kiss. There's something about kissing a woman when you're inside her that's intensely gratifying. It's the hottest echo of fucking her.

Sophia's hands travel down my body as I do, grabbing and clawing my shoulders, my biceps, my arse, like she can't get enough. It seems our hunger for each other is a raw and desperate thing.

If I'm going to go full throttle with my self-indulgence here, I may as well treat myself to the best view in the house. I force myself to still inside her for a moment and roll us over so she's lying on top of me. All that dark hair of hers falls around us, blotting out the daylight for a moment.

'Ride me,' I order her. 'Show me how badly you want this.'

She pushes herself upright with a pained little laugh, using her hand to scoop her hair back in one big flick.

Holy fucking hell.

She is spectacular.

She sits astride me, hair everywhere and eyes molten. I'm not sure where to look—at her flushed face, or her magnificent tits, or at the spot where my dick disappears inside her body.

All I know is that she's the best show in town. She rears up and slams back down, and the pleasure courses to every extremity in my body. I slide my hands along her thighs so I can grip her hips hard, controlling her movements, ensuring she stays on track. And, like the pro that she is, she does. She works my dick with slick slides, the pleasure she feels every time she sits fully down on me painted all over her face.

Then she's falling forward, planting her hands either side of my face so she can really go for it. Her hair tickles my chest, her tits bounce inches from my face, and I realise that she's not servicing me at all. God, no. She's working me for herself, wringing every bit of pleasure she can from my body like the greedy little thing she is, and I fucking love it.

I release her hips so I can palm her tits roughly. When I pinch her nipples, her entire face contorts, and she lets out a long, low moan. Christ, she's such a beautiful, sexual creature.

Her entire body is made for fucking, for giving men—and, it seems, herself—pleasure. I thrust up into her as savagely as I can from my supine position and, through my shockwaves of need, deliriously congratulate myself on an epic fucking hire, because Sophia really is the full package.

'I need you to come, sweetheart,' I beg her brokenly, because what I *don't* need today is to shoot my load before she does. From the strangled sounds she's making and the desperate way she's grinding against me, it seems she's close. 'I need you to keep milking my cock and taking what you need. Keep grinding that greedy little clit against me and show me what you're made of.'

'Oh Jesus,' she groans as she gets herself upright. I manage to keep hold of one of her breasts, using my other hand to find her clit and rub. I'm not taking any chances here. Our skin is slick with sweat. Her fringe is sticking to her forehead. I track her movements, keeping my hands on her as she rides me, chasing her orgasm. Our eyes are locked. Hers are wild, desperate with her need to come. I've never seen anything like it.

She rides me harder and harder, lost to whatever need is fuelling her right now. Her cries grow louder. More fevered. I lie here and I thrust, my entire body shaking with the effort of holding myself back, of keeping my—

Fuuuuuuck.

She breaks.

She bucks and she screams and her clit grows impossibly harder, slicker, and she slams down on me over and over and over *and I fucking detonate.*

I jerk on the bed, powerless beneath this goddess to do anything but let the orgasm she's milked from me course over my body. My hips rut uselessly, the most unearthly bellow breaks from me, and I'm dimly, blissfully aware of Sophia thrashing around above me as I fill up the condom in great, angry spurts.

Jesus fucking Christ, I'm hollowed out and reborn. I'm nothing and everything and so flooded with wellbeing that I feel weightless and thoughtless and... done. I'm done for. I let my arms fall outwards onto the sheets.

Then Sophia's smiling down at me, a majestic, sated smile that strikes me as the biggest triumph I could possibly have wished for, and she's lowering herself down on top of me. Deep inside her, my dick twitches happily as her breasts settle against my chest and her lips find mine.

With difficulty, I find the use of my arms, burying my fingers in her hair and smoothing them down her back as I kiss her, slowly, lazily. Our tongues entangle. Our breaths mingle. And I sigh my bone-deep contentment into her mouth.

Fuck the Montagues.

This is what I call a win.

CHAPTER 21

Sophia

'How does that feel?' he asks, shooting me a dirty grin as he smiles down at me.

I wince. 'Intense. It's a lot.'

'I think you can take a bit more.'

'No, honestly, I—'

He bears down harder, and I grimace. 'Jesus, that's painful. You went hard on me today.'

'Because I knew you could take it, beautiful girl.' He's still smiling, and I'm putty in his hands. This man is delicious.

My new personal trainer, Caio, is the polar opposite of my boss: warm, smiley, and emotionally competent. He's also as big a whore as I am, if his stories are to be believed.

Sadly, I'm not his type. Nowhere close.

'If I can't walk tomorrow, I'm coming to find you,' I warn him.

'You'll be fine. Caio's stretches are infamous. And don't forget an Epsom salt bath tonight. You did great today.'

We beam at each other, and I know he's right. That's why I'm taking this pain now, allowing my hamstrings to scream at me as he bears down on me, pushing my right leg so far forward that I could lick my knee if I wanted to. I force myself to breathe through the discomfort. The more confronting it is now, the less tight I'll be tomorrow.

Caio hinges his weight forward and pushes my leg a little further. If he were straight, this position would be incredibly dirty. I'd forgotten how fun it is flirting with gorgeous gay guys.

'I want an arse like yours by the end of the year,' I tell him.

'You'll get it. But it's a lot of work, baby. I didn't just get this in the gym, you know.'

I sigh. I know. Caio is a go-go dancer at Electric Dreams, a fabulous-sounding, Eighties-themed gay nightclub in Soho. His buns of steel are the product of hours and hours of shimmying up and down poles (and, presumably, hot guys' bodies) as much as they are of weights.

'I'd come and dance there if I didn't think I'd clear the room,' I say with a pout.

He laughs. 'Everyone would fucking love you. You should come one night. Bring your girlfriends.'

That's not a bad call. It's exhausting to go out with the seraphim. We get hit on everywhere we go. A gay club would be gold—we could dance all night, safe in the knowledge that we have zero sex appeal for any of the other punters. Maybe it's an outing for another weekend. Tomorrow night we have a group outing to the elite Mayfair sex club, Alchemy. One of its founders, Genevieve, is married to Anton Wolff, billionaire entrepreneur and the dirty bastard who dreamed up—and founded—Seraph. Gen gave all the seraphim membership over the summer.

I think she figured that having objectively hot women go there to blow off steam could only be good for business.

'Seriously?'

'Anytime. Breathe, baby. It's a lot to take.'

'That's what he said,' I quip, as he stays braced above me

in this weirdly intimate and totally asexual position. I turn my head to stare at his arm. 'If I were you I'd spend far too much time measuring the girth of my biceps.'

'I spend far too much time measuring the girth of a lot of things,' he admits with a grin, and I full-on cackle like the classy chick that I am. I'm still sniggering to myself when a shadow falls over my face, and I look up to find my boss glaring down at us, arms crossed over his chest.

He looks cranky and morally outraged and hot as hell.

Ugh.

'What the fuck is going on here?' he demands, and my mouth drops open. The nerve of this guy. He's been a total cunt to me since our hotel interlude on Tuesday, distant and dismissive and demeaning, and now he's trying to muscle in on my downtime?

I don't think so.

'Um, excuse me? I'm on my lunch break. What the hell is your problem?'

Caio eases off me and helps me lower my leg down. Fuck, my hip flexors are tight. He scrambles to his feet and holds out his hand to Ethan as I rear up onto my elbows with difficulty.

'Hi, Mr Kingsley. I'm Caio. We haven't met. I started four months ago, I...'

He trails off as Ethan shakes his hand in the rudest and most cursory way possible before glaring back down at me.

'It doesn't look like you were working out.'

'Caio was stretching me because he just worked me like a motherfucker.' I can't help it if that sounds risqué. Ethan is entitled to precisely zero disclosure about what I do in my lunch hour, whether I'm on his premises or not.

'Well, if you're finished "stretching", get showered and come upstairs. I need you on the Montague stuff. *Now*.' Without waiting for an answer, he turns and flounces out of the gym as I lie here and fume. The Montague transaction may be front and centre this week, but I'd bet my life savings that this little emergency comprises nothing more urgent than my boss' mystifying need to throw his weight around.

Caio squats back down next to me. 'Do you need to go?'

'Jesus, no. Do the other leg.'

He kneels like the obedient and rational human being that he is and lifts my other leg. 'Is he always that... grumpy?'

'Yes.'

'And hot?'

I sigh. 'Also yes. Unfortunately, the two are directly correlated.'

'Hmm.' We both turn to see Ethan's fine arse disappearing through the glass doors. 'Tom trains him. He says he works out like a psycho.'

'Nothing could surprise me less.' *Especially because I have borne witness to the results of whatever demons spur him on in the gym.*

'I think he was jealous. Maybe he wants you. You should definitely fuck him.'

I laugh. Sadly, my need to uphold contractually enforced confidentiality is greater than my desire to gossip with Caio.

'Not jealous. He just likes to remind me who's boss at every possible opportunity.' I don't add what's obvious to me:

Ethan is still suffering from a vulnerability hangover after those things he said and did on Tuesday, the way he allowed himself to need me.

And I'm the one who has to bear the brunt of it.

'WHAT THE HELL was that down there?' I ask as I stride back into his office, banging the door behind me. I've showered, fixed my makeup, and run some straighteners through my sweat-frizzed hair, vibrating with outrage the entire time.

Damn Ethan and his ability to ruin my post-workout endorphin hit.

He stands up and shoves his hands in his pockets. 'That guy was all over you. Have some self-respect.'

My mouth drops open. 'Like I told you down there, he was *stretching* me. And it's none of your business. Who the fuck do you think you are?'

'Your boss. I don't need gossip circulating that my EA is fucking everything that moves. When you behave like a slut in your place of work, you damage my reputation.'

I take a few steps closer, so we're almost toe to toe, and will myself to remember that I'm far too high maintenance for prison food, because the chances of me strangling this man are going through the roof.

'Oh no you didn't. You did *not* just slut-shame me.'

His look of alarmed regret is truly excellent. 'I wasn't slut-shaming you. I was pointing out that, as my EA, you have a duty to behave in an appropriate way.'

'There is nothing appropriate about the way I behave with you, and you know it,' I hiss. 'It wasn't very appropriate when you got me naked "in my place of work" and came all over my tits yesterday, was it?'

His lips press together, and he grabs my jaw in a pincer grip between his thumb and forefinger. 'That's different, and you know it. We have a particular relationship, and I pay you a fuck-tonne of money for that privilege. So excuse me for not being thrilled when I see you giving away the goods for free in the office gym.'

I reach up and wrap my fingers around his wrist, my nails digging into his skin. Good. I hope it fucking hurts.

'Firstly, he's gay, dickhead. Not that it's any of your business.' He's still gripping my jaw, so I can't nod to make my point, but I raise my eyebrows. 'Yeah. That's right. That guy probably loves dick even more than I do, which is saying something. So the only person whose reputation is at stake is you, because you're the one jumping to conclusions and throwing public hissy fits.'

I take the opportunity of his clear shock to wrench myself out of his grasp and back away. 'And let me make myself very clear. We do not have an exclusive relationship. I can flirt with whomever I want. I can *fuck* whomever I want. So don't for a second assume you have any jurisdiction over me when I'm not in this office. Do you understand?'

He visibly deflates. I've quite literally knocked the wind out of his sails, it seems. He points to the chair behind me. 'Sit down. I want to talk to you about that.'

I glare at him to ensure he understands he's not the boss of me, and I reluctantly sit. 'What.'

He flops into the chair behind his desk and picks up a manila folder that's sitting on his keyboard, lobbing it across the desk to me. 'I want to renegotiate our terms.'

I frown and flick open the folder. It's our Seraph contract. 'How so?'

He clears his throat. 'I want exclusivity.'

I laugh. I actually laugh. He came upstairs after our little altercation, and his first reaction was to pull this thing out of his filing cabinet? You've got to be kidding me. 'Hard pass.'

'Why?' He leans forward, gripping his armrests. 'You can't possibly be getting better orgasms elsewhere.'

I stare at him, at the memory in those grey eyes. Because I remember too, and it's very fucking unhelpful. 'It's not about the orgasms.' There's no point in lying, after all. We both know that he fucks me like no one else can... when he wants to play ball, that is.

'What is it about then? Money?'

'No. Not exactly.'

I can't exactly tell him that it's really about my determination to ensure that I reserve a decent portion of my time and energy for healthier, more regulating relationships with people who've worked on themselves and aren't the emotional equivalent of traumatised five-year-olds. It's time to deflect. 'What is it about for you?'

He stiffens further. I know this is hard for him. I'm sure he's been hoping that I'll just roll over and he won't have to divulge any vulnerabilities.

But I'm not about to make it easier. He has to understand the parameters of this relationship, and he has to respect my need for space and boundaries. That's the crux of it.

So I cross my legs and wait.

'I need to have more... certainty with you. More control of the situation. I appreciate that I may have... jumped to conclusions down there, and I apologise, okay? But I find that things work best when I'm in the driving seat, and so I'm afraid I require that. Control, I mean. Over, er, you.'

I would like it noted here that I deserve a very shiny gold star for not laughing. Wow, this handsome, infuriating Eight would make a fantastic case study for an Enneagram course. Instead, I lean forward and attempt to engage on a rational basis.

'Do you remember when I told you you needed a sub? That's what a sub would give you. Full control. That's not me. The only way you get me is as a free agent.'

'I don't want a sub. I'm not kinky like that. But I need more power over you,' he insists. I wish he didn't look so forlorn. He's making this far harder than it should be, even if he is being an overbearing wanker.

'Ethan.' I interlace my fingers and rest them on my crossed legs. I feel like a therapist which, honestly, is what it seems I'm becoming for this guy. An unqualified therapist. 'I say this with respect. You saying I should give you more control because you "need it" is like a heroin addict telling me I should give him more crack because he "needs it". Do you understand?'

I mean, as messages go, it's pretty hard-hitting, but sometimes you need to go for a blunt delivery. My instincts tell me anything less brutal would fall on deaf ears.

That said, his expression is blank. 'I'm not an addict.'

'No, you're not a drug addict. But we all have our coping mechanisms, and yours, it seems, is control, and the feeling it gives you can become addictive. When you're in the driving seat, as you said, you feel safer, and when you're not, you feel unsafe. And none of that is shameful or problematic or your fault. Actually, it's a really fantastic self-protective mechanism that your nervous system has developed. But the more unsafe you feel, the more and more you'll want to control everything. Especially your relationships.'

I pause, because this is a hell of a mirror I'm holding up for someone who's not remotely self-aware. 'And my job isn't to enable you. It's to uphold my boundaries so that I can be well and regulated and able to function properly. It's not to feed your excessive need for control.'

'I don't have an excessive need,' he insists. 'I just—I would like to know that we were exclusive so I don't need to worry about sexual health issues, and also I'd like to negotiate that I get to go bare with you. The condoms are bothering me. Oh, and I'd like to be able to see you some evenings, for sex, if that's an amendment you're willing to negotiate.'

I sigh and push myself up to standing. This guy is gaslighting me less than he's gaslighting himself. He hasn't heard a single word I've said except for *no,* and it's not his fault. It's really not. Those bodyguard, or protector, parts are so firmly in the driving seat that he's operating with very little sense of Self, and those parts will be working very hard right now to ensure that he doesn't try to derail their agendas.

'It's a no, Ethan. I'm enjoying this job, honestly. The sex is great, and the work is interesting. But my take is that you're in a very dysregulated place, with little to no interest in tackling that, and that makes it less enjoyable for me to spend time with you. I'm sorry, but it's true. It's important that I have the freedom to seek healthy relationships—and sex—outside of this.' I pause and deliver my punchline. 'And I'm heading to Alchemy tomorrow night with the seraphim, so there's no way I'm negotiating any kind of exclusivity agreement today. Not on your life.'

CHAPTER 22

Ethan

Sophia may be off on what strikes me as an ill-advised and irresponsible night out tonight at Alchemy, but she's here right now. A small part of me feels marginally guilty that I'm making her work a second consecutive Saturday, but a far larger and more forceful part needs to know she's safe and here and within my orbit.

The sense of conflict between those two emotions has me wondering, for just a moment, if that's what Sophia means whenever she bangs on about my 'parts'. I'm damned if I'll give her the satisfaction of asking her to elaborate on her psychobabble. I'd rather die.

We've moved from my study to the kitchen where we're poring over the list of questions and issues that my initial meetings with the biggest Montague investors have yielded. Our aim is to go back to each party as soon as humanly possible with the answers they require, but some of their queries require serious number-crunching on our part. I have my Strategy team and my Finance Director on the case, but Sophia is helping me compile all the information in one folder, organised by theme, so we have it to hand.

The reception overall has been warm, I would say. It's better than a tepid or outright icy reaction, but it's not a foregone conclusion. Our success in persuading the most influential investors to swap their Montague Group shares for Kingsley Hotel shares will depend on our ability to forecast mega cost efficiencies... and to persuade them that we will execute on these once we get the keys to the Montague kingdom.

It's a tough sell and, as war correspondents would describe it, a highly unstable situation on the ground. None of which is remotely appeasing to me. Of course, the more the investors smell value creation and the more they demand we slash costs between the two groups, the more the Montagues will dig their heels in.

In a word, messy.

Very fucking messy.

Sophia doesn't seem particularly happy with my current behaviour, but the feeling is mutual. When all around me a shit show of epic proportions is waging, I'd like to think the EA I'm throwing six figures a month at could rise to the occasion and provide a bit of fucking stability, but no. I admit I made a tit of myself yesterday over her PT session, but I'm extra sensitive right now. I'd like everything to be just so, in my office at least. I'd like to know someone in my life has the ability and the desire to meet my needs, but Sophia is far too busy psychoanalysing me to offer any actual comfort. She's just another moving part in this chaotic mess, and it's very fucking disappointing.

We're absorbed in breaking down the follow-ups from my meeting with Legal & General on Thursday when, to my discomfort, in walks Elena, my ex-wife.

Excellent.

I'd forgotten she was coming. I'd forgotten Jamie was here, truth be told. He stayed over last night because she had an urgent meeting in Brussels, and I haven't actually seen him yet today. I also didn't hear the doorbell ring. One of the staff must have let her in. She looks tired but perfectly groomed, as always, and, as always, distinctly displeased to be back in the house where I apparently made her so unhappy.

I close the laptop with a sigh and stand to greet her.

SOPHIA

Ooooh.

So this is Ethan's ex-wife?

Fascinating.

I sit up straight and pull my sweater cuffs down over my hands as Ethan rises to greet her, because this kitchen is like the Arctic Circle.

'Hi,' he says, his voice quiet but not what I would call intimate. Weary, more like. Resigned, maybe. He kisses her on both cheeks and breaks away to gesture at me.

'This is my new EA, Sophia. Sophia—Elena, Jamie's mother.'

Is that an odd way of putting it? I dunno. I'd expect him to call her *my ex-wife*, but maybe that's unnecessarily brutal. It's not exactly my area of expertise.

'Hi!' I say as brightly as I can, hopping off my bar stool. Ethan may be the last person on earth with whom I'd want to attempt a relationship, but at the end of the day, we're fucking, and I'm only human. I want to check this woman out and, at the very least, try my psychoanalysis party trick on the person who actually did attempt a relationship with him. I kind of wish I could give the poor woman a badge that says *AT LEAST I TRIED.*

I shake her hand. 'It's so lovely to meet you. Jamie's a very sweet boy.' Although I had no idea he was here.

'Hi, Sophia,' she says, giving me a smile that looks frankly exhausted but is also undeniably genuine. 'It's lovely to meet you, too.'

'How was Brussels?' Ethan asks her. To me, he adds, 'Elena is a translator for the UN.' There's no pride in his voice. He's merely stating a fact. He's not getting off on having an accomplished wife.

'Oh, how interesting,' I say, although I already knew this. Ethan's father, Richard, told me as much when he was asking his son about Elena the other day in front of me. Clearly Ethan doesn't remember. Richard definitely *was* getting off on Elena's accomplishments. I bet he thought it helped his family's optics. Even if she's run for the hills.

'It was fine, thanks.' She rubs her forehead tiredly. 'It went on ridiculously late, but I got the first train back this morning.'

My hot takes are as follows:

One, Ethan hasn't done what the offspring of so many parents with DPD—dickwad personality disorders—do and repeat the pattern by seeking the mirror image of what they believe love looks like by shacking up with another dickwad. Elena looks to be genuinely undickwaddish. And she's a translator for the UN, so she's presumably altruistic in nature.

She's possibly a Two or a Three Enneagram—The Helper or The Achiever—or a combination of the two. Hmm. Her obvious exhaustion suggests she spreads herself too thin, puts others' needs first, and has issues upholding boundaries. I bet she could have used a lie-in and a later train this morning.

Two, I'm not getting any vibes of affection or pining or regret from Ethan. He's respectful rather than tender towards her. A bit awkward, too. Whatever shit went down between these two—and I'd give a lot of money for the full scoop—he's not in love with her anymore, nor she with him.

And three, Elena is beautiful. Like, really stunning in a genetically blessed, can't-be-faked way. Not that I'd expect less from Ethan—whatever he lacks in the personality department, he's objectively gorgeous and loaded. He was always going to marry and procreate with a beautiful woman. Elena is tiny and slim, almost bird-like, from what I can see through her gorgeous Max Mara camel coat, which hangs open. She's wearing small but impeccable pearls and tan Tod's loafers and some tailored trousers with a merino-knit polo neck. Everything is classy and understated, unlike yours truly. Her bone structure is stunning, her eyes the same clear brown colour as her son's, and her shiny nut-brown hair is pulled into a neat chignon.

The woman is fucking gorgeous, even after an early commute from continental Europe.

'How's Jamie?' she continues, looking up at Ethan quizzically. He really does tower over her.

'Fine. I haven't seen much of him.'

'How did his maths assessment go?'

Ethan frowns. 'You'll have to ask him.' Code for *I have no fucking clue.* I wonder if they spent any time together last night.

'Well, I'd better get him.' She gestures awkwardly at the door to the hallway. 'I'd like to get as much of the day with him as possible.'

Something softens in my heart—Jamie's mother rushed back from an overseas trip on the first possible train so she could spend the weekend with her son. I'm just so damn happy to know he has one parent who can't get enough of him.

Before Elena can go off in search of him, there's a thunderous disturbance on the stairs on the scale of someone ripping out a bathroom and chucking its contents down the stairs.

'Don't run!' Ethan roars in a Dad voice.

Jamie enters the room at a fair clip, slowing down as soon as he sees the three of us and doing his best to look cool as he shuffles across the kitchen. He's in a dark green hoodie—hood up—and black scuffed jeans. He goes straight to his mum and folds her into a hug, dwarfing her entirely. She clings on to him tightly.

'Hi, my gorgeous boy. Oh my goodness, such a good hug. You ready to go?'

'Sure,' he mumbles against her. I risk a glance at Ethan. He's watching them with what looks like a stricken expression. I wonder if seeing Jamie's easy affection with his mother reminds him of how lacking his relationship with his son seems to be.

'Excellent.' Elena releases him. 'Do you have all your stuff? iPad? Phone? Chargers?'

He looks down at his feet. 'Yeah. Think so.'

'Sketch pad? You can't forget that. I can't wait to see what you've been working on.'

He smiles, bashful. He's such a sweetheart. 'Got it.'

'Great. Say goodbye to your father, then.'

'Bye, Dad,' Jamie mutters, making no attempt to go to Ethan.

'See you soon, mate.' Ethan steps forward and gives him an awkward slap on the upper arm. 'Have a good weekend, yeah?'

'It was so nice to meet you, Sophia,' Elena says.

'You too!' I say brightly. 'Have a great weekend, Jamie.'

'Bye,' he manages.

'I'll walk you out,' Ethan says stiffly. Boy, this is all very awkward. My inner Seven wants to run for the hills... or straight to Bond Street at least, to drown out all this Kingsley dysfunction in some good old hedonism. Thank god I have Alchemy tonight. I'll need it after this house and its master have finished sucking the very soul out of me.

'Honey, why don't you go wait in the car?' I hear Elena say from the hallway. 'I want to talk to your father for a sec.'

There is no way I'm not listening to this. I tiptoe over to the kitchen table, which is nearer to the hallway and is where I've left my handbag. If Ethan comes back in, I can pretend to be looking for my lip balm.

The front door opens, and Jamie presumably leaves.

'What's this about?' Ethan asks. I know that tone: feigned disinterest.

'I called him last night to say goodnight and he said he'd barely seen you!' Elena hisses. 'He said he had dinner alone in his room.'

'I have the biggest transaction of my career going on, for fuck's sake. I had him as a favour to you—doesn't mean I could drop everything to hang out with him. He knows I've got a lot on.'

'Jesus Christ. Can you hear yourself? He's your son! It shouldn't feel like a favour, but honestly, it does. He doesn't think you want him here. What do you have to say to that? Why the hell can't you make him feel welcome in his own home?'

'Of course I want him here. I'm just distracted. I'll do better when all this is over.'

'You'd better bloody do better. I could strangle that fucking father of yours for fucking you up so royally. Jamie will be withdrawn for the rest of the day now, you know? But don't worry, I'll pick up the pieces like I always do.'

The door slams.

Holy fucking shit. That was horrific. I honestly feel heart-broken for all three of them: for poor Jamie, who thinks his dad doesn't actually want to be with him; for Elena, doing her best to get Jamie through all the Kingsley trauma from which she's basically rescued him, and for Ethan, my controlling, gorgeous, avoidantly attached boss who fucks up everyone he touches.

Jesus. I wouldn't have expected Elena to deliver F-bombs with such aplomb, but she seriously read him the riot act, and I have to admire it. I suspect she won't be the only one picking up the pieces. Ethan won't be a happy bunny *at all* after that.

Sure enough, he stalks back into the kitchen, crosses it angrily, flings the fridge door open, stares inside, and slams it again. Okaaay then. On the plus side, he doesn't seem to have registered my blatant eavesdropping.

'Back to work,' he snaps, taking his seat at the island.

'Sure.' If he wants to numb his pain by burying himself shoulder-deep in the exact work that he's claiming is the reason for his rift with Jamie, that's great. Just wonderful. He won't be the first person to have done that. In fact, I suspect Ethan's bodyguard parts are responsible for the vast majority of his professional success to date, whether that's because he worked his arse off to gain his bell-end father's mercurial approval or because productivity is the ultimate society-sanctioned addiction, I'm unsure.

'Are you still planning on going to Alchemy tonight?' he asks about half an hour later, apropos of nothing. He doesn't meet my eye.

'You know I am. It's a Seraph night out.'

'What happened to meeting up at a regular bar—not good enough for you guys now?'

'We want to go check it out.' I shrug. 'Anton's wife, Gen, gave us all membership a few weeks ago. It sounds fun. And the bar's supposed to be gorgeous.'

'They have a two-drink limit.'

'Only if you want to go through to The Playroom afterwards.'

He stiffens and rolls his pen towards him across the marble. I personally think the setup at Alchemy sounds great —a lovely, sophisticated bar to hang out in (fully clothed, of course) and eye-fuck people, and then the option to go through to The Playroom next door afterwards for full-on naked fun.

'And do you?' He finally looks at me, spinning the pen between his fingers. His eyes are burning.

'I don't know. I haven't decided. And it's not exactly any of your business.'

That might be true, but it's also provocative. I know it'll piss Ethan off, and I want to push his buttons, for some reason.

He purses his lips. 'What a dirty little slut you are. I've been banging your brains out all fucking week, and it still isn't enough for you. You need so much dick that you're going to spend your evening crawling around a sex club in the hope that as many blokes as possible will dick you up. You're a fucking disgrace.'

To my horror, my eyes prick with tears. Man, his protector parts are *mean*. Mean, and seriously ugly, and so damn entrenched.

This is exactly the kind of behaviour that had Talia and her predecessors in floods of tears every week, that had them walking out that door and never coming back.

I take a deep breath and blink the tears away. It's less about Ethan knowing his cruel jibe has landed and more about showing him that he doesn't fool me. Not for one second.

And after that little stunt, he's put the ball firmly in my court. I twist my body around so I can look him in the eye. He's looking at me like I'm a worthless piece of shit on the floor, and I marvel at how many seemingly functional adults are actually walking around this planet every day with their most fucked-up, egregious parts uniformly running the show.

Ethan's nervous system is like a kindergarten class when the teacher has left the room, and I will not be that teacher figure. Only he can provide that for himself. But I can damn well step in for a moment and bring the class to order.

Before I do, I take a slow inhale and exhale in an attempt to regulate my own nervous system. I may be emotionally robust, but I'm only human, and it's hard not to interpret what Ethan said as an outright attack.

'Listen to me very carefully.' He rears back slightly on his stool as if he's expecting a bollocking. Good, if not strictly accurate. 'I'm only going to say this once. *I* know what you're doing, pal, even if you don't. You might think you're lashing out at me because you're feeling exposed or shamed right now, and you're in need of a power flex.

'But that's not exactly what's happening. You don't realise it, but you're testing me. You're pushing me away in the most horrible, insulting fashion to see if I bail. Because that's what Talia and the others did, didn't they? They couldn't hack your tests, so they bailed, and no blame to them. That stuff you just said to me was really fucking nasty.'

He goes to speak, but I cut him off. 'Nope. I'm not done. You can test me, but I won't abandon you. I know that was your fiercest, most burdened inner bodyguards talking just now and not you. I warned you when we met that I'm not broken. I'm strong enough to stand up to those bodyguards. I'm not afraid of them. That said, I have far too much self-respect to sit here and let you speak to me like that, so I'm going to give you some space.' I gather my phone and lip balm and slide off my stool. 'I'll see you on Monday.'

With that, I walk out of the room without a backward glance.

CHAPTER 23

Sophia

'So what I'm hearing,' Bree surmises, 'is that Ethan is far too dysfunctional for you to ever fall for him.'

I stare at her, horrified. 'God, no. He's good for one thing, and one thing only.' I shrug. 'And the work is interesting, I suppose.'

Given that this fabulous sex club, Alchemy, has a strict two-drink limit for those of us wanting to partake in the good stuff next door in The Playroom, we're engaging in a thoroughly enjoyable character assassination of my good boss instead of getting hammered. Athena and Marlowe are the only ones getting stuck in. Athena, of course, is heading home after this to the lovely Gabe. Saintly he may be, but I know he enjoyed Alchemy's 'facilities' before he employed Athena. Marlowe's boyfriend Brendan, on the other hand, apparently had one extremely short and deeply unfortunate visit here before he came to his senses over Marlowe, and is also apparently horrified that she's here tonight.

She didn't give him much choice in the matter, but we all know she'll be catching a cab with Athena later so they can slink back to their delicious Sullivan men.

I've spent the past quarter of an hour regaling the seraphim with my tales of Ethan 'Eight' Kingsley. It's not merely that I'm feeling frustrated and bitchy after my morning with him, but that it's useful to process this shit before it takes up too much headspace. If I don't talk it through with the girls, get a little validation from them, and, ideally, have a good laugh about it, I could end up stagnating or, worse, spiralling.

We've already covered the nuts and bolts of the Montague deal—the bits that are in the public domain, at least, Ethan's mounting stress levels, his majorly dysfunctional family dynamics, and his little hissy fit at the gym as well as his somewhat sweet but totally deluded proposal that we go exclusive.

When I let drop the bombshell of his nasty, hurtful outburst today, it's met with the horror and righteous indignation I knew my girls would serve up.

'He said *what?*' my friend Maya says.

'Yeah.' I screw my face up. 'So demeaning. And he meant it to hurt, too. He lobbed that grenade for maximum effect.'

'I'm so sorry.' Talia puts a hand over mine. She looks beautiful tonight in a powder blue silk slip that offsets her olive skin perfectly. 'That's exactly the kind of shit he used to pull with me. I don't know what the fuck is wrong with him, because I know he doesn't actually believe what he's saying. He's a decent guy at heart, but when he lashes out, it's so... I dunno. *Toxic*. Like he's rotten inside.'

Talia may not be familiar with parts work, but she's hit the nail on the the head. Unforgivable as that kind of behaviour is, it's not the real Ethan. No wonder she and he were a nightmare together. She's a brittle Three Enneagram—an outward-looking overachiever who's overly focused on seeking validation from other people. Add to that that I suspect she has a strong Six part—The Loyalist, who craves connection and security and is also a gigantic worrier, and their pairing was a fucking nightmare.

'You're right,' I tell her. 'It's not who he really is. And, weirdly enough, he's not trying to wound. I think he's trying to test people, see how hard he can push them before they abandon him. Think about it: if security for him is being in control of his relationships, then intimacy threatens that control. So it makes sense that he'd push the people he gets close to, to stress-test those relationships.'

Marlowe rolls her eyes. 'You're far more evolved than me. I would've slapped him across the face. I could tell when I met him that he was a cold fish. I don't know how you put up with it.'

'That would have been incredibly unprofessional and insanely tempting.' I take a sip of my champagne. 'And don't think I missed your euphemistic choice of the verb "met".'

Everyone laughs, not unkindly, and Marlowe goes instantly red. I bet she wishes she'd never had that threesome with Ethan and Brendan. Unlike me, she's pretty virtuous.

'Still,' Talia says, 'that feeling that he was constantly trying to break me was what I just couldn't handle, you know? It was so horrible. I felt like he was constantly setting me up to fail.'

'Of course he was,' I tell her. 'And you absolutely did the right thing by jumping ship. He wasn't good for you.' What I don't say, because there's no point, is that, in my experience of humankind and with the benefit of my psychology degree, testing someone to see if they're breakable is entirely different from wanting to break them. It's the opposite, in fact, because, wholly ignorant though Ethan may be of this fact, *he wants people to pass his tests.*

Every escalation is basically him asking *will you stay?*

And *that's* the heartbreaking part.

Because Talia and Elena and all the others who bailed didn't fail the tests because they were weak.

They failed because they mistook being tested for being abused.

And who can blame them? Why should they suffer mistreatment because another person doesn't have their shit together? They shouldn't, of course. Most abuses, most crimes, come from a place of trauma, and that may be unspeakably sad, but it categorically does not mean that any of us should tolerate them for a single moment. The impact of Ethan's behaviour on the people he hurts is the same either way, and they have every right to protect themselves.

Believe me, I'm hyper-vigilant to our dynamic. Right now, I'm staying because I think I can handle him. I believe I have the necessary skills and boundaries. But the moment his behaviour escalates, I'm out of here like a scalded cat. I'm choosing myself. I'm not a martyr, and I'm no one's punching bag, regardless of the psychology that's driving them.

'Here's the interesting takeaway for me,' Athena muses, breaking my reverie. I catch her eye. She has her thinking face on. Uh oh. She's about to make some deadly observation, I can tell—probably to get me back for ribbing Marlowe. 'Soph here has got herself a gorgeous billionaire boss, who wants to spend every waking—or at least working—moment with her. Marls and I are both poster girls for falling for your boss. *But.* Soph has managed to find a guy who's so spectacularly fucked up that there's zero chance of her being tricked into settling down with him. If that's not a quintessential Seven, I don't know what is.'

I give her my most unimpressed frown. 'Kindly fuck off.'

'Remind me what a Seven is?' Bree asks, tilting her head.

'The Enthusiast,' Athena tells her with glee. 'AKA the vivacious social butterfly who hates standing still, and hates pain, and will chase all manner of new, shiny things to avoid anything real and uncomfortable.'

Bree's laughing. 'Oh, man. Busted, girl. That's you to a T.'

'At least I know how to have fun, unlike you Threes. Your

Doer parts are running the show so aggressively that they won't let you rest for a minute.'

'And we wouldn't have it any other way,' Athena says happily. 'Also, I'm now engaged to, and employed by, a saintly Two, so I can over-function on the Audacity Foundation to my heart's content and call it altruism. Happy days.'

Talia's been listening, head cocked. 'So you're saying Soph chose Ethan on purpose, even if she did it unconsciously, because he's damaged enough that there's no risk of her being tempted to commit to him.'

Athena raises her glass. 'Precisely.'

A guy wanders over, smiling at us. 'Hey, ladies. I wondered if—'

Athena cuts him off with a raised hand. She doesn't even look at him. 'No.' He shrugs and meanders off sheepishly.

Talia is still staring at me in fascination, and I want to tell her to knock it off. Just then, opposite me, Marlowe does the most comedic duck-and-dive, scrunching her entire upper body over while her neck disappears between her shoulders.

'What the hell are you doing?' I ask laughingly.

'Speak of the devil.' She gives the tiniest jerk of her head in the direction of the door. 'Ethan's here.'

Oh, for fuck's sake.

ETHAN SITS ALONE at the bar doing a most excellent impression of Hades, having slipped up from the Underworld for a night of debauchery. I acknowledged him with a nod and a tight smile as he walked across the room, because I'm not totally immature and he is my boss, after all. He certainly hasn't undertaken any debauchery yet, though. As I continue to chat and laugh with the girls, I watch him rebuff woman after woman at the bar with Darcy levels of imperiousness.

He's dressed all in black, as befits the ruler of the Underworld, in a form-fitting shirt and trousers. No jacket, no tie. A few buttons open on the shirt. All very austere and dramatic and sexy.

And, if I'm totally honest, his eyes seem to be trained on me—or us—most of the time. I wonder how he's handling the gorgeous riot of colour in here. The bar is pink onyx, backlit so it glows wonderfully, the bar stools Kelly green. It's far too warm and sensual for Ethan.

'He's totally here for you,' Talia says.

'No he's not,' I argue, although I know she's probably right. I studied enough Attachment Theory in my degree to know that if Ethan's parenting attachment style is all-out avoidant, his attachment style to me seems more disorganised, which, to any of us on the receiving end, would look like blowing hot and cold. Push her away and then run after her to make sure she's not really going to abandon him, you know? Then have a moment of vulnerability, feel desperately unsafe, and freeze her out again.

That kind of attachment style tends to stem from a person's caregivers representing both safety *and* danger. Not knowing which way a parent figure will go makes for a chaotic upbringing. That said, the output is always equally chaotic and draining for everyone involved.

If I force myself to have a moment of introspection, I'll admit Athena had a point earlier. She called out one of my blind spots—that I'm attracted to people who won't tempt me to settle down. And, when people whose opinions you value show you your blind spots, it's worth paying attention. There's nothing more satisfying than knowing you've met one of your unknown unknowns face to face. For me, anyway.

None of that changes my current situation, which is that my boss is a majorly hot and majorly dysfunctional arsehole who has followed me here tonight like a little lamb who's lost his mama. It grates, and it also makes me feel guilty, which is really fucking unfair. His behaviour earlier was beyond demeaning. If I was anyone else, I would have called Camille straight away and demanded out of my contract. And now all I want to do is have a fun night out with my girls, and here he is, cramping my style and probably planning to cockblock me.

I don't even know if I want to go next door. Ethan was right when he called me out on that aspect earlier—it's not like I haven't had enough orgasms this past week. But what I would like is some sex on my terms, with a guy who knows what he wants and doesn't view his own emotional world as the Bogeyman.

Or guys.

Just saying.

What I do know is that, now Ethan's turned up, I'll have to go next door just to prove a point.

Marls and Athena are making noises about going home, anyway, so I sigh and turn to face the others.

'Come on, girls. Let's go see what all the fuss is about.'

Ethan

The decision to follow Sophia to Alchemy wasn't actually a decision. Not when I'd spoken to her earlier in that unforgivable way. The option of waiting until Monday to see her was unfathomable.

But now that I'm here, it's clear she's not thrilled to see me.

Far from it.

It shouldn't come as a surprise. I lashed out, saying things that were as disgusting as they were untrue, and she responded by giving me the kind of grace I neither expected nor deserved.

Any other woman would have slapped my face or thrown a glass of water in it.

Any other woman would have handed in her notice there and then.

But Sophia didn't.

And, as I slunk off to the den and collapsed on the sofa in a gigantic puddle of shame and self-loathing, I forced myself to confront some harsh truths. I owed her that, at the very least. I was out of line—way, way out of line—and I didn't know why

I had said those things or where they had come from. I really didn't. I was shocked and disgusted the moment they came out of my mouth.

I didn't understand what she'd meant when she'd said I was testing her. I was lashing out, I suppose. What was that saying? *Hurt people hurt people.* I was feeling shitty after Elena called me out on my inadequacies as a father, and I had some childish, petty impulse to hurt Sophia, too, to make her feel some level of the shame and inadequacy I was feeling. Not rocket science, but inexcusable, nonetheless.

Even now, I genuinely don't understand what she means when she talks about these 'parts', but I can concede that there's some kind of war being waged inside me, that there's a conflict. I hope that means I'm not all bad, that the rot hasn't spread to my core.

That there's hope for me yet.

Sophia is magnificent, and I don't just mean her looks, although tonight she's hard to look away from. Amid the group of undeniably stunning women, several of whom I've been intimate with, she stands out. Her dark hair is sleek and straight tonight in a long ponytail that only enhances the beauty of her face. She's wearing an emerald green silky dress that, from what I can see, has an alarming plunge at the front and is completely backless. It barely contains her curves, and I absolutely hate to think that she's chosen to wear it to this place for that particular reason.

No, she's magnificent because of the power of her self-belief, of her emotional fortitude. She would absolutely have been entitled to crumble earlier. She's unlike any woman I've ever met: the most enthralling mix of femininity and strength and compassion while taking no prisoners. She makes being well-adjusted look easy, and it's about time I stopped fucking around and taking her for granted.

It's time I started investing in her wellbeing beyond mere orgasms.

Which is why, when she and a few of her glamorous friends head for The Playroom's double doors, turning every head in the place as they do, I call out her name from my perch at the bar.

'Sophia. Wait. *Please.*'

~

HER HANDS ARE on her hips, showing every spectacular curve off to perfection, and her dark eyes are flashing with irritation and, I suspect, the anticipation of tearing me a new one, and god is she a vision. I take her in, the vibrant green silky fabric hanging loose around her neck and framing a sliver of the underside of each breast before plunging almost to her navel.

Now that she's right in front of me, I can see that this dress is seriously easy access. A sideways swipe of the neckline would free a breast, or I could just reach behind her and yank the entire halter thingy over her head so the dress pooled around her waist, suspended only by the perfect curves of her hips.

She's dressed to be naked in seconds, and it seriously pisses me off.

'What the hell are you doing here, Ethan? What do you want? Because you must know you're the last person I want to see this evening, and you could at least do me the courtesy of staying well away.'

'I know.' I dismount from my stool so we're practically toe to toe. I stare down at her lovely pinky-red mouth for a moment before meeting her gaze again. 'I came here to apologise in person for how I behaved earlier. It was completely unacceptable, and I couldn't let it slide until Monday.'

'Although respecting my wishes would have been a better way of acknowledging my need for some distance, don't you think? Because I assume you have enough emotional intelligence to understand that when I said I'd be giving *you* space, it was a tactful way of saying *I* needed space. Yet here you are.'

'You're right.' I swallow. 'I know you needed space from the prick I was earlier, but I was hoping… that if I, er, apologised, you might overlook the interruption.'

She narrows her eyes. 'Go on, then.'

Apologising is hard for me. I'd like to think it's less because I'm a dick—at least, not completely—and more because it involves vulnerability. And while Sophia seems to think I'm totally lacking in self-awareness, I know enough about myself to know that being vulnerable, in any form, makes me nervous. Splaying yourself open, admitting wrongdoing, putting yourself in the hands of someone else's mercy—all these are things that make me deeply uncomfortable.

That said, all these things are less terrifying than the alternative, which is alienating Sophia. I've fucked up every major relationship in my life, and I'm not about to make the same mistake quite so quickly. She may irritate the hell out of me with her lack of basic respect and unwelcome psychoanalysis and generally unwarranted levels of vivacity, but I'm man enough to admit that she's good for me.

Besides, the sexual chemistry between us is like nothing on earth, and I'd be an idiot to sabotage that.

I put a palm on each of her upper arms and gaze down at her. Her skin is so warm and soft. She hasn't said I can touch her, but I'm hoping she'll understand that it's part of how intentional, how genuine, I want to make this apology. I hope she can see the sincerity on my face, too, and hear it in my voice.

'Sophia. I am truly sorry for the disgraceful things I said to you earlier. I was pissed off, and I took it out on you. Not only were they incredibly disrespectful, but they were patently untrue.' Her mouth stays in a thin, unimpressed line. I clear my throat and push on. 'The way you own your sexuality is one of my favourite things about you, and I suppose I've been the main beneficiary recently. I know I can be... difficult, but I genuinely thought that was one area where I was getting it right, so it doesn't exactly feel great to know that you're coming here in search of other guys. On the contrary, it feels pretty shite, actually.

'But that's on me, not you. We have a contractual relationship, and I need to remember that you're a free agent. You're not my girlfriend.' The word sounds fantastical to my own ears. 'I shouldn't have taken my bad mood out on you. I can't tell you how sorry I am if I made you feel in any way lacking because I couldn't handle my own issues.'

She says nothing, but her face softens into a small smile.

'Say something. Please.'

She blows out a breath. 'Wow. It's very, very good for me that you're not this sweet and introspective most of the time.'

I frown. I have no idea what she means. I'd have thought she'd far prefer it if I was rational and respectful instead of volatile and controlling and emotionally inadequate. 'How so?'

'Never you mind. But thank you. As far as apologies go, that was a pretty good one.'

I nod my acknowledgment a little awkwardly. I'm not used to getting it right with anyone I'm close to—not Jamie, not Elena, not my father, and certainly not my EAs. 'So you're, um, going next door?'

'I am.' Her tone is somewhat defiant. She's expecting me to throw my toys again.

'All right. Anything in particular you're looking for in there?'

She shakes her head as if she knows my game and has no

intention of being tricked into disclosure. 'I don't know yet. I've never been in there. I assume you have, if you've managed to get in here?'

I incline my head. 'Brendan proposed me over the summer during my dry spell. It's... effective.'

That gets me a smile. 'I see. So of the two of us, it's you who's the pro tonight. Who'd have thought? Any recommendations?'

My throat constricts. Jesus Christ, the idea of Sophia being next door, tied to a cross, or bent over and shackled to the club's infamous banquette, or fucked up against a pillar, or laid out on a padded bench for several guys to use as they wish—the idea of it makes me feel faint with jealousy and desire. Because if I knew she was a prize the very first moment I saw her, then every depraved fucker in there will see her in this scrap of green silk and reach the same conclusion pretty fucking quickly.

She's playing her cards close to her chest. I know she's come here primarily to catch up with her girlfriends, but I'd be naïve to think the choice of a renowned sex club as a venue was incidental. I have no say over what she does in there; I know that. But I stand by my comments just now. It's been electric between us, physically speaking, since she started working for me.

So maybe, just maybe, she'll allow me to be her host next door.

'A few things spring to mind,' I confess. 'If you're looking to push some boundaries, you're in the right place.' I swallow hard. 'And I say this as someone who has your best interests at heart, but what could be more convenient than having a man who knows what gets you off, and knows what your beautiful body is capable of—or suspects it, at least—being the one to show you the ropes?'

She rewards me with her signature full-wattage smile, and

it makes me so weak with desire that my knees are trembling. Her eyes, black in this light, are shining. That easy-access dress of hers, which seemed like a personal affront when I first saw it, suddenly represents a world of possibilities. She's fucking gorgeous. I meant what I said. Her ownership of her sexuality is one of the most attractive things about her, and right now she's lit up, alive with the prospect of what tonight could hold.

And goddammit, I need a piece of that.

'And are those ropes literal or metaphorical?'

'Either. Both. Think about it. You just admitted that I'm the pro tonight, after all.'

She sighs. 'But it's my night. Not yours. I don't want you getting all controlling and hijacking it. What if I want to play with other guys?'

I flare my nostrils as I force myself to abandon every last boundary I'd need if I were to stay in my comfort zone with Sophia. Because no, I don't fucking want to share her, even if I can admit to myself that the prospect of watching other guys fall over themselves to give her pleasure is somewhat arousing. I force the truth out.

'I won't be thrilled, but I'd rather be a part of it than be excluded, and I won't mess it up for you. I won't cockblock you.'

I release her arms and hold my hands out in a gesture of surrender. Of truth. There you have it.

She stares at me in disbelief.

'I won't cockblock you,' I repeat, 'but I know there are times when you love me being in control, and I'd like to think I could manage the situation in a way that makes it even better for you.'

'So, what, you're saying you want to take the reins next door?'

I nod curtly, my stomach a roiling mess of arousal and possession. 'Exactly. Consider it my way of making amends. I made a very inelegant attempt to denigrate you as a sexual being earlier. Let me show you how I really feel. Let me give you a night you won't forget.'

Sophia blows out a breath. 'Then I suppose you have yourself a deal, Mr Kingsley.'

CHAPTER 25

Sophia

Well, that was the easiest *yes* I've ever given.

If Ethan Kingsley wants to fall on his sword and make tonight all about me, then who am I to deny the man?

The appeal of The Playroom lies in its mystery. Its potential. I want that roller coaster ride of fear and anticipation and thrills. I want nameless, faceless guys—in theory, anyway—but I'd be stupid to think that many of them would have more bedroom skills than Ethan. The man is, sexually speaking, a god.

This gives me the best of both worlds: an excellent insurance policy. If the randoms in here can't deliver the goods, I know for a fact that Ethan will finish me off with his trademark skill.

Besides, the idea of my very own Eight MCing sexy time for me is honestly very intriguing. Clearly, the man is possessive. I could have guessed that even before he asked for exclusivity. But I know from his threesome with Marlowe and Brendan that he's open to sharing, and he definitely has that Alpha Daddy vibe in spades. The idea of him commanding a scene for me next door, conducting a sexual symphony for me like a true maestro, is a scenario so spectacular even I couldn't have dreamed it up.

He puts a hand on the bare skin at the small of my back, his touch light, and leads me towards a pair of heavy oak doors. A bloody enormous security guard looks at the drink stamps on our hands—two each—before nodding at us and swinging open one door.

And, just like that, we step over the threshold and into a different world.

Holy *crap*.

The Greek orgy Thad organised for my leaving party felt positively benign compared to this. Organic, if you like. You know, lots of naked people frolicking in the great outdoors and letting things take their course. This is far more intense. *Intentional.* A roomful of London's elite stripping off and getting down and dirty?

I fucking love it.

I stand just inside the door, hyper-aware of Ethan's cotton-covered torso skimming my bare shoulder blades, and take in the scene before me. The air is thick with the smell of sex and the valiant efforts of masses of Diptyque *Baies* candles attempting to drown it out. The beat of trance music thumps out a carnal pulse in this large, high-ceilinged space that's dimly lit but airy, its huge white pillars and gauzy white drapes adding sensual drama.

And, all around, the beautiful people of London dance and sway and strip and touch and fuck. I've observed a steady stream of partygoers making their way through over the past hour, and it looks like things are really getting going. Take the (presumably wipe-clean) white sofa nearest me. Two guys are spit-roasting a redhead whose back is arched in such a clear expression of pleasure, of overwhelm, that my entire pussy clenches with FOMO.

I cannot *believe* I've only just unearthed this place! Although, to be fair, I have largely been playing in the Med for the past four years.

Ethan's hand slides over my skin and around to my waist, tugging me against his side. His voice is smooth in my ear, his breath warm. 'Anything take your fancy? Or would you like a tour?'

'Let's just—um—see where the evening takes us,' I suggest, and I take a step further into the room.

As we weave more deeply into the throng of bodies, Ethan keeps a hand around my waist, a move I'm sure is far less about protecting me and more about demonstrating to everyone that I'm with him. He leads me over to a trio of huge St Andrew's crosses carved from blonde wood, and I eye them with interest. There's a woman currently trussed up on one cross and a guy on the other, but the nearest one is empty. A hot blonde guy in a tight black t-shirt and black trousers approaches, his grin wide and flirtatious. He has swirling Celtic tattoos weaving up both arms, while on one very firm looking pec is pinned a little black badge with the Alchemy *A* in gold.

He's staff. One of the infamous Alchemy hosts. Makes sense.

'You guys need any assistance tonight?'

I smile at him. I'm fully expecting Ethan to tell him where to go, but he pauses beside me. When I glance up at him on instinct, he seems to be studying the guy. Assessing him.

'I think the lady could use some assistance getting up on this thing.'

I freeze, but in a really good way. Ethan's going to tie me to a cross? For all my experience, this is one thing I've never done. I continue to stare at him, and he laughs. He really should laugh more. It's so ridiculously sexy.

'You look like I've just given you the doors to a sweet shop. A first for you?'

'It is.'

He looks inordinately pleased by my answer. 'Well, well, well. I get to corrupt the ingenue tonight, it seems.'

I snort, because clearly that's not the case. 'I mean, you're welcome to try.'

He slaps the upper arm of the cross, assessing its robustness. 'These are a good option for you. They'll keep you nice and still for me.' He leans in. 'Means I can do *whatever I want* to you.'

Most of my sexual interactions with Ethan have been limited to what we can pull off within the confines of his office. Our tryst this week in the suite aside, he's made it clear that I'm there to relieve him of his stresses in the most efficient, perfunctory way possible. Self-indulgent this man is not. So for him to suggest that he's tying me to a cross so he can go to town on me is the best kind of revelation.

My night is looking up.

The ripped blonde guy grins. 'You going to strip her first?'

Ethan turns back to me. 'Ready to get stripped?'

The guy on the next cross along moans as another guy on his knees sucks his dick. With his shoulder-length dark hair, he really does look like Jesus. Weird. In front of us, a couple is gyrating, her back to his front. Her dress is hitched up around her waist, and I'm pretty sure they're having vertical sex.

I'm so ready to join the merriment. I hold out my arms. 'Have at me, sir.'

'That's my girl.' His face is soft with approval as he steps closer, and there's already a promising bulge in his trousers. He slides his fingers around the stretchy halter neck of my silk jersey dress and pulls it so he can weave it through all my hair and bring it up and over my head. When he lets it fall from his fingers, it pools around my hips, leaving me topless.

Ethan's gaze drops to my boobs, his gaze rapt. My nipples are already hard, which will surprise precisely no one, and he goes straight for them, palming me hard, his skin warm against mine.

'Nice,' Host Guy says appreciatively. Ethan ignores him, sliding his hands down my body so he can push my dress the rest of the way down. It falls to pool around my ankles with a soft, slinky whoosh.

'No panties,' Ethan muses, eyeing up my bare body. 'You really did come ready to play, didn't you?'

'You know I did.'

'Let's get her cuffed,' the blonde guy says. 'Heels on or off?'

'The heels stay on,' Ethan says in a tone that brooks no argument. He's the boss. I shrug and daintily step out of my gorgeous Halston, kicking it to one side. It's one of my favourite vintage pieces, sourced for my friend Lotta's legendary Studio 54 party a few years back. I hope it doesn't go AWOL. With his hands firmly bracketing my hips, he marches me backwards until I'm up against the cross.

The wood hits my bare skin, smooth and cool, the point where the cross, um, crosses solid against my bottom. I realise that my four-inch heels will provide me some much-needed height here.

'Secure her,' Ethan says, standing in front of me and rolling up the sleeves of his black shirt. His feet are planted wide, and I defy any woman in this place to find a hotter guy to service her tonight. He looks every inch the alpha Dom, no matter how much he swears blind that he's not that kinky.

The host makes quick work of my ankles while Ethan watches me, appraising me. I raise my arms so the host can fold the soft leather cuffs around my wrists and fasten them. As he does, Bree and Talia pass by behind Ethan. They're still dressed, but, judging by the carnal looks on the faces of the four guys they're with, that state of affairs won't last long. They wave maniacally at me and mouth *OMG!* I giggle, and Ethan twists around to look at them. When he looks back at me, there isn't a jot of interest on his face. Talia is definitely dead to him. Instead, he steps forward, somehow making it feel menacing. He brushes the sensitive skin of my stomach with his knuckles.

'Every man in this room is going to wish they were me,' he says without inflection. 'They're going to be fucking begging me. But no one touches you tonight except me.'

What the actual fuck?

'I thought you said tonight was all about what *I* want,' I say with a pout. Trust Ethan to pull a bait-and-switch stunt in a sex club.

'It is. I know you, sweetheart. You're an attention whore. Trust me, you'll get plenty of attention while I'm making you come. You know how pretty you are when you're having an orgasm. They won't be able to stay away.'

My blood thrums hotly in my veins at his filthy promises, rising to the surface of my face. Okay, so maybe he knows me better than I'm giving him credit for. I can roll with this. I am, after all, an epic attention whore. But I have to object on principle.

'You literally just told me you wouldn't cockblock me.'

'That was before I got you like this,' he says. 'You have zero leverage now, except your safeword. Besides, I don't want to share you.'

'You shared Marlowe,' I hiss. 'With Brendan.'

His face goes all stern and sexy. 'Marlowe isn't you.'

Oh, Jesus. For a woman who outright rejected his plea for exclusivity, even transactionally based exclusivity, my body has a funny way of reacting when he gets territorial. What an effective way for him to shut down the discussion.

I'm fully restrained now. I can twist my wrists inside their cuffs, but there's no way I can pull my hands out. Looks like our tattooed helper here is a bit of a Boy Scout. The delicious reality of my position starts to sink in. My legs are spread wide enough for me to feel cool air on my pussy. My body is completely naked, completely exposed to everyone in the club like this. My nipples are tingling, my pussy is already throbbing in anticipation, and Ethan is looking at me like he doesn't know where to begin. He takes a few steps back and rubs his hand along his jaw as he surveys me. He's barely touched me, aside from that featherlight graze along my stomach and his very quick grope of my breasts, and already my entire body is alight.

Ethan turns to our host.

'Get me a feather, would you?'

CHAPTER 26

Ethan

S he's breaking my brain.

Having turned up at Alchemy in the certain knowledge that she wouldn't be happy to see me, I now somehow have my beautiful assistant shackled to a huge wooden cross for me to do with as I like.

The lushness of her naked body, spread-eagled like this, is quite extraordinary. Her olive skin and perfect tits and generously curved hips, and that red mouth, parted in aroused anticipation: every part of her screams ripeness and fertility and all those other things we're hardwired to desire. Her black hair falls loosely around her shoulders, cascading down her arms, tendrils teasing her nipples. Her eyes are dark and sparkling with need as she waits for me to make my move.

It's no surprise to anyone that we're drawing a crowd.

She's drawing a crowd.

She's magnificent.

It can't be every night that these horny fuckers get to ogle a woman this spectacular, laid out for them in all her natural glory.

I twist the large white feather our host has given me

between my fingers. It must be a foot long, its ends softly curling. It will do perfectly. Last time I was here, a month or so ago, I saw a guy using a feather like this to tease the woman he had mounted on one of the crosses for his pleasure, and it seems my diabolical brain filed that tip away for future visits.

I am indescribably happy to be able to put his technique to good use tonight, and on *Sophia*, of all people.

Without taking my eyes off her, I close the gap between us and press my body flush against hers. I can't not. Every part of me is positively screaming to cover her. To know her like this. To enjoy her, just for a second, in a purely selfish way, before I give her all the things I know she wants tonight.

My lips find hers, and she opens for me immediately. Such a greedy, wanton little thing. She's in the zone already. She'll take whatever I give her. Our tongues dance desperately as I press my erection against her pelvic bone and my chest against hers. Where I'm hard and hungry and unyielding, she's soft and pliant, her tits smushed against me like the perfect cushion.

I knew as soon as I saw her that a man could get lost in this body, could *perish* in this body, and I was right.

With my free hand, I stroke along the side of her body, brushing over the velvet skin of her arm and the smooth niche of her armpit before caressing her waist. Her hip. I'm rutting into her, I realise. My dick has a mind of its own tonight. In return, she's kissing me back like a woman possessed.

'Do you like it like this?' I murmur against her plush mouth. 'Being tied up for me? Knowing you're at my mercy? That all your pleasure depends on me?'

'I love it,' she whispers with a broken moan. 'I'm so turned on I think I might die.'

'Don't die. That's an order. Just take it. Take it all. That's another order. Are your hands okay?'

I unglue myself from her enough to observe her wiggle her fingers.

'Yeah. All good.'

'Excellent. In that case...' I slide one hand into my pocket and use the feather to trace a line down the side of her body I haven't just caressed. This time, it's the soft, curling feathers that stroke downwards from the cuff shackling her wrist, down the skin of her forearm, the dimple of her elbow, down, down, skimming over her armpit until I reach her breast. Slowly, deliberately, I circle it, tracing its underside with the feather. She lets out a little whimper, and I smile to myself in delight at how responsive she is.

That said, she'd better pace herself. I haven't used the feather anywhere interesting yet.

Ignoring her lovely, pinched nipple, I trace a line further down her body, brushing over the soft curve of her stomach, circling her navel. She watches me, rapt.

'You are extraordinarily beautiful,' I tell her in a voice that's a little too husky for my liking. I blame the sheer volume of blood that's vacated my head for my dick. Her face lights up at my words.

That fucking smile of hers will be the death of me.

There may be two of us dead by the end of this evening.

'You're not so bad yourself.' Her eyes rake over me hungrily. 'It's like Hades killed a swan just so he could come up to earth and use the feathers to torture the maidens.'

'You're really calling yourself a maiden?' I swipe the very end of the feather downwards over the raven strip of hair, withdrawing it before it can get anywhere near her clit, and she shudders.

'Fuck. And *rude*.'

A guy has shuffled up next to me. 'Need any help? She could really have some fun if a few more of us grabbed feathers.'

'Don't even think about it,' I growl at him. Not only do I have no intention of letting anyone else touch her, but I intend to remain in full control of how slowly and tortuously I edge Sophia. Obviously I don't have unlimited time—I have to keep an eye on the circulation in her arms, after all—but I have no plan to rush this any more than I have to. Because, until this dickhead piped up, my mind has been blissfully clear. All there is is the stunning woman in front of me, and this feather, and the privilege of playing her body and watching it respond.

It's such a beautiful, clean situation.

Me.

Her.

Cross.

Feather.

And I'm conducting this symphony. I'm in full control. The feather is my baton, Sophia's body my orchestra.

'I wonder how wet you are. I bet if I dragged this thing between your legs, it would come out soaking.'

'Why don't you try and see?' she asks, and I grin evilly.

'I'm not stupid. And I don't want you to soak it yet. I want it nice and fluffy so I can do this.'

I raise my hand and begin to stroke one nipple with the lightest touches before brushing the feather across the valley of her breasts to stroke the other. The sensation must be such a tiny proportion of what she actually yearns to feel, but the effect is immediate. Her entire body jolts, and she moans.

'Oh my god, that's so good, oh my god.'

'Poor girl, so starving that she's grateful for the smallest scraps,' I croon. But such a lovely response merits a reward, so I ramp up the flicks, the brushstrokes, over one nipple and then the other as Sophia thrashes around as best she can.

'Now let's see how soaked you are,' I tell her, letting the tip of the feather graze her in a downward trail until it finds that landing strip again. This time, I follow the trail, coaxing the feather between her legs. They're open, of course, on this X-like structure, but they're not spread to the extent they would be if I had her laid out on a bed for me.

All the better to torment her.

The feather bends as it drags through her flesh. I long to bury my fingers in there, my face, but I long to edge Sophia even more. Just for a few more moments.

She begins the staccato gibbering that I know means she's seriously turned on. 'Oh—oh—oh—oh. *God.*'

'Tell me how it feels,' I command. My dick may be close to ripping the fly of my trousers open, but I'm holding onto my control with every ounce of strength I have.

She dips her head to look down at where the tip of the feather has disappeared between her legs.

'It's so... teasing. It's so not nearly enough. Ugh, it's fucking torture.'

'Really.' I step closer and burrow between her legs to the soaked flesh I knew I'd find. Holding her open with my free hand, I use the feather to tickle those deeper, hidden parts, brushing it back and forth over her clit.

'Shit.' She bucks against me, into my touch, as best she can, which is to say not very well, given how flush her body lies against the wooden cross. 'Ethan, please. Seriously.'

I've done far more hardcore things than this in my past, used more aggressive toys. I'm employing a fucking feather, after all.

But never has it felt this heady to edge a woman.

Never have power and delight and gratification coursed so warmly through my veins.

Because this is *Sophia,* the ultimate free spirit, the woman I can only have a small part of on her terms, and here she is, tied to a cross at my behest on a Saturday night, moaning and writhing for everyone to witness in all her naked, shameless, splendid glory.

She's made herself vulnerable to me because she *knows* I get off on it, and she *knows* I'll deliver for her, and that trust she's given me burns me up.

~

SOPHIA

Every inch of me is aflame as this netherworldly king continues to edge me with the most innocuous of props. Heat licks over my sensitive skin, mapping me. I'm sweating like the last cucumber in a women's prison, to be honest. And, as unbearable as the ache, the desperation is, I'm in love with this feeling. I'm consumed by this anticipation.

Never has sex felt quite so sacrificial. He could throw a lit match at my feet and finish the job, and I'd happily go up in flames for him. He's barely touching me, yet the stakes feel sky-high. After all, he has me stripped and lashed to a cross in a sex club.

And it seems we're attracting quite the audience. Of the two of us, I have the outward-facing view, and watching the members drift towards us has my arousal ratcheting up tenfold. They're mainly guys, staring at my body with thinly disguised hunger. One guy has his dick out and is stroking himself firmly as he watches me react to my gorgeous boss' teasing. A man and woman stand together behind Ethan. He has his hand down the front of her leather skirt, and the way she's squirming against him tells me she's feeling it.

I'm not surprised.

She's getting a pretty fucking good show. A voluptuous woman splayed out naked on a cross and a hot-as-fuck guy commanding her body, reducing her to a puddle on the fucking floor with nothing more than a simple feather?

I'd pay good money to watch this.

But I have the best view in the house, because Ethan's face as he stands inches away from me and explores my most sensitive flesh with the silken strands of his feather is noble and stoic even as it's etched with indescribable longing. I'm not the only one in pain here.

'I need more,' I whisper. He's close enough that he can hear me above the music.

'What do you need, sweetheart?' He brushes the feather lightly, lightly, over my clit and stares at my mouth.

'Anything. Your mouth. Your fingers. Just *you*. I want *you* to touch me.'

'This is all for you. All of it. All you have to do is ask.'

He takes a step back, dropping the feather theatrically so it floats to the floor. There's no doubt this man knows how to command a room.

'Your fingers okay?' He frowns up at my shackled hands, and I wiggle my fingers for him.

'Yep. But the rest of me isn't. Make me come.'

'Certainly, madam.'

He grins down at me, and it's so damn sexy. Some of his hair has fallen over his forehead, and I wish I had a hand free to rake through it. Then he's kissing me, pressing his taut body up against me once again, and I give myself over to all of it—the heat radiating from his body, and the supple power of his tongue, and the strokes of his hands as he slides them up and down my raised arms.

He breaks away and gets elegantly to his knees before me, glancing up at me through his lashes before sliding a couple of fingers deep into my pussy and twisting them. The angle at which my legs are fixed may not be conducive to full access, but the burn is instant. It's a *very* good burn, an incredible feeling of fullness. I really hope he fucks me right after this.

Then he's twisting his head for better access, and I hang my head and stare down, a mess of ravenous hormones as he starts to lick me. I'm not sure I've ever seen anything hotter than the sight this angle affords me of his jaw working as he does. He has a little stubble tonight. It makes him look more undone, and *fuck* if the sandpapery rasp of it isn't giving me all the friction I need.

I'm aware that the little crowd of voyeurs is growing more excited, and Wanking Bloke's hand on his dick grows faster in my peripheral vision. I can't even imagine what fate would befall him if he hit Ethan with his load, and I stifle a giggle. I hope for his sake that he doesn't.

But whatever little show he thinks he's putting on is nothing to the real performer at my feet, licking me and finger-fucking me so hard, so skilfully, that every nerve ending in my body is singing an aria. The heat coursing through my body intensifies, the crescendo inside me builds and builds, Ethan's tongue and mouth and stubble abrade the very core of me, and I know I have mere seconds before I detonate.

I arch into him as well as I can and let my head fall back into nothingness as I squeeze my eyes shut and allow him to play my body like the fucking maestro he is. The pleasure races, wild and raw, through my veins, Ethan's licks as devastating as throwing a lit match into a summer meadow during a drought. I ignite, bursting into flames around him, the constraints of this crucifixion only serving to intensify the sensation as my body attempts to contain the onslaught.

Ethan eats me through it all, his own arousal evident from the desperate hunger of his licks. I'm still lost in the aftermath of my violent orgasm as he and the host guy uncuff my wrists and then my ankles, and as floppy, as pliant, as a kitten when he hauls me against him.

'So fucking amazing,' he rasps in my ear. 'So beautiful. I need to fuck you now.'

I agree wholeheartedly. He needs to fuck me now. So when he walks me over to a big white ottoman thingy covered in a pleather Chesterfield pattern and lays me down, I put up no resistance. No matter how desperate he is to get inside me, he's so gentle with me. So *reverent*, even.

I lie back on the ottoman and luxuriate in being free from my shackles and flat on my back, stretching like a cat and rolling my hips from side to side. In a stroke of genius that has me tipping my imaginary cap to the designers, there is a mirror affixed to the ceiling right above us. It's dim in here, but I watch, entranced, as my shadowy reflection undulates above me, my silhouette clear against the white ottoman beneath me.

I don't miss the dangerous intensity in Ethan's eyes as he gets his dick out right there in the middle of the room of debauched partiers and sheathes himself with a condom from a bowl on a waist-high stand that's giving freestanding wine bucket vibes.

As he crouches before me, I raise my knees and part my legs so he can crawl over me. I'm still feeling exceptionally sacrificial, especially now that the Devil in black is braced over me, fly undone, huge, angry dick pointed straight at me like a loaded weapon. His pristine shirt and trousers make me hyper-conscious of my nakedness, my vulnerability, in the best possible way.

'Stay just like this,' he orders me.

Right on cue, I begin to salivate. 'Yes, sir.'

'You'll do whatever I say, won't you?'

'Yes, sir.'

'So desperate to get fucked that you'll let me call every single shot, even though everyone's watching.'

'One hundred percent.'

It's true. Our crowd of voyeurs is only growing, even if

there's no sign of Aggressively Wanking Guy. Maybe he's dealing with his after-spill.

I want them to watch.

I want them to see my gorgeous boss command my body the way only he can.

I want to put on a show for them, but more so for Ethan. And for me.

'I want to watch, too,' I add. 'There's a mirror up there.'

His face lights up with understanding. 'Gorgeous, filthy girl.' He shifts his weight to one arm and runs a leisurely fingertip around my nipple. It's still pinched tightly from my orgasm, and it's so sensitive. I suck in a pleased breath. 'Body from heaven. I could fucking drown in you.'

'Then do.' I bat my eyelashes at him defiantly. *What are you waiting for, then?* Honestly, sometimes this man's self-control is very disappointing indeed.

'Fuck. I will.'

And with that dark promise, he lowers himself down so he's lying on top of me, reaching between us and notching himself at my entrance.

Our eyes meet.

I nod. *Do it.*

He thrusts forward.

And my breath catches.

It's so good with him. So damn good. Who am I kidding? I don't want anyone else. I've barely given anyone else a second glance in here. It's impossible to want another man when Ethan Kingsley is wedging his fat cock inside me. It's unthinkable to hanker after group fun with total randoms when he's pressing his forehead to mine as he inches deeper, when his ragged breathing against my mouth is erotic beyond compare. Because no one else has this effect on me in any way.

He bottoms out, and I ignore his command to stay perfectly still, sliding my hands over his shoulders and down the muscular planes of his back before grabbing his arse cheeks and willing him to stay here. Just like this. Just for a moment. He kisses me hungrily, entangling his tongue with mine, before pulling away enough to make eye contact.

'Watch how well you let me fuck you.'

Oh, Jesus. 'Yes please,' I manage.

And he's away, dipping his head into the crook of my neck and giving me a clear line of sight to what is a truly excellent show: his black-clad body working above me, shoulders broad and hunched as they hold him in place, waist narrow, his perfect arse pumping up and down as he grinds into me over and over, making this fuck every inch as hard and dirty as I need it to be.

He fills me up in the perfect, profound way only he knows how, and I in return spiral higher around him. Burn brighter.

Being able to watch him fuck me is hotter than hell.

I'm less clear on why the spellbound expression on my face terrifies me almost as much as it gratifies me.

CHAPTER 27

Sophia

'This room looks like *Mamma Mia* threw up all over it,' Ethan observes from the comfort of my huge bed. It takes up most of the room in this bijou doll's house, but it's worth it.

I whack him on his very nice chest, but it's pretty ineffectual. I can't get a good angle, snuggled as I am into his side. 'Rude. And also borderline racist.'

He laughs. Smug bastard. 'Because you're Greek? Come on. Even you must admit there's a *lot* of blue and yellow.'

'Better than living in a great big mausoleum, like some people I know.'

I happen to love my room and the rest of my house. I may still be getting this place just the way I like it, but it's cheery and colourful with Mediterranean vibes. Opposite the bed stands an aqua blue chest of drawers, while from the free-standing mirror on top of it hang colourful Hermès scarves and my oversized Loewe straw hat. I will never admit in a million years that Ethan may have a minuscule point about the chest having *Mamma Mia* vibes.

Besides, Donna would never have forked out for Loewe.

Or Hermès.

He laughs again, and I decide I like this mellow Sunday morning version of him very much. It's definitely vindicating my admittedly dubious decision to let him come home with me last night. His body is so warm and hard and... mmm. I stroke his chest hair absently, wondering why the sensation of his hair and skin makes everything feel right with the world.

'That renovation cost a fucking fortune, I'll have you know.'

'Hmm. Pity you ran out of funds before you were actually able to furnish it.'

'She's snarky on Sundays.' He tugs me closer and plants a kiss on my forehead, and the sweet intimacy of it gives me the courage to divulge the diabolical plan I've been hatching since Ethan escorted me home last night.

I lay my palm flat on his chest and gaze at him as I wind my calf around his. His face is gently creased, open, his hair tousled. All those weekday walls are down right now, and I really hope this conversation doesn't have him resurrecting them.

'I have some news for you,' I tell him.

He arches an eyebrow sexily. 'Go on.'

'I've decided to go ahead with the exclusivity thing—if you still want to, obviously.'

It's quite something when someone's face literally lights up. His smile is shocked and pleased and stunning. 'Seriously?'

I nod. 'Mmm-hmm. And that's quite a smile you have there, mister.'

'Well, the most beautiful woman in the world has just said she'll go steady with me.' His smile falters. 'Even if I have to pay for the privilege. But that's more than okay.'

My heart goes pitter-patter. Oh Jesus. It's so much easier when he's an arsehole. Vulnerable Ethan is way too much to handle. 'I don't want any more money,' I clarify quickly.

Because, while we're clearly talking about a transactional, contractual arrangement, it would feel extra shitty to extort him as we lie here together, doing an awfully good impression of an actual couple.

He frowns. 'So what's the catch?'

'It's more of a condition.' Here goes. I'm surprisingly nervous about bringing this up, and I don't want it to land wrong. I clear my throat. 'I'm making a commitment to you by doing something out of my comfort zone, so I'd like you to pay it forward... and commit to seeing a therapist. Of my choosing. Once a week.'

He stiffens and pulls his arm out from under me, and I feel instantly bereft.

'I see. Yet another woman trying to fix me, because you think I'm a tyrant.'

My take is that society has a crystal-clear understanding of how Enneagram archetypes show up in the world without having one iota of understanding of or compassion for the very deep, very real fears that shape those archetypes. And so what we have are cruelly reductionist clichés that in no way explain the dynamics driving these behaviours at their core.

Eights, like Ethan, are bullies or steamrollers. Twos are martyrs or doormats. Threes are cut-throat workaholics. Sevens—like me—are party animals or commitment phobes. Sixes are hopeless piles of neuroses (hello, Ross Geller). I'm fully conscious of this, but it feels particularly cruel to hear Ethan use this kind of language against himself.

'No. *No.*' I push myself up onto one elbow. 'Listen to me very carefully. You are not broken, and you're not a tyrant. And I see you, probably more fully than you see yourself. I see a beautiful man, with so much integrity, who cares far more deeply than he lets on. But I think there are some tools out there that could help you, especially where your relationship with Jamie is concerned.'

At the mention of his son, he actually flinches.

'I'm not trying to "fix" you, and I'm certainly not making this request for my benefit. I know a therapist. He's amazing, and I think you'd like him, actually. Maybe you spend a few hours with him, and maybe he gives you some food for thought. Some tools, as I said.'

He's quiet for a moment. I suspect he's desperately trying to find a way to negotiate his way out of this. 'So you're bribing me with sex to get what you want. Don't you think that's unethical?'

'It's no less ethical than you paying me for sex. And I don't feel bad about it. The end justifies the means, and anyone who says that's not true at least some of the time is flat-out lying. My body is the only leverage I have here, so I'm not afraid to use it. You're not the only one who's freaking out. I'm the one handing myself over to a control junkie after telling him that more control was the opposite of what he needed.'

We're not quite glaring at each other, but it feels like a standoff.

'Why do you care who I see?' he asks, pulling me down so I'm lying in his arms again. 'Why can't I just see who I like? Why can't I just get Topher to go through the highest-rated therapists in Harley Street and book me into one?'

'Firstly, Topher doesn't have a psychology degree. I'd like to think I can steer you right here. Secondly—' I hesitate. It's crucial that I get my words right here. 'Traditional talk therapy and CBT are really fantastic. My regular therapist is amazing —she's based in Athens, but I still speak to her every week. That said, I think a different approach might work well for you at first.'

He narrows his eyes. 'What do you mean, *different?*'

'Well, I think you might benefit from something more... strategic.' The word is, appropriately enough, a strategic one. I don't want to say *emotional* or *somatic*, because I'll lose him.

But the truth is that CBT works brilliantly for people who can identify their thought patterns, whereas Ethan's trauma responses are happening in his nervous system, well below his conscious levels of awareness.

Besides, he's already in his head too much. He's already highly analytical on the surface. This guy personifies the T for Thinking in the Myers-Briggs framework. In fact, it's his Thinking dominance that protects him from any perceived vulnerability. Emotional cues? Danger. Logical thinking? Safe.

CBT arguably focuses on rationalising your way out of emotional patterns, but this dude's bodyguard, or protector, parts are running the show here. There's no way traditional talk therapy will land—his internal protectors will intercept and reframe any messages before they ever touch his core.

The human nervous system is ancient. These systems evolved long before we humans developed complex spoken language. Instead, they run on sensation, movement, and reflex, which is why a modality that accesses memory and emotion through felt experience as well as cognitive insight feels like the right approach for Ethan.

I press on despite the look of outright distrust on his face. 'So, imagine a time when you feel conflicted. Maybe Jamie reaches out to you, and a part of you wants to connect with him, but another part of you, a more forceful part, puts paid to that because you think you should stay away from him. To protect him, right?'

A small, tight nod. He really hates it when I bring up his relationship with Jamie and I get it, I really do. He feels vulnerable and self-conscious, and whatever protector parts are forcing him to keep his distance, I bet there are other parts shaming him for doing just that.

'Well then, imagine you have a conflict at work. Say your board members all have different agendas, and everyone's emailing you and complaining and weighing in, and it's getting chaotic. What would you do?'

He shoots me a *don't be stupid* look. 'I'd call a board meeting.'

'Exactly!' I give him a huge smile, and he blinks. 'Because everyone deserves their say, and you have to get everyone around a table and hear them out before you can move forward. Right? Because you'd never just tell any of them to shut up. If something's bothering them, even if it's irrational, you'd still give them airtime. But that's what we do when we don't like what our parts are saying to us. We shut them down, we drown them out, we shame them.'

He's quiet for a moment, and I hope that he's choosing to process this. 'So what's your point?'

'The kind of therapy I'd suggest you start with is called IFS, or Internal Family Systems. It's the idea that we have lots of parts inside us, all with different agendas, and that we're a system rather than a mono-brain. A lot of the parts are younger, and they haven't got the memo that you're a forty-year-old—'

'Forty-one.'

'Forty-one-year-old man who's got this.'

He's still looking incredibly sceptical, and I daren't psychoanalyse him any further to his face, so I pivot. 'Take me, for example. Like everyone on this planet, I have younger parts that were hurt when I was a kid, and protectors, or guards, that formed to make sure those younger parts never had to feel that hurt again. You following?'

He nods slowly, dubiously. I give him a shaky smile, because, no matter how much work I do on myself, no matter how many times I meet these young parts now, it always makes me feel vulnerable and sad. I may have had a life of extreme privilege, but my heart still bleeds for these little-girl versions of myself.

'Okay, so until I was seven, I was educated at an international school in Athens, and then we moved to London so I could finish the rest of prep school here. My parents were around most of the time, mainly to make sure I applied myself to my schoolwork. But once I got into St Paul's Girls' at eleven, their jet-setting started back up again. They mainly left my older brother and sister and me with nannies and house-keepers.

'There were tonnes of staff around—I was never neglected —but apart from the occasional awards ceremony, they just weren't around much during term time.'

He frowns and covers the hand I've laid on his chest with his. 'That's awful. I'm sorry. My dad may be a shit, but at least he was around. Too much, arguably.'

'It's okay. And they're not bad people. They're wonderful. That was the world they operated in—when you were that rich, you didn't let your kids cramp your style. But the reason I'm telling you is that there's still an eleven- or twelve-year-old girl inside me calling a lot of the shots, because she remembers how awful it felt to be abandoned. And she has a lot of very fierce protectors who still struggle to accept that I'm an actual adult who can handle myself.'

'What do you mean, protectors?'

'Well, other parts who don't want her to feel alone again. There's my party animal part—I call her Elizabeth Taylor— and her MO is to be so fabulous and sparkling and enter-taining that no one will ever want to leave her again.'

He gives me a tender smile. 'She does a great job.'

My eyes are prickling with unshed tears. I clear my throat. 'And, let's see, there's the jet-setter, the one who doesn't want to put down roots so that she can always be the one to leave before anyone else gets a chance to leave her. That's why I always need to have holidays booked and lots of social events in the diary. And, of course, there's Miss Hyper-Independent.

If I can take care of myself, I'll never need anyone to look after me anyway. Those are the main ones.'

In fact, those three protectors run my show so comprehensively that they shape my Enneagram type, just as Athena's Doer part relentlessly shapes hers.

'Jesus, you're self-aware. So this is why you do a job where you travel a lot and you're answerable to no one, really?'

That makes me laugh. 'Look at you! You get it! And yeah, I am self-aware, and it's taken a lot of work. But here's the thing. When I feel unsafe, or my nervous system is out of whack, these protectors kick in. They start booking holidays and shunning help and going to loads of parties to basically dissociate. And now that I know them so well, I can spot what they're doing a mile off. So when I notice any of those things happening, I stop and ask those parts what they need to feel safe, because *I* know it's definitely not another night out. The key is not to try to shut them out. Their fear is genuine, even if it's irrational, and we can't ignore it. We have to offer to listen to them.

'Often, these parts just want to feel seen and heard. They're working *so* hard to protect us all the time, and it's exhausting, but usually their protection is what's holding us back. Because no one could expect a five-year-old, or an eleven-year-old, to run the show and do it properly. They're kids. That shouldn't be their job.'

He blows out a breath. 'I get what you're saying. But honestly, I'm not sure all that *inner child* stuff is for me. It makes me cringe.'

'I totally get that,' I say quickly. 'And I'm not a fan of that fluffy language either. Look, this may not be the stuff I studied in my degree, but it's rooted in sound psychological principles. If you want it in adult terms, it's about your nervous system's threat detection system. It's decades out of date, which is why our adult brains get hijacked and our executive function goes out the window. You're basically running outdated operating software, and IFS helps you to update it.' I pause and sneak in my bespoke-to-Ethan mic drop moment. 'It's about taking back control within your system.' *Take that, you gorgeous Eight.*

He nods, and it's a good nod. I think it's a *you've given me some food for thought* nod. 'It still sounds pretty painful.'

I laugh. 'It can be. But it's also beautiful and very, very effective. It's unbelievable, actually. I still cry in every single session.'

'Oh, Jesus. But I think you're incredible. I don't know many people who'd be willing to look at themselves that closely.'

'Thank you,' I whisper. This compliment from this man hits hard.

'So who's this therapist then, anyway?'

He's getting there. I inwardly punch the air. 'Philip. He's my IFS therapist, too.'

'Wait—you have two therapists?'

'Yeah, and I speak to them both every week, because this shit is important. It's the most important thing I do, and doing this work on myself allows me to control the lens through which I see absolutely everything in my life. Because if I can stop my nervous system from being hijacked by old software left, right, and centre, I can feel safe and well and abundant, and that's... everything.'

'I admire that. I really do.' He slides a hand around my waist and tugs me closer towards him. The heat of his body is, in fact, giving my nervous system all sorts of warm, snuggly safety cues. 'But what's to say I won't run for the hills as soon as he starts probing?'

'Mainly that I plan to stand outside the door with a taser,' I tell him. 'But also because he's a really good guy. Very thoughtful, cerebral—he has a PhD in something to do with

Game Theory as well as a clinical qualification—but also very compassionate. He's an under-reactor. The opposite of me, basically.'

He sighs. 'And this is the only way I get you to myself.'

'To yourself and *bare*. How about that?'

He rolls me onto my back and buries his face in the crook of my neck, settling his delicious weight between my legs. 'I suppose that's a pretty compelling carrot.'

CHAPTER 28

Ethan

Much as it pains me to admit it to myself, the man representing Sophia's appointed therapist for me sounds like the real deal.

On paper, at least.

Dr Philip Hicks has a doctorate in Behavioural Economics from LSE and apparently used to advise the Bank of England on decision-making psychology while also acting as a consultant to what feels like every top-tier investment bank and management consultancy firm in the City on why smart people make predictably irrational choices.

He *then* went back to school to complete a doctorate in Clinical Psychology before later doing his IFS training.

Ouch.

The guy must be a hundred years old.

I got Topher to fact-check his qualifications thoroughly before I continued with his bio, and I pull it up again on my phone as I sit in his waiting room, which is comfortable but not so luxurious as to make me suspect I'm being ripped off. I once took Jamie to his first orthodontist appointment to find the guy standing outside his Wigmore Street practice, showing off his brand new Bugatti to his assistant. It wasn't a good look on him.

Anyway, I begrudgingly admit that this guy has a wealth of experience, even if he no longer operates as a regular shrink. Apparently, his PhD thesis was entitled *The Paradox of Executive Control: How Childhood Survival Strategies Undermine Adult Decision-Making in Financial Markets.* Honestly, I'd like to take a read of that. And it harks back to what Sophia was talking about in bed the other morning: that idea that we may not be able to control our executive function as fully as we'd like to think we can if it's being consistently hijacked by old software. I'll admit that the concept of improving my own efficiency isn't unappealing. However brutal the next hour is, this guy can potentially give me an edge in business. And, god knows, I need any edge I can get right now with all this Montague bullshit consuming my every waking thought.

Not my *every* waking thought.

I allow myself a little smile as I contemplate what my reward will be when I get back to work.

Sophia.

On her back in one of my suites.

Bare.

PHILIP, as he has instructed me to call him, has the personal gravitas that his bio would suggest. He's Black, extremely tall, and wearing a pale blue button-down under a beige crew-neck jumper with khaki chinos so old they've lost any crispness. He's also not a hundred years old. I'd put him more in his mid-fifties. His general demeanour strikes me as far more professorial than commercial, although he must have made a killing in the City before he jumped ship. Maybe it's the frameless glasses that give him his *thoughtful academic* vibe.

In any case, he doesn't look like a quack, which is the main thing. Nor does he look too woo-woo. There's no incense burning, no weird cats prowling around, and not a crystal in sight. Rather, his consulting room feels more like a study with its twin broken-in armchairs and bookshelves bursting with books on game theory and psychology.

I'm really glad I'm not expected to lie on a couch like in the movies. That would have been a deal-breaker.

We make small talk for a few moments, the point of which is, I assume, to put me at ease. I can't say it's working.

'So, Sophia referred you,' he comments, 'and she's working for you?'

'Yes to both. She's very persuasive.'

He gives me a genuine smile, showcasing teeth so white and even that it makes me wonder if he was on Bugatti Guy's books once, too. 'She's a very special human being.'

'She is.' That's something we can agree on.

'How much do you know about IFS?' he continues.

'Very little,' I admit. Perhaps if I stall, we can use up most of the session on him getting me up to speed and I won't have to actually do any of the 'work', whatever that is.

'Not a problem,' he says easily. 'I'll give you a bit of background, if I may, but you'll find that the best way to come to an understanding of it is in practice.'

Drat.

Philip goes on to explain, in an economically articulate way, how the framework was developed from more established concepts by a former family therapist called Dick Schwartz, who was working with families whose teens had eating disorders. His reference to family therapy reminds me uncomfortably of my conversation with Sophia on Sunday morning. When I tried to get out of doing this by explaining to her that Jamie already saw a therapist, she actually laughed. *No one in the history of the world has ever treated a kid successfully in isolation of his or her family unit* was what she said. In other words: *Jamie's not the problem. You are.*

Anyway, Dick noticed when talking to his patients that they would consistently refer to distinct "parts" of themselves: the parts who wanted to use food to control or numb, and the parts who would immediately afterwards shame those other parts. It was the beginning, Philip tells me, of a radical shift in thinking from the belief that we operate with one single mind.

'For so long, we've been taught to ignore our inner critic, or silence our intrusive thoughts, or seek a higher plane through meditation and spiritual practice. The main aim of IFS is the opposite. It's to listen to these younger parts and understand their fears while helping them to unburden them-selves so that you can function in a more regulated, rational way like the adult you are. Does that make sense?'

I nod, even though we're veering into distinctly uncom-fortable territory here. I'm not even wearing my suit jacket, but I'm starting to sweat. I hold onto his use of the word 'rational' like a drowning man.

'One of the first things we do in our practice is attempt to unblend. That means that we try to find some distance between ourselves—we call it the Self in IFS—and our parts, because our parts are often very tightly blended with ourselves.

'So when someone cuts you off in traffic and you react with the temper tantrum of a fourteen-year-old boy, and you just want to ram your car into their tailgate as hard as you can? That's not you. That's a part jumping, quite literally, into the driver's seat. But, god knows, it *feels* like you. And yet, as soon as that flare of anger has subsided, you think *where the hell did that come from?* That sense of dissonance, of being able to feel the disconnect between your Self and the part that just acted out, is how we know that we can unblend.'

I make a noise of acknowledgment, because that actually does make sense. God knows, I lose my temper. I have a sudden flashback to that day I interviewed Sophia, when Miles Montague had just hung up on me and I'd shoved all those research reports to the floor like a pissed-off toddler. I literally had felt about three years old in that moment. The injustice of the situation, the helplessness I felt, made me feel like a small child with no agency.

'One thing I'll ask you to do when we get started is to imagine a place where you'd feel comfortable unblending. It's a matter of visualising a way to give ourselves physical space from our parts. Some people imagine a waiting room, and every time a part pops up, they ask that part to take a seat across from them. Others imagine that they themselves are a great, solid oak tree, and their parts can find shelter on the grass across from them. Do you have any ideas as to what format might serve you?'

I frown. 'Sophia mentioned... something about a boardroom?'

'That's a perfect analogy. So how about every time you meet a new part, you can politely ask them to take a seat around the table in the boardroom. How does that sound?'

That sounds like utter bullshit, but I choose not to share that with this kind, earnest man who clearly believes what he's saying. 'Okay.'

Philip cocks his head. 'Please know that you can say anything in here, and I won't judge. This is a safe space for all your parts to share. Is there anyone in there who has something they want to say?'

Me. *I* have something I want to say. I twist my mouth before answering. 'It sounds... extremely far-fetched. Ridiculous, actually.'

He nods. 'I hear that. Your parts are making themselves heard. So it sounds like you have a part who's feeling judgmental, or sceptical, perhaps? Is that fair? Feel free to close your eyes if it helps you.'

I let my eyes drift closed, mainly so I don't have to look at Philip's kind, patient gaze. 'Let's see. Um. I just find the idea of... sitting around some imaginary boardroom table with various mini versions of me to be...' *Unhinged.* 'Ridiculous,' I repeat.

'Yeah. And that's absolutely acceptable. I get that. This is all very new. Also, if I may.' He clears his throat, and I open my eyes. 'Our parts have been running the show for many, many years, often very efficiently. Of course there will be parts who don't want to be exposed or questioned. That's perfectly natural. How do you feel about asking this sceptical part to take a seat at the table for now? Is that something you're comfortable with? Remember, you can close your eyes.'

I nod and let my eyes drift closed again, attempting to hold myself together. I feel on edge, unmoored. I grip the wrist of one hand with the other and imagine Sceptical Ethan walking away from me and angrily pulling out a chair at the main boardroom table in our offices. He flops down, unimpressed. I can feel the intolerance coming off him in waves.

'Okay,' I tell Philip. 'I'm—er—he's sitting down.'

'Good. That's really excellent. Why don't you thank him in your head for being willing to take a seat and give your other parts some space?'

I do so, awkwardly, and he rolls his eyes at me and crosses his arms. *Let's see where this gets us, jackass.*

'Is there anything else he wants to say?'

I knit my brows together as I focus. 'He has his arms crossed. He's not very happy. But... no, I don't think so.'

'That's fine. He's allowed to be unhappy, and he's allowed to be sceptical. Can you see him clearly? Can you see what age he is?'

I focus inwardly again. To my surprise, he seems quite a lot younger than me. 'Oh. That's odd. Late twenties, maybe? Thirty?'

'I see, and does he know who you are? Does he understand that there's a forty-one-year-old version of you who's older and wiser and who's capable of managing challenges like this without him needing to overburden himself on your behalf?'

I frown. I can see him. But I don't feel any connection to him. 'No. Don't think so.'

'No problem. If he's okay to sit there for now, let's see who else has something to say. Is there anyone else we should hear from?'

I cast my mind away from that pissed-off version of me and draw a blank. There's only grey matter in my mind, nothing clear. I feel a cold wave of panic wash over me at the prospect that I may not be able to deliver what Philip wants from me in this moment. I excel at everything I do. I'm absolutely not going to fail at this, even though I have no idea what he wants to hear. Maybe I can make something up—but my mind is still a giant grey cloud of nothingness.

I don't like this. Philip is running the show here, and I can't take the lead as I usually would.

'No—nothing, I—'

'Are you okay?' he asks gently, and I open my eyes.

'I don't know what to tell you,' I snap, my fingers twisting harder around my wrist. 'I don't know what I'm supposed to say.'

Honestly, I just want to get up and walk out of here. This is excruciating.

He glances down at my hands in my lap. 'That's more than okay. This is very new, and you're doing great. Often, our parts won't want to speak up. They don't want a light shone on them, because they don't think it's safe. As we've just discerned, they don't know who *you* are yet. They don't know that they have access to this amazing adult who can protect them, so it makes sense that they want to stay quiet. None of this is a problem. As we get to know each other and your parts better, you'll discover that sometimes they'll be shouting over each other to have their say, but sometimes we'll need to work backwards and access them through something that's been bothering you in your daily life.'

'Okay.' I nod and blow out a decidedly shuddery breath.

'May I ask you something?' His tone is even more gentle, and I nod again.

'Is it fair to say that this inability to produce the answer you think I want is causing you a spot of anxiety or worry?'

God, he's perceptive. It's borderline freaky.

'Possibly,' I hedge.

He nods. 'Well done for acknowledging that. I know it's not easy. How would you feel about delving a little deeper into that part of you that feels worried about not delivering? Perhaps it has something it wants to share?'

I rub my wrist, back and forth. I'm practically giving myself a Chinese burn at this point. 'I'm not sure.'

'No worries. Go ahead and close your eyes again if that makes you feel more comfortable, and try to take a couple of slow breaths in and out. You're safe here. It's just you and me.'

From anyone else, I might find that sentence creepy, but Philip's vibes border on the paternal, and I realise I do feel safe with him, or as safe as I could feel with any stranger who's asking me to bare my innermost fears and vulnerabilities.

'What can you tell me about this part?' he asks, his voice slow and steady. 'Can you ask him for more detail on why he feels anxious about not delivering?'

I squeeze my eyes and my wrist equally hard. 'He—uh—is worried you might be... displeased.' Actually, what I was about to say was *he's worried you might get cross with him,* but that sounded incredibly babyish, so I paraphrased just in time.

'I would never be displeased. I'm not here to judge you, Ethan. Not at all. But why does he think I'd be unhappy with him?'

'It's unimpressive that I can't come up with the goods. Disgraceful. And—*humiliating.*' I have the strangest feeling that I'm parroting the words.

'Those are strong words. Is that part saying those words to you?'

I screw my face up in concentration. 'I think… he's remembering them? Or someone is saying them to him?'

'Okay. Can he tell you who is saying them to him?'

The revelation is a bucket of freezing water to the face. 'Oh. My dad.'

'Ah. I see. And can you see this part? Can you see or feel how old he might be?'

Fuck. He's little, I realise. A lot younger than Jamie. 'Ten? Nine?' I have the strangest sense of young energy inside me. A little boy. A little boy repeating words to himself like *humiliating* and *disgraceful.* Over and over.

'Does he know why his father was saying those things to him? Can he tell you?'

I don't speak for a moment. I can't. I'm so paralysed with the shame of it all. I'm an ice block, totally isolated in my humiliation, frozen out by my father's icy rage and powerless to thaw. Days and days and days of it. The pain is so fresh, so visceral, it's as if it's just happened.

'Um, he took me to lunch to meet his friends, as a special treat, because he said I'd be running the company one day. He'd given me extra pocket money to invest—he said it was going to be our investment club that we did together. And at lunch he told me to tell him and his friends about the stocks I'd chosen. But the companies I'd bought that month had done really badly, and I'd lost money.'

I remember it so clearly. The smell of cigars at the golf club where we went for lunch. My blue exercise book lying on the table, *Kingsley Investment Club* written in my best handwriting on the front. The neat rows of the stocks I'd chosen, columns pencilled in with the share prices updated daily. Every evening, Dad brought home the *Financial Times* from work and I copied the previous day's closing share prices into my little model portfolio.

But clearest of all is Dad's face when I told all his friends that I'd made the wrong calls that week, lost our little club fifteen percent. It was like thunder, like a black storm cloud. I didn't know much, but I knew a fifteen percent loss in a week was humiliating. *Disgraceful.*

You'd be out on your ear if you were a real fund manager, was all he said in front of his friends. Someone laughed, Dad lit another cigar, and Charles Montague leaned over and spoke kindly to me.

Fuck, Montague was there. I'd forgotten that. They were still friendly enough, back then.

No one in the market saw that profit warning coming, he said, or something to that effect. *Don't be too hard on yourself. My boys wouldn't know a stock portfolio if it hit them in the face.*

'Dad held off until we'd said our goodbyes,' I continue, my voice scratchy, 'but he laid into me when we were walking to the car. Said I was a disgrace, and that I'd humiliated him back there. But'—I clear my throat—'the worst bit was that he didn't speak to me for two weeks afterwards. Not at all. He completely ignored me at dinner every night. It made Mum really sad, but he told her in front of me that I didn't deserve his attention. I hadn't earned it.'

I break off then and hang my head, screwing my eyes as tightly shut as I can and pressing my lips together, fighting for control. There's a pause as I do. When Philip speaks, his tone is filled with compassion.

'That is an incredibly painful memory to share, and I'm so sorry. Can you—can you feel that that little boy is separate from the adult version of yourself? Do you have a clear view of him?'

I nod. The pain of reliving the memory might be tearing me apart, but I can see him so clearly. Blonder hair. A skinny, anxious little thing. I hadn't had my growth spurt by then. And so fucking eager to please.

'How do you feel towards him?'

'I just—I just feel so fucking sorry for him. I want to give him a hug.'

'So do that. Take all those paternal feelings that you have for your own son, and give this very brave younger version of you a hug. You are absolutely allowed to parent these younger parts in a way that they've been lacking until now.'

It's the weirdest thing, but I imagine myself doing just that. The compassion, the love, I feel for him is pouring out of me. In my mind, I hug him tightly.

'Okay,' I say, nodding.

'When you can separate from your parts and find your Self, that's when you can bring qualities like curiosity and compassion to them. There are eight of those Cs, in fact. Now, if you feel ready, I'd like you to try showing or telling him who you are.'

I stiffen. 'How do you mean?'

'Just that you're *him* all grown up—a fully grown adult— and that you can handle your father perfectly well, and that that memory has passed. It's done, and he survived it. Your father can't make you feel less than anymore, and you live an independent life now. He doesn't have to go back there again, and if he does, you'll be with him.

'What you're trying to do here is divest him of this burden he's been carrying around all this time, so that you gradually learn that when you're in a situation where you feel you "can't deliver" in the present day, that's perfectly okay. You won't be punished or frozen out, because you're an adult, and it's safe to fail. It's human to fail. Does that make sense?'

I nod and inhale deeply. The little nine-year-old guy is still hugging me. I get the feeling he likes me being kind to him. *It's okay,* I tell him. It feels awkward as fuck, but the tightness in my heart is giving way to a warm glow. It actually feels like my heart is expanding. I persevere. *You don't need to deal with Dad anymore. He can't hurt your feelings. You're a grown-up now, and you're taller than him. You're me.*

He looks up at me, his skinny little arms still around my middle, and beams, and I find myself wishing my own son would look at me that way.

After a long silence, Philip speaks. 'How did that go?'

'Yeah. I think he kind of gets it. He seemed happier, anyway.'

'Well done to him for sharing. That can't have been easy. It might take time for him to grow to understand that fully, but perhaps you can hold him close this week, show him that you're all grown up. Does he have anything else he'd like you to know?'

I think. The blankness is still there, but it feels lighter. Less ominous. 'I don't think so.'

I open my eyes.

'You did very well.' Philip cocks his head. 'Very well indeed. Once your sceptical part agreed to take a seat, you really opened up. It seems like that little boy who was scared of failure very much needed to be heard.'

I nod, because I don't have anything to add.

'You know,' he says, 'if that instance of your father withholding love from you was in any way a regular occurrence, I suspect we'll be hearing more from that part.'

I shift awkwardly in my armchair. I've been squeezing my wrist all this time. It's sore, and the fingers gripping it are cramping. I realise it and give it a gentle rub instead.

'*Withholding love* sounds... aggressive,' I say.

He shrugs and taps his glasses on his knee. 'What would you call it?'

'I don't know. Um, emotional punishment? Freezing out?'

'All characteristics of emotionally immature parenting.' He states it as a fact. 'And all indicative of a parent who makes their love conditional.'

'My father's a complex man. He's very... outwardly focused. He hates being shown up in public. And yeah, he definitely had his own brand of teaching me a lesson.' Still does, in fact. 'But he's not violent, you know? He never hit me or anything.'

Philip arches an eyebrow at me. 'From what you've told me, it sounds like he didn't need to.'

CHAPTER 29

Sophia

'How did it go?' I ask, handing Ethan a flute of champagne as soon as he reaches me. Dude is definitely deep in his sympathetic nervous system—he's practically crackling with restless tension. He texted me from the car telling me he'd need a stiff drink as soon as he arrived, so I'm sure neat whiskey was more what he had in mind. You know, forty percent proof instead of ten percent.

Tough.

He wants to numb after laying himself bare?

He can binge on me instead of drinking through it.

We're in a smaller junior suite today. The Jubilee Suite wasn't available, which is fine with me. All we need is a bed, and this room is stunning, done out in the elegant neutrals and impeccable finish at which the Kingsleys excel.

I have to admit, I'm dying to know how it went. What he thought. How he found Philip, who I consider to be an actual genius. I've been thinking about Ethan non-stop for the past couple of hours, wondering and worrying and hoping that I did the right thing by pushing him towards IFS therapy. It's not like I gave him much choice in the matter.

'It was fine.' He takes a hurried slug of the champagne.

Uh-oh. 'Do you want to talk about it, or...'

'No.' He takes another generous swallow and sets his flute down on the console with the restless energy of a caged panther who's decided he's not messing around anymore. 'Come here.'

I take a step towards him, admiring the devastating hunger in the way he's looking at me, although I probably should take it as a warning sign rather than a personal compliment. It's clear the man needs a hell of a distraction, and I'm happy to be that for him.

He took a huge step today. Often, when we push our nervous system like that, we regress instantly. Retract. And while it can feel like going backwards in terms of progress, it's very normal. We take a risk, then we scurry back to what we perceive as safety, to our cave, until we feel secure enough to venture forward again. And so on. One step at a time, until we build our tolerance, until we gather enough data to prove that these steps forward are safe.

If Ethan feeling safe means circling back to what he knows —that he can command my body; that I'll take everything he needs to give me; that I'll be putty in those very capable hands of his—that's fine by me. He's a beautiful man, and I must admit he's impossible to resist when he's like this: all wound up and intense and in need of blowing off some steam.

I'm wearing a new favourite dress today. Last weekend, I reluctantly did some winter shopping, and I have to say this Gucci number is spectacular. It's a Seventies-style shirt-waister dress in ivory wool, with the brand's trademark navy-and-red striped trims on the collar, the cuffs and the pretty pocket flaps. It's giving *retro air stewardess,* and I could totally get on board with stripping for an autocratic Ethan on his jet sometime. Huge gold buttons complete the look. I may have undone another one while I waited for my boss, meaning he now has a perfect glimpse of the ivory lace beneath.

He holds his champagne flute imperiously to my mouth. 'Drink.'

I let my eyelids flutter closed as he feeds me a mouthful of champagne.

'Swallow.'

It's a lovely Bollinger Grande Année. There are definitely worse ways to spend a weekday afternoon. Dutifully, I swallow, and he watches my mouth as I lick my lips afterwards. I've matched my lipstick to my Gucci trim today—a classic cherry red.

'Good. Now take off the dress for me. Nice and slowly.'

Nicely, slowly, like the obedient little thing he longs to dominate right now, I slip the big gold buttons through their buttonholes and shrug the dress off my shoulders. Ethan eyes my body like a very hungry lion might size up a juicy little wildebeest.

'Lovely. Now reach behind and unhook your bra.'

Micromanagement has never been so hot. I reach behind myself, thrusting my boobs at him as I do, and unhook it, letting it slide over my shoulders and down to the floor.

He raises the arm holding the flute and dribbles a little champagne over my left breast. It's a cold, wet shock, and I let out a little giggle of surprise. Without missing a beat, he bends and licks a trail down my chest before sucking my nipple into his mouth hard. The ravenous sound he makes at the back of his throat has my pussy clenching just as much as the sensation of his hungry pulls do.

'There is *nothing* better in the world than drinking champagne off your magnificent tits, sweetheart,' he tells me hoarsely, glancing up at me through his lashes. I moan in response and grab his shoulder, widening my stance to keep my balance. He proceeds to give my right breast the same treatment, and I stand there, clutching his shoulder and grabbing at his hair and arching into him as he sucks and licks, his tongue flicking over my nipple in a way that makes me need it on my clit *now*.

He straightens up. 'Lose everything and get on the bed. I don't want a scrap of clothing on you.'

'Yes, sir,' I tell him, pushing down my thong and unhooking my suspender belt so quickly it's positively indecent. I shove off my shoes and stockings and practically vault onto the huge white bed before flipping so I'm on my back, up on my elbows, legs akimbo. I hope Ethan sees the mental equivalent of big flashing neon arrows pointing straight at my pussy.

NUMB HERE ⬇⬇⬇ *CUM HERE* ⬇⬇⬇

He stands at the end of the bed looking flushed and gorgeous, his mouth already swollen from his suckling. Without taking his eyes off me, he wrenches off his suit jacket, throwing it on the floor, and makes fast work of his shirt buttons. What he lacks in dexterity he makes up for in general hotness. He tugs his shirt out of his trousers and finishes the job before wrestling his belt and fly open. Down go the trousers and boxers. He bends, gets everything else off, and straightens up.

Holy fuck. So hard. So gorgeous. So good.

He points. 'Don't move *a muscle*.' Then he's grabbing not his flute but the actual champagne bottle and climbing onto the bed. Rearing up on his knees, he takes a swig, and I ogle him. Head thrown back, throat working sexily, pecs and abs and delts and biceps looking for all the world like the craftsmanship of the gods, so finely honed are they.

'Hmm.' He launches forward so he's crouched over me, bracing himself on one taut forearm, and covers most of the bottle's mouth with his thumb, like you would a bottle of olive oil. Then he's drizzling champagne in cold splashes over my boobs, my stomach, and between my legs. I squeal and flinch, smiling widely, and he bends so he can place the bottle on the floor.

'I knew you'd be the best fucking distraction ever,' he tells me, bending to slurp champagne from my bellybutton. 'But you are fucking useless at following instructions. *Don't. Move.*'

'Yes, sir.' I snap to attention, ignoring the rivulets of Bollinger trickling down my sides, into my pussy. Having a guy lick vintage champagne off your body is a sure-fire way to remind yourself that you are, in fact, a hooker, and I'm here for it. It could be worse, I suppose. At least he's not doing lines of coke like one of Thad's sleazy friends used to insist on doing.

No, Ethan here is getting his rocks off by making it all about me. It's not alcohol he's craving a hit of—it's control. And it's my job to give it to him. To lie here like a good girl and take every ounce of pleasure he's giving me as his tongue laps at my skin, as he moves up my body to feast on my breasts like they might actually lactate Bolly if he sucks hard enough.

And if that pleasure grows too intense, if my body starts to struggle with all this need banking inside it, if I begin to shake, to moan, with the effort of staying still when I want to flail and writhe when his fingers push roughly inside me, then I'll give him that, too. His victory will feel all the sweeter if he knows how hard it is for me to yield all this power over to him.

I'll be his prize.

The prize he told me I was all those weeks ago, the first night I met him.

The prize I know he needs in this moment as he reassembles the vestiges of his control from the shattered shards I suspect his session with Philip produced.

Ethan

Sophia's entire body is shaking with the effort of staying still for me. The inner walls of her cunt are so plush, so slippery, against my fingers that I cannot fucking imagine how they'll feel when I wedge my bare dick inside her.

I remove my fingers and crouch between her legs, running my tongue down her dampened strip of hair before hitting glorious, champagne-soaked pussy. *Fuck.* I get stuck right in, using my hands to push her legs further apart and burying my face in her satiny cunt.

Like a truffle pig, I rub my nose against her clit, eliciting a sharp gasp from her and a grunt from me. I really am a pig, but my sole intention here is to feel more animal than human, to turn off my thinking brain and seek relief for the most primitive parts of my body—the parts that know a good fuck is the cleanest, quickest route to total oblivion.

She may have served me up champagne instead of scotch, but boy, if her magnificent body won't make up for that.

And so I feast.

This is for me, not for her.

All of it.

Every lick and suck and sniff, the slide of my tongue against her slick, supple flesh, the delicate musk that invades my mind as I snort my fill of her: it's all to sate *me*. To drown out everything else there is in the world. She knows it, too, but fuck me, if the little minx isn't getting off on that. I know Soph, as I call her in my mind, and I know being used like this, being gorged on, is absolutely what gets her going. I know she's torn between going for it and taking it. Between clawing at my hair, shoving my head further between her legs, and abandoning her agency in favour of being at the mercy of a man like me when he's unleashed.

Right now, her body is my entire world, a magical kingdom the rulership of which she has granted *me*. I can do whatever I like to her, and the knowledge courses through my veins with the headiness that only the acquisition of absolute power can deliver. I may not court power in the outside world, but here, on this bed, with this woman, I'll take it, and I'll wield it, and I'll make fucking magic with it.

With difficulty, I unglue my face from Sophia's cunt. She makes a little whimper of disapproval, the whimper of an entitled princess who's used to getting everything she wants. I fucking love it.

'You don't get more until you're on your hands and knees for me,' I tell her. 'Get that beautiful round arse of yours in the air, and then we'll see about making you come.'

Looks like the princess approves now. She beams at me, her huge black eyes so captivating. They're eyes I could get lost in if I was another man and this was another time. But I need intimacy like a hole in the head given the afternoon I've had.

I want this as filthy as possible.

Dirty, feral rutting.

If she's letting me take her bare, I need to make this first time count. Honestly, it's the greatest gift she could give me in this moment.

The greatest service.

The greatest distraction.

I move aside and watch with extreme gratification as Soph flips over and pulls herself up onto all fours with the graceful efficiency of an athlete.

A beautiful woman like her, spread out on crisp white bedsheets, black eyes and hair and scarlet mouth and smooth, golden skin... it's a lot.

You'd think it was the ultimate pose of subservience.

But having her crouch before me on all fours, her peachy backside right there, her tits hanging heavy and swollen, her silken hair tumbling over her shoulders, cunt presented for me to do with as I please... now *this* is what I call submission. She's a rich, sumptuous banquet.

And I intend to fucking feast.

I step back between her legs and run proprietary hands down her spine, palming her waist, her hips, her arse cheeks. I run a couple of leisurely fingers down her crack, pushing in hard when I get to that sweet, pulsing cunt. Then I'm crouching as much as I can, twisting my head to the side to get full access, and burying my mouth and nose right where they belong once again.

I'm in sensory overload.

Her smell; her taste; the sounds of her little moans as I eat her; the satiny handful of her arse as I squeeze it: I'm addicted to all of it.

I need inside her.

Now.

God knows, she's wet enough.

'I'm going to fuck you now,' I tell her, raising myself back up onto my knees. She turns her head to look at me, face flushed, hair everywhere, eyes glazed.

'Do it. Put your big, bare dick inside me. I bet I'll be able to feel every vein.'

Fuck, she's filthy. I have a sudden and wholly unbidden image of my ex-wife—a woman I loved deeply and yet with whom I was incapable of communicating effectively. We had a satisfactory sex life, but it wasn't like *this*. Elena would never have said something she perceived to be that crude, but it's more than that. She would never have let herself go enough to even have that desire, let alone voice it.

She was also the last woman I was bare with.

I shut the door on that intrusive thought pretty damn sharply and turn my attention to the sensual goddess before me, the goddess whose over-the-shoulder smile and dirty encouragements are kindling on my fire. Sophia has not an ounce of inhibition, and it's one of the most intoxicating things about her.

'You'd better fucking believe it.' With my fingers wrapped firmly around my rock-hard dick, I drag my tip through her wetness. She's hot and slippery and sublime, and the sensation of all that welcoming flesh sliding against my crown has me inhaling sharply. I recover enough to growl, 'How does this feel?'

'So much better than a condom. Fuck me with it.'

I position myself at her entrance. Every fibre in my body is pulsing with the need to shove myself inside her and eradicate every sensation, every thought, in favour of the clench of her cunt around me.

So it's with a perverse sense of pleasure that I control myself enough to hold right where I am. Just for a moment. Just long enough to prove to myself that I can.

Engaging every abdominal muscle I have, I crouch over enough to massage one full, heavy tit, my skin scraping over her diamond-hard nipple. 'I didn't hear you asking nicely.'

'Please, Ethan.' She arches into me, trying to back up onto my dick. 'Let me have that big, angry cock. Show me how well you can fuck me when you're really, really wound up.'

'Better...' I push in the tiniest amount—not even half an inch.

'No one can fuck me like you. Why d'you think I signed that fucking contract? Yours is the only dick I want. I'm begging you for it. I *need* it. I—'

Without warning, I push right in, and fuck—oh my *fuck*. My head swims with the visceral, molten pleasure of ramming my dick exactly where it needs to be. I may have taunted her that she'll feel every vein, but it's the same for me. I'm sheathed in the warmest, tightest, wettest channel, and fuck if I can't feel every inch of it. Soph's as plush, as decadent, on the inside as she is on the outside.

There's nothing like this.

This is the real deal.

She is the real deal.

I kneel here, bottomed out in her, and for a moment there's only the blissful swirling of sensation as it pulls me into its vortex. I look down at the magnificent woman before me, at the wealth of abundance in her glorious body, at the place where we join, my dick buried deep inside her and my pelvic bone flush against her peachy arse.

But just for a moment, because every primitive instinct I have is telling me to *move*.

And move I do.

I grab her hips hard as I pull out and ram straight back in. Jesus, that's good. With nothing between us, her body is lighting up my dick. It feels like a bloody lightning rod. With a sob, she lowers herself down, arms outstretched and one cheek braced against the sheets, dark hair trailing everywhere.

'God, yes. *Harder*.' Her words are muffled by all that hair, but I've got her.

'Fucking *yes*,' I manage, pulling out again so I can slam back in even harder. Surely there isn't a narcotic on the planet equal to this? My entire body is consumed by the sweetest, most potent pleasure. My skin prickles with sweat, and I'm breathing heavily already. But she's telling me she doesn't want me holding back, and I need this hard. Need to fuck my way into oblivion.

I go for it. I undoubtedly freaked out in the car on the way back here, and I unleash every ounce of that on Sophia. This is who I am. This is when I know myself best. Here, on a bed like this, I trust myself to deliver every last thing she needs from me. I can do whatever the fuck I like to her and she'll take it.

More than that. She'll *love* it.

As I find my rhythm and grind into her, slow and hard and filthy, I let my hands go wild. I grab at her arse and drag them up her sides. I squeeze her tits hard, pinching and pulling at her nipples. I palm one tit while releasing the other to snake a hand through her hair and push her cheek further into the mattress. I grunt, and I thrust, and I fill myself up with all this incredible bounty.

I'm crazed with desire, delirious with it. I've never wanted anyone like I've wanted Soph in this moment, never wanted to drown in another person's body like I've needed to submerge myself in hers. The sounds we're making are fucking filthy— gasps and moans from her, pants and grunts from me, the dull, rhythmical beat of flesh slapping against flesh, and my God, is it amazing.

I throw my head back as my body seeks and seeks and seeks. I'm so deep inside Soph at this angle, and the sensation of bottoming out in her, bare like this, is a level of pleasure I've simply never known.

Her cries escalate, and the knowledge that I'm undoing her too, that she's right there with me, has me hurtling towards orgasm like I'm on a fucking vertical ski slope.

'Fuck, I'm going to come,' she says with a sob. 'Please, Ethan—fuck.'

I slide my hand around her neck and grip it hard, holding

her in place so I can really go for it. I'm leaving nothing on the table. I'm damn well milking this fuck for every last drop of annihilation it can provide—for both of us.

'Damn right you are.'

I piston harder, deeper, slamming into her over and over. I am one-hundred-percent out of control, completely unmoored, and I'm totally fine with it. I dig my fingers hard into her hip so I can hit her exactly where she needs every time. And as she falls apart, those exquisite, heaven-sent inner walls contracting as she screams out her release, I'm catapulted into another plane entirely.

Finally, I allow myself to detonate too. My dick fills with cum, going so impossibly rigid inside her that I may not survive this, and there's a moment of stillness, of exhilaration, so potent it feels like asphyxiation, need coursing around my body and threatening to take me under. And then I'm releasing deep inside her, my entire body shuddering with a violence I've rarely known, and I'm coming and coming and coming, pumping rope after hot rope *inside her body*, and the relief, the pleasure, obliterates everything that is not it.

Every last thing.

CHAPTER 31

Ethan

I'm lying on my back, boneless and weightless and sated, Sophia's body draped half over me. She's lying on her stomach in the crook of my arm, cushiony breasts pressed against my chest and face against my neck, one leg thrown over my thighs and her long black locks painting my torso, my upper arms. My cum trickles slowly out of her body, pooling stickily on my inner thigh, but I couldn't give a shit. I like that it's been inside her. With what tattered shreds of energy I have left, I pull her tighter in against me and let the fingers of my other hand drift idly through her silken strands of hair.

Never in living memory have I felt quite so replete. So at peace. From the way Soph is sprawled across me, I suspect she feels the same.

'That was exactly what I needed,' I confess after a few moments of blissful silence.

'Good. Clearly, it was my pleasure.' She hesitates. 'You doing okay, though?'

'Yeah. I am now.'

'Was it really that bad?'

I'm unsure if it's the lingering effect of my orgasm, or the fact that we're not making eye contact in this position, but I feel marginally better able to handle the idea of discussing my therapy session. 'No. Not at the time.'

It was... good, actually, in an odd way. That vision, or whatever you'd call it, of myself as a little boy was seriously unexpected and extremely discomfiting. But as Philip wrapped up our session, I felt a strange sense of something I suppose was peace. Or relief. Like I was the slightest bit lighter.

That all disappeared in the car. I tried to bury myself in emails but found myself instead looking out the window as my driver inched slowly back through the centre of town from Philip's practice in Russell Square.

The thing I didn't raise with him, the thing I couldn't get through my head, was how angry I felt. Angry with my father for being such a gigantic cunt, for bullying a kid like that, stacking the odds against him and making the stakes so high. It wasn't fair, any of it, and while Philip had me relay that message to my younger self, I couldn't help but think in the car that I'd slaughter anyone who treated Jamie like that. I'd fucking tear them limb from limb.

But here I am, so terrified of any kind of intimacy with my own son that I can't engage with him in even the most basic way. Philip's chilling line is still with me. *Sounds like he didn't need to hit you.* Sure, my father is an egocentric bully, but am I any better? Am I damaging my son irreversibly with my own brand of cruelty? Am I no more deserving of being a parent than Richard Kingsley?

I didn't love today. It was miles out of my comfort zone, and I'm still not entirely convinced it's not weird shit, but I do know this: I need to do something to repair relations with my son, and if Soph thinks this is a decent place to start, then I'll damn well sit my arse in that saggy armchair once a week until I can look myself in the mirror again.

I blow out a shuddery breath and smooth a palm over Sophia's hair.

'I can practically hear you spiralling,' she observes into my neck.

She's not wrong. I sigh. 'I got a tiny glimpse this afternoon into the infinite void of my fucked-upness. What if I'm too broken to fix?'

She pushes herself up onto one arm and looks down at me. Her face is still flushed, her lips swollen from the kisses I gave her after pulling out of her and tugging her down on top of me, and her dark eyes are soft.

'Woah. You are not broken, mister, you hear me? Nowhere near.'

'I don't know about that,' I say feebly. This eye contact thing isn't so bad after all. Whatever is in her eyes, it's not pity. It's fiercer than that, which is a relief. I don't think I could bear it if it was.

'Listen to me. I know a lot about this stuff, okay? Every coping mechanism that you've developed, you've done for a reason. Even the ones that aren't serving you anymore or are holding you back. Look, I don't know a tonne about your childhood, but I'm beginning to get an idea. The truth is, if you had a parent who withheld love or who felt like a source of danger at times, the chances are you developed beautiful, self-protective strategies that allowed you to survive before you were even old enough to dress yourself. How amazing is that?'

She smiles at me, and it may be the most stunning sight I've ever seen. 'That is not the hallmark of someone who's broken,' she continues. 'In fact, it's precisely the opposite. All you're doing now is working on shedding all that armour so you can live the life you're meant to live, full of love and connection and wonderful relationships. And I promise you, the scariest part is showing up. Over and over. It's scary for all of us to dig deep like this. But we practise, and we develop those muscles, and—this is super important—we learn to regulate in between so that we build our capacity to hold all these confronting things. And the more you regulate, and the more grace you give yourself, the more you'll find you can handle this. Yeah?'

To think I hired her for her looks. Her sexuality. Her vibe. She might just be an Oracle. To be honest, everything she's saying sounds terrifying, but the thought of carrying on like this is even more terrifying. That memory of my father today really rattled me. I have to find a way to be a better man than him. I owe it to Jamie and Elena. And, if I'm entirely honest with myself, I need to find a way to control all these demons that seem to hijack me. I can't be at their mercy anymore, and that's what's galvanising me.

'Yeah.' I extricate my hand from her mane of hair and stroke her neck. Her shoulder. Her skin is so, so soft. 'When did you get so wise?'

She tosses her head, her smile turning coquettish. 'Well, my name literally means *wisdom*, but like, a higher state of spiritual wisdom.'

I groan, but I'm smiling too. 'Fuck's sake. Of course it does. So all this regulating stuff you're talking about—I assume that includes fucking you senseless? Because that totally sorted me out.'

She laughs and lowers herself down so she's lying in the crook of my arm again, her long, elegant fingers brushing over the hair on my chest. 'Sex can definitely be regulating, but that just then sure as fuck wasn't. That was numbing of the highest order.'

'What do you mean?'

'Well, when we feel vulnerable or unsafe or dysregulated, we have two choices: regulate our nervous system, or numb it. That, my friend, was the sexual equivalent of bingeing a triple cheeseburger. You can eat your feelings, or you can ejaculate them.'

I laugh and nudge her. 'That's ridiculous. That was positively medicinal.'

'It wasn't medicine, it was anaesthetic. And it's not ridiculous. You were majorly in your sympathetic nervous system when you came in—anxious, twitchy—and I don't blame you in the slightest. And when you're activated like that, you can choose to find a way to work that stress out of your body, or you can numb: sex, alcohol, gambling, shopping. *Working*. Whatever. The difference is that you're trying to make the pain go away instead of dealing with it.'

'Fuck that. So sex can't be regulating?'

'It can be *very* regulating, when it's intimate. That was a quick, dirty fuck. When you use someone else to help you feel safe and secure, that's called co-regulating. That's what we're doing right now.'

'What are we doing?'

'Cuddling. Skin-on-skin.' I attempt to pull away, because I do not cuddle, but she wraps an arm around me like a koala. 'No. Don't do that. Allow yourself to just enjoy it for a few minutes. It's good for you, and you deserve it.'

I exhale deeply and reciprocate, banding my arm more tightly around her. I still maintain that that fuck was precisely the medicine I needed and the reason my equilibrium is restored, but this is... nice, too. Relaxing.

'You know a lot about this stuff,' I tell her. 'You're good at it.'

She rubs her forehead against my chest. 'If you must know, this is what I want to do eventually.'

'Seriously? What—therapy?'

'Yeah. IFS therapy. You can become a practitioner, or, like a coach, directly through the IFS Institute, but I'd like to go back to uni at some point and get licensed as a psychologist first. I honestly believe IFS is the way I want to go, but I want to have all the clinical basics in place first, you know?'

I don't know why I'm stunned. Like I said, she's good at this. And no matter how well-paid or intellectually rigorous this role is, there's no doubt she's overqualified to be anyone's EA. The woman is a trailblazer with a devastatingly sharp mind. Of course she doesn't want to fuck men like me for money forever.

Still, panic rears its head swiftly, harshly, and I instinctively withdraw my arm, tugging it out from beneath her body and scooting back across the bed, putting distance between us. I'm right back to being that little boy again, just for a moment— the one who can't depend on anyone to give him what he needs. Not permanently, anyway.

I want to support her. I really do. She should have everything she wants. She should follow her purpose and be lit up by it. But, for some reason, all I can hear is the screaming in my ears that she'd leave me.

'Nice of you to inform your boss of your professional plans.' Even to my own ears, my voice sounds flat and strangled and harsh. Honestly, if I was her I'd kick me in the shin for behaving like such a dick.

But she doesn't.

She hoists herself up onto one elbow and cocks her head, surveying me. And then she reaches for me, wrapping a soft hand around my neck.

'Hey. It's okay. Note my use of the word *eventually*. This isn't imminent in any way.'

I lie here and stare at her, stony-faced. I'll be damned if I'll let her see the slightest crack in my facade.

She strokes her hand along the ridge of my shoulder and down my arm. 'That reaction is a part,' she says softly. 'Because I know you, Ethan, and you don't like it when people fail your tests. Or maybe you do like it, because then they've proven you right by bailing on you. I'm telling you again, I'm not going anywhere. That's a long-term plan. I'm only thirty, for Pete's sake, and I love this job.' She strokes over my pec, and my jaw works. 'I'm not leaving. I'm simply sharing what I'd like to do long-term, because we were having a moment of connection, and you paid me a lovely compliment, and I thought I'd reciprocate by sharing a confidence with you. That's all this is. Okay?'

Those dark eyes of hers are soft. She has no problem at all looking me in the eye. She hasn't thrown a hissy fit, or gone all defensive on me, or flounced out of bed. She's here and, much as I hate to admit it, everything she's saying is eminently sensible.

I nod, shame coursing through me at the hateful way I just reacted. Fuck, she's got my number. And maybe she's right about the parts stuff, because I can't deny I feel conflicted, and I know that, deep down, the man I am is as happy for her as he is excited to see what she'll achieve in this field. 'Yeah. Of course. Sorry—I'm so sorry. You're right.'

'No need to apologise.' She closes the chasm I've created between us and puts her arms around me again. 'Like I said, that was a protective part flaring up—one of your bodyguards. They do a great job of keeping you safe. And it's so much easier once you know what it is.

'Because you took the first step today to building an open line of communication with these guys, and once you have that, you can build trust. And once you have trust, they'll start to understand that it's safe to lay down their weapons. That you've got them. And *that*, my handsome friend, is when the real magic happens.'

Fuck, she's incredible. She's like a soothsayer. *Sophia, she of ancient wisdom.* I can feel the power that lies within her as if it were a tangible thing. I lay a hand on her back, revelling in the sensation of being chest to chest with her, of our hearts beating together, and clear my throat.

'Let me try that again, please. You'll be amazing at that. You definitely have a special gift. I can't imagine how many people you'll help.'

'Thank you,' she whispers. She raises her head a fraction so she can put her lips close to mine. 'And for what it's worth, I'm so very proud of you for the step you've taken today.'

With that, she kisses me.

CHAPTER 32

Ethan

Over the last few days, I've felt the presence of that small, devastated boy I met in that consultation room. Philip told me to keep him close this week, to show him my life. To demonstrate to him that I'm a grown man and I've got him. I love him. I can fight his battles so he doesn't have to be scared anymore. Basically, he explained that I can learn to parent myself, to be the father figure for those stuck younger parts that they didn't have. He even said something about rewriting my childhood.

All of it still strikes me as just this side of batshit crazy, but I can't help but be moved by it somehow. In business, I'm always on the lookout for that silver bullet—the single act or decision or efficiency that will change the game. And while none of this stuff is easy—on the contrary, it seems excruciatingly hard—it's certainly *clear*. It's a path. And the idea that this path might lead me to a new future, if I'm strong enough to follow it, one step at a time, is as entrancing as it is terrifying. I'll admit that much.

The sense of conflict lasts until my next appointment with Philip. He starts by asking me how I've been feeling about our first session, checking in on that little boy we met last time, and then asks whether I have anything in particular I want to discuss. I'm far from ready to bring up the reason I'm here in the first place—my abysmal failure at parenting my own son—so I raise my reaction to Sophia's admission that she'd like to continue her studies at some point.

I intentionally keep things as vague as possible. Rather than disclose the nature of my contractual relationship with Soph, I mention that we're seeing each other on the side and were in bed at the time. Neither do I divulge her interest in IFS as a career. I'm unsure if she's previously discussed that with him. But I do talk him through my knee-jerk, and pretty fucking nasty, reaction.

He cocks his head and surveys me, tapping his folded spectacles on his knee in what I'm beginning to see is a habit of sorts. 'Okay. So she shared her future plans with you, and it sounds like a part was instantly activated. Can you recall how that moment felt in your body?'

I think for a moment. 'Instant withdrawal. *Instant.* I just wanted to get away from her as soon as possible. She was, um, lying on my arm, and I actually pulled it out from under her. And there was some kind of screaming in my ears that made me want to abort. It almost felt like an ejector seat,' I add sheepishly.

'Mm hmm.' He says it without judgement, without inflection. 'Anything else?'

'I felt extremely hurt. But in a really childish way, like it was personal. It felt as though she'd hurt my feelings. That sounds ridiculous when I say it out loud.' I snort, forcing myself to keep going. 'But at the same time, I was angry, and I wanted to ice her out. So I got really huffy and distant with her. I could feel my entire body going completely rigid, as if I wanted to punish her. It was the kind of lashing out that I seriously despise about myself—you know, she hurt me, and I couldn't let that stand, not for a single second, so I had to turn the tables and make her feel as shitty as she made me feel. It was really uncalled for.'

'So'—he taps his glasses on his thigh again—'I'm hearing a few parts there. There's the part who feels hurt and abandoned —sounds like a younger part, possibly the little guy we met last time. Then there's the very fierce protector, who wanted to armour up immediately and both withdraw from Sophia and punish her—or that's possibly two protectors, even. And, finally, there's a part who's observing all this and shaming you for the way you reacted—probably another protector.'

When I feel overwhelmed at work, my most tried-and-tested trick is to grab a pen and a notepad and write it all out. Make lists. Do a mind map. Bullet points. Circling things. Underlining. Whatever it takes to get the mess out of my head and wrangled into some sort of order.

Oddly, that seems to be what's happening here.

Philip has taken my unstructured word-vomit of how I perceived that interaction with Soph and created a list of characters who each have a very specific agenda. It's astonishing, actually.

I nod slowly, attempting to process this cast of, well, parts of me. 'Yeah. That makes sense.'

'How do you feel about shutting your eyes and seeing if any of them have something more to say? If that boardroom analogy still serves you, maybe you could ask those guys to take a seat, and we can see if anyone else shows up, too.'

'All right.' I shut my eyes and take a deep breath, balling my hands into fists in my lap.

'Feel free to take a couple more slow breaths,' he advises. 'If you can, visualise them sitting across the table from you. Whatever you can do to experience some degree of separation from them. They may be parts of you, but they're not *you*. Try to bring them to mind one by one as separate entities. The hurt little boy. The harsh critic. The icy one. And the angry one, if you feel he's separate.'

I do as he says, slowing my breathing and focusing on getting those other entities to sit down. That hurt part does indeed seem to be the nine-year-old I've been hanging out with this week. He's sniffing and he wipes his hand across his nose. His eyes are red and puffy, but there's a mutinous aspect, too. He's sulking, I realise. Poor little guy. Not for the first time, I wonder how the hell my brain is capable of this kind of visualisation.

The ice king, as I'll name him, seems older. He's maybe in his early twenties? He's wearing a suit, and he has an off-putting energy—a *come anywhere near me and you'll regret it* energy. He's radiating tension and twitching with his need to control this situation, but is he angry? No. No, I can't feel it. It's more that his walls are sky high. An ice king in his castle. Mentally, I make him take a seat. He sits at the head of the boardroom table and crosses his arms, unimpressed.

Following him, my inner critic sits down. He's older still. It feels like he might be the age I was when my marriage started imploding a few years back, when I was failing epically with my son and my wife was in pieces all the time. He feels seriously bitter. Wounded, maybe? He's muttering to himself that it's all my fault. That I drive everyone away. Nevertheless, I have him across the table from me, thank fuck.

'Okay, um, I've got the hurt little one and the ice king sitting down. And the critic.' I blow out a breath. 'Jesus, this feels like herding cats. Or being a kindergarten teacher.'

He laughs softly. 'Funnily enough, that kindergarten analogy is a familiar one in IFS. When your parts are running the show, it can absolutely feel like a classroom of little kids where the teacher has stepped out for a minute. But never fear, there is an adult in charge, and it's you. We just need to make them aware of that fact.

'Now, see if you can observe how you feel for a moment. Does it feel a little less busy in there, now that you've managed some separation?'

I consider. 'Yeah. It feels like... less of a circus.'

'Great. That's wonderful. Now, why don't you see if you can identify anyone else. Is the angry part still in there, do you think?'

Squeezing my eyes more tightly shut, I cast my mind inward. Why was I so angry that day? Why did I want to lash out at Soph, to make her feel like shit?

Oh, fuck.

'Yeah.'

Silence. He's waiting for more.

'I'm... a teenager, I think? I'm still at school. Sixth form, maybe. I'm so sick of my dad being a twat. He won't fund a gap year unless I promise to take over the family business.' Fuck, we went up against each other at that age. He still had the power to freeze me out, to withhold love and money and attention, and fuck knows what else, but I was so bloody sick and tired of being his fucked-up emotional toy that I started fighting back.

Anything was better than being helpless.

'And that made you angry.'

'Yeah. *Yes.* He was so fucking egotistical, and he still had all his old tricks, but I was as tall as him by then so I just felt... more equal, I suppose. Less scared, anyway. But I was so angry all the time that he behaved like such a giant bell end.'

Bell end. I haven't used that term for years. It's a good one.

'It sounds like this part has a lot to be angry about, and, of course, he's determined to halt the pattern of abuse his younger self suffered. Do you think he's willing to take a seat for a moment, and then he can share anything he wants to get off his chest?'

I nod, eyes still closed, and focus on imagining my adolescent self sauntering around the table and flopping down in a chair. I had swagger by then. The sheer amount of female attention my looks and fortune and sporting prowess afforded me saw to that. I had an identity beyond Richard Kingsley. And, while he fucking loved it when I came home with medals and achievements, he didn't like that I was becoming my own man.

Not one bit.

And when he didn't like something, he sure as fuck tightened the screws.

'Okay,' Philip says when I've been silent for a few moments. 'In your own time, see if you can go inward and notice if anyone has something they want to say. Does your angry teenager want to keep sharing?'

Angry teenaged me is currently slumped in his chair, kicking the table leg. I frown in concentration. 'Um, he's saying he was pissed off with Soph for pulling the rug out from under me, but that's about it. I'm not getting much else from him.'

'Mmm-hmm. That's fine. We can try showing him who *you* are, if you like, unless there's someone else you need to hear from first?'

My brows knit together again. When I cast my mind's eye over the motley crew sitting across from me, most of the energy is coming from two of them—the little boy with the reddened eyes and the ice king.

'The little one,' I say, almost on instinct. He has to be my priority. After several days of holding him close, I feel responsible for him.

'Good. See if he's prepared to share anything, and perhaps remind him first that he knows you. That you're him all grown up, and he survived, and he's thriving. That he's safe now.'

Thriving is hardly the word I'd use to describe my current status in life, but I take his point. After a few moments of trying to telepathically communicate with him, I ask him what he'd like to tell me. I'm surprised by the clarity with which his voice hits me. I have no idea what I sounded like when I was a kid, but he sounds like he might be an even younger version of the nine-or-ten-year-old I met last time. He's eight, maybe? Seven?

'He says grown-ups always make promises and never keep them, and they always go away.'

'That's right, that's right.' He says it soothingly, as if he's reassuring the younger version of me. 'Any idea what he's referring to? Can he tell you more?'

With a jolt of realisation that sickens me, I plant my elbows on the armrests so I can drop my face into my hands. Yes, I have an idea.

Grown-ups always go away.

So. Many. Times.

I clear my throat, battling for my composure. 'He's looking at me. He's absolutely heartbroken. Yeah, I know what he's talking about. I mean, he's not exactly short of examples.'

As I breathe deeply, trying to pull myself together, Philip speaks. 'If you feel in your heart that you'd like to comfort him, feel free. Give him a hug, or have him come and sit on your lap. Whatever feels right for you and for him.'

Head still in my hands, I nod. I'd like that. He looks so bereft. I can't leave him there on that office chair. In my mind, I hold out my hand, and he slides off the chair and comes willingly. I gather him up and settle his skinny little body on my lap. He melts into me, his head lolling against my chest.

Now I can breathe more easily. I raise my head, keeping my eyes closed so I don't lose the line of connection to him. One memory in particular stands out in lurid, agonising Technicolor.

'Once, we had a special morning at school the week before Father's Day where the dads could come in and see our work, and our teacher said we could all introduce our dads to the rest of the class. We spent so much time in the run-up making them special cards. Mum printed out lots of photos of Dad and me for my card. They said we could swap ties for the day, and Dad said I could wear his favourite one and he would wear my school tie.'

Fuck, there's a stinging in my sinuses. I screw up my nose. 'Oh, it was my first year at Westminster. I must have been seven, then. Dad said he'd come. He knew I wanted to tell the class about his hotels business, and also, he was an OW—an Old Westminster—and he loved coming back to the school. He was super proud of me for getting in, because the entrance exam was really hard.

'But on the day he didn't come. I was the only boy with no one there. My friend Alex's dad couldn't come, so his grandpa came instead. So I wasn't allowed to present, and I had to sit with Miss Davies when we had our special Father's Day cupcakes. I took his card home and gave it to him at dinner, but when I asked him where he'd been, he said he got stuck at work.' Tears are stinging my eyes now, and I screw them more tightly shut in an attempt to keep them at bay. 'He said I didn't understand how hard he worked for this family and that I was an ungrateful little arsehole. And—he said that if I was at all grateful, I would stick to my job and work hard at my school subjects so I could do my family proud rather than wasting my time doing arts and crafts.'

I can't help it. I shudder out a huge breath and, to my utter horror, the tears come, silent but devastating, wracking my body. In desperation, I open my eyes a fraction, squinting at the tissue box I know to be on the coffee table between us. Without a word, Philip holds the box out to me, his face stricken. I can feel the compassion radiating from him. I nod my thanks and yank a couple out, holding them to my face and blowing loudly. I'm as embarrassed by my outpouring of emotion as I am shocked by it. I never, ever cry. But, more potent than anything else, the heartbreak of reliving that moment crowds my mind and squeezes my heart in a vice.

I can still see the card. It was blue, with several photos that I'd painstakingly glued to make a montage. Front and centre was a shot of Dad and me grinning at Stamford Bridge, during an incredible VIP trip to see Chelsea play Man United at home.

I was so proud of that photograph. Of that memory.

But the happiness it brought me had nothing on the pain of that Father's Day celebration at school. Of being left alone, with no father to proudly show off and no tie to swap. Of being gaslit and belittled when I got home as Mum, in her usual style, tried to brush my pain under the carpet and priori- tise keeping the peace over giving me the comfort I so desper- ately craved.

'I'm so very sorry that happened to you,' Philip says after a few moments. 'What would your adult self like to say to him?'

I let my eyes drift closed and my head fall back, exhausted. 'That it's not his fault, none of it. That his dad let him down, and it was inexcusable. That'—more tears leak quietly from my eyes—'his dad is an egotistical twat, and I'm so sorry he had to survive that shit, over and over.'

'Good. And what's in your heart towards him?'

'So much compassion. And love. I'm so proud of him, but my heart bleeds for him, you know? It just *bleeds*.'

'Yeah,' he says quietly. 'Does he know that? Can he feel your love?'

In my mind, I wrap my arms even more tightly around that little boy who was so cruelly rejected by his arsehole father. He sags against me. He seems exhausted, but calmer. 'Yes. I think so.'

'Please thank him for his bravery in sharing.' He clears his throat, and I open my eyes to see him cock his head. 'And does your ice king part have anything to say about this? Or your angry part? I'm curious to hear how they feel about your father's mistreatment of you.'

'The angry part's still angry.' I wipe my eyes with the balled-up tissue. I, too, feel calmer. 'He's spitting fire. But... the ice king part is saying, "See? The only thing you can do is take all the power back and hold it for yourself".'

Philip frowns. 'Who's he saying that to? The little one? Or the angry guy?'

'Both.' Wow. 'He's telling them both that this is the only way to get ahead. That if you let yourself get hurt or angry, he gets all the power.'

'He being your father?'

I nod. 'Yeah.'

'Interesting. So what else does he have to tell you? How does he cope?'

'Well, um, he says that if you leave first, you have all the power, so it doesn't matter if the other person then leaves.'

'Ahh, I see. So is that why he withdrew when Sophia told you about her future plans, when that little boy got hurt? Can he tell you more about that—about how he felt in that moment? What does he see his job as?'

I let my eyes drift closed again. My inner ice king is still sitting at the head of the table. Fittingly, the *froideur* emanating from him is intense. I'm getting mixed signals—it's as if he wants to tell me to fuck off and at the same time is keen to share what seems eye-rollingly obvious to him.

'Well, he says that he has all the levers, and that means he has the power to control everything about the situation, and if you don't pull those levers then you're fucking stupid and you're leaving yourself wide open.' That actually sounds quite chilling—sinister, even.

'And what levers are those?'

'Well, you control the physical distance first. Withdraw. Get as far away as possible. Then you control the emotional temperature. When you freeze someone out, they can't touch you. You're in control of the situation, not them. Make them feel bad—you're showing them that you won't stand for any bullshit stunts. Show them you're not vulnerable to attack.' My spine grows straighter as I speak, as if I'm absorbing his power.

'He sounds very strategic,' Philip observes mildly. 'What else does he have in his toolkit?'

I consider for a moment. 'Well, a lot of it's about controlling what you give to others. If I don't show my feelings, then you can't use them against me. If I keep you at arm's length, you can't pull the rug out from under me. If I pay you for your time, then I don't owe you anything.' A vision of Sophia fills my mind and I shake it off.

'He's very persuasive. Very impressive. Clearly he believes very much in what he's saying. But that language is also very armoured language, Ethan. Can you hear that from where you're sitting?'

I relax my spine again and exhale. 'Yeah. It is, I suppose.'

'He's very certain that he's found the winning formula, but we know that certainty isn't in any way correlated with correctness, don't we? How old did you say he was? Early twenties?'

'Yeah. I think so.' There's an arrogance there for sure, a *once bitten twice shy* kind of certitude. 'I think it was after my dad had hired me to Kingsley Hotels, so he'd kind of given me the keys to the castle. But I was still very much on probation.'

'I see. So you realised your anger didn't serve you and that this kind of armouring up was the way forward?'

'Something like that, yes.'

'And you had exactly this reaction when Sophia inadvertently triggered a much younger hurt part.'

'Yeah.' I shift uncomfortably in my seat.

He blows out a breath. 'Well, first of all, what an incredible bodyguard you've created for yourself. How spectacularly effective. He's essentially weaponised emotional withholding to the extreme. I wonder if you can take a moment to reflect on just what a wonderful job this protector part has done of ensuring that no one is allowed to hurt your younger parts, over all these years, and tell him how grateful you are? I mean, in many ways he's magnificent. If you see fit and you feel that gratitude in your heart, take the time to thank him for his service.'

My entire life, I've been made to feel like my tendency to withdraw, to control, has been one gigantic character flaw. *Control freak. Ice cold.* My ex-wife, who, alongside my son and my previous EAs, has borne the brunt of my emotional coldness, used to weep and rail. *You freeze people out. It's like living with a robot. You punish people for caring about you.* And, honestly, I can't blame her in the slightest. She was right. I did punish people for caring about me. For daring to get too close.

But this is the first time in my life that anyone has suggested that this ice king-slash-bodyguard is in any way positive. Beneficial. *Necessary.*

And that may be one of the most beautiful gifts a fellow human has ever given me.

I drop my head, shoulders sagging, entire body softening, curving inwards. *Thank you,* I say to myself. *Thank you for keeping me safe. Thank you for saving me from him.*

'The thing is,' Philip says gently when I've finished my internal prayer of gratitude and met his eyes once more, 'that we can now start to release this part from a lifetime of extreme service so he's free to choose a role he actually wants to do.

Maybe he becomes your most brilliant, dispassionate strategist or your clearest-headed leader.

'If we help him to understand that you're safe now, then he can lay down his arms and stand beside you rather than in front of you. Because your adult self is whole and strong and worthy of connection, and shields don't foster connection. They prevent it. How does that sound?'

I feel hopeful for the first time in a long time.

Hopeful that I can change.

Hopeful that I can free myself from whatever fortress I've erected around myself.

I nod my agreement. 'Yeah. It sounds great, actually.'

'I'm glad. You've worked through a lot today, Ethan. And here's what I want you to sit with this week. Your ice king learnt that emotional withholding gives you power. But every time he does his job—every time he withdraws, punishes, controls—he's teaching someone else that love isn't safe. He's creating the very wound in others that he was designed to protect in you. So perhaps, this week, it's he whom you keep close.'

His words don't just land.

They detonate.

I'm sure he means to speak in generalisations, but I can only think of one thing.

Jamie.

Oh, God.

Jamie.

Sophia

Across the broad stretch of the bar in the Austen ballroom at the Montague Knightsbridge, I spot Ethan.

We're firmly in enemy territory here in this vast, beautiful room. No matter that the seraphim often congregate in the Montague bar for drinks—when we're not playing in our new Alchemy sandbox, that is. Tonight, I'm here as part of the Kingsley Hotels delegation, and I can't help but feel like a Trojan horse. Or maybe Switzerland is a better metaphor.

There's nothing to be done about it, of course. It would be unthinkable for the Kingsleys not to show tonight for the prestigious Golden Keys awards. The Golden Keys are the last word in luxury British hospitality, and taking a table is a prerequisite for every major player in the industry.

Taking a golden key home is the ultimate endgame, but everyone pretends that they're merely here to network. To support. Ethan has explained the politics to me at length.

For this year's awards to be located at the Montagues' beautiful Knightsbridge flagship smarts, just as the open secret that Charles Montague and not his old frenemy Richard

Kingsley is receiving this year's Lifetime Achievement Award tonight must smart.

Still, in my view, Ethan and Richard and their team can afford to hold their head high. Their hostile takeover is very much in motion, Montague Hotels' top five shareholders have declared themselves in favour of the deal if the price is right, and, much as it saddens me, the poor Montagues have egg on their faces. I wouldn't admit as much to Ethan, but I'm glad they're the ones to host tonight's awards. I'm glad Miles and Theo's dad is going out in a blaze of glory, that he's being lauded by his peers for what I know has been an exemplary career, his staggering achievements matched only by his consistent reputation for integrity.

In my opinion, Richard Kingsley could do worse than to take a few leaves of out Charles Montague's book.

In any case, here we are. And while I may suspect, deep in my gut, that I'm batting for the wrong side overall, I know I'm batting for the right man. And I'm glad I'll be here for him tonight.

He's walking towards me, cutting intently through the throngs gathered at the bar as if he has tunnel vision, his posture perfect. The financial press these past few weeks has declared the deal financially sound but ethically dubious. Going full hostile on one of your oldest and closest rivals is deemed a little unseemly for the Brits' liking. So turning up here tonight, to a roomful of press and peers who all have an opinion, can't be easy for him, even if he's currently on the winning side where the deal is concerned.

Fuck, the man is fine. This is the first time I've seen him in black tie, and he wears it well. He's devastatingly urbane in the bespoke Givenchy tuxedo I saw hanging on the back of his office door earlier. His hand-tied bowtie is perfect, the tiny black-and-silver studs punctuating the crisp whiteness of his shirt. His body shape is made to wear black tie—the beautifully broad shoulders and trim hips have the tailoring hanging perfectly. His light brown hair is swept off his face. If he swapped out that champagne flute for a martini glass, he'd be the perfect Bond.

Most arresting of all, though, is the way he's looking at me. Like I'm the only person in the room. I'm probably doing much the same.

He stops in front of me.

Let me say at this point that, while Ethan met his parents for a drink (on friendly territory) straight from work, I hurried to my local hairdressers in South Ken where one of their geniuses wrangled my hair into an elegant updo before racing home to slide into an incredible red satin number by Suzanne Neville, whose Fulham Road boutique is far too close to my home to be safe.

The corsetry in this thing is a work of art. My waist is tiny, satin drapes beautifully over my hips, my boobs are on a platter, and a chiffon sash makes its way diagonally across one shoulder before billowing out behind me when I walk. It's stately, it's grownup, and it's also sexy as fuck. Thad's diamonds glitter in my ears and around my wrist—he was generous like that. And, judging by the look Ethan's giving me, I've hit the mark like a sniper.

'Evening,' he says, his casual tone studied amid all these people.

'Good evening.' I turn my head so he can kiss me first on one cheek, then the other, his free hand brushing my upper arm.

Before he pulls away, he whispers, 'You're always beautiful, but this is something else.'

I smile, and I preen internally, because we may be at some awkward industry awards, and I may be his secret hooker, but every girl loves standing in a beautiful dress as the most handsome man in the room whispers adoring words while eye-fucking you to perfection. It's a Cinderella-meets-*Pretty-Woman* mashup, I suppose. Even if I fall decidedly closer to the latter.

'Thank you.' My gaze drops to his mouth as he pulls away. 'You look very debonair.'

'I try.' His smile is wry. 'But you're the first and last person in this entire godforsaken place who makes me glad to be here.'

I meet his eyes. 'I'm not going anywhere.' It's an echo of what I told him in that bed after his first session with Philip, but it's also particularly relevant tonight. 'I'm not leaving your side.'

He nods a little stiffly, as if he's pleased but doesn't want to show it. 'Glad to hear it.'

'All you have to do is play nicely for one evening. You're a classy guy. I know you'll behave perfectly. Smile sweetly for the cameras. And don't punch anyone whose name is Montague.'

'It's a sad state of affairs when I'm unsure if I'd rather be sitting with that lot or with my parents.'

'It's not a great choice, I'll give you that. But it'll be nice to meet your mum.'

It won't be *nice* at all to meet Ethan's mum, but it will certainly be fascinating. I console myself with the knowledge that I can psychoanalyse her to my heart's content when we're at dinner. Any woman who can stay married to Richard Kingsley for half a century, who can raise a man as impressive and yet as emotionally dysregulated as Ethan, had better have a damn good reason for it.

DAMN IT, I wish there were Enneagram sweepstakes. I wish I could call it, could estimate someone's number and then put a few hundred quid on my bet at Ladbrokes before hauling them off for a quiz to see if I've got it right.

Alas, betting on people's personalities is still considered both uncommercial and, I suppose, unethical, so I have only my dopamine hits to reward me.

We're sitting at a large table towards the back of the room. The Austen ballroom is a stunning feature of this old hotel. It was built in the late Victorian era, sinking into disrepair for decades and becoming more and more of a budget hotel before the Montagues bought it, poured astonishing amounts of money into it, and brought it back to life in the most wonderful way. Now it's the jewel in their crown.

No wonder Ethan and Richard can't wait to get their hands on it.

The ballroom is high-ceilinged, with creamy, intricate Rococo mouldings on the ceiling and walls and antiqued glass mirrors reflecting a million sparkles from the chandeliers and candles. In keeping with the traditional decor, the snowy white circular tables are decorated lavishly with crystal, candelabras, and huge silver urns filled to overflowing with tumbling pink and white roses and anemones and ranunculus.

Green-and-white ivy trails from the bowls and onto the tables, echoing the muted greens and whites and silvers of the Christmas trees and plump garlands dotted around the periphery. It's the first week in December, and the entire hotel is decorated to the nines.

I love it. I love London at Christmas, and I didn't realise how much I missed it until the shops started decorating properly last month. I've been deliriously happy these past few weeks, strolling down Bond Street and enjoying the benefits of the dick-swinging competition Dior and Chanel and Louis Vuitton and Ralph Lauren hold every year as they seek to outdo each other on the festivities front. I've been Christmas shopping for Mum and my sister Ria in Fortnum's. And I've bought up most of Harrods' Christmas shop so I can decorate my home.

As I gaze around the beautiful room, I have a sudden stab of pride in the Montagues. Good for them for not rolling over. They may be fighting for the future of their company, and possibly their jobs. After all, the combined entity won't need two CEOs or two chairmen. Still, they're hosting this evening on their turf with every bit of the aplomb for which they're renowned, and I say good on them.

Even ballsier is their decision to stick the Kingsley table near the back of the room. It's kind of hilarious, if you think about it, and I'm sure it has chins wagging at every table. If tonight is the only time they get to call the shots, it seems like they're damn well going to enjoy it.

Richard, however, is *not* happy.

'It's a disgusting lack of respect,' he's blustering now from across the sea of flowers. 'I can barely see the screen! It really does show their true colours. Should be bloody ashamed of themselves. It was probably that joker Theo's idea.'

I press my lips together and try not to laugh. I'd put money on Richard being right (clearly, I'm in a betting mood tonight). It's totally a Theo move. With every toy his father throws, a stick rams itself further up Ethan's arse, but I'm finding it all rather amusing, actually. There's nothing I adore more than a roomful of people wearing beautiful clothes and drinking expensive champagne and acting like toddlers. Nothing at all. The gowns and tuxedos may be decidedly grownup, but people's younger parts will be out in full force at an event like this, and it'll be a hoot to watch.

I will say at this point that my general prophecies about Ethan's mum, Imogen, were right. She's beautiful, firstly— think perfectly styled ash-blonde hair and Faye Dunaway-level cheekbones. She's in what I know to be a current season beige Armani Privé column dress, which is pretty badass when you're in your sixties, and looks fucking knockout, with a black pearl necklace that has to be Mikimoto. I bet she and Elena always twinned aesthetically—says the literal scarlet woman.

Secondly, she's openly hyperviligant, especially where Richard is concerned. His unhappiness is causing her anxiety levels to ratchet up notably, and we're still on our starters—a lovely crab, radish and apple salad, if you must know. If the Enneagram was a roulette wheel, I'd be throwing all my chips down on Six.

Earlier I suspected she might be a Nine—the Peacekeeper —but that's not it at all. As a Nine, she would have emotionally checked out of this little scene, but she's actively trying to manage the situation. Healthy Sixes value connection, security, and family, but there's no way this woman is healthy. Not when she's stood there all these years and allowed her husband to fuck up her son to the extent that she has. Nope, Imogen is absolutely prioritising how things look over how they feel. She's absorbed Richard's toxic Three behaviours, and all she cares about right now is optics. Keep him happy. Keep him quiet. Smooth things over. Who gives a fuck how badly her son has spiralled out of control all these years; who cares that her former daughter-in-law has had to physically remove her son from the family circle to protect him.

God, no.

All that matters to Imogen is maintaining appearances. I suspect she lost touch with her true feelings a long time ago.

Some old fart with a combover stops by and slaps Richard heartily on the shoulder. 'Oh my! You've been put on the naughty table, Dickie boy! Haven't you just! Someone's set the cat among the pigeons, haven't they?!'

Richard plasters a smile on his face and pushes his chair back, the picture of jovial tolerance as he stands and shakes the man's hand. 'Crispin! My man! How the hell are you. Yes, it's rather cheeky of them, isn't it?'

'Well, very sporting of you, old chap. Very sporting indeed. You'll be front and centre next year, mark my words.'

After he's bidden the old codger farewell and sent him on his way, he takes his seat, smile erased and face like thunder. The about-turn is extraordinary, and I can see, in a way I haven't properly been able to appreciate during our work interactions, just how infectious his mood must have been when Ethan was growing up, how easy it would have been for Richard to hold his family emotionally hostage.

'Everyone has noticed. We're a laughingstock.'

Imogen lays a hand on his arm. '*They're* a laughingstock. Like you said, it's infantile behaviour.'

He shakes out his napkin and lays it back on his lap. 'They will rue the day they pulled a stunt like this. The Kingsleys will take no prisoners, and they should know that.'

Across the table, the company's finance director, Theresa, shudders. I like her. She's extremely direct and terrifyingly competent. I'm glad Ethan has her as his number two.

'You and Ethan will show them, darling,' Imogen says. Her tone is one you might use with a truculent toddler. 'Of course you will. Now'—she flashes her megawatt smile at her son—'tell me how my lovely grandson is. I haven't seen him for ages!'

Theresa and the other members of the board who've joined the Kingsley delegation tonight take this as a signal to chat amongst themselves. She turns to Frank Taylor, one of the non exec directors, and engages him in conversation, and it strikes me that I have no real business being here. I'm the only guest at the table who's neither board nor spouse. I suspect I'm here purely to distract and morally support Ethan, and the thought makes my heart squeeze a little.

I glance at him as he answers his mum. His posture is perfect, shoulders tense.

'Jamie is fine. We've—ahh—we've actually been working together on his Christmas list, because he wants to build his own computer as his Christmas present.'

His mother's face goes blank. 'I don't know what you mean, darling. How on earth could he build a computer?'

'It's a hard drive. They're modular. You buy a glass case and you choose the components and assemble them. It means if you want to upgrade the RAM or the graphics card at some point, you can just replace that single part. It's all quite clever, actually.'

'It certainly is! How did he get interested in that?'

'His Computer Science teacher, apparently. They've been watching YouTube videos together. His teacher built one and told the class about it, and they've all got the bug. He's going to spend Christmas morning with Elena, but she'll drop him off with me for the afternoon so we can work on it—she said she's not touching it with a bargepole.'

I smile to myself. Ethan's actually pretty excited about this gift—by his standards, at least. He hasn't divulged much to me about his sessions with Philip, but I know he feels like he's making progress and is ready to start taking bigger steps with Jamie. This computer strikes me as a fun project for them to get stuck into together.

Imogen smiles fondly. Whatever her issues, she seems to genuinely adore Jamie. 'What a clever boy. My goodness! Building his own computer!'

'That's all well and good,' Richard snarls. 'But you really ought to be grooming him to get involved with the family business. He's shown zero interest so far, and it's not good enough.'

'The word *grooming* has pretty different connotations

these days, Dad,' Ethan says, and I press my lips together to stop myself from smirking.

'Don't be flippant. You know what I mean. The boy hasn't a commercial bone in his body, and that has to change. When you were his age, I had you analysing our monthly P&Ls to spot trends. And we started you with that investment club aged seven. Do you remember? You're just lucky I didn't beat your lessons into you. My old man was far too partial to the philosophy of sparing the rod and spoiling the child.'

Ethan's entire body goes from stiff to downright rigid, and he stares at his father like he could happily strangle him with his bare hands.

'I remember.' He spits the words out. 'And Jamie will choose the career he wants. He'll follow his own path. I have no intention of letting history repeat itself. Do you understand?'

CHAPTER 34

Ethan

The problem with doing the work, as both Philip and Soph have told me, is that once you start to understand more about what's really going on with yourself and with others, you can't unsee any of it.

Yesterday, I watched from outside our offices as a perfectly respectable-looking middle-aged woman assaulted a stranger in the street because he'd been going what she perceived as the wrong way down the road on his bike and had almost run her over. When he stopped, she pushed him so hard that his bike toppled over and he fell to the ground. Out of nowhere, a crowd gathered, and much screaming ensued as other strangers tried to stop the two of them from beating the crap out of each other.

Before, I would have shaken my head and muttered *nutters* as I went about my business. But yesterday, I was struck by the fact that I'd likely had a front-row seat to very young parts being triggered on both sides. It made the occurrence even more disturbing, I think, because it had me musing on whether we were all leading our daily lives without our adult Selves being in the driving seat in the slightest.

I suspect the answer to that is probably affirmative. I can certainly think of many world and business leaders whose toddler selves are behind the wheel, constantly terrified that someone else will grab their toys.

And now, as my dad casually dredges up his past cruelties to me, something that, a month ago, might have caused me an unwelcome but non-specific pang, the memory of my past distress is so very specific, so very intense, that I can't let it slide. I've met my younger self. He's real to me, and he's still stuck in that place of pain, a place filled with bewilderment and shame and intense loneliness. Now that I've met him, I'm his protector, and if I know one thing, it's that my father will never get his toxic, egotistical claws into my son the way he got them into me.

No fucking way.

Jamie doesn't have an iota of interest in the "family business", and I'll be damned if I don't spend every last ounce of my energy shielding him from Dad's toxic brand of nepotism, which Philip recently explained to me is more like enmeshment.

According to him, my father likely enmeshed my identity, my values, with his, viewing me as basically an extension of himself and punishing any efforts I made to forge my own individuality with his tried-and-tested manipulation tactics. You know: guilt. Shame. Gaslighting.

Even the word sounds sinister. *Enmeshment.* Jesus.

Yeah. Richard Kingsley will enmesh my son over my dead body.

～

MY EVENING CONTINUES TO WORSEN, the only bright spot, quite literally, the dazzling beauty in scarlet who's sitting next to me. I can't wait to follow her home later like a pitiful puppy and bury myself so deep inside her that the desire in my veins drives out all this poison.

We're forced to endure a delightful, humble and moving speech from Charles Montague alongside a vitriolic stream of consciousness from my father, mumbling his heckles from where he sits.

No wonder they put us at the back of the fucking room.

Charles is a true patriarch—a man who's used his influence to create jobs and build careers and change lives. He's a born leader. Integrity and passion seep from his every pore.

'Tonight marks the end of this chapter for The Montague Group, as you are all aware,' he says, removing his glasses and wiping his eyes. His voice has grown a little scratchy. 'It's been a long chapter, filled with adventures. Wonderful, joyous highs and devastating lows.

'Sometimes I think it's a good thing that none of us has a crystal ball. The memory of our hotels standing cold and empty during the pandemic is one I'll take with me to my grave. But today, they are alive with people intent on making memories with their families, people who entrust us with the privilege of making those memories, and it's a privilege my family will never take lightly.

'It may not be our name on the door this time next year. The market has spoken, and I respect that. But I also know that, in the hands of our very capable new ownership, our hotels will continue to thrive. Our *employees* will continue to thrive. And our guests will continue to make new memories, to connect with their loved ones, and to enjoy our hospitality as they do.

'And, at the end of the day, that's all any of us can ask for.' At the lectern, he raises his champagne flute. 'To the next chapter.'

'To the next chapter,' the room choruses. Flutes are raised. The toast is drunk. My father is sitting, stony-faced, in my periphery. Of course he's not happy. Charles may have publicly passed the baton, but there's no denying that his words felt more like a victory speech than a concession speech, and quite right. He should be proud of what he and his family have built. Not only that, but he's openly daring us to uphold their standards, not just of the hotels themselves, but of the kind of integrity and leadership that have put a man like Charles on that podium. What it must be like to have a man like that for a father, I can't imagine.

As the great and good of the luxury hotel industry rise to their feet to honour him, so do Soph and I. We stand and applaud him until our hands are sore.

'Sit down!' my father hisses, and we ignore him.

He's showing his true colours tonight.

And I can't unsee any of those colours.

As soon as the interminable meal has ended, I escape from Dad's belligerence and Mum's exhausting efforts to smooth everything over and prop myself up against the bar. I nurse a neat scotch, although it's probably the party doing most of the nursing. Damn Soph, making me second-guess everything I do. I'm sure she'd call this *numbing*, and she'd be right. God knows, I need something to take the edge off this wretched evening.

I watch with intense unhappiness as she catches up with the Montague clan at their table at the front of the room. So far, she's hugged Charles and his wife Laura, that awful Theo and the pretty brunette I assume is his wife, Soph's friend, and Miles and his wife Saoirse, who I've met a few times in passing.

Seeing Miles in black tie reminds me with a pang of the first time Elena met him. She observed to me afterwards, with far too many giggles, that she thought he looked exactly like

Theo James. *Exactly like* is a long fucking shot, but clearly he's done well for himself. Saoirse is beautiful.

He hasn't done nearly as well for himself as I have, though. I refuse to remind myself that I'm paying for the privilege.

The truth is, I'd be lost without Soph, especially tonight. It stings to see her in her element, laughing and joking and hugging, keeping the Montagues in her thrall as she regales them with god knows what stories. She's an impossible woman to look away from, and they're soaking up every bit of her dazzling personality.

I wish I felt more certain that we're on the right side of this thing with the Montagues. It's hard to look at Charles Montague and Richard Kingsley side by side and believe that I've chosen the right ally. Not that I've actually *chosen* him— not for a second. But I wish I felt less shitty. I didn't miss Charles' heavy-handed dig at our plans to cut his employees. It would have been impossible to miss.

And I wish, at the very least, that Soph didn't have to feel as though she was sleeping with the enemy. I wish—entirely for her sake—that there was a reality where we could socialise with them as a couple. These people are her friends, after all. She's known them for years and years.

Unlike my father, I'm mature enough to understand that things aren't always black and white, good or bad. The Montagues are good people—better than we are, without a doubt, which explains why their cost base is more bloated than ours. Dad may be right that softness doesn't drive excellence, but Charles and Miles' brand of integrity has to count for something.

~

As I stand there, completely alone in a roomful of people I know, I realise to my intense discomfort that Miles

Montague is making his way to the bar. Too late, he spots me, but he doesn't give me the cold shoulder. Unlike some members of my family, he has basic manners. Basic decency.

He nods curtly at me and turns to where the servers are milling about behind the bar.

'That was a great speech,' I say. It's an olive branch, albeit a lame one.

He doesn't look at me. 'Yeah. It was. Scotch, neat, please,' he says to a server.

'I could barely see it from where we were sitting, but still.'

His mouth twitches, and he looks over.

'My brother's idea, but I wholeheartedly approved it.'

'I bet you did.' I try to laugh, but it's more of a sigh. 'My dad was fuming. Still is.'

'So my work is done. What did you expect? A front-row seat? A spotlight? You'll get that next year.'

'No, mate.' I shake my head. 'Didn't expect anything less. I'd like to think I'd have had the balls to do the same, if the tables had been turned.'

He accepts his scotch, thanks the server, and looks at me properly then.

'That's the thing. The tables would never have been turned. We would never have pulled a stunt like that, because we're not led by our egos. We have nothing to prove. I mean, your father's behaviour is no surprise, obviously. He's a fucking narcissist, if ever I saw one. But I thought you were more decent than him. Relatively speaking, anyway. So what the hell your excuse is, I have no fucking clue.'

He goes to walk away from the bar, but I stop him with a hand on his arm. There's something about that word, and the way he said it, that has alarm bells ringing. 'Wait—what do you mean by that?'

He looks at me blankly. 'I meant what I said.'

'Was it a turn of phrase, or... narcissism, I mean? You didn't mean it literally?'

'Well, it's always a hard one to diagnose clinically. Narcissists aren't exactly known for their introspective natures. But I was married to one, and let's say I've read every book there is on the subject.'

I'm extremely confused now. 'You're saying Allegra was a narcissist.'

Miles' ex-wife is a beautiful socialite. Truly stunning. I didn't know her well enough to judge her character, although I do know she abandoned Miles and his daughter Bea, who was then two years old, during lockdown, taking off to LA for a new lover and a yoga empire. It was all over the tabloids at the time.

His lips press together before he answers. 'I am. And I'm the oblivious dickhead who not only married the woman but waited for her to walk out on us instead of taking Bea and running for the hills.'

'Shit. I'm so sorry.' I truly am. There may be beef between us—a lot of it—but I wouldn't wish that on my worst enemy, even if Saoirse seems like the sweetest woman ever.

He nods awkwardly.

'And you think my father is a narcissist—like a proper one?'

That gets a humourless laugh out of him. 'An absolute textbook case. I can recognise them at a hundred feet now. Sorry to be the one to break it to you, pal.' He picks up his glass and goes to leave again. 'But like I said. Doesn't give you an excuse to follow blindly in his egotistical footsteps. Look, I have to go find Saoirse.'

With that, he turns and vanishes into the throng.

CHAPTER 35

Sophia

Ethan ushers me into his office as soon as I turn up. He stayed at my house after the awards dinner last night, and I distracted him from his unique brand of melancholy stress the best way I knew how: with sex. He fell asleep in my arms almost immediately. Early this morning, he went home to shower and change. He looks tired this morning, but he still beat me in here. His beauty routine is a little more pared-back than mine, I'll warrant.

I get on my tiptoes and kiss him lightly on the lips.

'Do you have many plans for next week?' he asks by way of greeting.

I think. 'A few social plans. A dinner, and a Christmas party on Thursday. Why?'

'Cancel them.'

I don't grace that unreasonable command with a reply. Instead, I fold my arms over my chest and raise my eyebrows. I'm wearing a scarlet cashmere sweater dress this morning. I've sexed it up with a black Alexander McQueen belt and some gorgeous black boots, but I still wish I didn't have to dress for frigid temperatures. It's utterly miserable out there—there's barely any sunlight.

He sighs and runs his hands down my woolly upper arms. 'Look, I thought we could work out of my place in Mustique next week. We could go tomorrow, even. I don't have Jamie this weekend.'

I gape at him, a thrill running through me. I had no idea he had a home in Mustique. 'But why?'

'I could do with putting some space between me and this shit-show. And'—he shrugs awkwardly—'I know you've been struggling with the cold. I thought you might like to spend a few days being warm.'

Be still my heart. The king of the underworld understands that I have a Mediterranean pulse, that I need heat. I give him my widest smile, showing him how much his thoughtfulness means to me.

'You had me at *warm*.'

He grins, pleased, and immediately he looks younger. Lighter. What might Beach Ethan be like, hmm? All golden and carefree? I can't wait to find out.

'So, will this be like in *The Thomas Crown Affair*, when Thomas sweeps Catherine off to his charming little shack in Martinique, and she cavorts around topless all day, and he's all like *I never bring anyone here?*'

He frowns. 'Yes to you cavorting around topless. But I'm not sure I'd call it a shack.'

VILLA AURORA IS MOST DEFINITELY *NOT* a shack. What it is is an absolute stunner, perched on a leafy hill overlooking L'Ansecoy Bay. We pull up in a 'mule', which is apparently the local term for a beach buggy. The villa's very smiley butler, Kelvin, picked us up from the airstrip. Apparently there's a team of staff, so I guess I won't be cavorting around topless that much after all.

The flight in Ethan's jet was memorable—my Gucci dress and retro-slash-porno flight attendant role play made sure of that. But I also managed to glean from him that his villa is one of the original Oliver Messel-designed homes on the island. This knowledge has been breaking my brain a little, because if I think about Ethan's 'minimalist corpse' aesthetic and Messel's Sixties-style theatricals, then there's zero overlap in that particular Venn diagram. None at all. The Holland Park mausoleum isn't exactly overburdened with silk-fringed lamp-shades or coral motifs, is it? I spent the non-sex part of the flight using the jet's Wi-Fi to research Messel's work further. Ethan has assured me that there are a few relevant coffee table books at the house, and I can't wait to dive in deeper, to learn more about the flamboyant hallmarks of the man who created *the* Mustique aesthetic.

I gaze in astonished delight at the stunning, low-level building as Kelvin rounds the circular drive, bringing us to a brisk stop in front of the villa. It's perfectly symmetrical, with a single-storey wing jutting out on each side from the central part of the structure. But more than that: it's lavender. Ethan owns an actual lavender home! The pastel walls are the pretti-est, most feminine foil for both the vibrant green palms every-where and the impeccable white lattice work all along the balconies. The once-reddish tiles on the pitched roofs have weathered almost to grey.

'I feel exactly like Princess Margaret,' I announce as Kelvin helps me down from the mule. I swapped the Gucci for vintage Pucci somewhere over the Atlantic, and my multi-coloured kaftan is making me feel even more like the island's most famous—or infamous—fan. The sensation of suddenly being in light clothing, of being enveloped in warmth, is more blissful than I can say.

'Well, you certainly act a lot like her, so that's no surprise,' Ethan grumbles, but when I look back at him, he's grinning at me. He seems lighter already, and, as we saunter towards the front door, through which I already have a clear line of sight to the sea, he slings an arm around my neck, pulling me closer towards him so he can press a kiss to my temple.

~

'Apparently this was a thing for Messel,' I tell Ethan around fifteen minutes later, waving my hand back towards the house. We're sitting on the idyllic veranda whose pitched roof is lined with white-painted tongue-and-groove planking. The housekeeper, Esmé, who seems thrilled that Ethan has brought a woman along, has shoved an excellent mojito in my hand, and he plonked a glossy Messel coffee table book in my lap before taking a seat next to me on the bamboo sofa. I'm happy as a clam.

'What was?' He leans in, looking down at the book. His arm tightens around me, fingertips brushing my bare shoulder.

'This concept of being able to see straight through from the front door right to the sea. So indulgent, and what an amazing first impression it makes.' I recall from my Oscar de la Renta book at home that he had the same thing going on in his dreamy Dominican Republic house. 'It says he loved positioning doorways and windows just so to frame a view.'

This book is a riot of colour and drama and gorgeous detail. Greek columns. Gratuitous trompe-l'oeil. Pastels. Pavilions. Shells. Scallops. It's just so fucking fabulous.

'I should probably have lived in the Sixties,' I tell him. 'I would have been one of those heiresses that Slim Aarons photographed with my mojito and toy poodle in my over-furnished house.'

'Is there a man in this life?'

'Definitely. You probably would have lived in a speedo, though.'

'Small price to pay.'

We grin foolishly at each other before I turn my head to gaze out past the lovely turquoise pool and over the lush greenery that covers the distance from here to the cobalt-blue sea. The air is thick with the scent of flowers, of vegetation.

'You like it here?' he asks.

'I love it already. I could die happy. How can you ever bear to leave?'

He laughs a little and drops a kiss to my forehead when I turn back to him. He, too, changed mid-flight, into the palest blue linen shirt and white chinos. It's such a billionaire-on-holiday look, and it makes me feral. He has his aviators on, and honestly, Ray-Ban should sign this guy up. He was born to wear aviators in the same way that Brad Pitt and Tom Cruise were. It's something about his razor-sharp cheekbones.

'It's a lovely place. But I'd lose my edge here. London gives it to me.'

He doesn't sound happy about that, merely resigned.

'Right now, having an edge sounds overrated.'

'It probably is.'

'But how the hell did you end up with this place? I thought you'd have some kind of Bond villain lair, all bunker-style, built into the side of the mountain. Nothing frou-frou. Like an Aman resort.'

That puts a smile back on his face. 'I love Aman.'

'Of course you do. I'm more of a Beverly Hills Hotel kind of girl.'

'Nothing surprises me less.' He sighs and pushes his avia-tors up onto his head. 'And you're right. This isn't me. I bought it when I was married to Elena. We rented it one Christmas when Jamie was a baby, and she fell completely in love with it. And, honestly, I fell more in love with how we were here. Relaxed. So when it came up for sale, we jumped on it. I thought maybe it would be good to have something in our lives that was more... chaotic. Not chaotic, but organic, maybe. Softer. More fun, I suppose.'

He smiles softly, wistfully. He's remembering. He's remembering a tiny, chubby version of Jamie toddling around this place. Him and his wife when they were presumably happy, in love. My heart squeezes for him, and for the happy little version of Jamie who seems to me to be long gone, and for Elena, too. I think I feel most strongly for her, oddly enough, because she's the one into whose shoes I can put myself most easily.

Imagine walking away from this man. From this life. From a house you fell in love with, a house full of memories. I don't know how she felt when she asked Ethan for a divorce. I don't know if she still loved him, if she made the ultimate sacrifice for her son, or if she was so disillusioned by his shortcomings as a father that it killed that love.

Either way, it must have been horrific.

I put a palm to his face and stroke it softly. 'Sometimes, a little chaos and colour and fun can be good for you,' I whisper.

'I've worked that out.' He raises his hand, his fingers closing over mine. 'It's exactly how I feel about you.'

I'VE BEEN to the Caribbean several times before, but never to Mustique—never to any of the Grenadines, actually. My parents favoured the BVIs for winter getaways when we were kids, and Thad was a fan of St Barths, but I'm quickly falling for Mustique's particular brand of Sixties-style sugared-almond chic.

Trouble is, I could also fall hard for the magic this place seems to hold over Ethan, for the version of himself he is here. Before we've even finished our delicious late lunch of pineapple and spiny lobster salad, served by Esmé on the shady veranda with the killer view, I'm marvelling at the lightness of his demeanour, at the easy smile that plays on his lips. Mustique is the polar opposite of his London lifestyle—all colour and warmth and relaxation—and I'd say it's damn good for him.

'Try this.' He holds what looks like an arancino ball up to my mouth. I take a bite, and delicate flavours explode on my tongue. I moan in delight.

'Oh my God,' I say when I've swallowed. 'What the hell is that?'

'Squash and coconut arancini. They're a speciality down at the Cotton House. You can try their version tonight, but Jamie loved them so much when he was little that our chef, Irving, was determined to master them.'

'I'd say he succeeded. They're incredible.' It strikes me once again that this past life Ethan has painted with the broadest brushstrokes of happy family memories is so vastly different from what I've observed of the Kingsleys' lifestyle these days—the carefully drawn custody agreements, the tension between father and son.

'You know, maybe you should bring Jamie back here if he likes it so much. Do you bring him here often?'

'Not really.' He removes his gaze from my face and pushes a piece of pineapple around his plate. 'I only get a couple of weeks a year of holiday time with him, so this year we did active stuff—a week of skiing at Easter and water sports this summer.'

I nod, even though he's not looking at me. 'Makes sense.' But it's so sad. Two weeks a year and occasional weekends is nothing, even without Ethan's particular issues. No wonder they're disconnected.

He clears his throat. 'Elena asked me if they could come here next Christmas. I said of course. It's a good idea, I think. They both love it. But it's only been a year since—since we finalised the divorce, so we're still finding our feet, all three of us.'

'Of course you are.' I grab his hand on the table and brush my thumb over his knuckles. 'And you'll figure it out. You're doing great.'

He smiles, but it's forced. 'Thank you, but that is most definitely not true.'

'How long were you and Elena married for?' I venture.

'Almost fifteen years.'

'Wow.' Fifteen years is a heck of a long time. I take a sip of my sparkling water. Ethan strikes me as such an isolated figure. I can't really imagine him living in matrimonial bliss, with a wife and a kid, even if it all ended badly. At the same time, I can't think of anyone I'd love to see happy more than him. Under all that trauma and all those walls, he's such a decent guy. He's a man of extreme integrity, even if he doesn't want people to know that.

'Yeah. Wow.' He looks bleak, and I don't want that. Not here. I've put that look on his face with this line of questioning.

'You must have some very happy memories of this place,' I say softly, still stroking his hand.

He looks out at the pool, at the glorious gardens framing that extraordinary view of the sea, and I swear he's watching little ghosts running through the gardens and splashing in the shallow end of the pool. He doesn't speak for a while.

'The best,' he says eventually. He turns his hand over on the tablecloth so it's palm up and he can squeeze mine.

I smile at him. 'Do you want to share them? I'd love to hear them.'

'Just'—he shakes his head—'the simple things, you know? I realise it's a cliché that the billionaire buys an obscenely expensive house so he can sit on its beach and find himself while playing with shells, but it really is like that. Or it was, anyway.

'Jamie loves this house so much, and the team here always treated him like their own kid. He used to follow Kelvin around with a tiny watering can when Kelv was telling the gardeners what to focus on.' He smiles at me, eyes crinkling with all that love, all that memory, and I'm not sure I've ever seen him look quite so handsome. 'He'd be stark naked, waddling around, peeing left right and centre. I think he watered the plants with his pee more than he ever managed with water. That must have been the first Christmas after we'd bought it outright.'

I laugh. 'Nice.' I've spotted a couple of baby photos of Jamie at Ethan's London home, and he was adorable. Huge brown eyes. Big smile. Chubby as hell—so different from the shy, subdued boy I've met.

He continues talking, still holding my hand. 'He loved knots. Loved them. Not sure how many knots we learnt one year. He must have been six? I was so out of my depth, watching YouTube videos of how to tie the damn things so I could teach him. One of the guys down at Basil's Bar took pity on me and showed him the literal ropes, thank fuck. He still has some of the knots hanging in his bedroom at my place.'

Silence hangs between us. 'You're a great dad, you know,' I tell him. 'It's obvious you love him very, very much.'

'I do, but I don't know how to talk to him, and that's no fucking good, is it?'

'You will,' I urge him. 'You've taken this huge step with Philip purely so you can reconnect with your son, and that is a *big* act of love, my friend. It'll pay dividends. I have faith in you.'

He raises his beautiful, solemn face to me, his grey eyes shining with emotion, and, leaning over, kisses my forehead.

'I need you to have faith in me, because I'm not sure I have it in myself. Not when it comes to Jamie, not when it comes to whatever the fuck I'm doing with this deal. But I'm tired, and I dragged you here so I could forget about all my shortcomings for a few days.'

'So let's go explore then. Let's go and enjoy ourselves.'

He brushes his lips over my forehead once more before pulling away. 'We should head down to the beach. I'd enjoy myself far more if you were in a bikini, even if I'm not sure I'll survive the experience.'

CHAPTER 36

Ethan

I t turns out that lying with a bikini-clad Sophia in the warm, shallow waters of this beautiful turquoise sea, that kissing her, letting my hands roam over her body, is most conducive to forgetting my woes back in London.

Her bikini is yellow and extremely skimpy.

She's a goddess.

And, as I lie here on the shore, with the waves lapping softly over my legs and Sophia crouching over me, sandy and tangle-haired and flashing white teeth as she laughs, I have the truest sensation of peace that I can remember in quite a while.

This was a sound decision. A really sound one. I have a tendency to double down when I'm stuck in the reeds, but these reeds were so fucking torturous that I had no choice but to turn and run.

I'm very glad I did.

The oddest thing is that, while none of my problems—not Jamie, nor my father, nor the Montague deal—are, in reality, forgotten, they're... distant. Manageable. As though I'm seeing them through a telescope. And it makes them seem less fearful. Less overwhelming. It reminds me a little of what Philip calls 'unblending' from my parts—that when I can persuade them to take a seat at that boardroom table, it gives me breathing space. And with that space comes perspective, the reminder that they may be a part of me but they're not actually *me*. And that makes them less all-consuming, somehow.

Back at lunch, when Sophia was asking about my memories from here and I could feel myself spiralling in return, I would have said that I'd rather not talk about any of this shit. That I'd rather shove down all the painful stuff and focus on the here and now—on being here today, with her. On the seven days and nights of sunbathing and sex we have ahead of us. But now, lying here as I stare up into her face, her dark hair backlit against the sun with an actual halo, I feel the opposite. I feel like it's safe to talk. Rather, *I'm* safe, even if I talk about some of the things that are bothering me.

London and my family are at the other end of the telescope, after all.

I reach up and tuck a strand of hair behind Soph's ear. It falls instantly back down again, hanging over me. The sea has made it all wavy, and I like it. It adds to the beach goddess vibe.

'Do you think my dad's a narcissist?'

She spits out a surprised laugh. 'Bloody hell. Um—yeah? Very possibly? What brought this on?'

Quickly, I fill her in on my short conversation with Miles at the bar. It was only two nights ago, but it feels like longer. She sighs and flops down beside me, turning her body towards me and propping herself up on one elbow. I turn into her and mirror her pose.

'So, narcissism's one of those concepts that gets bandied about, like sociopathy. And if you're talking about actual Narcissistic Personality Disorder—NPD—then we don't even a hundred percent know what causes it. It's most likely some combination of neurological predisposition and a shitty upbringing—nature *and* nurture, basically. You think your dad might have that?'

'I have no clue. But it seems Miles has some experience with it, and he made out that he could spot it at fifty paces where Dad was concerned.'

'I mean, that makes sense. Once you know what to look for in a condition, you get attuned. My older brother has ADHD, and my mum used to say she could spot an undiagnosed child across a playground, or from any throwaway comment we made about kids in our class.'

'Like the parts stuff.' I told Soph about seeing those parts come out when I was watching that cyclist and that woman have their bust-up.

She pokes me in the chest. 'Exactly. Once you see it, you can't unsee it.'

'So you think he could be? My father?'

Soph blows out a breath. 'It's very possible. I mean, he's either a raging narcissist or just a gigantic wanker. Neither is great for you. Do you have a take on why you need to know?'

I allow myself to flop back down on my back, to let the sand hold me. 'I've been trying to work that out. It's not that it's bothering me—more the opposite. Because it's an explanation, I suppose. And if there's an actual, clinical label that I can attribute to him then it absolves me more. It means none of it was ever really about me, or what I did wrong. It was about him.'

Her face creases with emotion, and she brushes her knuckles oh-so gently down my stomach. 'Listen to me, babe. It was never about you. None of it. And I really hope that the work you're doing with Philip will show you that unequivocally. No matter what the fuck is wrong with Richard, it was all about him.'

I nod, but I'm not entirely sure I'm processing that. I know, having met my younger self several times now, that she's right, but it's extremely hard to absolve myself. To know that I couldn't have done anything differently, that the way my father treated me—treats me—has always been out of my hands. 'Still, it would be nice to get some... validation, I suppose.'

'You'll never get it from him. You'll never get an apology. There are certainly lots of online tools and questionnaires you can use to get a clearer idea of what you've been working with for all these years when it comes to your dad, but he'll never admit that you didn't deserve any of it.'

I blow out a breath. 'I know. Sorry.'

'Don't ever apologise. But we can work on it this week if you like—there are checklists that will validate your experience. When you see all those behaviour patterns written down, my guess is that it will resonate really fucking hard. But that's why the work you're doing with Philip is so important—because it's about reparenting and unburdening those parts yourself. That's how you find your peace. Not from him, never from him.'

I slide a hand around her bare waist and pull her down towards me on the sand so that our foreheads are touching. 'Thank you.'

'Always.' Her forehead still pressed to mine, she rakes her fingers through my hair. It feels so amazing that it gives me shivers. 'For you, I think, it's about how you respond going forward, how you want to reclaim your life. Boundaries, for starters. Honestly, walk away tomorrow if you like. Cut off all contact with the worthless dipshit. It's nothing more than he deserves.'

I laugh a little nervously, because the thought of blocking my father from my phone and walking away from the giant ego-trip of a company that he's built feels so fantastical, so insane, that it has my head spinning. But Soph's not done.

'And also, for you, I suspect a lot of it is about recalibrating your relationship with control.' Her voice is gentle; I can tell she's being careful with her choice of words. 'Historically, it's been a way to keep you safe, but as you heal you might find you don't need to hold onto everything so tightly.'

I close my eyes and rub my nose gently against hers. 'Thanks for the free therapy session,' I whisper, and she laughs softly.

'Well, you've brought me on holiday. Let's call it even.' She pulls away, and I open my eyes, staring up at her. She's looking at me with so much care and concern. 'Bottom line—none of your past relationship with your father was your fault in the slightest, and going forward, everything is up to you. He doesn't get to define how you move through the world anymore. For fuck's sake, don't let him take another day of your happiness or your peace. Remember: *it's not your fault.*'

My eyes dampen instantly. 'That's basically what I want to say to Jamie. That none of this shit is his fault. He's just a kid. I've fucked up so badly, yet I've stuck him in therapy, like he's the problem. How the hell am I supposed to make it right?'

'You will. I promise you you will. Showing up, doing the work—that's how you make it right. Before long, you'll be in a place where you can have that conversation with him, and you can start to prove it to him through your actions. And don't knock the therapy—it's great that he's doing it. If you both have professionals who can help you, it will give you both far more emotional literacy. Your relationship will be all the better for it. I promise you.'

'Thank you,' I mouth before pushing myself back up on my side. I hook a leg around her legs and close the gap between us. 'You know, you're really good at this stuff. You have a very special gift. I'm so sorry for that hissy fit I threw when you told me you wanted to move into this at some point. God, it was so fucking childish.' I screw my face up at the shame I still feel over that memory.

'I accept your apology on behalf of the part that was working very hard to protect you,' she says with a beatific smile. 'And it's all good. Honestly, you probably can't see it, but you've made such massive progress in just a couple of weeks, babe. It's incredible. Goes to show what strides you can make when you put your mind to something.'

I trace a line over the sand-dusted curve of her shoulder and down her arm. I was worried I'd regret opening up, that it would spoil this bubble we have, that laying myself bare would make me want to instantly clam up again, but none of those things have happened. We had what I would deem a very fucking deep conversation, and as a result I feel closer to her than ever. It helps that she's so wise, so brilliantly articulate about these matters and so firmly supportive. I meant what I said. She'd make a brilliant therapist.

But right now, it's a different kind of therapy I want from her. And so it's gently that I sit up and lay her down flat on the sand, dark hair splayed in tangles around her and her sea-damp skin glistening in the sunshine. I pause for a moment to drink in the sight of her, because she's a fucking vision, before lowering myself on top of her and pressing my lips to hers.

CHAPTER 37

Sophia

Our week of a Mustique lifestyle is quite the antidote to the bleak midwinter of London. We cover the bare minimum of work—Ethan was definitely lying when he proposed working from here—but it doesn't feel so bad when 'work' involves swimming costumes and bare feet and a cup of Irving's excellent coffee as we check our laptops on the veranda each morning after breakfast.

We swim in the sea. We stroll down to Basil's Bar most evenings and work our way systematically through the excellent cocktail list. After an indulgent first night dining at the Cotton House, we tend to come home for dinner. It's more chilled out here, and I want Ethan all to myself. He seems to feel the same.

And we talk. God, do we talk. Here, in his safe, happy place, his tongue is loosened. We lie in a large hammock in a shady area of the garden, top-and-tailing as he haltingly tells me about his first few sessions with Philip, opening up about his fucking father, and his fucking investment club, and his fucking Father's Day celebration no-show, and I'm so furious that I cry helpless tears of rage.

Maybe I wouldn't make such a good therapist after all, if I can't hold space for Ethan without losing my shit.

He describes his younger self in the most starkly beautiful language, and I'm incandescent with wonder that the emotionally walled-off man I met just a couple of months ago has already found the courage and open-heartedness to connect so deeply, so beautifully, with the burdened parts of himself who've been running his system for all these decades.

And we talk about me, too, because Ethan is worried that he's making it all about him. I laugh at that, because I suspect this man hasn't dominated a conversation with his introspective observations probably ever. And he doesn't get this, but it makes me so happy to see him do that, not just because it means he trusts me, but because with every memory, every realisation shared, he's processing his trauma in a way that's manageable for his nervous system.

But he insists, so I tell him all about my family. My upbringing. I tell him about Camille scouting me at Stanford and my decision to put pause on pursuing my clinical studies and instead follow an infamous, married fuckboy around the playgrounds of the Med for years and years while being hand-somely rewarded.

I'm just glad he's not familiar with the Enneagram, so he can't laugh at how ridiculously Seven-ish I am.

I tell him, too, about my reasons for being so fascinated by IFS, for wanting to pursue it professionally. I attempt to explain why I find it such an incredibly powerful, empowering modality, why I believe so wholeheartedly in the way it can change lives. And, this time, rather than facing a wall of cyni-cism, I'm preaching to the choir.

This time, he gets it.

Because I'm me, and I have more Achiever parts than I'd like to admit to Athena, a clinical practice won't be enough for me. I have a dream to start an app while I continue my studies, an app that pulls together all sorts of therapeutic and coaching and somatic modalities into a trusted directory that hooks individuals up with professionals.

I even have a secret dream to include an optional personality profiling section for the ultimate in therapy matchmaking. Take Athena, for example. She recently began working with a new coach, Amy, and she loves her. The reason? Her coach is a raging Three, just like her. Sometimes, it's helpful and healthy to work with people who are your opposites, who have perspective into your blind spots. But sometimes, we want someone who'll get us. Amy gets why Athena wants to work all day long and achieve more, more, more. She understands the strength of the impulses that drive that relentless achievement, and she also understands the fears and the pain points that come alongside it. They're kindred spirits.

I gloss over the personality profiling aspect a little with Ethan, except to explain that I'd use a variety of tools to triangulate people's unique character (because *triangulate* sounds more professional and less creepy than *obsessively psychoanalyse them from every angle*). Still, he seems impressed. More than impressed. I'd go so far as to say he finds the entire concept inspiring.

'If anyone can pull this off, you can,' he tells me, his hand over mine as we lie on the gigantic white daybed next to his pool one afternoon. 'It's the perfect intersection for your skills, I can tell. And if you ever need a backer, you just let me know.'

And this is why I love holidays. Because you don't talk about this kind of shit when you're grabbing lunch from the cafeteria or having a quick bang on your boss' desk. That's real life (though, admittedly, the desk-banging is a niche aspect of that), and when you're living your real life you're simply too stuck in your rut to think much about your dreams.

Somehow, lying on a soft white mattress under the

Caribbean sun makes everything seem possible, whether it's launching apps or reprioritising your life's relationships.

Maybe not *everything*. One morning, I chuck my phone across the daybed with an angry growl. Ethan, who's reading the paper, looks over, amused.

'What's up with you?'

'Fucking Connections. I crapped out.'

He gets himself upright, a move that has his abs rippling in a deeply gratifying way, and picks up my phone so he can take a look at the screen.

'Which one didn't you get?'

'I didn't get purple or blue. But it was purple that fucked me up.' I throw an arm over my face in self-disgust. 'Give me a homophone any day of the week—I'm the *queen* of homophones, because I always read the clues out loud. But it's that dratted kind that gets me. Every. Bloody. Time.

He reads aloud. '*What "trip" might mean. Journey. Fall. Drug. Switch.* Ha! Very clever.'

'Yeah. Too clever for me.' I remove my arm from my face and push myself up onto one elbow. 'Do you know what I'd give a lot of money for? Like, a lot.'

'Tell me.' He puts down the phone and scoops me against him with an arm hooked around my waist.

'I would kill to see their database.'

'Who? The *New York Times*?'

'Yup. Think about it. Think about the tagging system. Like this gigantic semantic web.'

'She rhymes now.'

'That's how badly I want to see it. Imagine playing with it. Imagine *building* it. God, it blows my mind.'

Ethan's looking at me as if I've lost my marbles and yet he's quite fond of me, anyway. He probably has a point. My obsession with peeking under the hood of this game makes sense to me. After all, my entire brain is a giant meaning-making machine. But for normal people, it may be a little much.

'Imagine the matrix, babe!' I practically shout. 'Okay, imagine in their matrix, they have the word *bear*. Like the animal. So that could also be tagged as a homophone for *bare*, like naked. Let's see. It could be a finance term—*bear market*. A verb—*to bear*. It could even be in words that begin with conjugations of the verb *to be*. They really like fucking around with prefixes and suffixes, you know.

'Imagine seeing all those tags cross-referenced with thousands upon thousands of others. And don't get me started on the red herring tags they must have. Honestly, it makes me horny just thinking about playing with it. I'm not kidding.'

He's full-on laughing now, his fingers stroking my back. 'You've thought about this a lot.'

'I have. Have you never?'

'Can't say I have. I don't play it much. I prefer Wordle.'

I stare at him, aghast. 'You're what they call a basic bitch. You know that? You're not even living! What is this bleak, Connections-less existence you call a life?'

He laughs again and kisses me. 'I'd better start playing, then, hadn't I? Now, what shall we do about all this horniness you have going on?'

I AWAKE one afternoon from my nap in our enchanting white bedroom to find Ethan gazing at me from his spot next to me on the bed, an experience that is altogether sexier and less creepy than it should be. My nap was a *just because I can* kind of nap: the very best kind. It was a floaty nap, the type where you're not entirely sure how deeply you slept but you do know that you were all up in those delicious alpha brain waves.

He wasn't here when I lay down. He had some calls to do. But he's here now, and he's so gorgeous. He's wearing only a pair of board shorts, his already golden skin newly sun-kissed and hair tousled and face soft.

'Did you sleep?' I ask him, rolling onto my back so I can stretch. Above me, the ceiling fan whirrs lazily, framed by the sides of the teak four-poster.

'Nah. Just came in. Sorry for waking you.'

'That's okay.' I stretch again, feeling like a cat, and roll back to face him. I'm still in my bikini—coffee and white zebra stripe today, with gold hardware—and his eyes rove over my body once more. 'So you just came in to perve?'

'Something like that.' He brushes his fingertips down my upper arm.

'Well, perve away, mister. I like your eyes on me.' I give him a lazy smile. 'You're so fucking hot.'

He smiles in return, but it's not the smirk I'd expect. It's more tremulous than that. I snuggle in closer, and he hooks a hairy leg over mine.

'You alright?'

'Can I ask you something?' he says stiffly by way of answer.

'Of course.'

He purses his lips like he's thinking about what he's going to say, then he speaks. 'Do you think that if I wasn't... if I wasn't paying you, you'd still be here with me?'

'*What?*' I ask, stunned. A second later, it hits me: I shouldn't be stunned, because this is the Eightest thing he could ask. If an Eight's biggest fear is being betrayed, then letting me get even this close to him is a huge step for Ethan. I recover before I force the poor man to respond to my stupid question. 'Babe, of course I'd be here. You can't think for a second that I wouldn't—can you?'

I falter on that last part, because of course he can. That's what he does. That's why he tests the important people in his life over and over. I may have passed all his tests to date—I wouldn't be here otherwise—but he's still entitled to have his doubts. And the very question he's just posed is such an immense act of vulnerability for him.

Here's the thing. It's always the thing. Our nervous system doesn't understand words—it's hundreds of millions of years old in parts. It needs to *feel* to understand.

So I need to make him feel. And in order to do that I need to tamp down every Seven part of me that wants to make a joke, to grab his dick—anything to lighten the atmosphere, to move away from the discomfort that being vulnerable necessarily elicits.

First, I start by using my words, because I'm not about to leave him hanging.

'Sorry,' I amend. 'I heard you the first time.' I shimmy my body forward, wedging myself further under his leg, and I slide my top hand through his hair so I can cup his head. My bottom hand I place on his taut pec, right over his heart.

'Listen to me,' I whisper. 'Nothing about us, here, is about what you pay me for. You hear me? *Nothing.*'

His beautiful grey eyes go hard and cold, and I know he's already regretting flaying himself open. He removes his leg from mine, and I feel instantly bereft. 'That's not entirely true. I asked for exclusivity. We agreed I'd go bare when I fuck you.'

I keep my hands where they are, pressing my palm against his rapidly beating heart. Grounding his body in safety. 'You did. Both of those things are true. And if I'd wanted to keep things very boundaried within that arrangement, I would have fucked you on demand, sure, but I would also have requested my own room, or I might even have refused outright to come here on the basis that it would blur lines.' I slide my hand over his jaw, over the muscles tensing between his skin and his stubble. 'But none of that is what's happening here, and I know that, and I think you do, too.'

I sigh, because his insecurities—and I mean that in the most literal sense that he has a perceived lack of safety—are prompting me to have to be very vulnerable too, in a way that I never was with Thad and had no intention of being with Ethan. Not that I ever imagined I'd *feel* vulnerable to the feelings he's evoking in me.

'I'm here out of contractual obligation just as much as you've brought me here for a convenient fuck. Both things may technically be true, but they're not the *reason* for us being here.' My hand smooths over that tense jaw and down his neck. Over the domed, muscular shoulder I love so much. And, in response, his hand finds the crook of my waist and settles there. 'I think we're here together because we're both deeply, ridiculously attracted to one another, and because, despite all initial signs to the contrary, we feel seen by each other, which makes us drawn to each other on a totally different level. I'd say this is pretty special. What do you say to that?'

His eyes flicker over my face, moving from my eyes to my mouth and back again as if he's trying to perform a visual polygraph test. I'm walking a tightrope between reassuring him and freaking him out. He may need to know that I'm here because I want to be, but who the fuck knows if he's ready to admit to himself that this thing between us is escalating out of both of our control?

My guess would be that he'd like our dynamic contained in a Goldilocks space where he knows I won't betray him but he also knows he can control his emotions—and mine. Then again, he's displayed a textbook disorganised attachment style to me throughout the past few weeks, so god knows where he'll land on this.

'Special,' he repeats slowly, as if trying it on for size.

'That's right.' Right now, his rock-hard dick is the only part of Ethan unafraid to state its agenda. Slowly, as if he's a skittish horse, I slide in more closely against him so our bodies are flush, my palm trapped between us. 'I can lie here and psychoanalyse us until the cows come home if you want, babe. You know me. But I'd rather show you. And I'd rather *you* show *me* what you're thinking, too. What do you say?'

'Show you? How?' In spite of himself, his fingers flex on my waist.

With difficulty, I roll us so I'm on my back, his weight on top of me. 'Like this.'

CHAPTER 38

Ethan

'Feel me,' she tells me. 'I want you to see what effect you have on me when we're together. And I don't just mean sexually. Just... touch me. Explore my body. *Enjoy me.*'

I'm not entirely sure what her endgame is here, but then I'm not entirely sure what my endgame was when I asked her that stupid question. That said, if she wants to stop talking about this shit and start enjoying the hell out of each other's bodies instead, then I have no problem with that.

I lift my weight off her, getting to my knees so I'm crouching over her. She's right. I need to see with my own eyes what effect I have on her. When my call ended, I found myself sitting on the terrace and spiralling, wondering if Sophia was going through the motions every time she let me fuck her. While my instincts—and ego—said not, some part of me that sounded pretty bloody loud begged to differ.

She's breathtaking against the white sheets, her long, dark hair splayed around her. Her tan has built over the past few days, her naturally olive skin growing darker. Her nipples are already hard through that dratted bikini. It's impossible not to be hard around Soph, especially like this, but like she said, the physical attraction between us is irrefutable. I owe it to her to show her how entranced I am by her before I go to ram my dick inside her.

Instead, I reach up and gently, slowly, rake my fingertips through her mass of hair. It's so soft, so silky. She stares up at me, eyes molten, pink mouth pursed in anticipation.

'When I first saw you,' I tell her as I stroke her hair, 'my very first thought was that you looked like perfection. And my second was that you couldn't possibly be that good up close.'

She presses her lips together in a pleased little smile and places her hand back against my heart, where it feels so good and right and true.

'You were, obviously.' I pause to brush some strands of hair off her shoulder, focusing on the gold starfish attached to her bikini strap. 'But what I failed to appreciate at the time was that your looks aren't even the best part of you.'

My eyes flick back up to hers in time to catch the flash of shock on her face.

'And that's what makes me feel inordinately lucky to have you here with me.' I clear my throat. 'In any capacity.'

Her fingers flex against my heart. 'That's what I'm trying to tell you. I feel the same. There's nowhere else I'd rather be, honestly.' And when I look into her beautiful brown eyes, it is indeed only honesty that I see there.

She said this thing between us was *special*.

She asked me to *show* her just how special.

So I do.

I dip my head, and I seal my mouth over hers. My kiss is slow enough that I can savour every moment, every sensation. The soft pressure of kissing those pillowy lips. The tiny hum of approval she makes as I do. The slick glide of my tongue against hers as she opens easily for me, and the silken wet as I explore her mouth. I let a hand trail down over her breast, grazing over the triangle of fabric and taut nipple between it, but I don't stop. Instead, I make it my business to roam my hand over her skin, so warm and soft, using my fingertips to map her.

It proves such a pleasurable experience that I break our kiss, enjoying the frustrated little whimper she makes as I do, and make my way down her body.

For me, sex is one of two extremes, even with Soph: a quick, perfunctory means to an end, that end being release and blessed oblivion, or a prostrated affair where I edge myself or my partner or both in an effort to show everyone involved who's boss. Philip would have a lot to say about that part, but I have no interest in thinking about Philip while Soph's glorious body rises and falls beneath me.

Right now, I want neither of those things. I merely want to see where this interlude takes us. I want to simply *exist*, for a moment, in this airy room, with the gentle humming of the ceiling fan, and Sophia undulating beneath me. I want to cast off every last exhausting burden I seem to carry every fucking day, and I want to just be.

I want to get lost in her. In this.

So I do.

I crouch between her legs and kiss my way down the valley of her chest, between her breasts, marvelling at the satin that is her skin. Her stomach, as I stroke and kiss it, is even softer, the area around her navel achingly so. I rub my cheek over it, my hand brushing over her waist, and she sighs indulgently, her fingers working through my hair.

I've known since I hired Soph that, if I was ever going to allow myself to indulge, she would be the ultimate decadent playground. Her body is a carnal Disneyland, lush and rich and abundant. As I continue to make my way down it, hooking my arm around one thigh and gluing my nose to her fabric-covered cunt so I can inhale sharply, she lets out a shuddery moan. Arousal is pumping off her, and the scent of it is like nothing else.

But she's more than just a cunt, no matter how honeyed, how musky, how ready, and so I continue my languorous journey, kissing one inner thigh and then the other before I slide my hand down one satiny leg before cuffing her ankle and licking her instep.

She huffs her impatience. 'Ethan.'

'What?' I peer up, smiling at the naked frustration on her face. 'You told me to enjoy you. That's what I'm doing. Just roll with it.'

'Just roll with it? Are you serious right now? Fuck, this is not the time for you to discover your inner zen.'

'*You're* my inner zen.' I run my nose along the arch of her foot before releasing it and turning to the other one. 'But if you want me to *show you*, then I will.'

I brace myself on one arm and slowly untie one side of her string bikini bottoms, then the other, folding the triangle fabric down as if I'm unwrapping the most precious package, which I essentially am. A glance up her body shows her watching me avidly. I keep my eyes on her as I slide a single finger inside her. Her lips part, and I groan.

When I do this slowly, when I really focus, I can feel every aspect of her as if it's a singular miracle. The astonishing wetness. How snugly she fits around my finger. The glide of it against her slippery inner walls. These few inches where our flesh meets contain multitudes, entire worlds. My dick may be throbbing, weeping, but the rest of me is entranced.

'How does it feel?' I murmur as I slide out and back in, slowly. Keeping my finger exactly where it is, I carefully bend and plant my free hand near her shoulder, so I can watch her face more closely.

'*Incredible.*' It's a whisper.

'Yeah?'

'Yeah.'

The room is quiet, the only noises the breeze through the greenery beyond the open French doors and the ceiling fan. It allows me to focus on our breathing and on the obscene, addictive sounds of her body sucking me in. I slide my thumb lightly over the glossy button of her clit, watching for her reaction.

Soph has a highly expressive face, but observing the ripples of desire that pass over it as I touch her in this leisurely way may just be the most mesmerising thing I've ever seen.

'What do you need?'

She swallows, looking up at me through her thick eyelashes. 'You, inside me. But like this.'

I'm already removing my fingers and kneeling up to push down my shorts. 'Slow, you mean?'

'Yeah. Slow and, like, intentional. Make me feel every thrust.'

Her face is a plea just as much as her words.

Holy fucking hell.

Make me feel every thrust.

That I can do.

As soon as I've wrestled off my shorts, I'm back to crouching above her, our faces inches apart. She arches on the bed, restless, as I notch my crown against her entrance and proceed to feed her my dick. Not for the first time since we renegotiated terms, I thank heaven for no condoms.

I press myself inside her in small, shuddering increments.

Beneath me, she trembles. She has one hand clutching my shoulder and the other flexing in my hair.

The feel of burying myself inside her is exquisite. Otherworldly. It's astounding that two bodies can together produce such intense pleasure.

I bottom out inside her, and it's a symphony of sensation.

I watch her face, and she watches mine.

I dip my head to kiss her, just fleetingly. Her lips, her tongue, feel like a rain-soaked flower.

And then I begin to move, slowly. I may be hyper-aware of what my body wants to do, but I'm not in its thrall. I'm not blindly, savagely seeking release. I allow my head to fall into the crook of Soph's neck, to inhale the scent of her perfume and her post-nap skin. With the arm not supporting my weight, I gather her up as best I can. Our bodies slide against each other as I fuck her, her ragged breaths in my ear and the grip of her fingernails against my shoulder, my back, the best barometers for gauging another person's pleasure that I've ever known.

The build is so fucking good. It has my skin prickling with sweat, my joints growing molten. The rhythm of this dance we're doing is an ancient tattoo, a timeless inner knowledge.

Soph's hand drags down my back until she's grabbing my arse and holding me closer. Pressing me deeper inside her. I get it, I really do. *Sublime* does not begin to describe the sensation of bottoming out in her every time. With an anguished sigh, she lets her other arm fall out to the side, smacking the mattress.

'Dear *god*. I never, ever want this to end.'

'Not sure I can manage that,' I grit into her hair before turning and kissing her jaw. 'But I get what you mean.'

With difficulty, I lift my head so I can see her face. She's flushed, mouth swollen and huge eyes almost all pupil. She's the most spectacular sight I've ever seen, caged in as she is on this bed by my body. This is chemical. The very air feels charged. It's intense, this feeling. Overwhelming in a way that goes beyond the physical. I don't use drugs, but this weird, expansive, addictive high that I'm experiencing certainly feels like drugs. Like everything in the universe is as it should be.

'I'm close,' she whispers, eyelashes fluttering closed for moment. 'Oh, Jesus.'

'Look at me,' I command. 'Show me.' I need to see this,

need to be able to look into her eyes when she comes apart for me. She opens her eyes, her breaths coming in pants, and it strikes me as extraordinary that I can have this effect on her, that she's as overcome as I am.

I slide out and thrust back in, and it's slow and deep and so fucking dirty, with this weird, elemental overlay that's happening, and I swear the sight of her face as I fuck her, as she climbs that onset of her orgasm, makes this doubly erotic. There's something about undoing a woman as strong and unapologetically sensual as Soph that stokes my desire like nothing else on earth.

Her entire body is shaking. Our eyes stay locked. She looks almost terrified of what's to come.

Good.

She should be.

I remove the arm I have banded around her and reach between us so I can pinch her nipple hard. Her face contorts, her eyes darting frantically over my face, mouth open in a silent scream. I twist her nipple, biting down on my lip savagely in an attempt to hold myself the fuck together, and drive myself harder inside her.

She breaks, falling apart in spectacular style, body bucking and bucking below me, crying out her orgasm. I press my forehead to hers and urge her on as I piston into her, my thrusts coming faster now. I've lost all control.

'That's my girl. That's my girl. Give it to me.'

She's practically weeping, and I know how it feels. There's a ball of pressure in my chest almost as great as the one in my dick. As she claws at me, rolling her hips over and over so her greedy cunt can milk me and milk me, the heat in my lower body fucking ignites, my balls tightening impossibly as I go rigid inside her and then start pumping. And pumping. Emptying myself violently. Endlessly. Roaring out my own orgasm.

I find her lips as I rut through the rest of it, licking into her mouth, fucking her at both ends, palming her breast. Anything, everything, to prolong her pleasure and mine, to draw out the moment she told me she wanted never to end.

When I finally flop down on top of her, sated and depleted and mindless with what feels like peace, she's breathless and giggling.

'What?' I mutter against her cheek, inhaling the scent of her hair.

She wraps her arms loosely around my neck. 'I think the infamously cold-hearted Ethan Kingsley has just mastered the art of sex as a co-regulation technique.'

I lift my head so I can roll my eyes at her, but she's not done.

'Otherwise known as *making love*.'

CHAPTER 39

Ethan

'You look even more pleased with yourself than usual,' my old mate Brendan observes as he pulls out a chair opposite me.

I'm not sure self-satisfaction is a state I permit myself that often, but if he's referring to my Caribbean tan and my relative level of relaxation, then he may have a point.

'I could say the exact same thing for you.' I stand and slap him on the back as I bro-hug him.

We've arranged to have a drink in the Parliament bar at the Kingsley Westminster. It's been a while since we caught up—a function of my preoccupation with the Montague deal and his preoccupation with his EA-turned-girlfriend, Marlowe.

He'd never admit it, but I suspect it's also partly due to the fact that he brought Marlowe in for a threesome with me before he'd admitted to himself that he was seriously into her. As far as I'm concerned, it was an amusing interlude, now forgotten, but I suspect he wishes he'd never done it. From what I can tell, the bloke is head over heels.

And *I'd* never admit how much I've been looking forward to catching up with him. When did I become the kind of man whose social calendar consists of business dinners and oblig-atory family functions? Brendan's one of the few people who knew me before I became... whatever the hell I am now. In a life full of barely tolerated networking, Bren's a breath of fresh air. And god knows I need that.

'I'm feeling pretty fucking smug, actually,' he says with his trademark wide grin as he sits down. He's like a big, good-natured golden retriever.

'Popped the question, did you?'

'Nah. Although, between us, I went ring shopping last week. Brought Gabe's fiancée Athena along to make sure I got it right—I think I told you she and Marlowe are best mates from school. She fucking *fleeced* me. To say I got upsold is an understatement. I'll need to work till I'm eighty to pay it off.'

I let out a genuine laugh. 'That's amazing, mate. Seriously, congratulations. When are you popping the question?'

'I'm taking her and Tabs—that's her daughter—to the BVIs after Christmas to give the new catamaran a whirl. Thought I'd do it then.'

'Brendan Sullivan, family man. I never thought I'd see the day. No wonder you're so pleased with yourself.'

He crosses one ankle over the other knee and picks up the scotch I have waiting for him, saluting me with it. 'She has to say yes first. But that's not why I'm pleased as fuck. I had a very interesting day in Nottingham today.'

I frown. 'What were you doing in Nottingham?' As far as I know, Sullivan Construction's business interests are solely focused on London.

'You may well ask.' He leans forward conspiratorially. 'Marlowe has no clue about this, by the way. I'm not sure how she'd react. But get this. Tabby's biological father was Marlowe's music professor when she was at uni. The pathetic fuck seduced her and then showed her the door when she told him she was pregnant. Tried to strong-arm her into getting an abortion.'

I grimace. 'Jesus. What a prick.' Brendan has filled me in on his girlfriend's daughter's health issues, and the fact that he dropped everything to go to the US and be with them when the little girl had a heart valve replacement. Sounds like Marlowe, who seems to be a lovely woman, has had a shitty run of things.

'Yeah. He was married at the time. Fed Marls a load of bullshit about how he was unhappy in his marriage, but when push came to shove, he was just a fucking predator. Clearly he was scared shitless that he'd get busted, because Marls told me he moved to a different uni that summer. But she wouldn't tell me which one.'

A slow smile spreads over my face. 'Let me guess. Nottingham?'

'Got it.'

'How did you find out?'

He snorts. 'Hired a private investigator. It wasn't exactly difficult for him to find this twat, but I wanted some extra leverage from him too, shall we say.'

'So you've gone full vigilante, basically?'

'Yep. Paid him a little visit today in his faculty.' He screws up his face. 'God, what a worthless piece of shit he is. How the fuck you walk away from a woman like Marls, I don't know. But his intense stupidity is my gain.'

'What did you say to him?' I'm enjoying this yarn immensely. It's such a Brendan thing to do: the stubborn side of his default golden retriever mode. His lack of impulse control has caused him problems in the past—there's no doubt about that—but I find his cavalier, *fuck it* attitude far more refreshing than I would if I'd spent more of the past decade cultivating realness in my relationships.

'We had a little chat.' He grins at the memory. 'Reminded

him of his spectacularly poor life choices. Told him that he'd donated sperm to the most amazing, resilient little girl to ever walk this earth. Told him he wasn't worthy of scraping the shit off her shoes, or her mother's. He seemed pretty affronted until I pulled out my trump cards.'

He pauses, smiling broadly as he nurses his scotch. His Irish genes have made him a highly entertaining storyteller, so I'll allow him this pause for effect as he spins his yarn.

'First, I put down a photo of the PhD student he's currently fucking.' He shakes his head. 'Randy old fucker. He must be pushing fifty. But the *pièce de résistance* was when I showed him a piece of paper with his wife's name, mobile number and email address on it.'

I bark out a shocked laugh that has the people at the next table looking over in alarm. 'Holy *fuck*. Remind me never to cross you.'

He starts to laugh, his shoulders shaking. 'Genuinely one of the most satisfying moments of my life. I let him know that Marlowe was now in my care, and that I was one of the wealthiest and most influential people in the British Isles. I told him I was *this* close to making a donation to the University of Nottingham's Music Department, the only condition of which would be the immediate termination of his contract and an investigation into his abuses of power so thorough that he'd never work again.'

'Jesus Christ. Weren't you tempted to just crack on and do it?'

He shrugs. 'Nah. He has a wife and two kids. The poor fuckers have enough on their plates dealing with that gobshite without being on the breadline, too. But I told him if he doesn't cease all romantic relationships with his students *for good*, then I'll know about it, and the axe will fall swiftly.'

With that ominous pronunciation, he sits back and takes a swig of his scotch. Here's the thing about Bren: he's larger than life and so full of bluster. He definitely isn't known for thinking through consequences before acting on his impulses. But he also has a heart of gold. Sparing that jackass for the sake of his family is classic Brendan. I give him an approving nod.

'Classy. That was the right way to go, I suppose.'

'Yeah.' He stretches and yawns. 'Shame. Would have been fun to destroy the useless cunt. I did get Marlowe's old boss from the Royal Academy fired last week, though. He fired her when she left early too often to take Tabs to A&E. Pathetic tosser. So I pulled some strings and had him axed. Probably the second and last time our family's patronage of the RA has actually served any useful purpose—my first meeting with Marls there aside.'

I chuckle. Despite an elite education, Bren hasn't a cultured bone in his body, and he's not afraid to admit it.

'But enough about me.' He pours us each a generous slosh from the bottle of Macallan I had the server leave on our table. 'I'm dying to know how it's going with the lovely Sophia.'

The discomfort is instant. Obviously, things between me and the lovely Sophia are going very fucking well. Mustique was, undeniably, a kind of turning point, even if I'm unsure yet *what* kind. All I know is that there is, for want of a better word, an intimacy between us now that goes beyond mere chemistry.

And if I'm not ready to analyse any of it too closely, except to say that I feel lighter, more contented, than I'd expect given the immense work headaches I've got going on, then I'm *certainly* not ready to analyse any of it with Brendan.

Deflection it is.

'Have you met her?'

'Once. Briefly, last month. Marls had her and Athena over for a girls' night when I was out at a dinner, but I caught them before they left. They were pretty hammered.' He grins knowingly. 'She's very entertaining and *very* hot.'

I purse my lips together before replying. 'No argument here.'

'So it's going well? I don't have much to go on except what I've heard from Marls, but I understand she has a Mustique tan to match yours?'

I'd like to slap that smug grin off his face. 'Didn't realise you were such a gossipy little bitch, Sullivan.'

'Just looking out for my mate. But if she survived a week away with you and she hasn't run for the hills yet, that's a good sign, surely?'

He's nowhere close to the truth.

Sophia.

I allow my mind to drift back to my favourite memories.

The sunset on her face.

Her filthy cackle whenever I said anything that amused her (which was a lot, apparently).

Kissing her. On the shore. In our bed. In the hammock.

I've spent the entire day with her, and I still want more. Bren doesn't need to know that I'm going back to hers for my next fix when I'm done here.

It seems my face betrays me, because Bren slaps his knee with a loud guffaw. 'Holy fuck! That's the goofiest grin I've ever seen. You've got it bad.'

I roll my eyes. 'Look. It's going well, alright? She's really amazing. We're... seeing how things go.'

He shakes out his wrist. 'I knew it! I'm thrilled for you, mate, honestly. It's been a rough year for you—you deserve it.'

'Thanks. The rough year isn't over yet. But yeah. She's a bright spot in it, there's no doubt about that. She even has me going to therapy—it was one of her conditions.'

To be honest, I'd love to tell him more about all of it— Soph. Therapy. The small green shoots of hope that have started to spring up when I consider that my future may actually have the potential to be anything other than a write-off.

But even if Bren is one of my closest mates, there's still an element of holding myself back. I give him what I think he wants, which really amounts to easy banter. He doesn't want or need to know what the darkest corners of my soul look like. I'll reserve that for Philip, given I'm paying him handsomely for the privilege.

He gives a low whistle. 'Fucking hell. You in therapy—I never thought I'd see the day. Good on you, mate. So you're dating?'

'Kind of. I suppose so.' If *dates* look like lingering dinners at the Cotton House, our legs intertwined under the table, or champagne picnics on the beach at sunset that morph into skinny dipping and sea sex, or the strangest feeling that every meal, every drink shared, is a moment I wish could last forever. 'We have a thing this weekend, actually—as a couple. Some friends of hers are having a Christmas party, and I promised I'd go with her. Aide Duffy—do you know him?'

'We're going too,' Bren says, and relief rushes through me.

'Thank fuck. I think some of the Montagues will be there —not my idea of a relaxing night. How do you guys know each other?'

'I've met him a few times in passing at various fundraisers. He's a good guy. And Marls met Aide's wife Lotta a while ago through your girlfriend and it seems they hit it off.'

I ignore his use of the G-word. He won't get a rise out of me. 'Well, as long as you're prepared to act as a human shield if things get ugly,' I mutter instead.

He grins. 'I'm fucking massive. I can cover you easily, mate.'

The thing is, I know he means it. This may just be the only friendship I have that isn't transactional. He doesn't need anything from me, doesn't fear me, doesn't want to impress me. He just... likes me.

I'm not sure when that became so rare.

CHAPTER 40

Sophia

bviously, I'm nervous about engineering a social situation where Ethan meets my friends. I'd be nervous even if Nora and Theo weren't going to be at Lotta's party. After all, my gorgeous boss isn't much of a people person, and I'm fully aware that the walls he erects around himself when he's uncomfortable can come across as a bit... prickly, let's say.

But it's tough shit, because I'm damned if I'm going to fly solo at a fabulous Christmas party where everyone else will be loved up. Besides, he's so handsome! I want to hang off his lovely strong arm far more than I should. I want to show him off.

And I definitely want a masterful, Ethan Kingsley-branded kiss under the mistletoe at some point.

I've had to have a serious chat with my Seven parts about this burgeoning 'thing' between us. Philip guided me through it earlier this week. The story I tend to tell myself is that, when I next enter a romantic relationship, I'll only do it with someone who's done sufficient work on themselves.

I'm pretty strict about this, actually. I've put in the hours,

I've done the work, so why should I put up with someone else's unresolved trauma? That's not cruel, it's self-protective. I don't want to be with a guy who's clingy because he hasn't worked on the sources of his attachment style issues, or one who's avoidant for the same reason. I want to be in a relationship of two grown-ups who know how to parent themselves.

The teeny problem with this is that the vast majority of people, of course, have not done the work. As Athena loves to point out with irritating regularity, that's not actually a problem for me. It's a get-out clause. It allows me to remain free as a bird while absolving me of all responsibility for my lack of meaningful, non-transactional relationships.

Of course, Athena was just as bad as me until she met Gabe, except that her motivations were different. She was too scared that a boyfriend would eat into her precious time meant for achieving.

See? It's never about actions with my beloved Enneagram. It's always, always about motivation, baby.

Anyway, because I *have* done a lot of work on myself, and because uncovering my blind spots through wonderful epiphanies is part of how I get my dopamine kicks, my freakout when my double Seven confrontation hits is relatively contained.

Why double?

Because not only do I have to *sit* with uncomfortable feelings without running away to do something distracting, but because the *subject* of said uncomfortable feelings is that Ethan may, horrifyingly, be morphing from a bit of a mess, let's face it, into a guy who is doing the work and may—*may*—actually be a keeper, if he stays on this path.

Yeah.

Bummer.

The absolute worst part is that Athena called it that night at Alchemy.

Look, I'm not your average Seven. I've done the work. I may be a butterfly, but I understand the importance of feeling safe enough to land somewhere (in theory, at least). I may operate firmly in the happy half of the human emotional spectrum, but I make a real effort not to shy away from dark thoughts. A permanent fixture on my bedside table is a book literally called *Healing Through the Dark Emotions.*

See? I'm trying here.

The really, really scary part of all this is that I've seen enough chinks of light in Ethan's character, in his fragile nervous system, to realise that, fully healed, the guy may even be the perfect foil for this little Seven.

Calm to my chaos.

A safe container for my mess.

Consistency to my abandonment fear.

Stability that stops me from wanting to chase the next shiny thing.

Protective without controlling.

Okay, okay—I admit the last one may be a stretch. This is Eight we're talking about, after all. But it's not beyond the realms of possibility.

He told me one night in Mustique that my belief in him is the reason he has the strength, the courage, to undertake this journey of healing and self-discovery. That I'm the first person in his life to truly see him. To get past the walls and the protectors and the tests and truly see the man within.

And the worst—or best—part is that I think it might be true for me, too. The guy knows bugger all about this stuff. He's never heard of the Enneagram. He's super new to parts work. And he's still standing at the very base of the mountain range that houses emotional literacy and self-awareness and nervous system regulation. He's barely begun his upward climb.

Despite all that, *it feels like he truly knows me.*

And that is fucking terrifying.

~

LOTTA DUFFY, née Carlotta Montefiore-Charlton, has been the self-styled queen of parties since her parents infamously hired out the Hard Rock Cafe for her eleventh birthday, but she's mellowed a lot since meeting Aide, who's a grumpy self-made billionaire with a heart of gold. He comes from a pretty impoverished background, so excess and entitlement still don't sit well with him (his wife, a tech heiress, has no such problems). I'm embarrassed to say I've never made it to the home they share, the home Lotta's property development firm actually built for him before they ever met, but I haven't exactly spent much time in the UK in recent years.

Besides, it's somewhere out in the sticks. Only the certain knowledge that any party hosted by Carlotta Duffy is bound to be a hoot would have me venturing out of central London on a freezing night the week before Christmas.

And oh, has Lotta gone to town. Holy crap.

Ethan's driver pulls into a sweeping driveway, the trees and shrubs lining it all dotted with the prettiest, tiniest white fairy lights. The exterior of the house itself is modern and stunning, and when we enter, my gaze is immediately drawn to the enormous Christmas tree that dominates the vast, double-height hallway. It's decorated only in white and gold, the reflection of its twinkling lights muted on the fabulous poured concrete floor.

My tastes usually run a little more traditional, but I could totally get on board with this. And it's so much fun to imagine Lotta here. She's told me before how much she loves this place, even if her home growing up was full of Hermès china and Versace rugs, thanks to her flamboyant Italian mother.

The place is already filled to the brim with glamorous

looking people, and Shakin' Stevens is pumping out. I would have been very disappointed if Lotta's taste in music had matured beyond the cheese I remember from uni. I accept a coupe of champagne from the server hovering by the entrance and grin up at my handsome date. He looks so dashing with his hair combed back and his Tom Ford burgundy velvet smoking jacket. And, honestly, I don't care if they all hate him. I don't care if he gives them nothing, because why should he open up to strangers if he doesn't feel safe? I don't care if they think he's standoffish or arrogant or a corporate raider, because they haven't taken the time to get to know the man beneath. They may be my friends, but they haven't earned the right to judge him.

I have. And I know just how incredible he truly is.

'You ready for the Inquisition?' I ask him.

He leans in and kisses me on the forehead. 'For you, yes.'

I swoon. I know he'd rather be anywhere but here tonight, and I'm touched beyond belief that he's here for me. That he's comfortable enough with me to admit it.

'YOU HAVE A BEAUTIFUL HOME,' Ethan tells Lotta and her yummy husband, Aide, as we stand in their glorious kitchen. She met him during a community project and she actually thought he was a builder for a while and not a billionaire. He's definitely the kind of hyper-masculine guy who can pull off a tank top with aplomb.

'Thanks!' Lotta says with a megawatt smile. She looks gorgeous in a slinky, winter-white floor-length dress, her dark hair in huge, bouncy curls. 'I shouldn't take much credit for it —Aide had it before we met—but I will, because my company actually designed it.'

Aide rolls his eyes. 'Not that you had much input, clearly. You didn't even realise.'

She hits him on the arm. 'I worked it out in the end.' They stare at each other with hearts in their eyes.

'You know, Ethan's pad makes this place look positively over-furnished,' I offer. Aide has definitely gone for a minimalist mid-century vibe, but his home exudes a level of warmth that Ethan's simply doesn't have. I point to the riot of greenery tumbling down from a cool wooden platform suspended above the central kitchen island. 'Look, babe, those are called plants. P-L-A-N-T-S. They are living organisms known for their ability to improve air quality and promote emotional regulation.'

Before he can issue a snarky response, Lotta's face lights up at something behind me. 'Nor!'

Oh shit. So Nora and Theo are here.

This should be interesting. I squeeze Ethan's arm before turning around to greet them.

'Merry Christmas!' my friend Nora says, throwing her arms around me. 'Bloody hell, you look stunning!' She releases me and clocks Ethan, giving him a curt nod. 'Hi.'

'Hello.' His reply is cool but polite. Thank heaven no one tries to shake anyone's hand. I couldn't handle it if Nora left Ethan hanging. I really detest awkward situations like this.

'Merry Christmas, gorgeous,' Theo says, pulling me into a giant hug. He's wearing a hideous Christmas jumper of Rudolph that features a giant light-up red nose, but he still manages to look hot, his dark hair raked messily off his face. It would take a lot to make Theo Montague look ugly. He jerks his head in Ethan's direction. 'Spectacular dress. Pity you brought Ebenezer with you, though. Your taste in men is appalling.'

'Not cool, Theo,' I say warningly, but Nora's already on the case, tugging him to look at her with a hand on this arm.

'We talked about this!' she hisses. 'Remember what we tell the twins: if you can't say anything nice, don't say anything at all. If you can't behave in a way fitting of this lovely party, you can go and sit in the car.'

I'm grateful to her. Still, watching married couples arguing is always uncomfortable as fuck. Talk about a quick way to put a downer on the party. I glance up at Ethan to make sure he's okay. After all, I dragged him behind enemy lines. He gives me a little smile that I think he intends to reassure, but it doesn't reach his eyes.

'I'm going to see if Bren has arrived. I'll catch up with you shortly.'

With that, he kisses me on the cheek and backs away through the crowd.

I glare at Theo. 'Happy now?'

~

ETHAN

I make myself scarce for a good half an hour, taking my drink outside and finding a perch on the terrace, which is surrounded by outdoor heaters, thank fuck. I can't deny it's a beautiful plot of land Aide has here—very peaceful. After I've scrolled mindlessly for what feels like ages while pretending to check my emails and studiously avoiding the friendly, well-meaning smiles of anyone who wanders outside for a smoke, I force myself to brave the party again.

Here's the thing. I can't blame Theo for being antagonistic. The takeover is going full steam ahead, and I'm always going to be the big bad predator in the Montagues' eyes. I probably shouldn't have come, but here's the other thing.

I want to make this work with Soph. She's the one good thing I have in my life right now, the one relationship I haven't yet fucked up inexorably, despite a couple of excellent efforts. If I can do the work on myself, prove to her that I'm worth taking a proper chance on, then I'll do it. And letting her come to a party alone because I'm scared of getting a hostile reception isn't the way I want to move forward.

To my intense relief, I spot Aide and Bren in a quiet corner of the kitchen. I don't know Aide, but something tells me this is his preferred party mode: hanging out quietly and enjoying some decent one-on-one conversations, rather than flitting around like a social butterfly. Sophia mentioned on the way here that he's far more introverted than Lotta. In that, I suspect our couple dynamics—if I can presume to call them that—are alike.

'Mate!' Bren says, pulling me in for a bear hug as he whacks me hard on the back. His friendly mug and overt physical affection are far more welcome than I'd like to admit. I may hate socialising, but usually I'm sought out at whatever events I drag myself along to. I don't pretend for a moment that people want to converse with me, but they usually want something from me. Tonight, most people are oblivious to me and a handful actively despise me. I'm a spare part at best and a liability at worst.

I'm even more relieved to find that Marlowe is nowhere to be seen. I couldn't give a fuck about that threesome we had, but I'm sure Bren doesn't want any reminders of his past errors of judgement, not when he's so close to proposing.

'We're talking about work, I'm afraid,' Aide says sheepishly, holding out a bottle of champagne so he can refill me and Bren. He's on bottled beer.

'That's alright. There aren't many other people here who'd want to talk to me about work these days.'

Bren guffaws. 'You're not wrong.'

'What is it you do again?' I ask Aide. 'Medtech?'

'Medical data. I run a company called Totum.'

'Of course, that's right.' I know of Totum, in that it's a member of the FTSE 100 index. As I understand it, it allows all the trusts within the NHS to share patient data, which shouldn't be complicated and yet, thanks to the vagaries of our National Health Service, is near impossible.

'Aide's the real deal,' Bren says cheerfully. 'Not like us nepo babies.'

I grimace. 'I can imagine. How'd you get into it, anyway?'

He shakes his head. 'Nah, you don't want to hear that.'

'Actually,' I say, 'I'd like to. Here I am, running a family legacy I don't really give a shit about and ruining another family with a deal I'm honestly not even sure I want. So hearing from someone who's actually leading from the heart would make a nice change.'

Where the fuck did that emotional vomit come from?

Bren and Aide both stare at me.

'Fucking hell, Kingsley,' Bren says. 'Therapy's definitely loosened your tongue.'

I shrug. 'I think I'm just past caring. Honestly, I'd love to hear your story, mate.'

Aide sighs and embarks on his tale with the reluctance of someone whose ego is in no way tied to his—clearly extraordinary—achievements. He tells us about how there was a kid at his school who was being systematically abused by his father. Because the dad always took him to different emergency departments at different NHS trusts after he'd beaten the shit out of him, the pattern of abuse was never picked up on by the authorities.

The kid ended up dying.

Jesus *Christ*. My blood runs cold, and I feel sick to my stomach.

'That is so wrong on every fucking level,' I say gruffly.

'Yeah, it is,' Aide agrees. So he went on, while at uni, to build a software programme that could translate and share all patient data widely while remaining highly secure. Totum—the Latin word for *all*. Lotta's father, who is a well-known software billionaire, ended up seeding him his first round of capital. He dropped out of uni, and the rest is history.

I frown. 'Hang on—so you must have known Lotta before, no?'

'We met at her house once. She was sixteen, and I was a petrified twenty-year-old. She has no recollection of it.' He shakes his head fondly. 'Clearly, I wasn't memorable enough for her back then.'

I'm mulling over the rest of the story. 'You built a business because of a social injustice that you wouldn't—couldn't—let slide, and you've saved lives and totally overhauled the NHS.'

'I definitely haven't overhauled it, mate. It's still a fucking shitshow.'

'Agreed. But you made a real difference. You addressed a real problem.'

'Your hotels address a problem, too,' Bren argues. 'You may not be saving lives, but you're offering a service.'

'I suppose so.' I look down at my glass. 'Would you ever want to take early retirement?' I ask Aide. 'Spend more time with your family?'

He purses his lips. 'Nah. Not at the moment. I've stepped back from a lot of community responsibilities—Lotta taught me the meaning of the word boundaries when we got together. But the company itself—I really believe in it, you know? There's still so much work to do. I'm pretty evangelical about it. So no, I'd struggle to hand over the reins.'

I stare at him. 'Sounds more like a calling than a career to me.'

He shrugs. 'Feels more like it, too.'

What would that be like? To get out of bed every morning with a fire in your belly? To know that you're doing good, to be excited for the day ahead because you truly believe in your cause?

I have no fucking clue.

I run a company that I inherited.

I run it in the precise way that my father ran it, that he instructs me to run it.

He tells me to jump; I ask how high.

Since starting my sessions with Philip, I've begun to realise that many of the voices in my head are actually my father's voice. Sitting here listening to Aide talk about his calling, I realise I don't even know what my own voice sounds like anymore. Every decision, every strategy, every fucking thought has been filtered through *what would Richard want?*

And I'm finding, like with many discoveries in therapy, that once I am made to see something, I can't unsee it.

I may be the CEO of Kingsley Hotels, but it's very clear to me that I'm still the puppet, and Richard Kingsley is the master.

Ethan

Christmas arrives, and, with it, my biggest parenting test to date. Worse, Soph has gone to Athens for a few days to spend well-earned time with her folks. I can't resent her time away, but I miss her. The house feels particularly soulless at this time of year, and I must admit that Soph's mausoleum descriptor feels apt, even after the company I've hired to decorate the place for the holidays has done their work.

I sent Soph off with a bold token of my appreciation—a Spinelli Kilcollin ring stack in white and yellow gold, dotted with diamonds and emeralds. It reminded me of her when I saw it in Harrods: exceptional craftsmanship in playful packaging. It's serious jewellery, but I could imagine her wearing it as soon as I saw it.

She'd probably say it was another of my 'tests', and maybe she was right. A stack of rings is an intimate, serious gift. Would she freak out when I gave it to her?

The answer to that was an unequivocal no. She seemed thrilled with my gift to the level of being besotted, and I have to say it looks pretty sexy on her long, slim fingers.

It looked even sexier when said fingers were wrapped around my dick on her last day in the office.

She in turn gave me a very fine Brunello Cucinelli sweater and—shocker—a stack of self-help books for my bedside table. I'm sure I'll get around to reading them at some point. There are two on the Enneagram, whatever the fuck that is.

I spend as much of Christmas Day alone as I can, popping over to my parents' place in South Ken to make a brief appearance at their champagne reception before making my excuses. I've told them that Jamie is coming over to assemble his computer today, and I may have falsified the start time to engineer my escape from the godawful conversation with Dad and his self-satisfied golf buddies. I take a bracing walk around Holland Park, muttering *Merry Christmas* to the parents of all the rosy-cheeked kids who are inevitably road-testing new bikes and scooters. I eat alone—a lovely slice of the Beef Wellington that my chef, Davide, insisted on cooking for me yesterday before I sent him home.

What was it that irritating shit, Theo Montague, called me a couple of weekends ago? *Ebenezer*. I'd like to think I've never been miserly—not in the slightest—but I can't help but feel like Scrooge as I sit alone at the semi-festive dining table that Susan set for me yesterday: place mat for one.

It's fine, though. I'd rather be alone than enduring my parents' grotesque insincerity and their friends' congratulations over the Montague deal. Besides, I'm a bundle of nerves over my afternoon with Jamie. All the components for his PC are wrapped separately in jaunty red-and-white candy-cane paper, thanks to Topher, who procured the cheeriest paper he could find. I need to get this right, dammit. Building this thing is the perfect chance for us to find common ground, to enjoy some proper quality time together, as long as I don't sabotage myself.

I've spent several sessions now with Philip, unravelling the strands of my dysfunctional relationship with my only son. Somehow, my time away in Mustique with Soph gave me the perspective I needed to crack on. Jamie is the reason I agreed to put myself through this, after all. And I've known for longer than I'd like to admit that my relationship with Jamie won't fix itself.

I need to step the fuck up.

~

HE TURNS up with Elena around five, looking more animated than I've seen in some time.

'Merry Christmas, Dad! Did everything arrive?'

His lip service to basic festive etiquette has me chuckling. I'm not sure I've felt enthusiasm levels like his in a long while —except for when I've had Soph laid out before me, that is.

'Get in here, you little scamp. Merry Christmas.' I pull him into a hug and plant a smacker on his temple. He's too tall for me to kiss the top of his head. 'Yeah, everything's here, hopefully. I'm sure you'll tell me in about thirty seconds flat when you've ripped all the paper off like a savage.'

I release him and go to kiss Elena on both cheeks. As usual, she looks stunning and immaculately turned out. This is bittersweet. It's only the second Christmas since we separated, and the wounds were very new last year. We're far better apart; I know that much. I was never able to give my wife what she needed, but my burgeoning relationship with Soph tells me that Elena, through no fault of her own, was hopelessly ill-equipped to deal with my particular brand of lingering trauma. Most people would be, to be fair.

That is to say, we're better off apart. But it seems that the ache of being part of a splintered family feels all the more acute at Christmas.

My wife left me.

My parents disgust me.

And my son is so remote it sometimes feels as though we're speaking different languages.

I hold out a hand, gesturing for Elena to head through to the drawing room. 'What time did he wake up this morning?'

'This *morning*? Try lunchtime.'

I laugh out loud, and she grins at me. 'Silver linings.'

'Agreed.' God, there were Christmases when Jamie woke us in the dead of night, such was his level of hysteria over Father Christmas having been. Today, he's a world-weary fourteen-year-old with no reason to get out of bed. It's convenient, and helpful for Elena's sleep quota, but there's something sad about it, too.

'The main event was here,' she says. 'He's been asking me all day if it's time to come over yet.'

The flush of pleasure is instant, even if I'm only too aware that the attraction is not *me*.

'In that case, let's not keep the man waiting.'

I pour Elena a small glass of red and grab a can of Jamie's favourite brand of lemonade from the fridge. Elena and I perch on the sofa next to the tree while Jamie collapses on the rug. It seems odd that my ex-wife and I aren't exchanging gifts. All those years of lavishing her with expensive presents in desperate attempts to make her feel seen and valued and even cherished—all the things that my issues caused her to doubt.

Not sure I'll ever forgive myself for the myriad ways in which I've hurt the people I love.

I thought about getting her something, of course, but ultimately decided against it. It would only have embarrassed her, or worse, upset her.

I clear my throat. 'Alright, mister. Show us what all these mysterious components are, then.'

I have to say, I've been impressed with the way Jamie pitched this entire project to us. Elena and I have always been very strict on gift budgets. We don't ever want our son to have a false perspective on the value of money. So when he presented me with an Amazon gift list of components that ran to four figures, my first reaction was *hell, no.*

But Jamie surprised me with his ability to argue the concept: he'd need an extremely powerful computer for his Computer Science and Design Technology studies. This way, he argued, we'd take the pain of a hefty initial outlay but could replace the individual parts at will at a fraction of the cost. The environmental benefits weren't lost on me, either. And here we are.

He makes rapid work of tearing the paper off parcels ranging from the huge glass case that will house the entire machine to a tiny package containing the thermal paste and brushes. I hope he knows how to use all this stuff, because I haven't a bloody clue. His genuine *oohs* of happiness are all I need to hear, though.

'I'll be off, then,' Elena says, getting to her feet after he's laid out his unwrapped gifts in a reverent array. 'It looks terrifying!'

I see her to the door once she's done hugging Jamie. She's heading to Paris first thing tomorrow to see her parents. 'We'll see you in a few days.'

'Have fun.' She kisses me on the cheek. 'Rather you than me.'

I laugh drily. 'You're not wrong.'

'Seriously. I think it'll be good for you two.' And with a brisk little nod, she's gone.

WE TURN the kitchen island into PC Build HQ, unpacking every single component from its layers of protective packaging. For the next three hours, I find myself astonished as my fourteen-year-old son proceeds to put together a powerful computer with calm proficiency. It's truly staggering.

'I don't get how you know how to do this,' I tell him as I watch him apply thermal paste painstakingly.

'I watched a lot of videos.' His gaze remains steadfastly fixed on the job at hand. His attention to detail is really something.

'What's that for?'

'You need it as a layer between the CPU and the CPU cooler. But if I don't do it right it could overheat, so this was the bit I was most nervous about.'

'Well, you're doing a great job. Seriously, mate, I'm so impressed. This is incredible to see. You've obviously done your research.'

He halts his painting and glances up at me, a pleased grin on his lovely little face, and I feel as though my heart could burst through my chest with the amount of love I feel for my kid. Who knew that he would grow into this particular human being, with this personality and these interests? All I know is that my most important job as a parent is to encourage this, to give him the support and the agency he needs to pursue the dreams that make him *him*.

When the machine has been fully assembled inside its glass box, aside from the front panel, Jamie looks over at me, his face alight. 'It's ready.'

I give him a huge grin. 'Time for the moment of truth?'

'Yeah.' He grimaces and nervously plugs the computer into the socket on the island. 'I'm really scared.'

'I know. But it's not the end of the world if it doesn't work first time. We can tinker until it does, okay?'

'Okay.'

Frankly, it would be a miracle if this random selection of components turned on, but who am I to predict the outcome?

He presses the power switch on the side of the machine.

There's a taut moment of silence, and then the damn thing whirrs, springing to life. The fans light up and start spinning in multicolour.

'Holy shit!' Jamie shouts, and I laugh. Now's not the time for a swearing lecture.

'Look at it!' I say instead. 'It's incredible!' It really is. He's opted to have almost everything in white, and it looks positively futuristic, the soft RGB lighting of some of the components glowing prettily within the glass case.

'I'll be able to change the colours of the lights and everything,' he says. 'I might change it all to pale blue. That'd look nice and relaxing.'

I shake my head. 'Consider me gobsmacked. I can't believe you built that thing.'

'We built it,' he corrects. 'I would've been too scared to do it on my own.'

I've done fuck all, but I'll take it. We grin at each other. I feel giddy for him.

'What's next?'

'We need to take it up to my room and connect it to my monitor, but it should be fine. Oh, and I'm going to change these, too. They look ugly.'

He points to some flat black wires attached to one of the components. They are indeed ugly, at odds with the sleek white of everything else.

'Those ones came with the GPU, but I got spares in white just in case,' he explains. 'Look.'

He unwraps the replacements, which I agree will match the rest of the components far better. With the same efficiency, he disconnects the black cables from the part they're attached to.

Immediately, the entire computer powers down.

I freeze.

'What—did you just trip the fuse?'

'Ohmigod ohmigod ohmigod,' he chants. 'No no no no no.'

'What's happening?'

'I just tried to hot-swap them.' The pitch of his voice rises to panic mode, and he begins to jump around on the spot, shaking out his hands.

'What does that mean?' I can feel, hear, the panic in my own voice.

'I took them out while the power was on. I think I just fried the GPU.'

Now, I don't know much about hardware. But I know that *fried* is not good.

'What's the GPU?'

'That box. The graphics card.' He starts to cry. 'Ohmigod, I'm so stupid. So fucking *stupid*.'

'Is it fixable?' I ask, staring in horror at the now inert PC. The PC that cost over a grand and has just taken Jamie months to plan and almost three hours to assemble. I'm pretty sure the graphics card was the single most expensive compo-nent of this entire piece of kit.

'I don't know!' he wails. He presses the power button, but nothing happens. He shakes his head, tears rolling freely down his cheeks. 'I don't think so. I think it's fried.'

'You mean it's ruined?'

He presses his lips together and nods his head.

'Are you serious right now?'

My tone has him looking up at me, his eyes huge. 'I think so,' he says in a small voice. He presses the power button. Again. Again. Nothing. 'It would have caused a power surge.' His voice grows even smaller. 'I might have damaged the motherboard, too.'

I stare at him in horror. My devastation on his behalf flares bright and hot inside me. I want to pull him into a hug, to shield him from this brutal kick in the nuts. But within a fraction of a second it's ignited into something far uglier, something that makes me want to shake him in frustration.

'You told me you had this in hand. I've just watched you assemble the damn thing like a professional! How the fuck could you have been so stupid?'

He's shaking his head, shaking his hands, jiggling on the spot. 'I dunno, I dunno. It was an accident. I didn't think.'

'We've just spent over a grand on a piece of kit that you said you were ready for, and you've gone and blown the entire thing up with one stupid, childish mistake! Well, I'm not replacing the parts. Let that be a lesson to you. You can save up or wait till your birthday. Fuck's sake.'

I slam my hand down on the island and it makes an effective thwack against the marble. I'm not sure why I'm so furious. Maybe because I've seen how capable he is, how much he cares and how fiercely he can focus when he's really passionate about something. This gift was a massive gamble, and he's just ruined the entire fucking thing over a stupid fucking error, before we even got it upstairs! It's madness, that's what it is.

Jamie stares at me, tears cascading down his cheeks. His nose is running, and he wipes it with the back of his hand. 'I hate you! I hate you! Why do you always have to be so mean? You're a fucking psycho, just like Mum said!'

Before I can react, he turns on his heels and sprints out the door. I hear the panicked thud of his footsteps up the stairs, and then the slamming of his bedroom door.

I stand, shell-shocked, next to the inert ruins of his labour of love. What the actual fuck just happened? I feel sick to my stomach, but I nonetheless down the rest of my glass of red.

Slowly the anger abates in great, toxic waves, leaving me even more sickened.

His face. Those things he said. That name he called me.

He messed up. He made a stupid mistake in his excitement, and I tore him limb from limb. I chose to punish him rather than comforting him like any normal, emotionally healthy parent would. What the utter fuck is wrong with me?

Even when my heart was bleeding for the poor kid, my knee-jerk reaction was to eviscerate him. To humiliate him. To pile on. I was angry *for* him, but I unleashed my fury *at* him.

An image flashes into my mind.

My dad, excoriating me for my poor investment club performance in front of his mates. The loneliness I felt. The shame. The anger. The sheer, unnecessary cruelty of it all.

Jamie was already devastated. The little lad knew he'd done badly as soon as the bloody PC powered down. He had that sickening realisation that, with one tiny lapse in concentration, he'd undone all his painstaking work and probably ruined his new prized possession.

But I'm the one who's just ruined my son's Christmas.

CHAPTER 42

Ethan

I don't see or hear from Jamie all evening. He doesn't come down for the homemade sausage rolls Davide made specially for him, and when I knock on his door around ten, he shouts at me to go away in a voice so fragile, so tear-filled, that it has me choking up.

'I'm sorry,' I tell him uselessly, pressing my palm against the door as if it's his heart. 'I'm so sorry I lost my shit. We'll find a way to get it fixed, okay? I promise.'

Nothing.

While I want to bulldoze in there and try to make this right with every fibre of my being, I recognise that this is about my son's needs and not mine. I'm a fucking mess. I've been doing the work, putting in the hours. I've talked this over with Philip several times. And at the first sign of a fuck-up from my poor, beleaguered kid, I go fucking nuclear *on Christmas Day* and unleash all my issues on him.

I have a feeling Philip would tell me to have some compassion for whatever parts clearly want me to fail at having any kind of relationship with my son, but he can go to hell. If I'm incapable of showing compassion to my amazing kid, I sure as fuck don't deserve to show any to myself.

I pace around downstairs for another hour or so, cleaning up the wrapping paper mountain Jamie left and neatly sorting the packaging for all his PC parts, blasting some godawful Christmas music to drown out my thoughts of self-hatred. I can't call Elena. I can't put that on her. Besides, she'll be furious with me, and she'll probably insist on aborting her trip and coming over to collect Jamie.

I'm half delirious with heartbreak, so I do the only thing I can think of. I spoke to Soph first thing this morning to wish her Merry Christmas, but I message her now as I trudge up to my room.

> Let me know when you've finished dinner
> and are free to chat x

She calls me immediately, and I flop on my bed.

'Hi, babe! How's it going with your fellow titan of tech? You guys having fun?'

Even her voice sparkles. She sounds animated and relaxed and maybe the tiniest bit tipsy. She sounds like how people should sound when they're spending Christmas Day with their loved ones.

My voice cracks. It's hearing her voice, feeling her presence and her absence equally keenly. It's the knowledge of how gravely, how terrifyingly, I've erred.

'I fucked up big time. I lost my shit with him and I'm sick to my stomach over it. I don't know what to do.'

Silence. And then: 'Oh, honey. God, I'm so, so sorry. I know how much your plans for today meant to you.'

She floors me. No judgement. No lashing out. Of the two of us, I've messed up far, far worse than Jamie today. And while I couldn't find an ounce of compassion for him, here is Soph holding it for me.

I don't deserve it.

'Thanks.' I can barely get the words out.

'Hey, I'm switching to video. Okay?'

I hold the phone in front of me and watch as it connects. There she is. She looks like she sounds—tinkly and glamorous and flushed and gorgeous. I smile, despite myself, but her huge eyes shine with sympathy.

'You wanna tell me what happened?'

I sigh and fill her in tersely. Jamie's excitement. The successful build. His split-second error. And my disgraceful reaction. 'I did exactly what my dad used to do to me,' I say. 'I made him feel like making a mistake was unforgivable. I was so fucking cold.'

Her lovely mouth twists in sympathy. 'All those bodyguards really came out to play, huh?'

'Exactly. But honestly, even saying that feels like a cop-out. I can't blame some "parts". It's *me* who's the problem. He called me a psycho, and honestly, I can't blame him. I'm exactly like my fucking father.'

'You're exactly the opposite, and here's why.' She points a finger at the screen, and I see the ring stack I gave her sparkle. 'You think your father has wasted a moment on self-recrimination? Has he fuck. For a man like that, everyone else is the problem. You, on the other hand, have stepped up. You're doing the hard work. You're trying. You're only human, and let me tell you, babe, that until you learn to show yourself some compassion, you're not going to find it easy to extend compassion to anyone else.'

I suspect her words have a grain of truth to them, but like I said, I'm not in the mood for anything like self-compassion. Not even slightly. I push myself off my bed and walk to the window, looking out at the quiet serenity of my street. Everyone is behind closed doors, celebrating with their families. It's not until I look down at my own driveway that I realise the front gates are open.

'That's odd.'

'What?'

I glance back at the screen. 'The gates are open outside. I closed them after Elena pulled her car out.'

She frowns. 'Could Jamie have gone out?'

'Nah. I would have heard him. Hang on.'

I open my bedroom door and pad to the other end of the hallway. His door is wide open, as is the door to his ensuite across the room.

'Jamie?'

No answer. I shout it again. Phone in hand, I sprint downstairs and work my way through the ground floor. 'Still nothing,' I tell Soph.

'Could he be in the basement?'

'Yeah. Maybe.'

I head down to the obscene basement we had dug out a few years ago, when we bought this place. The home cinema is empty. Same for the games room. The door to the garage is ajar, and I walk through, where I stop dead between the Defender and the Aston.

The icy wall of fear that hits me almost steals the breath from my lungs. I feel like I've been winded. In shock, I turn to Soph.

'The Tesla's gone.'

CHAPTER 43

Ethan

'W*hat?* Fuck.' She looks as stunned as I feel.

'It's just—gone.' I stand rooted to the spot, looking stupidly around the garage as if it'll materialise.

'D'you think he—how would he...' Her voice trails off. 'Can he even drive? He's fourteen!'

'He knows how to turn it on and get it in gear.' Realisation hits me. 'Oh my god.'

'You really think he could drive it, though?' Her voice is quavery with panic.

'It's like driving a fucking golf buggy.' My throat is constricting with terror. I can barely get the words out. 'He could probably work it out. Fuck, he must have taken the keycard.'

The keycard tends to collect dust in a drawer in the hallway console, because I operate the car exclusively from my phone.

My phone.

'Wait.'

I minimise the video to one corner and pull up the Tesla app, staring at it in horror.

It shows a journey underway to Markham Street, SW3. Elena's house in Chelsea. ETA: eighteen minutes from now. He's already heading down Kensington Church Street. My heart begins to beat so hard in my throat that I might throw up.

'Oh my fucking god. He's en route to Elena's.'

'Jesus Christ.' Soph's eyes are wide with shock. 'Can you call the police?'

I think frantically, willing myself to calm down and adopt logic, but I can't. My body is screaming at me too loudly.

'If I call them, they'll arrest him, surely.'

'Yeah.' She falters. 'But at least he'd be safe.'

I'm already running back up to the ground floor for the keys to my Aston, which is far more analogue than the Tesla. She's right, of course, but I cannot have Jamie's already disastrous Christmas ending in flashing blue lights and a squad car.

I just can't.

'I'll follow him.' I wrench open the relevant drawer and grab the keys. Sure enough, the black Tesla keycard is notably absent. 'The roads will be dead tonight. I can catch him up.'

As I head back down to the garage, my brain is a whirling dervish of catastrophic thoughts. Jamie, crashing dead-on into a lamppost. Into another car. There will be god knows how many drunk drivers out there tonight. Him losing control and totalling a pedestrian. Ending up festering away in juvie.

'Oh my god.' My breath catches.

'Listen. This is central London. He won't be speeding. Can you see how fast he's going?'

I look back down at the app. He's doing twelve miles an hour down Ken Church Street. I choke back a sob-slash-laugh of relief. As long as he continues to drive like a granny, I can catch him up. But it's so easy to speed in the Tesla without realising. The acceleration on that thing is insane.

'Twelve miles an hour,' I manage, unlocking the Aston.

'Good. Good boy, Jamie. He'll be fine, babe.'

I'm fastening my seatbelt and pulling the door shut, turning the key in the ignition. The Aston purrs nicely to life, but right now I could really use the efficiency of an electric car. 'I don't know. He's not very street-smart. My fault.' It's an understatement. He gets himself to school on the Tube with a plain-clothed security detail trailing him, but he's far from a streetwise kid. The thought of him in this state, white-knuckling a powerful machine that he's years too young to drive out on the streets of central London is almost too painful to bear.

'Where the fuck did he learn to drive that thing?'

I tap my fingers impatiently on the wheel as I wait for the garage door to rise. *Come on come on come on.* 'We did a few rounds out in Wentworth when I first got it. He thought it was great fun.' Who knew our rare father-son bonding time over our new toy at the golf club would enable the worst moment of my life? 'Listen, I've got to call him.'

I go to end the video. Jamie, I can see, is turning onto High Street Ken.

'Wait.'

It's only the urgency in her voice that has me pausing. I glance down at her stricken face. 'What? I need to go.' I squeeze the wheel like I'm trying to strangle it. 'What a stupid little *fucker.*'

'Just—this is a cry for help, yeah? He's acting out because he's feeling devastated. Okay? He feels gutted and ashamed and unloved and utterly wretched right now, and he's probably scared shitless. I know you are, too, but please don't lay into him, babe. I'm begging you. He needs his dad right now now. His dad who loves him. Please try to come alongside him rather than coming down on him like a ton of bricks, yeah?'

I nod curtly. 'Yeah. Later.' I end the call and pull out onto Elgin Crescent. Thank fuck for deserted Christmas Day roads. If I floor it, I can catch him.

'Siri, call Jamie,' I order. As Siri puts the call through, I floor it down an eerily clear Ladbroke Grove. The dialling tone kicks in.

Pick up pick up pick *up*.

It goes through to voicemail—an automated one, because teenagers don't know voicemail exists. *Fuck*. I slap the wheel with all my might, and the car jerks. I'm crawling out of my body. I'm so terrified, so overcome by this maelstrom of terror and fury, that it's likely *I'll* be the one who ends up wrapped around a lamppost. I force myself to pull up onto the pavement with a noisy swerve so I can pick up my phone.

My best bet right now is a text. Of course he doesn't want to pick up the phone to me. I'm the monster he's taken such desperate measures to evade. Soph's words are ringing in my ear, and honestly, I'm grateful for them, because I could cheerfully wring his neck. But I force myself to take a second, just one second, before I unleash my horror and fury onto a text message.

She's right, as always. He's terrified. He hates me. This isn't Jamie. He doesn't act out. If anything, he shoves it all down. Makes himself small. Disengages.

I've already fucked up to an unbearable level this evening. This is my only chance to redeem myself as a father.

With shaking hands, I type. Thank fuck for autocorrect.

> I love you. You're not in trouble. Promise.
> On my way x

I pull the Tesla app back up, throw the phone down, and swerve back onto the road, cutting a red light to bomb down Kensington Church Street with indecent haste. I'm doing almost forty. Jamie's crawling along Queen's Gate.

I can do this.

I tell Siri to call him again.

Nothing.

I'm so close. Thank fuck, the lights at the bottom of Queen's Gate are green. I tear across the crossroads, and there he is, making his way down Onslow Gardens, a quiet residential street.

Oh Jesus Christ. Thank god. Thank god.

I beep my horn, and he speeds up a little. Shit. I lower my window. 'Jamie! Jamie, stop!'

We're approaching the Fulham Road. It's now or never. I grit my teeth, put my foot down, and switch to the other side of the road, which is deserted. With a pull on the wheel that I hope I've calculated correctly, I swing left and brake hard so that I'm facing horizontally across the junction with the Fulham Road, cutting Jamie off. Through my passenger window, the Tesla comes to a emergency stop inches from my vehicle, which I suspect is thanks to the car's auto-braking function and not to my son's ability to anticipate my maverick stunt.

I did it.

Jesus fucking *Christ*.

I grab my phone so I can unlock the Tesla and exit the Aston on shaky legs. Jamie's face is white as a sheet, his eyes huge and terrified. I wrench open the driver's door and squat down so I'm level with him.

'Oh, thank god,' I say before he has a chance to say anything. 'Thank god.' I wrap my hand around his neck and kiss the side of his head before I start gabbling. 'You're safe. You're not in trouble, okay? You're not in trouble. Every single thing that's happened today has been my fault. All of it. And I'm so fucking sorry.'

He starts to cry: the big, noisy sobs of a child. Because that's what he is. He may be a gangly six feet, but he's still just a kid. A little boy who needs his dad and doesn't understand why his dad can't fucking be there for him. He shudders something out that I don't understand.

'What, sweetheart?' I reach across and unfasten his seatbelt. 'What did you say?'

'I scraped the hubcap. I got too close to the kerb. I'm really sorry.'

I sob out a laugh as I help him out of the car. 'I don't care. I don't give a flying fuck about anything except for you. Not hubcaps, not PCs. You hear me?' I haul him against me, hugging him so tightly the poor kid probably can't breathe. But I'll take my chances.

With my arms wrapped around him like a vice, I rock us side to side. 'I love you so much. I'm so sorry about earlier. You were right. I was a psycho, and I'm so deeply ashamed of myself. You're absolutely bloody perfect, and I love you, and I'm so sorry I don't tell you enough. You're the most important person in my life.'

'I love you too.' He lays his head on my shoulder, his skinny little body still wracked with sobs. 'I was really scared.'

'I know, mate. I know. I'm not surprised. But I'm here now.' I release my grip a little so I can pull back and look him in the eye. 'What do you say we get out of here?'

He glances over at the Aston, still blocking the junction. A bloke trying to turn into Onslow Gardens has got out of his car and is yelling *wanker* at me. I couldn't give a flying fuck.

'Will I need to drive the Tesla back?'

I honk out a real laugh, relief coursing over me in waves. 'No way. Not on your life. I'll park it here for the night. I'll jog down and grab it tomorrow. Right now, we should go home and heat up some sausage rolls. And then whenever you're feeling up to it, maybe tomorrow, we can do some triage on the PC and work out what replacement parts I need to order for you, okay? We'll get it sorted, I promise.'

His face crumples at that, his chin wobbling. 'Okay. Thanks, Dad.'

As I gently steer him onto the pavement so I can move the cars, he says with another look at the Aston, 'You drove like you were on *The Rookie*. That was fire.'

I think that's a compliment.

AFTER A QUICK TEXT to Soph to tell her all is well, I make us a midnight feast of hot chocolate and reheated sausage rolls. We eat them tucked up under a blanket on the sofa in the main living room so we can enjoy the tree while we watch *Arthur Christmas*. We may both be shattered, but I'm aware we need some serious decompression time.

He chuckles his way through the movie, some of the colour returning to his cheeks, but I mainly sit there and watch him. I'm still a mess. That could have gone so badly wrong. A kid driving a car, for fuck's sake. Seeing his journey pop up on the app was the most terrifying moment of my life. I can't believe we're here, that we got through this, that he's emerged from his harebrained adventure unscathed—physically at least.

I suspect we'll both bear the emotional scars for quite some time.

One thing's for sure: I need to text Philip first thing tomorrow and plead for an emergency session. It's weird how fast it's become my instinct to turn to him for help, but, god knows, I can't process a shitshow of this scale by myself.

CHAPTER 44

Ethan

I put Jamie in my bed with me last night. No way was I letting him out of my sight. He may no longer be a flight risk, but I don't want him feeling abandoned for a second. He slept like a log, the crash of all that emotional devastation and adrenaline wiping him out, but I lay there and stared at him for a long time. A couple of hours, maybe.

Last night crystallised a lot of things for me, but mainly that I can't let this kid move through life for one more day without understanding what he means to me. I won't.

I make him pancakes, which he eats at the island. He's fixated on the PC and has already looked up several YouTube videos on how to isolate the broken parts.

'I think I might need to replace the GPU and the motherboard,' he says, wrinkling up his face as if he's scared to say it out loud.

I nod. 'That's okay. Honestly. We can order the new parts as soon as we know for sure. I'll sit with you while you work it out, if you want.'

He spears a piece of pancake and dunks it in the maple

syrup that I had Davide pick up for him. 'But you said last night that I needed to be taught a lesson.'

He says it so forlornly, so resignedly, that the pain of hearing it almost brings me to my knees. I flinch.

'I shouldn't have said that. It was very cruel of me. It's no excuse, but I was absolutely gutted for you, and I lashed out instead, and I'm thoroughly ashamed of myself. I regret it so much. You were right to be angry and hurt.'

The nod he gives me is small, but if what I just said in any way landed with him then I'm grateful. Soph was correct last night. My dad never wasted a moment validating me or apologising to me or ruminating on his many, many failings. And it strikes me that, if fucking up as a parent is a very human crime, making it your kid's fault is downright evil.

'I mean it.' I take a sip of my coffee and twist my body so I'm facing him. 'Everyone makes mistakes, and my humiliating you over a simple error was absolutely not okay. You need to know that you can mess up and it'll still be okay. I'm your dad. If you can't count on having me on your side, then who can you count on? Except for your mum. She's amazing, and I've always been grateful that you have her.'

His face softens. 'Yeah, she is.'

'But having one great parent doesn't make it okay to have one shoddy one, and I'm going to do better, I promise.' I make myself press on. There's a balance, I think, in being a parent. I've already proven how damaging it can be to erect walls, but, while vulnerability is important, I can't totally fall apart. It's crucial that he knows I'm strong enough to handle my own shit. He needs a parent who thinks they're a victim just as much as he needs a parent who's totally walled off, which is not at all.

I should know.

I have one of each.

'I need you to hear me, mate. Every single problem we've had has been down to me, not you. I have a lot of issues from my own childhood, and I've never really tackled them. But I'm doing a lot of work on myself now, and it's helping. Most of the time,' I add sheepishly, and he gives me a small grin. 'Grandpa was a nasty piece of work when I was little, a really tricky character, which I think you know, but it's taken me a long time to work out that that's on him, and none of it was my fault.' I swallow, attempting to lodge the giant lump in my throat. 'So that's why I'm going to work so hard to make sure you know none of *my* shit is *your* fault. Absolutely none of it. And I'll do better. I promise.'

He stares at me, eyes wide, face open and trusting. 'Okay.' He stuffs an enormous piece of pancake in his mouth. His inability to hold a grudge is staggering, and I know we have a long road ahead, but I have no idea what I've done to deserve this level of openness from him given my track record. I clear my throat.

'I don't want to get heavy, and we should go and run those tests on your PC when you've finished your pancakes, but I wanted to say this, so it's out in the open. Grandpa really messed me up, and I think I've been so worried that I'd mess you up that I've tried to stay away too much. You have such a fantastic mother, so I think I leant on that, but I've been scared to get close because I didn't think I deserved you, really. I thought I was too broken to be any good to you.'

He stares at me, growing visibly alarmed, and I press on. 'I know now that I'm not broken, that I'm strong enough to be the dad you deserve, and I'm going to prove it to you every day. And I'm sorry from the bottom of my heart for not being around as much as you might have liked, and I need you to know that none of it was to do with how much I love you. Because I love you more than anyone else in the world.' I lean over and ruffle his already tousled hair. 'Do you hear me?'

'Yeah,' he says with all the enthusiasm any teenage boy would muster in the face of emotional diarrhoea from a parent figure.

I chuckle. 'It's okay. Sorry for getting weird. But I'm going to show you. We have a lot to catch up on, don't we?'

'I suppose.' He wriggles. 'Can we go to the driving range this afternoon?'

I sit up straighter. 'Absolutely. Did you bring that new driver your mum got you?'

He smiles, and it's a real smile. 'Yeah. It's fire.'

'Great. You can show me what you've got.'

'You sounded very distressed in your text messages,' Philip says over my computer screen. He's out of town for Christmas but has, bless him, readily agreed to an emergency Boxing Day Zoom with me. Jamie is watching *Top Gun: Maverick* for the millionth time down in the cinema room after what even I would admit was a highly successful trip to the driving range. He got on brilliantly with his new driver, and I wasn't too shabby, either.

I take a deep breath and recount the story as efficiently as I can: my high hopes; the successful build; Jamie's fatal error; my nasty meltdown; the car chase; my rescue of him. My heart rate is ratcheting up even as I relive it.

'I'm so sorry,' Philip says faintly. 'It sounds like you gentlemen have had quite the time of it. That must have been very upsetting for both of you.'

'Yeah.' I wipe my palms along my jogging bottoms. 'You can say that again.'

'How is Jamie doing, first of all?'

'He seems okay. He slept well last night, which is more than I can say for myself. He seems encouraged by the fact that we're sorting his PC out. And he was worried about my telling his mum, but I know she'll be far more furious with me than him.' I let out a shaky little laugh. 'I have to say, the more I learn about this stuff, the more paranoid I get that every instance like this is going to cause deep and lasting trauma for him.'

He pauses and looks downwards. He's probably tapping his specs on his knee, out of sight. 'That's a valid concern, and that's very possibly a protective paternal part talking. You do have one, you know, Ethan. I hear it a lot when you speak. Your Papa Bear part, for want of a better term, is always going to be extremely protective of your child. I think our parenting parts tend to be some of the most ferocious I've encountered in my years of practice.

'All of which to say is that Jamie's lucky that he has a father with those parts. It's not clear to me that your father did, from what I've heard. So you are not your father, and Jamie is not you. You're doing the work, and he has access to a wealth of resources to help him process all of these experiences when he's ready. But, more importantly, he is gaining more and more access every day to his father's Self Leadership, and that's a beautiful thing.'

I screw up my face. I've heard Philip talk about the Self, that higher piece of us that's not a part, but I'm not sure about the *Leadership* bit. Soph referred to the Self in Mustique as *divine energy*, which made me want to run for the hills. That's far too woo-woo for my liking.

My confusion must be evident, because he carries on. 'Think of the Self as your wisest boardroom member, the one who sees the big picture, who can think long term, who doesn't panic or lash out. Your parts can be more like reactive junior execs who have a short-term agenda. Self will listen to them, but he's not ruled by them. He leads from an adult, centred place.'

'I'm not sure that describes my parenting style recently,' I quip without humour, but he shakes his head.

'It's a journey. And what you have to know is that your Self is always there. Sometimes it just gets drowned out by the noisier voices. But as your parts learn to trust you more, you'll access that Self Leadership more and more easily. But first, do you want to tell me how you're feeling? Any observations you want to share? It's absolutely to be expected that you'd still be very shaken up after what you've been through.'

This is what I've come to expect and appreciate from Philip. It's why I messaged him. He's someone I can unload on with no guilt of overburdening him, no fear of judgement. More than anything, he makes it acceptable for me to have all my feelings. He makes them all feel normal, I suppose. And being made to feel normal when you're second-guessing every fucking thing about yourself is seriously underrated.

So I attempt to vomit out all my thoughts, my fears, in one big, messy outpouring. Obviously, there's the lingering feeling that we dodged a bullet, that Jamie could have been injured, or worse. The *what if* feeling that haunted me last night when I was trying to chase sleep. There's an enormous amount of guilt, not only at my outburst, but at the fact that I drove my son to such extreme behaviour in an attempt to seek comfort from his mother. It still makes me sick to my stomach that I caused him such intense pain.

On top of all that, there's, honestly, some residual fury at Jamie for taking such a stupid, unjustifiable and overdramatic risk. Why the fuck couldn't he have called an Uber? This emotion I've been keeping a tight lid on. I'm absolutely not about to unleash my wrath on him again.

Let me see: there's the worry that I'm basically my father, that when push comes to shove, I care more about saying and doing whatever the fuck I like than protecting my son. And there's an analyser who's in full panic mode. He feels a bit like a White House advisor who's been told he has to defuse a bomb with little to no information as to when and where it'll strike. As though this is all an impossible puzzle that he surely must be able to intellectualise his way through. I'm judging myself for failing on that front, to be honest. I relay all this to Philip as best I can.

'If you can, take a moment to thank your parts for being so ready to share,' Philip says. 'I'm sensing a lot of fear and vulnerability, quite rightly, so I appreciate that there's a lot going on in there.' His mouth quirks into a ghost of a smile. 'I'm not sure you're aware of this, but at some point, you stopped referring to feelings and started referring to parts, which is a sign that, even in the midst of all the emotions you must be going through, you can unblend from these parts enough to observe them.'

Huh. I hadn't noticed that, and honestly, I'm surprised that I've done that. I make a non-committal noise.

'Is there a name you'd like to give that White House part? The Fixer? The Problem Solver, maybe?'

'The Fixer sounds about right.' It's true. I pride myself on being able to fix things. I'm an established business leader overseeing a complex takeover, for god's sake. That I'm so out of my depth and so utterly fucking oblivious when it comes to my son is the thing that galls me most of all.

WE WORK THROUGH MY PARTS, one by one, and as we do, I feel a sense of something that's not quite peace settle over me. Nor is it lightness; more an absence of weight. We've gone through an hour already, but Philip tells me we'll take as long as I need, and I feel unfathomably grateful to this kind, wise man who's giving up his precious family time to deal with me and my fuck-ups. If Self Leadership really is the wisest, most adult board member, then I'd hire Philip Hicks for that role any day of the week.

'Let me ask you a question,' he says now, having worked through every voice in my head. In my mind's eye, they're all slumped, exhausted but somehow less burdened, around my boardroom table. 'If you continue on your current path, what do you think will happen?'

I blow out a loud, tired breath. Fuck knows. 'Um, a haphazard relationship with Jamie at best—well-meaning, but probably with a lot of fuck-ups on my part. A successful merger—in the market's eyes, at least—and, I dunno, same old, same old.' I trail off.

'And how does that make you feel?'

'Exhausted. Defeated. Like, I don't know why I'm bothering.'

'That's right, that's right. So, another question for you, then. What does your heart tell you Jamie needs right now?'

I sit up straighter and try to focus. 'He needs to know I'm there for him unequivocally. That he can be uniquely himself and I'll be there every step of the way, and that I love him unconditionally.' As soon as I say the words, it all feels very clear. Very straightforward.

'That's very beautiful,' Philip says softly. 'What else?'

'I dunno—more physical time together, I suppose. Which is tough because of our custody arrangement. And when Elena hears about what's happened, she will *not* be up for that. But I want to spend more quality time with him, not just downtime at the weekends when we're both knackered. He's in therapy, you know. I think I told you that. And I know now that it's me who needs to do a lot of the work, but still—I'm wondering if we want to do something jointly. Something like this. Even if it would be excruciating.'

'That's definitely possible. And yes, parts of it will be confronting, but parts can be beautiful, too. There are even little rituals that we do in the IFS space where a child can pass some of the burdens their parents have put onto them back to that parent.'

'Shit. That would be a lot of rituals.' And unspeakably uncomfortable.

He smiles encouragingly. 'It can wait until you're both ready. So I'm hearing: more quality time; more emotional connection and opportunities for you to demonstrate your unconditional love and support for him; and possibly even some kind of joint therapy as a way to process some of this shared trauma you may have.'

I nod. It sounds terrifying and insane and borderline undoable, but also exhilarating. Hopeful.

'If you feel comfortable, I'd like you to check back in with your ice king part, if you have access to him. Ask him what he would say to all this when he's at his most fiercely protective, holding up all those walls to keep you safe.'

I cock my head and try to consider. I can feel him more clearly than I can envisage him—an icy, impenetrable wall at the head of my boardroom table. 'He says *fuck, no.*'

He chuckles softly. 'He's always been your most extreme bodyguard, from what I've seen, anyway. And yet, when you were telling me what you felt in your heart that your son needs from you right now, I didn't hear him at all.'

I go stock still, because he's right. And that icy guy may be there, but it's as if he's off duty. He's observing, not wading in.

'What I did hear,' Philip continues, 'was courage, when it comes to doing right by Jamie. Clarity of purpose. *Compassion*. Those are all hallmarks of Self Leadership—in fact, they're three of the eight Cs, as I've mentioned before. That calm, clear voice is your Self, and it's not making decisions from a place of fear. It's making decisions based on what is *right*.'

I hum my agreement, because that's how I do feel, weirdly. I feel calmer.

'So, in that vein, I'm going to ask you: what would it feel like to prioritise Jamie over every single other thing? Not just your relationship with him for your own sake, but building him into a secure, Self-led adult for his sake?'

I shrug, feeling reckless and cavalier and everything else. My heart rate has slowed, but I'm filled with a sensation of vitality. Of possibility. I wave my hands in the air in a gesture of surrender. 'Fuck knows. Sack in my job, tell my dad where he can shove Kingsley, pull Jamie out of school, and go on a boys' trip somewhere amazing where all we do is bond and make incredible memories together for a decent amount of time.'

Through the screen, Philip's smile is megawatt.

'But I can't, obviously.' My shoulders slump, and I let my head hang, too. 'I have a lot of responsibilities, and a major transaction to complete, and an ex-wife who categorically won't let me steal her son away.' *And a brand-new girlfriend I can't fathom being away from,* but I don't say that.

'I'm curious—what if those obstacles weren't as fixed as they seem? What would it look like to explore whether this is actually impossible, or just difficult?'

As a CEO, I appreciate his question. Treating assumptions as fact is such a common error, caused by blind spots and an unwillingness to question the premise, and such an act is often the precursor to defeatist thinking and a failure to act boldly.

I sit up a little straighter. 'I mean, they're not impossible. They're just—messy.' I turn over the issues in my mind. So many moving parts. 'Our takeover of The Montague Group. The visibility—the market would go ballistic. The financial press would have a field day. The investors I convinced to back me would have my guts for garters.' I trail off. What a mess I would make. It doesn't even bear thinking about.

There's a moment of silence.

'I'm interested to know,' he says slowly, 'where *you* see your responsibilities. Different parts may be carrying different responsibilities, but if it's possible to access some of that Self energy, I'd like to know where *you* see your primary responsibility.'

I let my eyes drift closed. The first time I did this in a session, it was excruciating. I felt stupid and vulnerable and I couldn't stop worrying about what Philip must be thinking of me. But now it comes a little more naturally, and it helps me to shift away from the visual noise of his face and my twinkling Christmas tree and focus on what matters.

'Jamie,' I say flatly. 'There's nothing else. No one else.' All there is is a role at the helm of a company I dislike, founded by a man I've found the courage to despise, and a woman in my life who has been the starting point for every single gift that this work has given me. She's far too special to ever turn my back on, to ever risk losing... but she's for me.

She may want me, but she doesn't need me. Not like Jamie does. I strongly suspect she's my happy ending, and I can't think like that yet.

Not when I owe it to my son to give the rest of his life the absolute best shot it has of being happy and healthy and secure.

Philip is silent. When I open my eyes, he's smiling. It's a proud smile, almost fatherly. He presses his lips together and gives me a little nod.

Clarity.

That's what he said he was hearing when I spoke about Jamie.

Thoughts are pouring into my head now, clear and true. It's as though someone's turned on a tap.

My parts have agendas. They have responsibilities, driven by fear and shame and every other negative emotion. They have strong feelings about the things they should be doing.

But *I* only have one agenda. One responsibility. One true purpose.

If I'm going to act, I need to get hold of Miles Montague.

As soon as possible.

CHAPTER 45

Ethan

M iles' reply to my panicked text message is as unwelcome as it is predictable.

Merry Christmas. But you must realise you're the last person I want to hear from over the holidays

Of course I am.

I get that, of course. But I wouldn't ask if it wasn't absolutely critical. Also - I have a proposal for you that I really think you're going to want to hear

Short of you walking away from our company, that's highly unlikely

But if you insist

Little does he know.

I can come over tomorrow?

The gods of timing are on my side. Jamie's due to spend the day with some school friends at a place that offers go-karting and gaming arcades.

> We're up in Chipping Norton this week. But I can talk tomorrow morning if you're sure this can't wait.

> I'm sure. I'll drive up. See you then.

That makes sense. Miles has had a place in the Cotswolds for a few years. My stomach roils unpleasantly. Interrupting his family time to have this conversation makes the prospect even less appealing, but needs must. I have a very clear objective, and I won't let a lack of courage stand in my way.

Not anymore.

MILES' Cotswolds pad is fucking amazing, a beautifully proportioned Georgian sandstone manor standing in what look like lovely grounds, even if the trees are starkly bare. As I ease up the driveway, the gravel crunching under my wheels, I'm met with a painful reminder of how Christmas can look when someone gives enough of a shit to make an effort. The firs outside are dotted with white fairy lights, there's an enormous red and green wreath on the front door, and a tree twinkles through one of the long sash windows. It's also a reminder that I'm very much an unwelcome interloper.

Miles meets me at the front door, every inch the country squire in forest-green chinos and a beige sweater with leather elbow patches. He may look far more undone than I'm used to seeing him in London, but he also looks distinctly underwhelmed to see me. Nevertheless, he extends a hand and we shake.

'Sorry to disturb your family time. I appreciate you seeing me. I'll make this as quick as I can.'

'You're lucky that I have my folks and *all* my in-laws here and the twins are particularly grizzly today. You're almost looking like the appealing option.'

I know from previous conversations that Saoirse is from a large and chaotic Irish family. I respond to his olive branch with a chuckle and follow him away from the cacophony of voices and a child crying and across the hall to what is a lovely study overlooking the gardens. The wall-to-wall bookshelves are a rich burgundy, a fire is crackling in the grate, and a pair of wing-backed armchairs flank it. The overall effect has me thinking about Soph's distaste for my brand of minimalism. I find a lack of clutter eases my mind, helps me focus—but perhaps I should warm my place up a little.

Before the fireplace stands a small coffee table laden with a pot of tea and a plate filled with mince pies and shortbread. However displeased Miles is to see me, good hospitality clearly runs in his veins.

We take our seats, and he gets to pouring.

'How's Sophia?'

'She's great. She's back in Greece for the week.'

'Theo tells me you two are dating.'

I nod. 'That's right. We are.'

'She's fantastic.' His tone is mild, but I swear I hear an element of judgement. *Don't fuck it up when you don't deserve her in the first place.*

'No argument here.'

He hands me a teacup. 'So, what couldn't wait until New Year?'

Fuck knows where I should start. But Miles is known for being a straight shooter, and I owe it to him not to waste his time. I blow out a breath.

'It's been a tricky few days. I've had a bit of a crisis with

Jamie, and it's been a real wake-up call. It's been a long time coming, really.'

He glances up from adding his milk, a flicker of interest in his eyes. 'The crisis, or the wake-up call? And I'm sorry to hear that.'

'Thanks. And both, I suppose. I've been harbouring suspicions for quite some time that I'm not on the right path. I suppose you don't want to hear that.'

He makes a scoffing sound, and I force myself to continue. I had this all planned out in the car, but it's proving harder than I thought to get it out.

'Bottom line is, I have a lot of issues with my father, which we touched on briefly at the Golden Keys. I've been more and more unhappy about working my arse off to continue his legacy, which is essentially building an empire in ways I don't wholeheartedly approve of.'

I risk a glance at him, because he won't relish hearing about my delayed crisis of conscience. He sits back, expression inscrutable.

'Go on.'

'While I've been letting Dad fuck me up the arse, I've also been really struggling with Jamie. Things are bad, but Soph's got me into therapy, and it's—it's really helping. But not enough, because I was a shitty father to Jamie on Christmas Day. I blew up at him for something stupid, and he stole my Tesla and tried to drive to his mum's.' My voice cracks a little, and I clear my throat.

Miles' eyebrows wing up. 'Fucking hell.'

'Yeah. I got to him in time, thank fuck, but it was a big wake-up call.' I gesticulate with the hand not holding my teacup. 'The truth is, I don't know what the fuck I'm doing, but I do know that my loyalty needs to be to my son and not my father. Full stop. Starting now.'

'I can't disagree with any of that.'

'I need to put in some proper work with Jamie. Get away with him. I'm turning into my dad, basically, and it terrifies me. I can't keep perpetuating this cycle of narcissism, like you said.'

His voice is soft when he speaks. 'I never said you were a narcissist, mate. On the contrary. But if your dad is, then you owe him diddly squat.'

I nod. 'It's a complex issue, obviously. I haven't been in therapy for long, but I'm beginning to realise that he has a very unhealthy hold over me. It must seem from where you're sitting that I'm crazy to have any loyalty to him at all, but it's not that easy. He's—he's used a lot of nasty tactics to keep me in line—I'm talking carrots *and* sticks—and I'm only starting to understand just how well they've worked.'

Miles puts his cup down and leans forward, elbows on his knees and fingers steepled. 'That's the thing with narcissists. They can be very bloody clever, and they really fucking weaponise their love—or your perception of their love, at least. Because, of course, the plot twist is that the love doesn't actually exist. It's all a mirage, a projection on our parts.'

I study him. 'Did your ex-wife do that?'

'Like a fucking Olympian. But I'm not that smart. I didn't work any of this out until she walked and showed me and Bea her true colours.'

'That's rough. I can't even imagine.'

His smile is tight. 'Yeah. But it's hard to have perspective when it's someone you love. You think that's what love is, at least. I also choose to believe that it says we're fundamentally decent, trusting people who judge others by our standards. I don't know. It fucks with your head, that's for sure.'

'Yeah.'

'I'd be happy to share my encyclopaedic findings on the subject another time. I practically have a PhD in it. Let's see. They make you feel unworthy of their love. You know, the love that doesn't actually exist. Their blowing hot and cold creates so much emotional chaos that you start being a total control freak in every other part of your life, just to give yourself the semblance of control.'

I stare at him. 'Jesus.'

He laughs without humour. 'Yeah. Of course, it would have been worse for you. I was a grown man who showed precisely zero judgement of character. Allegra totally sucked me in. But you were just a kid. I reckon Richard could really fuck someone up if he chose to.'

I sit there, frozen. This is an odd conversation to be having with my long-time nemesis, a man who hates my guts right now. Perhaps he's just avoiding his noisy in-laws and cranky toddlers, but I'm staggered he's being this open with me. This generous, when he has no reason to be.

'Something like that. And when I behave like a dick to Jamie, I'm acting the exact same way as he did to me.'

He grimaces. 'Like I said, that's rough, but you're clearly not a narcissist. So your reasons for doing that will be different, and that's for you to work out with your therapist. But you were saying. About choosing him over your dad.' He takes a bite of his shortbread finger, watching me as he chews.

'I want out,' I say flatly.

Fucking hell.

I've finally said the words aloud to my counterpart in this excruciating deal, to the man whose family, whose entire company, I've put through hell these last couple of months.

I push on. 'Out of the deal, out of Kingsley Hotels, out of the industry. I don't know what the hell I want to do, except spend some time with my kid and find something to be passionate about that's not running Richard Kingsley's empire for him.'

He stares at me. There's a moment of stunned silence before he begins to cough as he chokes on his shortbread crumbs. 'Jesus, mate,' he protests when he's recovered. 'I mean, I'm all for epiphanies of the heart, but what the fuck? You can't walk away from this. It's way too far down the line for that—the market would crucify both our share prices.'

I force myself to hold his gaze as I shake my head. 'Not if I appointed you as CEO of the combined entity.'

CHAPTER 46

Ethan

'You're insane. Certifiably insane.'

'Maybe,' I say slowly. 'Maybe I'm insane to have come here and shown my cards to a guy who's always had good reason to detest me. Maybe this will all blow up in my face, but honestly? This is the first time in a long time that I've felt good about my actions.'

He's still staring at me in utter shock and bewilderment.

'You're serious.'

'Deadly. I can't go on like this.'

'You're actually considering walking away from everything you guys have built and handing it all over to me?'

'Well, first of all, I didn't build it. My father did. I'm just his evil henchman. Secondly, I don't see it as walking away from anything. I'm walking towards what's important, probably for the first time. And thirdly, why the hell shouldn't I hand it to you? You're by far the most qualified person of anyone to lead the combined entity, and that includes me.' I grin at him, and I suspect it's maniacal. I feel maniacal.

He barks out a shocked laugh. 'You're off your rocker.'

'You betcha.' I sit back and cross my ankle over its opposite knee. I've been tied up in knots since last night over having this conversation, but I'm enjoying myself immensely. I suspect Miles is right and I have officially lost the plot. But the sensation of having zero fucks left to give is really fantastic.

'Jesus Christ.' He drags a hand down over his face. 'I'm not sure I've outright hated you, mate—like I said, you're not a total egomaniac like your old man—but I've always found you a bit of a cold fish. You never give an inch.'

I nod, feeling fatuous. 'I know. My therapist has had a lot to say about that.'

'I bet they have. They'll probably be able to buy a nice gaffe in the South of France by the time they've finished sorting you out. Fuck—sorry. That was uncalled for.'

But I'm chuckling. 'I'm sure he's counting on it.'

'Look. You've really taken me by surprise, mate. People don't usually take me by surprise, but consider me gobsmacked. But, at the very least, I can tell you're serious about this. In that respect, I trust you. So honestly, if you have an idea for how the hell this harebrained scheme of yours should work, then please enlighten me.'

'It's like this. Of course I realise how shitty it is for me to walk away from a transaction I spearheaded. How much of a let-down that would seem to investors. But consider it this way. I'm a father, and I have a child in crisis. As far as I'm concerned, he has to be my priority. This is an emergency situation. This time it was stealing a car and joyriding. If I don't act, what could it be next time? Drugs? Cutting himself? I hate to think.

'If he was physically ill, there'd be no question that I'd remove myself from my job to focus on his recovery. Just because it's his mental health that's at stake, doesn't make it any less important.'

'Agree wholeheartedly.' He nods. 'And, for what it's worth, the market should take that as a valid reason. A family health emergency should be respected as a reason for making drastic decisions.'

'I'm glad you think that.' I square my shoulders. 'And if I was leaving the firm in the lurch, then I'd definitely feel more conflicted. But let's be honest here. We're acquiring The Montague Group because our organic growth is shite. Your strategic positioning is far superior to ours. And who's at the helm of that growth engine? You. I'd be delusional to argue that I'm more qualified to lead on that front than you. All I'm good for is slashing your jobs, which, honestly, is something I was never fully comfortable with in the first place, even if I knew it was the best way to get the market on board.'

He's shaking his head at me in disbelief. 'You cheeky fucker.'

I shrug. 'I don't pretend to be as passionate about our people as you and your dad are. I'm more cut-throat, and I suspect you're overly emotional. *But* I don't know for sure what I think, because my father's voice has been in my head for so long that it'll take a while to articulate my own values.'

'Seems like you're making a good start,' he mutters, taking a sip of tea.

I ignore the low-key compliment. 'So what do you think?'

'Fuck. I think it's insane, and you've turned my Christmas upside down, and my wife really wouldn't want me taking on two companies instead of one... but at the same time, I have to say, I have a lot of respect for you for being prepared to throw a lit match and walk away.' He nods thoughtfully. 'A *lot* of respect. I mean, Jesus, this shit could actually work.'

That gets a genuine laugh out of me. 'I'm very relieved I'm not the only one who thinks so.'

'What makes you think your board would support it?'

'Honestly, I'm cautiously optimistic. Dad aside, most of them are decent people who respect my leadership. Every one of them is a big fan of you and your father, and even your cocky little shit of a brother. I think they'll be pretty aghast, but I'd expect them to choose the successor that will upset the markets the least, and I believe that's you.'

'Good to know. But I have to ask—how big a part of your motivation is down to the fact that this will fucking destroy your father?'

'Not as much as you'd think. I'd never set out to destroy him. I'd rather just walk away. Disengage. But I can't say I don't feel a certain satisfaction that his shitty parenting methods have blown up in his face.'

'You wouldn't be human if you didn't, mate.' He blows out a breath. 'Okay, a lot to think about. How about this— you stay for lunch, and I'll get Dad in for a chat. I think it's time we got him involved.'

~

MILES DISAPPEARS for about twenty minutes, I assume to fully brief Charles before he joins us.

'I hear you're proposing a reverse takeover of sorts,' Charles says after he's shaken my hand. A friendly member of staff has been in to set a tureen of soup and a pile of turkey and ham sandwiches on the round dining table at the far end of the room. I usually try to avoid gluten, but it would be rude to decline these on every level. Not only is Miles' hospitality far exceeding what he owes me, but they look delicious.

'That's essentially what it is. It's unorthodox at this stage in the proceedings, but it's not uncommon when the target is superior.' I don't say it as if I'm trying to blow smoke up his arse. I'm merely stating a fact.

'Unorthodox it definitely is. And ballsy.'

I laugh grimly. 'Tell me about it.'

'The biggest problem that I foresee is not Miles taking the reins per se but the investors getting spooked that he'll backtrack on the job cuts,' Charles muses. He pulls up a chair, and we sit, too. As we tuck into the soup and sandwiches, we also get stuck into the finer points of how the announcement, the transaction, and the future of the combined entity could possibly work. It's ambitious on all fronts, not least because I've totally blindsided poor old Miles.

'I didn't even know I wanted this,' he groans at one point. 'I've never even thought about it. I just wanted you to bugger off and leave us to run our company in peace. But now I see it, I can't unsee it. Damn you, Kingsley.'

I chuckle. 'Sorry, mate. I appreciate I'm handing you a hell of a burden.'

'You're handing me a royal mess, but it's an itch I've got to scratch.'

'You know,' Charles says thoughtfully, 'it's a hell of a bombshell, and I appreciate you're scrambling to find a solution that works for your family, as you absolutely should, but it's genius, really. Not that you wouldn't do a fine job running the company,' he adds hurriedly. 'Of course you would.'

'Jamie's the catalyst. But, like I told Miles, I've been having doubts for some time, and a few recent conversations I've had have been clarifying. I actually think it might be the best thing for the business.'

He nods. 'It's all very unconventional, but by appointing someone outside of your faction as your successor, you're telling the market that you value finding the right person for the job. That should sit well.'

'Talent over nepotism,' I mutter.

'You have talent, too.' This from Miles.

'Of course you do. And, while I wouldn't want to be you when you propose this to your father, I can't deny there's a certain cycle that you're breaking with this very courageous move.'

He's too polite to say it, but I suspect the *cycle* he's referring to is that of the Kingsley men needing to dominate and destroy everything they touch.

'I'm not proposing anything to him. I intend to fill the board in, appeal to every member individually, and get my votes in the bag before I politely inform him of my intentions. I'll very much be telling, not asking.'

Miles presses his lips together in an unsuccessful attempt to hide a smirk. Charles laughs delightedly.

'Oh boy, oh boy. I almost feel bad for him. His entire business empire, handed over to his arch nemesis.'

'Don't feel bad. He's had it in for you for years. This takeover all came from him, you must know that. I'm just the idiot who went along with it.' I pause. This is difficult, but it has to be said. 'For what it's worth, I really am incredibly sorry. For everything. I regret all of it.'

Charles' expression grows sober. 'We're all adults, and we run public companies. This is the risk. We know that. Besides, he's not an easy man to cross, your father. I wouldn't like you to be too harsh on yourself.' He shakes his head. 'You were such a lovely little lad, back in the day. I remember you clearly, because you reminded me so much of Miles. So smart. So eager to please.

'He was... he was hard on you. Very hard. Cruel, even. It was difficult to watch, sometimes, especially as a father of boys. So, to see you come here today when none of this can be remotely easy for you—it's admirable. It really is. You've shown a great deal of principle, of integrity, and I know you'll go on to make a great success of whatever you try next, if we get this thing over the finish line. If it's not an overstep to say, I'm proud of you. Very proud.'

A hush falls over the table. I bow my head over my soup bowl, not trusting myself to speak for a moment.

I can't be sure what memory, exactly, he's recalling, whether it's the investment club disaster or another of the humiliations I suffered at my father's hands. For a moment, that ten-year-old version of me hovers right by my side. Coming from a man as noble, as fatherly, as Charles, this feels like nothing short of a benediction. A precious gift. The approval my father never gave, offered freely by the man whose family I tried to destroy.

He saw me then, and he sees me now, and he may not be my father, but he's twice the man Richard Kingsley has ever been. In this moment, I understand what I've been missing my entire life—and what Jamie deserves to have from me.

I'm worried about Ethan.

I'm worried about Jamie.

I'm worried about Ethan worrying about Jamie.

My original plan was to stay in Athens for New Year's. My family is on good form, after all, and I have a dozen invitations for New Year's Eve parties. My sister's fiancé is throwing one of them at a fabulous new rooftop restaurant that I've been dying to try out.

I really want to go along.

More accurately, I really want to *want* to go along. Because, actually, I just want to go back to London. I miss Ethan so much it's honestly pathetic, and I feel so helpless over here. I know his argument with Jamie and the Tesla stunt shook the shit out of him, and I hate that he's so alone. I hate that he doesn't have anyone looking out for him.

I've also been getting the distinct impression that he's up to something, and I can't for the life of me work out what.

So when he FaceTimes me three days after Christmas and spills the beans, I am well and truly gobsmacked. Turns out he spent most of yesterday with Miles and Charles Montague, thrashing out what equates to a kind of coup to blow up his father's legacy, put the Montagues in charge of the combined hotel group, and extricate himself in the process.

I have no words. It's audacious and brilliant and the epitome of evil genius.

Walk away.

Make reparations.

Fuck his father up the arse.

All in one swift move.

'But what will you do instead?' I ask in shock. He's grinning at me, amused, I suppose, by the expression on my face as I attempt to process.

His face falls. 'I'll need to talk to you about that,' he says softly. 'But I'd rather do it face to face.'

'That's settled, then,' I tell him. 'I'll come back first thing tomorrow.'

I don't love the queasy flip my stomach performed when he said he needed to talk about the future. I'm likely to be out of a job if Ethan walks, but that's not what's bothering me. I couldn't give a shit about the job. I have plenty of money between my Seraph income and my ample trust fund, whose investments I manage aggressively—the seraphim have an investment club where we pool ideas and share tips.

Like many things in life, when the universe forces our hand, it can be a good thing. I already know I'd never go and work for another man in the same capacity. I just couldn't. Not after Ethan. This may just be the kick up the arse I need to stop fucking around with billionaires and go back to uni to get my clinical qualification.

No, the feeling of foreboding that I can't shake is a direct result of ruminating over what Ethan means. What he wants to tell me.

The funny thing is that usually, at this (early) stage in a relationship, I'd be freaking out about feeling trapped. Now I'm freaking out for quite the opposite reason, and, even as I congratulate myself on the progress I've made at managing my Seven parts, I realise I don't like it. This is precisely *why* I have my Seven parts, for fuck's sake. They're there to protect me, to ensure that I don't become dependent enough on anyone that they could hurt me, and, obviously, to make myself so fucking adorable, so entertaining, that no one would want to walk away, anyway.

I feel as though, by opening myself up to Ethan and this precious fledgling relationship, I've also opened myself up to a world of potential hurt, even if I don't know why or how.

~

I GO STRAIGHT from the airport to Ethan's place. He's told me that he dropped Jamie back at his mum's earlier today. I fiddle with my beautiful ring stack for the entire flight. I haven't stopped fiddling with it, admiring it, since he gave it to me. It's gorgeous and insane and playful and so *me*.

He has his driver pick me up, and when we pull into his subterranean garage, he's standing right there. He yanks open the back door and tugs me out, pulling me into a tight hug as his driver opens the boot to grab my luggage.

I wrap my arms around his neck and breathe him in. He's wearing the sweater I gave him for Christmas, and it's so soft, and there's so much hard muscle beneath it, and he smells so good, but it's his face that hits me hardest.

That face.

He's so handsome. I pull away so I can see it, cup it in my hands, kiss his mouth. He hasn't shaved today, and a dusting of light brown stubble makes his jaw look even more defined.

'I missed you so much,' he says against my lips, and then he's kissing me, deeply, decadently, as if it's been a year and not a handful of days since he last got to kiss me. 'Let's get you warmed up.'

I reluctantly admit that the living room looks less bleak than usual, thanks to the beautifully—if monochromatically—decorated tree and the fire that's roaring rather than crackling as it consumes the borderline irresponsible mound of logs in its grate. The lighting is down low, and Bing Crosby is playing softly through the speakers. Ethan has his usual French press of coffee ready to go, and he pours me a cup just the way I like it—black, with half a teaspoon of brown sugar to take the edge off.

'Okay, so tell me everything,' I demand as he tucks me up on the sofa. I'm sitting sideways, my legs stretched out and covered with a large blanket while he proceeds to sit at the far end. 'I go away for a few days at the quietest time of the year and you manage to instigate a coup of epic proportions. I can't leave you alone for a minute.'

And so he launches into his account of yesterday's trip to see Miles.

'Oh my god, I'd love to have been a fly on the wall. His face must have been a picture!'

'He was pretty shocked. He definitely thought I was smoking crack. But he appreciated my motives, at least.'

He massages the instep of my foot through the blanket, and I arch into his touch as I process.

'So you want to spend more time with Jamie,' I prompt. 'Right? That's why you're getting out of the deal? The company?'

'Exactly.' He looks at me, his grey eyes soft. I can't believe I thought they were cold when I first met him.

'And is his mum up for that?' I know the custody agreement he has with Elena is strict. 'I hate to ask, but does she know what happened the other night?'

'She does now. We had a long chat earlier. I sent Jamie upstairs when we got there, because I knew she'd be furious with both of us, and I didn't want her taking it out on him.'

'That was nice of you. And was she?'

'Yeah,' he says shortly. 'She was fucking fuming, and also very upset, obviously. It really shook her up.'

'Of course it did.' I reach out to take his free hand. 'These things are awful for any parent. Do you think she'll let you spend more time with him?'

He hesitates. 'This is what I want to talk to you about. But the short answer is yes. She's conflicted. She desperately wants me to have a close relationship with him—almost as much as she wants to protect him from me.'

I wince. 'Ouch.'

'Yeah. But consider it from her perspective. It breaks her heart every time I hurt him, and it should. The thing that's carried me through all these years is that he couldn't have a more loving mother. But Elena's a very fair person. She's not spiteful, and she doesn't have it in for me. She listened to my entire pitch, and she's given me her blessing as long as I feel confident that it's the right thing for Jamie.'

I go still. 'What was the pitch, Ethan?'

He doesn't shy away from my gaze. In fact, his is clear and open and resolute. There's peace in his expression that I don't see often. 'That I pull Jamie out of school for two or three months—maybe even a full term—and he and I go off on a big adventure.' He swallows. 'Possibly Australia.'

Oh my god. It's a knife to the heart, but a small part of me isn't shocked. I've been gearing up to something like this since he told me we needed to talk. Not *this*, exactly, but I could sense he had something big up his sleeve.

But seconds after the agony comes the shock of something that feels joyous and heartwarming. The Ethan I first met was cold and walled up, numbing himself in his work while feeling no passion for it. He would never have walked away from his company, his shareholders, from a deal that would put his name on the map.

This Ethan is lighter, somehow. He's throwing in the towel on every single front, moving forward without a backward glance so he can invest in the thing he's deemed to be the most important one of all: his relationship with his son. He's a laser-focused guy. His intensity radiated from him as soon as I met him. But the *focus* of that intensity has been overturned, and I can't help but applaud that he's gone all in on this. Everyone, everything, else be damned.

Including me.

'Say something.' He squeezes my hand.

I shoot him what's probably a dazed smile. 'I'm processing.'

'Process out loud?'

That gets a little laugh out of me. I cock my head and survey him. His handsome face is filled with concern, but I'm absolutely not about to make this about me when it categorically isn't.

'It's amazing. That's what I think.' I shrug. 'If ever you needed proof that you are not your father, this is it. What an incredible thing to do for your son. All this time, you've worried that he feels abandoned by you, and you're not even telling him you love him more than anything else—you're *showing* him. I mean, wow! What a powerful statement.'

What I don't say is that the most impressive thing about all this is how terrifying a step it must be for Ethan. For so long, he's believed that, to protect his son, he needs to stay clear of him. Ethan's entire Enneagram type as an Eight has revolved around protecting people through controlling them rather than through connecting with them. I've seen him transform his relationship with me, choosing connection, choosing to trust, and it's a beautiful thing.

But Jamie is the person in his life who he most fiercely, most desperately, wants and needs to protect. It stands to reason that he would choose the most extreme ways to feed that need. Yet here he is, choosing deep engagement and real vulnerability so that he can show up for his son in a healthy way.

And it is blowing. My. Mind.

My eyes fill with tears, and he instantly misconstrues them. 'No. No, sweetheart.' He rears up so he can pull me along the sofa and into his arms. 'I'm so sorry. I don't want—I don't want to leave you. I feel *sick* at leaving you. That's not what this is about.'

I turn to face him and lay my palms along his cheeks, cupping his face. 'You misunderstand.' I smile through my tears. 'I think that's the most beautiful thing I've ever heard, and I'm feeling very emotional that you're choosing Jamie over absolutely everything else.' I press my forehead to his and scrunch up my face in an effort to keep my shit together. 'You're such a good man. *Such* a good man. And let me tell you right now, you're a wonderful father. No one makes a sacrifice like that unless they're a truly loving parent.'

He lifts his face and uses his thumbs to wipe away my tears. He looks stricken. I'm not sure he's absorbed any of the reassurances I've just given him. 'None of it's a sacrifice except for you. I don't give a shit about any of it but you. Good riddance to the deal—honestly, I feel bad landing Miles with it.' His voice drops to a whisper. 'But walking away from you will be the hardest thing I've ever had to do, and the most terrifying. Because I'm absolutely shitting myself that you'll get fed up and leave me. I'm choosing my son over you, after all, just as things were getting really serious. The timing couldn't be worse.

'I know I need to do this—and I will, I absolutely will, even if it means losing you. But I'm not sure I'll ever, ever get over it.'

We stare at each other. The tears are pouring down my cheeks now.

'I love you,' he whispers. 'I'm in love with you. Head over heels.' My lips part at the shock of it, but he presses on. 'I never, ever dreamed I'd meet someone who'd actually see me, and believe in me, and heal me. I never, ever thought I could be close to someone in the way I am with you.'

'Listen to me.' I grab his face harder and try unsuccessfully to blink away the tears. 'Okay? Just listen. First, I didn't heal you. Not in the slightest. You're healing yourself, babe, and don't you ever forget it. And secondly, you've basically just told me that you're choosing your son over me, that that relationship is more important than ours—'

He goes to interrupt, but I shake my head. 'No. Listen. You've just prioritised your son over me, and I'm assuming I'm out of a job, too, given that you're buggering off, and never'— I pause, my entire face crumpling at this tidal wave of emotion —'*never* could I have imagined that all that would be the proof I need to stick around for someone.'

His expression goes from devastated to bewildered. I need to do a better job of making myself clear. 'You've just chosen your child over your business, your deal, your father, your *money*. You've just sacked off trying to control everyone and everything around you and done the emotional equivalent of jumping off a fucking bridge. You've taken all the shit in your life that fucked you up and you've started doing serious work on yourself and taking massive steps to make reparations.' I stroke his face. 'If that's not the best proof I've ever seen that you are the man I'm proud to love then I don't know what is.' I erupt into slightly deranged, sobbing laughter. 'Even if you're leaving me behind.'

'You love me?' he asks, those beautiful grey eyes searching my face.

'I love you. And I love your beautiful heart. I love it even more when you let it shine. And I'm so fucking proud of you. I wholeheartedly support this. I know it will be the making of you and Jamie.'

'I want to ask you to wait for me. I can't make you, obviously. But I've been thinking about this obsessively. I know I haven't been great boyfriend material. But I'm going to keep doing the work while I'm away. I want to Zoom with Philip as much as he can bear, maybe get Jamie involved, if he's game. I want to keep working on all the shit that stops me from being able to get close to the people I love.' He rakes his fingers through my hair. 'I want to be worthy of you.'

His face is so full of love. Of tenderness. Here's the thing about Eights: when they fall, they fall hard. They give themselves over completely. If their entire personality is fearing abandonment and loss of control, if their tests really *do* test the people closest to them, then the rewards for passing their tests are beautiful in the extreme.

So I tell him what he needs to hear.

'I love you. I'm not going anywhere, I promise. I'll be waiting for you when you and Jamie are done with your glorious, crazy adventures.'

God knows, I understand better than anyone the importance of having a safe place to land when we're ready to stop moving.

He drops his head to my shoulder and holds me so tightly, muttering into my neck as I rake my hands through his hair. 'I was so fucking scared you'd tell me where to go. I was terrified, actually.'

'No way. You're not getting rid of me that easily.' I rock him in my arms. 'So, a few months in Oz, eh? What made you decide on that?'

He pulls away and grins at me. 'It was Jamie's idea. It's summer there, and he said he couldn't think of a better place for me to learn how to chill the fuck out.'

CHAPTER 48

Ethan

I have Elena's approval to take Jamie away for an extended period which, given how viscerally she'll miss him is, frankly, extraordinary and a touching vote of confidence in my ability to keep our son safe and happy.

I have Soph's love and her promise that she'll wait for me, which feels just as extraordinary. The two women I've loved, believing in me. Backing me.

I've spent the past forty-eight hours working feverishly with Soph on reaching out to each board member and apprising them of the situation. To a person, they have all agreed to honour my proposal and back Miles as CEO, which means I have the votes to pass this thing, even with Dad voting against me.

Everything else from here on in is a technicality.

I haven't yet informed Jamie's school that I'm pulling him out, but I don't really give a shit what they say. I'll be telling them, not asking.

The only obstacle remaining before I jet off with my son, the only piece of business left hanging, is to inform my parents of my *fait accompli.*

On my way to their house, I remind myself of what's at stake by texting Jamie a link to a TikTok of an Aussie guy performing a jaw-dropping surfing stunt.

> You and me in two months' time.

His reply is instant.

> It'll be me not u. Ur too old.

God knows how shite his punctuation will be after missing three whole months of school, but I have no intention of giving him a hard time. Instead, I send a laughing emoji as I chuckle to myself. Cheeky little fucker.

I've employed a high-end tour operator to put together the ultimate adventure package for us, factoring in plenty of opportunities for rest, healing, and relationship building in unforgettable surroundings. No doubt our two-week camping trip to K'gari will be a highlight, but I'm anticipating many other highlights, too.

The tour operator is aware that Jamie is leading the idea generation. He and I had a FaceTime last night that was enthusiastic, bordering on manic. He's so excited. I want to show him that this is for him, that this is my chance to spend time getting to know every aspect of my son in all his messy, perfect glory. So I'm not calling the shots here.

He is, every step of the way.

Now that I've committed to this, I can't fucking wait. If it wasn't for the need to stick around for the board meeting to get Miles formally voted in and for the acute nausea I feel at leaving Soph, we'd be hightailing it out of here tomorrow.

I've arrived at a double epiphany concerning my father. The first part is that, as Miles pointed out yesterday, the love you chase for so long, for which you bleed yourself dry, doesn't actually exist. That people like Dad and Miles' ex-wife will never love you as much as they love themselves. That realisation is brutal and liberating in equal measure.

The second part is just plain liberating.

Because if the love doesn't exist, then there's no point in chasing after an illusion. No point at all. Which leaves me free to move forward with my life and focus on real, lasting love, like the love I feel for Jamie and Soph.

I arrive at my childhood home, always a bittersweet experience, and am shown through to the formal drawing room by our long-standing—and long-suffering—butler, Andrew. My dad is big on pomp and ceremony. He believes that every advantage should be maximised, that the facade he shows the world is all that matters.

He never seems to understand that everybody sees right through it, but then self-awareness has never struck Richard as a sound use of his time.

My parents redecorate the house from top to toe once a decade. It's 'the done thing', after all. These days, the drawing room is trendy neutrals and linen-covered walls. Long gone is the rose-coloured damask upholstery of my childhood.

'I've got some news,' I announce once Andrew has set down the tea tray between us. I remain standing on the pretext of warming my arse by the fire, but really, I feel more at an advantage like this. Best just to come out with it. 'Jamie's been having some problems with his mental health, which are mainly my fault, so I've taken the decision to pull him out of school for a term. He and I are off to Australia for three months.'

I'm aware that this hat trick of bombshells is the most inflammatory Molotov cocktail I could have thrown at my folks. Mental health is not a thing as far as they're concerned (go figure). Neither is foregoing one's elite education for any reason. And, while I haven't spat out my decision to leave

Kingsley just yet, it's clear that I'm planning to abandon work for a considerable period.

Let the fun begin.

'What's wrong with Jamie?' Mum asks, right as Dad bellows, 'You can't take the boy out of school! He's weak, just like his mother. You're enabling him, making him soft. He'll never amount to anything if you coddle him like this. Mark my words—you'll ruin him completely.'

'He's fine, Mum. I'd rather not get into it.' I mean, what's the point? *I've fucked him up because you fucked me up?* That's a non-starter. 'And yes, I can take him out of school, as a matter of fact.' This to my father. 'And I'd "ruin" him if I ignored his needs. Seeing someone and advocating for them has never ruined anyone.'

He ignores that, obviously. 'He should be focusing on his GCSEs! He's barely started the syllabus. Why did I go to all the trouble of getting him moved up to the top set for Science if you're going to go and mess up his studies by gallivanting around for a whole term? Besides, you can't possibly get away from work right now. The transaction should be your number one priority. It's unthinkable, that's what it is.'

Here goes. My palms prick with sweat as I force myself to say the words. 'I'm leaving the company. I'm walking away. It's not good for me and it's not good for Jamie. I'm reassessing my priorities. Make no mistake—*Jamie* is my number one priority.'

I brace myself for their reaction. Mum gasps theatrically, but Dad just rolls his eyes. 'Don't be ridiculous, Ethan. What utter nonsense.'

My internet rabbit-holing around narcissism informed me that narcissists often refuse outright to accept information that threatens their worldview. If Richard Kingsley's worldview is that he and his empire are untouchable, then this tracks.

But it means I need to say the damn words twice.

Before me stands my ageing father, but all I can see is the bully from my childhood. Logic tells me I'm a grown man, but my body is responding with childlike terror.

I clear my throat. 'Listen to me, Dad. I'm done with Kingsley Hotels. I'm out—for good.'

Dad's face twists from dismissively condescending to downright thunderous. He gets to his feet with an agility I didn't know he still had, fixated solely on me. 'That is unacceptable! Have you lost your mind, boy? What a disgrace you are to the family name!'

Instantly, I'm nine years old again and sitting in the dining room at the golf club with my painstakingly written list of stock market losses. Richard Kingsley is a bully. He was then, and he is now. Now, I know that his reactions have nothing to do with me, or anyone else. They have only to do with him, and his demons, and his narcissism. But the little boy I feel myself to be doesn't know that.

I suck in a panicked breath as Dad stalks towards me, and grasp onto one of Philip's excellent pieces of advice from our last call.

Tell that little boy that he never has to go up against his father again, he said. *He never has to be scared of him, because you'll be there. He has you in his corner. You're a grown man. He can hide behind you. He doesn't even need to see him. You've got this, and you've got him.*

I force myself to imagine my younger self hiding behind me. Gripping the back of my trousers in dread. Blocking out the view of his furious father. Feeling the reassuring height, the solidity, of my adult self. I sense him squeezing his eyes shut, and I mentally applaud his bravery as I face up to my dad.

This time, I don't cry.

I don't cower.

Behind me, I sense that terrified little boy finally exhale.

I stand there, and I merely raise a sardonic eyebrow, and it infuriates him even more. He continues to rant at me, shaking his finger as if it's on him to impart an important life lesson.

'Kingsley men do not walk away. We are leaders. Leaders in business, leaders of people. We stick around and we show the world how it's done. Leaving the company, indeed! You're delusional. What do they call it these days? A snowflake. You'll humiliate all of us. Can you even imagine what the press would say?'

And there it is. The outright admission that my father wishes to be judged only on his public glory and not his private deeds. On perception and not reality. If it happens behind closed doors, he's not interested. And that's precisely why his actual success as a parent never preoccupied him for a single moment, while his perceived success as a business leader preoccupied his every waking thought.

I haven't taken this enormous life decision in order to spite my father. I really haven't. It's simply a pleasant bonus. But I can't deny that satisfaction courses warmly through my chest as I stand to face up to him. I have several inches on him now, a fact that feels more reassuring than it should. These days, I physically tower over the bully. I slide my hands into my pockets.

'I don't care what the press says. I don't care what your golf buddies think, or your old cronies in the industry. I care about my son's wellbeing and my own.' I clear my throat and fix him with my iciest glare. Today, I'm happy to have the protection of my inner ice king. He's a terrifying mother-fucker, and he's about to show Richard Kingsley that he's totally fucking impenetrable.

'Besides, I've found a supremely elegant solution: a successor who's far more qualified than I am to lead the combined company into its next phase. The press will love him.' I pause for effect. 'Miles Montague has graciously agreed to step up as CEO. After all, he's the architect of our main growth engine. The board has already approved him as my successor with immediate effect. We've drafted the press releases and we'll put it out as soon as the board has formally voted him in.'

My father appears to be physically unable to speak. For a glorious moment, I imagine him dropping dead, right by the fireplace. Alas, he turns a deep purple and belatedly finds his voice.

'Miles Montague! Over my dead body! Are you out of your fucking mind?'

My mother starts weeping, her default response to any family conflict, and I find myself feeling a spot of compassion amid the usual irritation. Philip would have a field day with my mum. For decades, she's made placating Richard Kingsley her entire personality. I'm sure her wounds run deep.

'It's okay, Mum,' I say. 'I promise.' I turn back to my father. 'Actually, I know exactly what I'm doing. I'm choosing my family over an empire that's only ever existed to serve your ego, and I've put in place a successor who's probably even stronger than I would have been.'

'He won't cut costs.' Dad's face is still purple, his eyes bulging out of their sockets. He may be furious, but he's also more rattled than I've ever seen him. The ground beneath his very feet is shifting; I've shattered the world as he knows it with a single sentence. 'You know that. He's too much of a pussy.'

I shrug. 'Maybe, but he'll grow the top line better than I could have, I'd put money on it.'

But he's not listening. 'You'd put their name on the door of my company. You're nothing more than Charles fucking Montague's Trojan horse, you disloyal little shit.'

'You should listen to your father,' Mum interjects pleadingly. 'Please, sweetie. He's so much more experienced than you. He can give you some guidance! He can help you out of this silly mess you've made.'

'A self-serving man once told me,' I reply smoothly, ignoring her, 'that loyalty never helped the bottom line. If I'm correct, that's what you told Charles in that board meeting, anyway.' Let's see how he feels about having his own bullshit served back up to him.

He's staring at me as if he doesn't know me, as if he's never set eyes on this quietly courageous, intransigent man standing before him. And he'd be right. I've never shown this side of myself to him. But I've finally chosen my son, fourteen years too late, and I'll be damned if I wouldn't go utterly feral to protect him.

'That's not what I meant, and you know it,' he spits. 'They don't have what it takes. I forbid you to propose that Montague boy. I'm the Chairman of the Board, dammit. Let's see what the little turncoats have to say when they're facing up to me.'

I shrug, unbothered. 'Feel free. But that's the wonderful thing about British corporate governance standards, Dad. They are all entitled to vote as they like.'

I don't think he's even listening. 'The Montague *M* on *our* doors,' he mutters, eyes glazed. I suspect his mind is playing him a vivid movie of how the future of the company he built will unfold, and I suspect it's a tough watch. He turns his gaze back on me, and it's pure poison. 'I built this company on *my* vision and *my* values, and Charles Montague thinks he can swan in and put his name over *my* doors? Have you no shame at all?'

I nearly laugh at that one. 'Your values are greed and glory. Charles Montague has more integrity in his little finger than you have.' Mum gasps at my impudence, and I ignore her. 'I spent the twenty-seventh with him and Miles in the

Cotswolds, hammering this thing out. He was incredibly gracious, considering you've spent years dreaming of destroying his legacy.'

And now he'll erase yours. He'll reimagine it as his own, and it will be all the better for it.

The words hang between us. I don't need to say them. Dad grips the mantelpiece and stares into the fire. He looks utterly lost, and I don't blame him. When you give all of your attention to things that don't actually matter, and they disappear, what's left? Nothing. Because the things that do matter are no longer available to you.

'It's done, Dad. Okay? You can rail all you want, but it's a done deal.'

He looks up and glares at me. 'You are no son of mine. I mean it. You're an utter disgrace. I would *never* have abandoned my responsibilities in favour of my son.'

I do laugh at that, but there's no mirth in it. 'Tell me something I don't know, Dad.'

'You belong to me. This company, this family, *you*—it's all mine. I made you, and I can unmake you. You think you can just decide to leave? You're nothing without the Kingsley name.'

'You're so wrong, on so many levels. None of it is yours. You have no autonomy over anyone but yourself, something Mum would do well to take on board. And you threatening me shows me just how despicable you are. I don't want your name. I don't want any association with you. And I certainly don't want anything you have to offer.'

He spits out an outraged laugh. 'After everything I've given you—the fine education, the opportunities, the bloody *company*—this is how you repay me? You're cut off. Both of you. Every trust fund, every inheritance. See how far your principles get you when you're living like a pauper.'

'You're entitled to do all that, if it makes you feel better,' I say with a tired shrug. 'I don't care about any of it. Honestly, good riddance.'

The tragedy is that my father truly believes he's given me the best start in life, just as he truly believes that what he's threatening to take away is in any way valuable. The reality, of course, is that his bargaining chips hold no value at all for me. Not only will I remain an obscenely wealthy man even without my inheritance, but I just don't give a shit about the trappings he's attempting to use as leverage.

One could argue that Richard Kingsley's toxic parenting style has lost him a son *and* an empire, but he never really had the former. I was a figurehead: the golden boy, the successor to his legacy.

This may be the end of the story for Kingsley Hotels, but it's the beginning of a new chapter for me and Jamie.

And I can't wait for it to start.

God knows, I'm far prouder to be known as Jamie Kingsley's father than Richard Kingsley's son.

Ethan braces on one arm, staring deeply into my eyes as he tenderly rakes my hair off my face. Being the focus of this man's attention is always quite something, but being the focus of his attention when he's buried deep inside your body is a whole other level.

We're in his bed. His bags are packed and standing by the front door. Tomorrow morning, he'll grab Jamie from Elena's and they'll fly halfway around the world.

'Fuck.' He shakes his head. 'I can't believe I'm about to walk away from this.'

'You mean you can't believe you're about to walk away from *me*.'

He grins. 'That too.'

'Some things are more important than getting your rocks off, babe. Like making amazing memories with your son. And if he can do without his new PC for three months, you can do without me.'

'Tell that to my dick,' he groans, and I laugh.

'It's not about the sex.' He eases slowly out of me, and my fingers flex on his shoulders, willing him to get back inside me.

'I know.' I whisper it.

'I'll miss you so much. You light me up.'

He pushes back in, and my eyes fill with tears. There's nothing like knowing he'll soon be ten thousand miles away to add a serious emotional punch to what is already excellent sex.

'I'll miss you too,' I manage brokenly. 'But you'll find a million things to light you up over there. I know you will.'

'God, please don't cry, sweetheart.' He lowers himself fully down, wrapping his arms around me and pressing all that delicious weight onto me. 'I can't bear it. I love you so much.'

I respond by holding on for dear life and rolling my hips as much as I can as he thrusts into me. He's already made me come with slow, beautiful licks of his tongue, but the second orgasm is igniting inside me, driven as much by my love for him as by his magical dick. He's above me, inside me, all around me, blotting out everything that isn't him.

He kisses me as he makes love to me, slowly, languorously. He's not edging himself or me like he used to; instead it feels as if he's savouring every moment. Committing it all to memory.

I'm not scared about Ethan going off and changing his mind about us. I'm not scared that our relationship won't survive three months apart.

I'm just scared of spending ninety days and nights away from him.

He's apologised a million times for the fact that he won't be inviting me out to join him and Jamie at any point, but the truth is that I'd push back if he did. He needs this. Jamie needs this. Elena is due to meet them for a week halfway through, a move I'm more than on board with. I can't imagine how much she'll miss her son, and I honestly applaud her for giving Ethan her blessing. It can't have been easy for her, and it definitely wasn't something she was obliged by the custody agreement to do. Quite the opposite.

I pull Ethan's head down and find his mouth. There's

something so intimate about having his tongue inside my mouth at the same time as his dick. I can't get enough; I want him to consume me completely.

Finally, when I can't withstand the onslaught a second more, I fall apart around him.

And I sob the whole way through it.

AFTER A MONTH of enduring my moping, Athena drags me out for a heart-to-heart. It's an early dinner in Victoria, because tonight she's dragging Gabe to watch her favourite show, *Hamilton*, at the Palace.

'I can't believe you're going to see it again,' is how I greet her. She looks fucking amazing as always, in a long, olive green silk dress that offsets her gorgeous hazel eyes and auburn hair. She really is one of the most genetically blessed people I've ever encountered.

She shrugs. 'It makes me feel seen.'

'Because Alexander Hamilton was the biggest raging Three who ever Three'd.' If Athena personifies The Achiever Enneagram type, then that particular Founding Father blows the stereotype out of the park.

'Exactly. I find it inspiring.'

I laugh at that. 'Babe, you know it's supposed to be a *cautionary* tale, right? Like, he lost everything.'

Her expression is mulish. 'But he achieved so much. He was willing to pay the price, although the real tragedy is that he never got to achieve everything he wanted to before he died.'

Clearly, Athena's work on herself is not done if she thinks Threes *ever* get to achieve all the things they want before they inconveniently die. No wonder Hamilton wrote like he was running out of time. But I'll leave that to her executive coach and her therapist to work through with her. In fact, she should probably play Billy Joel's *Vienna* first thing every morning just to calm herself the hell down.

'I don't know why you're dragging poor Gabe along,' I say instead. 'You'll just complain the whole way through that Hamilton married the wrong Schuyler sister. Although you know Gabe is the real-life version of Eliza, right?'

'I love my saintly Two fiancé.' She shakes out her napkin crossly. 'But you're right, he should have married Angelica. At least then they could have been unsatisfied together. She said it herself—theirs was a meeting of wits.'

I sigh and pick up the cocktail menu. We both know she'll go and hate-watch it the whole way through and have an absolute blast.

'So, how are you coping without Eight?' she asks with a sly look at me. 'You still have a job, right?'

'For the moment. Miles and the deal are keeping me busy, thank fuck.'

It's true. Ethan stuck around for the board meeting that voted Miles in (they were one person short of getting a unanimous vote, funnily enough) and attended key handover meetings with the top investors of both companies. The conversations weren't easy, but it seems the market's faith in Miles' capabilities is high, and the entire issue has turned out to be less of a crisis and more of a wobble for the deal.

Since he left, I've been working mainly on helping Miles and his team with everything from liaising with various financial PR firms on communicating his hastily drawn-up vision for the merged entity to working with our finance and strategy teams on delivering endlessly crunched numbers to the Montague side.

Quite honestly, it's been incredibly stimulating. Gone is most of the ill-feeling between the two companies, too. While there are a great deal of nerves at the Kingsley team's end over what it will mean for their jobs to have the Montagues running things, Miles tells me that his people feel like the executioner's axe is no longer hanging over them. Even Theo admitted to me that Ethan's stunt was *the sickest fucking stunt I've ever seen.*

'Have you had any time to work on your app?'

'A bit. Having no one to shag in the evenings frees up quite a lot of time. And I've got my doctorate all lined up for September at UCL.'

University College London is one of the best places in the country to do a clinical psychology qualification, and, while it will take me three or so years to complete, I absolutely intend to both launch my app and achieve my IFS Institute qualifications at the same time.

I guess I have a major Three part after all.

Athena nods approvingly. 'Excellent. And Ethan will help you with the app?'

'He wants to. He seems really excited about it, but I've forbidden him from committing to anything until he gets back from Oz. I want him to keep an open mind.'

'Who would have known that Ethan Kingsley, ice-cold tyrant and destroyer of seraphim, would end up in IFS therapy, of all things? By his standards, he's practically singing *Kumbaya.* You've done well with that one, girl.'

'He's done all the hard work himself,' I say defensively, and she smiles.

'So, does he call you for phone sex a lot?'

'Sometimes. The time difference is pretty rough. They're surfing in Noosa at the moment, so I get hurried calls from him when Jamie's down at the beach, begging me to show him my tits so he can jerk off to them. But mainly he just sends me silly presents from wherever they are and calls to tell me how much he loves me and how much he misses me. He'll go dark next week when they're on K'gari, though.'

I trail off, a little embarrassed at how sentimental it all

makes me feel. Still, knowing that Ethan is all the way over there, thinking about me—or my tits—is really something, even if I'll have a couple of weeks of no contact.

But Athena doesn't tease me. Instead, she raises her glass.

'So my favourite Seven has finally found a man she feels safe to settle down with. And the glorious irony is that she would have avoided him like the plague if he hadn't suggested at the outset, with every single word out of that lovely mouth of his, that he was the ultimate walking red flag. It's a stealth attack worthy of the history books, darling.'

I pick up my glass and clink hers. 'The man has moves. I'll give him that.'

CHAPTER 50

Ethan

If I close my eyes and think about the past few weeks, in my mind, the memories are golden and sun-drenched. You know, like a retro movie where sun flares keep hitting the lens.

I couldn't have chosen a better place than Australia to come with my son and work on our relationship. With every day here, we heal, and we talk, and we build. I don't mean to say that we're baring our souls—this is an introverted fourteen-year-old I'm dealing with, after all. There's more grunting than baring, at his end, anyway.

Still, I'd call this healing. Every time he feels my full attention on him, I hope it rewires his system a little in the direction of knowing deep inside how important he is to me. Every time he does some crazy stunt, or we celebrate a random achievement of his just for the sake of it, or he lights me up because *he's* lit up, I hope he understands that I love him for *him*. Just as he is.

I've talked a lot to him about myself. My dad. My upbringing. The extreme bodyguard parts that have had me in their grip for so very long. I've talked to him about unknown unknowns and known unknowns, about the difference it makes to develop an understanding of what you're grappling with as opposed to being blithely oblivious to it.

We can't always access Self Leadership. We can't always prevent ourselves from being hijacked by well-meaning but extreme protectors, or guards. But it's certainly helpful to know that they exist, to grasp their agenda, and to have an open line of dialogue with them.

I should know. Aside from this past fortnight on K'gari, Philip and I have been working hard on doing just that.

Even without the official therapeutic work, this place is like therapy all on its own. Elena and I may have tried to give Jamie as normal an upbringing as possible, but a billionaire father and an elite schooling and bodyguards (actual, not just emotional) barely constitute normal. London's an intense environment at the best of times, and this is a world away from that frenetic pace.

Starting in Sydney was a way of easing ourselves into the transition with big city energy and the delights of Bondi. We may not have visited the Opera House (Jamie has the cultural sophistication of a banana) but we scaled the bridge: terrifying and exhilarating in equal measure.

Since then, we've shed our city skins and morphed into surfer dudes—I'd like to think so, anyway. Noosa was good, clean fun of exactly the kind I'd hoped we'd find. Our surfing stunts may not have been worthy of TikTok, but we fell into bed exhausted every night, our hair crusty with sea salt.

And on K'gari, we became even more feral. I'm sure both Elena and Soph would have been horrified by our lack of personal hygiene. We got pretty attached to our 4WD camper van, watched both the sunrise and the stars at the incredible Tukkee Wurrow, and met some dingoes. There's something about stripping back all of the bullshit and the trappings to the stuff that really matters: food, water, nature, and human connection. Love. Not sure there's more to it than that.

We both had a thorough shower before Elena came to join us in Port Douglas for some beach time, and we reluctantly swapped our four-wheeled home for a swanky villa. My ex isn't a princess, but if she was coming all that way to get her Jamie fix, the least I could do was put her up in style. It was a successful visit, I think. She and Jamie were ecstatic to see each other. I was worried that hanging out as a trio would be awkward, but it wasn't. Not really. There was enough to do and see to keep us occupied and provide plenty of conversation fodder. A few times, I caught her observing us together with a mixture of what felt like bewilderment and happiness. It seems she liked what she saw, and if I've given her any reassurance that this was the right call for all of us, then I'm a happy man.

I SIT in my plastic folding chair, nursing a nice cold beer as Jamie struggles sweatily with our tent. I wouldn't mind, but I even got us a pop-up one. And yet he seems to be making a dog's dinner of it.

We're still in Port Douglas. Jamie argued that the fancy villa where we hosted his mum was 'wanky' and insisted that we redress the balance with a few nights in a super basic, 'normal' campsite. I can confirm that this place ticks that box: it's extremely low budget but has a chilled vibe that I appreciate. He's insisted on being on tent erection duties, something I've agreed to with pleasure and watched with great amusement.

'How's it going over there?' I enquire, crossing one ankle over my other knee. Thanks to the fleet of staff at the villa, my Noosa t-shirt is distinctly cleaner than it was, but that won't last long. I reckon we'll have to burn our clothes when we get home.

'Fuck off,' he mutters, and I snigger to myself before taking another cleansing sip of beer. Ahh, this is the life.

Finally, the tent is up.

'Well done,' I tell him. 'Make sure to hammer the tent pegs in nice and deep. We don't want to blow away in the night, do we?'

He gets to work, hammering away at the pegs one by one. Bless him, physical coordination is not this kid's skill. He may have built a little muscle with all that surfing we did, but he's still all gangly limbs, with very little control over his motor skills. I grimace as he attempts to bash one in. The ground is seriously dry, to be fair. I imagine it's hard work, trying to hammer aluminium into earth as packed as this, but he has the angle all wrong.

'Careful. Try and hit it head on.'

'Nobody asked you,' he grunts, and I chuckle.

'Fair enough.'

Thirty seconds later, after a particularly aggressive hit at an ill-advised angle, the damn thing snaps in two with a comedic *donk* sound. Jamie stares at it in abject horror and gasps loudly. He looks up at me, his eyes wide. I stare back... and then I lose the plot, laughing my head off. I don't know why it's so funny—it's low-key slapstick, nothing more— but I find it hysterical, for some reason. I'm crying actual tears.

'You should see your face.' I point my beer bottle at him. 'Absolutely priceless.'

'But what are we going to do?' His tone is panicked. He looks around at the tent wildly.

'Hmm, I dunno.' I pretend to think. 'If only we had a couple of spares—oh, wait.'

I push myself out of my chair and wander over to the pile

of pegs. 'Here you go. They tend to provide extras in case the person putting it up is a total muppet.'

'It wasn't my fault! The ground was too hard!'

'You tell yourself that.' I ruffle his hair, just to piss him off even more. 'But honestly, chill. It's just a tent peg. It's not like it's a five-hundred quid graphics card, is it?'

He sucks in a harsh breath that I've gone there. 'Such a dick.'

'Too soon?'

'Way too soon.' He picks up the spare peg and tries again.

I grin. It's far too easy to wind him up, and far too much fun.

Jamie gets the tent secured eventually, and we set up our bedding. I eye it with distrust. That foam pad does not look enticing. With the tent, we've rented the pads, sleeping bags, and pillows.

He points at the folded pillowcases. 'Should we put the pillow sheets on?'

That cracks me up again. 'They're commonly known as pillow*cases*, but yes.' Where the hell did I get this funny little human from?

'Oh yeah.'

'Sound familiar?'

'Yeah.'

'Go on, then.'

We kneel and unfold our pillowcases. He looks at his dubiously.

'Like this.' I ruche it up over my arms and show him how to hold it away from him and feed it over the far end of his pillow. 'I'll tell you an embarrassing story. When I went off to uni, I'd never changed my sheets. I had no idea how to do it. I got to St Andrew's, and Mum had bought me new linen and a new duvet, but I didn't have a clue how to get the duvet cover on. I was reading Economics, but I swear it took me an hour to figure it out. So let's make a man of you and teach you how to put on a real, live pillowcase, yeah?'

I WILL SAY this for the Aussies. Their barbecuing skills are worthy of their global fame. Even at a very basic campsite and caravan park, the barbecue they've laid on tonight is legendary. Jamie and I ate our bodyweight in sausages and burgers, and we're sitting side by side in our old man folding chairs, doing a little stargazing. We've pushed our chairs right up next to each other, and his tousled head is lolling on my shoulder while I have my arm around him.

We've done a lot of this recently—just hanging about and staring at the sky—and it strikes me how much more life-affirming it is than watching Netflix. It's prompted some big discussions too, about space and the meaning of life, as well as what should be straightforward questions from Jamie about the behaviour of the moon and the stars and the tides. His keen interest and smart questions have made me realise how woefully inadequate my working knowledge of astrophysics is.

There's been a lot of hasty googling on my part.

'What do you miss most about home?' I ask him. 'And if you don't say *Mum*, I'm going to tell her.'

He laughs softly. 'Mum. But also my PC, and playing Elden Ring.'

'I get that. The stars are pretty cool, though.'

'Yeah. They are. What do you miss the most?'

I consider. 'Macchiato from that place on Portobello. And Soph.'

'Oooh. You love her.'

'You know it.'

'You call her all the time, and you never want to hang up.'

This seems unfair. I've been consciously limiting my

phone time with Soph so Jamie doesn't feel as though I have one mental foot back in England. But it's always gutting to hang up on her. 'Well, I miss her. But also, we haven't been together that long. Being away from her is a chance to get to know each other properly, you know? To have some good conversations.' *Without constantly being distracted by trying to fuck her instead.*

'Are you going to marry her?'

I look up at the night sky. It's a lot better lit here than it was at Tukkee Wurrow, but it's still aeons better than the light pollution of London. I should probably be better at picking out the constellations by now. 'I want to marry her. I love her very much, and I think she's one of the best human beings I've ever met. That's a pretty good basis for spending my life with someone, I think.'

'Do you think she's a better human being than Mum?' he asks, and I jolt.

'No! God, no. Your mum is an amazing person—she's so loving. So warm. She's incredible. But I wasn't the best version of myself when I was with your mum, not by a long shot. And I didn't even realise. So that made things really tough on her, and I'll always regret that. Soph knows how to handle me. She has a lot of expertise in this stuff—in why we do the things we do, and why our different parts can struggle with different things. She's the reason I've been on this journey. I have a lot to thank her for.'

'She makes you really happy.'

'*You* make me really happy.' I rub my cheek against the top of his head. 'But yes, she does, too. How would you feel if I asked her to marry me?'

He shrugs against me. 'I dunno. It's fine. I'm cool with it.'

'Really? It would be a big step, one of your parents remarrying.'

'Loads of my friends have step-parents. It's not that deep. Would she be my stepmother? She'd be fun, I suppose.'

'Yes she would, if she said yes. And yeah, I think she'd be a lot of fun.'

'You're fun now, too. As long as you don't get back to London and turn all boring again.'

'Hey, I won't. I've given up work, remember? You'll be the one being boring at school all day, every day, while I'm living it up and doing whatever the hell I like.'

He groans. 'So unfair. You could even go to the cinema in the middle of the day.'

'I could,' I agree.

'So when are you going to ask Sophia to marry you?' He twists his head to look up at me, his grin cheeky.

'I don't know yet. I wanted to see how you felt first. And I have no idea if she'd even say yes. I buggered off and left her, remember?'

'Well, I'm fine with it. So don't use me as your excuse. Sometimes you've got to put yourself out there, you know? You didn't know Miles would say yes, but he did.'

'True. But I probably wouldn't have been heartbroken if he'd said no. I'm not in love with Miles.'

'Maybe. But you wouldn't be here, either.' He nestles back against my shoulder again.

I sigh. When did he get so wise? 'You've got me there, mate.'

'Is she going to come out and meet us?'

'No, I told you. This is just you and me, and I'm good with that.'

'But she could come and see us in Malaysia. You could pop the question then.'

'You're really shipping us, aren't you? I haven't even thought about how I'd pop the question.' That's technically a lie. I have thought about it, at length. I just haven't worked out the perfect plan yet.

He springs out of his seat and turns to me, his face alight.

'I know! You could use our secret project to propose!'

That gives me pause. Jamie and I have been working on something on and off for the past two months. It's extremely complicated but seriously enthralling.

And it could just make for the perfect proposal.

I sit up straighter. 'Go on. What do you have in mind?'

CHAPTER 51

Sophia

Every day brings a new set of requests for information from the Montague side. The transaction is in its final stages now. We're so close to the finish line. Miles actually offered me a job as a member of his Strategy team, which was incredibly touching, but I turned it down. I have my plans, and they don't involve the corporate life much longer.

Besides, the poor guy has no clue in what capacity my filthy boss-slash-boyfriend hired me, or what grotesque sum he's been paying me.

Ethan and Jamie FaceTimed me last night to invite me to join them in Langkawi, Malaysia for a few days as they break their journey home. It was the quickest *yes* I've ever given. I physically ache with the need to be close to him again, even though the pleasure at seeing how well they both look never fades. They're both tanned and healthy, their hair sun-kissed and their grins wide. There's an ease with each other that shines through even on a video call, and it tells me categorically that this trip has given them all the healing Ethan hoped for and more.

I cannot *wait* to see them.

~

THERE'S a knock at the door to my office. When I look up, I find to my surprise that Elena is standing in the doorway. She looks, as ever, stunningly beautiful and perfectly put together, if a little flustered.

'I'm so sorry for dropping in unannounced. I wondered if I could steal you away for a quick coffee. I totally understand if you're too busy.'

I am self-aware enough to know that I'm a nosy bitch. So when my boyfriend's ex-wife offers me an opportunity to chat, then you can bet I'm going to bite her hand off with indecent haste. Also, she saw the boys last week, and I'll be pathetically grateful for any additional scraps of information she can give me about how they're getting on.

'Definitely!' I force myself to push my chair in a calm, ladylike manner. 'Everything's under control here. And my awful boss is away, so he'll never know I'm slacking.'

She smiles awkwardly at that. I give her a double kiss at the doorway and we head out to a local coffee shop. First thing in the morning, it's insane, but it's quietened down by now.

'So, how was your trip?' I ask her once we're sitting with our coffees. She has a light tan and a smattering of freckles over her nose. The teeny part of me that isn't disgustingly in love with her ex-husband would love to have seen them together. No wonder Jamie is such a good-looking kid. She really is naturally, ethereally beautiful. Ethan told me that her mother is French. It explains the effortless chic she has going on.

'It was wonderful. Do you have everything you need?' She looks worriedly around the table. 'Sugar? Is this dark enough? I can go up and ask them if they have any other types.'

I smile reassuringly at her. 'I have everything I need. I promise.'

'Okay. If you're sure. Here.' She slides the bowl of light Demerara towards me and watches intently as I add half a teaspoon to my black coffee. The truth is that I'd have loved something darker—maybe muscovado—but my inner pop psychologist is already honing its initial analysis of Elena as Two Enneagram from that first time I met her, and I'm not about to take advantage of the fact that she'd absolutely go up to the counter and make them ransack their sugar stocks for me. She may have a Three wing—you don't get to be a translator for the UN without having major drive—but I'd bet that at her core she's a Two.

The Helper.

What must it be like to wake up every day with a deeply entrenched need to help others and be married to Ethan Kingsley Version 1.0?

Very fucking ungratifying, that's what.

'So the trip was great,' I prompt her, and she blinks.

'Oh! Yes, it was fantastic. The boys were on excellent form. That's why I wanted to buy you a coffee, actually. They were both so well, and I just...' She presses a hand to her heart. 'I just couldn't believe how relaxed Ethan seemed, and they were so *easy* with each other. I know you've been the one to persuade him to start therapy, and I can't thank you enough.' Her brown eyes fill with tears, and she shakes her head, frustrated. 'I didn't see us ever getting to this place when I walked out on him. I really didn't.'

'Oh my gosh.' I reach out and put my hand over hers. She strikes me as quite shy, but she's incredibly sweet, and my heart is bleeding for her. 'Honestly, I can't take any credit. I may have strong-armed him into therapy'—*using techniques I'll never tell you about*—'but the work has all been Ethan's. He's really, really intent on seeing this through, and you should know that his whole motivation comes from wanting to be a better dad to Jamie.' I squeeze her hand one last time and sit back.

'I wanted to talk to you about that. He explained what he's been doing with the therapist, and it sounds really powerful, but... I suppose I'm trying to get a sense for how much of this astounding transformation has come from him just getting away from Richard and the company and all that, and how much is—permanent. I can't help but worry that when he gets back to London, this chilled-out version of him will fade away again.'

I consider my response carefully, because it's a fair question. 'I think most of us would be a far more relaxed version of ourselves if we were surfing rather than navigating London traffic every day, and you've seen him far more recently than I have, but what's different for Ethan is that he now understands what's going on in his nervous system. He understands why he gets angry or controlling or walled up, and that gives him a fighting chance at working on those parts of him that are calling the shots.

'Previously, he was totally oblivious, from what I saw. And yeah, he'll come back to London, but he's cut ties with his dad and he's walked away from the company. Those are major, major steps towards finding his own path. If anything, I'd expect him to double down on his progress when he's back rather than go backwards.'

'Perhaps.' She takes a dainty sip of her coffee. 'I hope you're right. I'm very aware that...' She clears her throat. 'When I left Ethan, neither of us were in a good place, and my only priority was Jamie. Ethan was just so toxic. I begged him to go to therapy, but he wouldn't hear of it. He'd go through these cycles of lashing out at everyone around him, and then hating himself for it, and then withdrawing so much that it was as if there was no one at home. It was awful, and there was absolutely nothing I could do to help him.'

'It sounds so difficult,' I murmur. 'I can't even imagine.'

She shrugs in an elegantly French way. 'I was all out of options. I had to get Jamie away from Ethan and his fucking father. But I've never *wanted* to keep him away—I just thought it was the safest thing for his wellbeing. And Ethan seemed happy with that solution, too. Not happy, per se, but he seemed to think Jamie was better off without him, too, which broke my heart. So I pushed for custody, and he didn't fight me. But now... I wonder if I should reconsider. I've never seen our custody agreement as a power struggle or an act of spite. And if they truly end up having a relationship that's healthy and beneficial for Jamie, then it would be wrong to preserve that ruling.'

My heart starts to beat faster. Harder. 'You'd consider joint custody?'

'If.' Her voice is firm. 'If they come back and Jamie wants to see more of his dad, then I wouldn't stop him in any case. Besides, he won't be working all hours like he used to. It would make sense.'

Now it's me who's in danger of crying. 'I think that would be a very beautiful thing to do for your son *and* your ex-husband,' I say quietly, 'and I would be amazed if it didn't prove a huge success.'

She nods. Her eyes are still bright with unshed tears. 'I only want what's best for my son. He's amazing. And, of course, a close, loving relationship with his dad is the best thing for him.'

I give her a huge smile and raise my coffee cup in a salute. 'No arguments here.'

'So.' She cocks her head and considers me. 'You and Ethan —you're serious?'

'Yes.' It feels weird as fuck to sit across from his ex and admit that. 'Very.'

'And you didn't mind him taking Jamie away for so long?'

'If you could make the sacrifice, so could I. And if you must know, it's the swooniest thing I've ever seen. How could I not fall in love with him a little bit more when he said he was chucking in everything, me included, to show up for his son?'

She laughs a little, but then her expression grows serious. 'It was a wonderful decision. And, if you know Ethan as well as I do, a very shocking one. I have to say'—she stares out of the window for a beat—'that seeing them like this together was bittersweet for me. I'll be honest with you. I loved him very much, and when I married him, I saw glimpses of that man. Glimpses. But that's all they were. I could never— unlock them, I suppose. I could never unlock *him*. And it felt like such a waste, as if this amazing man was frozen inside this huge block of ice for years and years, and I had no way of melting it and helping him to escape. And I was so frustrated and so *angry* with him for so long, but at the same time, it would break my heart.'

I stare at her. What a stunning—and devastating—analogy. 'I'm so bloody sorry. It's tragic for all of you. I'm so sorry he didn't have the tools he needed back then, that none of you did. And I'm even more sorry that he couldn't be what you needed him to be. It's not his fault, and it's definitely not yours, but it's still shitty, and you're allowed to mourn it.'

She nods. 'It is a type of grief, really. I mean, I'm over him. I'm not in love with him anymore, just so you know. I'm very much ready to move on—I've been dating a colleague of mine for a few months, actually.'

'Oh, I'm so happy to hear that!' I really am. Poor, poor Elena, spending a decade and a half with a man who couldn't escape his demons. And to fly across the world only to find that the Self-led version of him, the one she always had faith was buried in there somewhere beneath all that trauma, is a living, breathing thing?

She's right. It's a very real kind of grief.

'Thank you. I'm happy. And if my son finally has the father he's always deserved, then I'm ecstatic. As a mother, that's all I've ever wanted for him.'

'You're such a good mother,' I tell her. 'It's not really any of my business, but I think you've managed this entire process with such grace and wisdom. Honestly, hats off to you.'

'That means a lot to me,' she says with an incline of her head. She gives me an enigmatic little smile. 'And from the expression on Ethan's face whenever he says your name, I suspect this family will be very much your business when the boys get home.'

CHAPTER 52

Sophia

The Datai Langkawi, where I'm meeting the boys, is nestled amid dense rainforest, right on the coast of the Malaysian island of Langkawi. I know many, many facts about this resort, because I've spent far too much time on its website and Instagram account over the past few days.

I have never been this excited in my life. I'm finally going to be reunited with my man, and in the most spectacular surroundings. I'm never letting him go again.

He offered to send the jet for me, but even I'm not princessy enough to demand a private jet for one. Instead, I graciously accept a first-class plane ticket. I shower in the airport lounge and change into my adorable hot pink sundress, and a driver from the hotel picks me up. Ethan and Jamie arrived here late last night. I strum my fingers on the Jeep's leather upholstery for the entire journey, because I. Cannot. Wait.

In the vast lobby, with its vaulted wooden ceiling, I stand for a moment, disorientated, until I hear a shout from behind me.

'Soph!'

I know that voice.

I swivel, and oh my God.

There he is!

But also—holy fuck. He is so *fucking* hot. He and Jamie are grinning at me, and he looks so tanned, and rugged, and muscular. He has a neatly trimmed beard, and his brown hair is sun-streaked, and, in a soft cream T-shirt and beige cargo shorts, he basically looks like some hot, ripped surfer dude.

I'm totally going to get railed by the ripped surfer dude.

We both start running, even though I'm in wedges, and we kind of slam into each other. The moment my body hits his, the moment he wraps his arms around me and I get to inhale the scent of his skin, it hits me like a tonne of bricks how much I've missed him. How shitty a facsimile of *this* our Face-Times and WhatsApps have been. How viscerally I need to be with him, to be close to him. I wrap my arms more tightly around him and tilt my head up to snort his neck, and he chuckles, low and soft.

'Hi, you.' He strokes my hair and then forces me away from his neck so he can kiss me. It's slow and loving, and it may be pretty PG, but it's perfect. Simply having his lips pressed against mine is perfect. When he pulls away to study me, I beam up at him like some kind of crazed koala bear, fisting his t-shirt in my hands. He smiles back down at me, his thumbs grazing my cheeks. 'Aren't you a sight for sore eyes.'

'Right back at you,' I retort.

'Jesus, get a room, guys,' Jamie grumbles beside us, and I laugh, embarrassed, and extricate myself.

'Oh god, sorry, Jamie! Hi!' I go in for a hug, which he returns awkwardly. 'You look fantastic!' I tell him. 'You both do.'

'Do you want to see the villa?' he blurts out. 'We got a beachside one. It's fire.'

'I would *love* to see the villa.' I put my hand in Ethan's and squeeze tightly.

The three of us walk through the hotel, Jamie loping ahead. I swear he's grown even more since I last saw him. The resort is spectacular, but I can't quite take it in, because I'm too busy gaping at my hot boyfriend, and it seems he's having the same problem. Every time our eyes lock, we grin like lovesick fools, which I suppose we are.

I've been dreaming of this moment for months. I'd come to terms with the fact that I wouldn't see him until he landed back on British soil, and I had detailed plans to go full *Love Actually* on him and Jamie at Heathrow, but this is even better, because this place rocks, and because I get to see him in full Aussie Ethan mode, when he's still chilled out and wearing shorts and flip-flops.

I *really* dig Aussie Ethan.

Every tiny thing feels like a miracle. The heady scent of the rich undergrowth that surrounds our path. The secure warmth of Ethan's hand in mine. The slap of his flip-flops on the wooden walkway. And then we happen upon the most beautiful low-level buildings, framed in lush gardens.

'This is incredible.' I turn in a circle, taking in the stunning landscape, the turquoise pool, and the two glass-and-wood structures that sit perpendicular to each other around the pool.

'I don't even have my own room, I have my own *villa*.' Jamie spins in front of the smaller freestanding structure, pointing through the open French doors to a chic bedroom. 'But yours is even bigger. It's massive. Come and see. Your shower is lit. Dad let me try it last night.'

He trots across the terrace and through the doors of our villa, and I marvel at the change in him. Gone is the hangdog demeanour, in its place a serious happy puppy vibe. It's amazing to see. I grin at Ethan as we follow him through into a stunning, neutrally decorated lounge area with vaulted wooden ceilings and then into a fuck-off bedroom. Oh, this will do very nicely for my purposes. I glance at Ethan again, and it appears we're on the same page, because he clears his throat.

'When's your golf lesson, mate? Two o'clock? Better go and get changed for it. I can help Soph unpack.'

Jamie frowns. 'But her bags aren't here yet.'

'I'm sure they'll bring them down any minute,' Ethan counters smoothly. 'They're very efficient.'

I suppress a laugh as Jamie shrugs. The kid has zero guile, bless him. 'Okay.' He bounds off with all the grace and exuberance of a Labrador puppy.

'Have fun,' Ethan calls after him. 'Try not to stress about about your swing too much. Just relax and enjoy the views. And don't forget your golf shoes!'

Poor Jamie is scarcely out of our villa when Ethan pushes the bedroom door shut and spins around, pulling me into his arms. His kiss is ravenous, as if he's trying to consume me with his mouth. *This man.* I return the kiss, clutching at his bicep for stability as I grab at his hair, our mouths sliding, tongues doing battle. He tastes like *Ethan*, and the beard is a new and very welcome addition, adding excellent friction. I want to climb my man like a tree and never come down.

'Bathroom,' he gasps into my mouth. 'In case the poor porters do actually show up.'

He backs me into a palatial bathroom before locking the door and slumping against it. He's already breathing heavily. 'Fuck, I love you so much. You're even better in reality. Now strip.'

I cross my arms. 'Ditto. And ditto. And no fucking way. You left me, and I've come all this way. You need to make it worth my while. *You* strip.'

He grins sexily and hauls himself off the door. 'The lady

makes a fair point.' He yanks his t-shirt off, and I can safely say I have never felt this smug in my entire life as I do watching Ripped Surfer Ethan prepare to get naked for little old *moi*.

He balls the t-shirt up and chucks it at me. 'I'm feeling objectified.'

'So you fucking well should.' He's huge and golden and all hard muscle and sculptural planes. His normally flat stomach is now an actual six-pack. He should never, ever go back to a desk job if this is how the outdoorsy lifestyle makes him look. I circle my finger at the groin area. *'Off.'*

He looks entirely too self-satisfied shoving down his shorts and boxers, as well he should. He kicks them off and straightens up, his lovely hard cock bobbing.

Jesus Christ, how I have missed that cock.

'Nice dick.'

'Thanks. What are you going to do about it?'

'This.' My very cute sundress has a ruched upper half and sweet little bows on the straps. I undo the bows, letting the straps hang loose, and work the dress down over my boobs and hips, unveiling my little welcome gift: no underwear was donned at the airport. 'Tada!'

'You little beauty.' He's on me in a second, and fuck me, if the shock of full-body skin on skin isn't the single best thing in the human experience, I don't know what is. Except for what comes next, obviously.

We go crazy, groping each other's arses and dragging our hands over each other's skin and kissing wildly, heads twisting and limbs everywhere.

'Shower,' he gets out, and we manoeuvre ourselves into the huge walk-in shower. He cranks up the water, and I yelp as the cold spray hits us, but I don't even care. I'm breathless as he kisses the life out of me, our skin growing slick. I grab his dick with zero finesse—Jesus *fuck*, that feels good—but he pulls my hand away laughingly. 'Don't. I won't last as it is.'

'Don't care, as long as you can go again.' I reach for it, and he cuffs both wrists with one hand. 'Seriously, sweetheart. I haven't had sex in three months. Much as I love your hand on me, I'd rather it was your cunt that was gripping me when I shoot my load.'

Okay, that's an excellent point. I nod and dive on him again, moving my mouth over his face, mapping him with my lips. How can he be exactly as I remembered and yet so much *better*? 'I love you,' I mumble. 'I love you, I love you, I love you. Don't ever leave me again. You're not allowed.'

'I have no plans to.' He slicks my hair back into a rope and twists it around his fist, tilting my head up. 'Not ever.' His face is grave, and the sincerity of his words hits me right in the heart. I can feel pressure welling up in my sinuses and behind my eyes.

'Good.'

'Good. Glad that's settled. Now back up against the wall for me like a good girl, and let's take a look at you.'

He may be a world away from the icy, dysregulated Ethan I met all those months ago, but he can still seriously pull out that BDE when he wants to, which is most excellent. I shiver and back up against the huge, cool limestone tiles.

'Spread your legs.'

I spread 'em faster than you can say *ho*.

Then he's coming towards me, looking at my body as though it's the single most exquisite sight he's ever seen. He comes right up close and bends so he can take one aching nipple into his mouth as he closes a strong hand around my other breast.

I practically shoot through the ceiling.

Holy fuck, the *relief* of having his mouth, his hands, on me after all this time. It's like nothing else. I must be squirming excessively, because suddenly he's cuffing my upper arms and pinning me to the wall as he alternates between my boobs with his beautiful mouth and tongue and teeth, sucking and licking and tugging and kissing, and then he's getting to his knees, peppering my stomach with kisses on the way down as he goes.

He hooks one of my legs over his shoulder and looks up at me, a torrent of water pouring over him, bouncing off his broad shoulders, his eyelashes wet and starry and his expression ardent, and I was wrong earlier.

This is the most smug I've ever felt.

It's also the most besotted, and needy, and ravenous. I inhale so raggedly as he slides a couple of fingers inside me that I almost choke on my own breath. I sound like I'm in respiratory failure.

'You are every fantasy I've ever had,' he tells me. 'And every fantasy I didn't know to imagine.' The candour of his swoony words is written all over his gorgeous face. I make some pathetic, whiny noise and, reaching down, grip his head and yank it forward to my pussy.

His gratified chuckle is the last thing I hear before his tongue hits my clit and I lose every last piece of my executive function.

How the *hell* have I lived without this for three months?

The best part about it is that Ethan seems as disinterested as I am in eking out this orgasm. The master of all edgers is hell-bent on delivering a flurry of climaxes all round with the efficiency and deadliness of machine gun fire. His new secret weapon: *stubble*.

'Rub your beard against my clit,' I gasp, 'and fuck me harder with your fingers. I need this hard and fast.'

'Spoken like my true soulmate,' he growls against me as he obliges on both fronts, abrading my most sensitive parts with his yummy beard and thrusting his fingers inside me so hard that the wet slaps are audible even over the torrent of water.

'Fuck. I need you to fuck me so hard after this. I want it

rough.' I pull on his hair, and he makes some strangled noise I think he intends to suggest that he may not actually survive that long. I let my head fall back against the tiles and give myself over to the sheer pleasure of it, the indulgence, the astonishing need my body has for his.

Ethan's not the only one who needs to worry about not lasting today. A few short minutes of his handiwork and I detonate, screaming out my release as my orgasm engulfs me like wildfire. I'm barely coming off it before he's scrambling to his feet, lifting my leg again with a hand under my knee, and shoving inside me like a fucking caveman. No finesse, no patience, just brute force.

I loop my arms loosely around his neck. In truth, I have no bodily strength left after that orgasm turned my limbs to jelly, so I hope his dick can impale me effectively enough to keep me upright.

My money's on his dick.

When he's fully inside me, we both bark out shocked laughs, because the reality of him filling me up is so over-whelming, so all-consuming, that it wipes out everything else. He's squatting slightly to line up with me, and I'm on one tiptoe, which feels ill-advised, despite the dick-as-prop situa-tion. It seems he agrees, for he hoists me up with a hand under my other knee and shoves me up harder against the tiled wall. It's smooth, but it could be a wall of nails for all I care.

If my spine has to be collateral damage while I receive the most satisfying railing of my adult life, it will all have been worthwhile.

'I'm too heavy—' I begin, but he presses his forehead to mine.

'Don't insult me or yourself.'

No argument here.

'Better,' he grunts, kissing me hard and parting my lips with his tongue as he rams up hard inside me.

Mmph is my impassioned agreement.

He breaks away. 'Sure you want it rough?'

'Don't you fucking dare hold back.' I dig the nails of both hands into his shoulders. I'm a cowgirl, and they're my spurs, and Ethan Kingsley is my thoroughbred. Time to take him for a ride.

'Hold on tight, then.' Like the keeper he is, he keeps his word, fucking me hard and fast up against the wall, his hips pistoning as his dick drags up and down me in the most perfect way. I'm not sure how it can feel like the filthiest and most intimate act on the planet, and all at the same time, but it does. I'm seeing stars and making farmyard noises as he fucks me and fucks me, all the while kissing me with a savage passion.

'Close,' I pant into his mouth.

'Thank fuck. Show me.'

If he's the thoroughbred, I'm the prancing show pony who's always ecstatic at the chance to show off. I writhe against him, my greedy pussy chasing every last drop of sensation as I exploit his glorious cock with every bit of shamelessness I possess. The heat is deeper this time, in some primal part of my body, as if every single sex organ I possess is colluding on some grandiose cymbal crash. He fucks me and fucks me, and I moan like a porn star as I thrust into him as best as I can which, honestly, is not very much. Still, desire is a great antidote to muscle fatigue.

'So good,' he growls in my mouth. 'Jesus, I love you. I can *feel* you.'

Yes, it seems he can, because the tremors grow and grow and suddenly I'm flying through the air like a big, slutty, orgasmic rock slung from a catapult.

It's probably worth clarifying, given this ambitious sexual position, that I mean that figuratively and not literally.

Oh my fucking Christ I am fucking done. *Done*. Dead.

Deceased. Ended. That was *the* best orgasm of my life. Meanwhile, my *amour* is emptying the juicy cum-fruits of his great big ball sacs into my pussy with staggering levels of virility. He gives up on my mouth and drops his head to the wall, roaring out his release as he pumps me and pumps me with borderline violent thrusts. As he does, his roars morph into something that sounds like *I love you. I love you. I love you.*

Honestly, he talked down his game just now, but this is a seriously impressive performance.

I'm totally marrying him.

CHAPTER 53

Sophia

The Pavilion restaurant at the Datai may just be the most incredible dining venue I've ever encountered, and I've dined in some pretty fabulous locations. It's basically this huge pavilion (oddly enough) that floats off the edge of the terrace into the rainforest while being held up by thirty-metre-high stilts. It's open-sided and dotted with candlelit tables, with beautiful views out to the canopy of tree-tops that surround it. The scent of the warm evening air mingles with the fragrant cooking smells courtesy of the restaurant's Thai chef.

A friendly server leads the three of us to a table at the far end of the restaurant. It's quiet and is perfectly positioned for us to enjoy this panorama, especially because Ethan insists I sit facing the rainforest. He and I are both still punch-drunk from this afternoon's orgasms—we went another round in our bed—and Jamie is on good form. Apparently, his golf lesson went great and his chipping is improving. He also told me on the way over that he's pleased I'm here to keep his dad company so he can spend some overdue time with his Nintendo Switch.

I let out a slow exhale as we await our drinks. This place is magical. I mainly travel in Europe. I've hit up Singapore and Hong Kong a few times, but being here, perched high above the soft earth of the rainforest with the man I love and the son he's forged such a strong, loving relationship with is the best kind of suspension from reality. London, and its bustle and noise and pollution, suddenly feels like a wholly unappealing prospect.

Our drinks arrive—champagne for Ethan and me and fresh lemonade for Jamie—and Jamie nudges him. 'Dad,' he hisses.

'Okay.' Ethan clears his throat. 'We've, uh, we've made you something. We've been working on it on and off for most of the trip, haven't we, mate?'

Jamie nods. His smile is wider than I've ever seen it, and I sit up straighter. 'Really? How cool!' I have a sudden vision of the boys working away on some old-time handicrafts together. You know, whittling me a homemade recorder out of bamboo, or something folksy like that. Stranger things have happened. So I'm extremely confused when Ethan hands me his phone.

'Check out the app at the very bottom.'

I glance down. There's an app called Lynx, its thumbnail a graphic of a metal link. 'Lynx?'

'Yeah,' Ethan says as Jamie says, 'Say it out loud again!'

'Lynx. Lynx. Oh.' I look at the graphic again. 'Links! It's a homophone!'

'Yes.' Jamie smacks the table in satisfaction, and Ethan nods. He seems quiet. Watchful.

'Open it.'

'*Links*. I love it.' I click on the app and it opens up. There are two grey bars across the screen. One says GAME and one DICTIONARY. Ethan cranes his head to see it.

'Okay. Click on DICTIONARY.'

I click, feeling some sort of nervous butterflies, though I'm not sure why.

'Can I tell her, Dad?' Jamie asks, and I look up to see Ethan nodding.

'Go for it.'

I click in, and a list of words comes up with the alphabet hyperlinked down the left-hand side.

'We've made you a game,' Jamie explains. 'Like Connections, because you're so obsessed with it. But Dad said you always wanted to see all the category tags, so we built them.'

I stare dumbly at him. 'What?'

He points. 'Click on any word and you'll see.'

'Oh my god,' I mutter, the butterflies turning to flutters of real excitement. 'Are you for real? You've built me a Connections game with a *back end?*'

'Yeah!' Jamie nods excitedly. 'Well, I built the code for it and Dad built the words part.'

'Because I'm illiterate at coding and you're illiterate at the English language,' Ethan supplies.

'That's rude.'

Ethan raises an eyebrow at him. '*Pillow sheets?* Need I say more?'

They both collapse into laughter, and I smile. Must be some insider joke. They're fucking adorable. I scroll through the As.

'Okay, I'm clicking on *arm*. Oh my god!'

When I click into the word, various tags come up.

> *Body part (v)*

> *—chair (n)*

> *Weapon (n)*

> *Weaponise (v)*

> *Division (n)*

'Holy shit!' I look up at them. 'This is amazing! Are you kidding me right now?'

They glance at each other again and smile. There's definitely something I'm not getting here—they're being cagey as fuck. Jamie pushes Ethan on his shoulder. 'Tell her to play the game. We set one up for you.'

'Why don't you give the game a go, sweetheart?' Ethan says in a sexy, sugared tone.

'Alright. But I want to play with the dictionary for a *lot* longer afterwards.' I click through to the GAME tab, and up comes a four-by-four grid, just like in Connections. There are sixteen words locked and ready to go. Below them, like in Connections, is a Shuffle button. I press it. 'Should I do it now?'

TESTAMENT	MI	WED	BEQUEATH
JOIN	EGO	YA	U
VOLITION	METHYL	HITCH	THOU
EWE	ESPOUSE	DETERMINATION	MYSELF

'Yes!' Jamie practically shouts. 'It's a special one, just for you.'

I shimmy in my seat and straighten my shoulders. 'Bring it. You with me on this, babe?'

'No.' He smiles at me and shakes his head. 'You're on your own for this one.'

I focus on the letters, reading them aloud to the boys so I can pick up any homophones. Once I've run through them once, I see a couple of potential patterns. Saying *ewe* aloud made the first one click for me.

'Ewe, ya, thou, U.' I hit them all and press Select. '*You*. Bingo! One down.'

'Nice one,' Ethan says.

'She's guessing them in the wrong order,' Jamie stage-whispers, and I look up.

'Am I? Oh, sorry.'

'No, you're good,' Ethan tells me. 'Keep going.'

'This is so clever. I can't believe you guys built this for me. Okay, let's see.'

I squint at the puzzle. *Mi* is probably the musical note—thank you, *The Sound of Music*. 'Anyone know what the abbreviation for Methyl is?' I ask them. I have my suspicions, but I'm not so hot on the periodic table these days.

'M-E,' Jamie says, drumming his fingers on the table.

I select Myself, Methyl, Ego and Mi and the answer comes up correct. *Me*. 'Yay! Go me!'

My eyes latch onto *testament*. 'Old Testament? New Testament? Last will and testament?' I muse aloud. Jamie's sharp intake of breath has me snagging on that one. Will. Ah, yes. Bequeath. Determination. Testament, and... Volition. Triumphantly, I hit Select. '*Will*. Three down, one to go.'

I highlight the four remaining words: Hitch, join, espouse, wed. No guessing required. '*Marry*. I did it! That was so clever, guys.'

Ethan licks his lips, his expression tense and watchful. He glances at Jamie like he's unsure of something.

'Read the answers out loud!' Jamie sing-songs, and I chuckle. He's ridiculously sweet.

YOU

EWE, U, THOU, YA

ME

EGO, METHYL, MI, MYSELF

WILL

BEQUEATH, DETERMINATION, TESTAMENT, VOLITION

MARRY

ESPOUSE, HITCH, JOIN, WED

'You. Me. Will. Marry.' I stop and freeze. Jamie said I was guessing them in the wrong order, didn't he?

You. Me. Will. Marry.

I look up from the screen.

Ethan is smiling at me. He's a handsome man, a beautiful man, but I've never seen his face so radiant with love, with a bright hopefulness.

'Will you marry me?' he whispers, and the world stands still.

My entire body begins to shake. Tears spring from nowhere and tremble on my lash line. 'What?' I'm officially a dumbass. 'Are you serious?'

He reaches across the table with both hands and sandwiches my hand between them, his touch warm and sure. 'I've never been more serious in my life.'

The words tumble from my lips. 'Well, yes! Of course I will! Oh my god! Oh my god!' I'm weeping, shivering, as feelings hit me like an emotional hailstorm.

He wants to marry me.

We're going to get married.

I'll be his wife.

He's out of his seat and rounding the table, kneeling beside me and covering my face with kisses as I laugh and cry and grab his head in my hands.

'You're going to be my husband,' I say, like a fool, and he rubs my nose with his.

'That's the plan. You're going to be my wife. God, I like the sound of that.'

'And you're going to be my stepmother,' Jamie pipes up from across the table, and we both burst out laughing as I glance up at him. He's wriggling, looking a combination of mortified and tickled pink.

'Oh, shit! Can I be a very wicked one?'

'No way,' Jamie says, just as his dad adds, 'Be my guest, sweetheart.'

~

LATER, I lie in the huge bed with my fiancé, two commas curled inwards as we gaze at each other from inches apart.

'I railroaded you, didn't I?' he asks, dragging a hand down his face.

I circle his wrist, pulling it away. 'No! You surprised the hell out of me, but you didn't railroad me.'

He groans. 'I wasn't sure about whether I should spring it on you so soon, and I definitely wasn't sure about doing it in front of Jamie in a public place. The Lynx app was just supposed to be a present for you. It started out as a fun project for the two of us, and it spiralled from there. And then Jamie had the idea of proposing to you via the clues, so I had to include him.'

'Wait—it was Jamie's idea?'

He nods, bashful.

'That's amazing!' My heart swells. The sweet little guy.

'To be honest, that was what spurred me on. I was nervous about how he'd react to my remarrying, especially since the past year has been so tough on him. I didn't want to undo all the work we'd done on our relationship, but he was all for it. He likes you. And he likes how happy you make me. So that was him taken care of, and then I just needed to worry about you running for the hills.'

I smirk. 'So you proposed on a small, remote island?'

'Yeah. Exactly.'

I snuggle in closer. 'I'm not going anywhere. And, while I didn't expect to leave Malaysia as your future wife'—saying it aloud again has me suddenly feeling shy—'I'm ready, babe. I'm more than ready. Bring it on.'

He kisses me, and I lose myself to the moment. Kissing him when I know he'll be my husband is a whole other level of intoxicating. Everything is a whole other level of intoxicating, even being in bed with him. This is how it'll be, forever and ever.

He pulls away from the kiss but leaves his hands on me. 'I haven't even got you a ring—I didn't want to rush it and grab something I wasn't sure about.'

'Hey. You built me a semantic database to make my weird

little brain happy. Nothing says *everlasting love* like that. Who needs a ring?'

'I love your weird little brain. It's incredible.' He kisses my nose. 'And you'll get a ring. A very big one. For now, maybe you can wear your stack on your left hand.'

I look down as he eases my gorgeous, shiny stack off my right hand and slides it reverently onto my left. Our eyes lock.

'You're seriously good at choosing rings. I have high expectations.'

'I wouldn't expect anything less.' He clears his throat. 'There was one more thing I wanted to say. I—we can have a long engagement, if you like. I walked away from you for months, and you've been amazing about it. I didn't want you trekking out here to meet us and then leaving not knowing that I want to spend the rest of my life with you.' His grey eyes are so soft, so loving. 'But I also know... that I'm still a work in progress. You're in such great shape, mentally. I've made strides, but I might not be husband material just yet. We can wait if—'

I put a hand over his mouth. 'No. Stop it right there. We've had this conversation, remember? You're not broken, you're not damaged. You are whole and perfect and wonderful, and it will be the privilege of my life to marry you. The second you threw away everything for Jamie, I knew you were it for me. Understand?' I remove my finger and smile at him.

He nods, his eyes growing wet. 'I'm going to keep working on myself.'

'Fine. But do it for yourself, not for me.'

'I will. I've grown to enjoy it, actually. It feels like I finally have some control over myself.'

I grin at the C-word. 'The right kind of control. The good kind.'

'Yeah.' He hooks a hairy leg over me and tugs me right against him, yawning. Poor guy with his young, insatiable fiancée. I've exhausted him. We lie like that, in each other's arms, and I feel an overwhelming sense of peace. I've finally found my forever place in the world, and it's beautiful.

When I'm almost asleep, he speaks, his voice slurred with tiredness. 'I meant to say, I've been reading one of those Enneagram books you gave me for Christmas. It's good stuff. I think I might be an Eight? What do you think?'

Epilogue

TWO YEARS LATER

'You're so amazing with her,' Soph tells Jamie as he bounces his six-month-old sister, Lola, on his lap, holding her under her arms. 'Look! She adores you.'

Lola's gummy beam is dazzling as she stares, bewitched, at her brother. Her tiny hands make grabby fists as she attempts to reach for his hair, his ears—whatever she can get hold of—but every time he bumps her on his thighs, her tiny bare feet flail, and she cackles her deep belly laugh.

The sound of my baby daughter's laugh may just be the best thing in the world. I have videos and voice notes full of it. I'll never, ever get over it.

Lola is her mother through and through—a ray of sunshine, genuinely captivated by everyone she meets, and determined to seize the maximum pleasure from every moment.

She's already a wonderful teacher.

My son tears his eyes from her for a second to glance up at me. 'She's so sweet. And it's good that she can sit up now.'

'It's very good,' I agree. Now, Soph and I can prop her up on a rug without constantly worrying that she'll keel over sideways. It makes entertaining her far easier—and lower maintenance.

'Can you take her for a sec? I want to grab another pizza.'

'Of course, mate. It's your party. Go for it.' I hold out my arms, but instead of handing her over immediately, he buries his face in her soft golden neck and lets out a loud raspberry. Her little body freezes as her mouth goes comically wide with delight and she lets out her signature fishwife cackle.

Jamie comes up for air, grinning like he's just won an Olympic one-hundred metres. I know how he feels, because I could blow raspberries on Lola's skin all day long for the rest of my life and never get bored.

'Just one more.' Banding one arm securely around her middle, he holds out her tiny arm and goes for a raspberry right in the crook of her elbow. Right on cue, Lola honks.

'Her laugh is as classy as her mother's,' I observe drily to my wife.

'Sounds about right.' Soph bends down to take our daughter, but I beat her to it, grabbing Lola and pulling her tightly into my arms so I can smother her soft cheeks and shock of black hair in kisses as my wife sings *Obsessed* by Mariah Carey under her breath.

She may have a point.

'Go and give your mum a hug,' I tell Jamie with an affectionate slap on the shoulder as he attempts to shoot off. 'She's barely seen you this afternoon.'

Elena is here with her newish husband, Raphael, a UN colleague she started dating just after I met Soph. I'm thrilled my ex has found happiness. I always knew she was a wonderful person, and far too good for me, a fact she underscored when she dropped by a couple of weeks after our return from

Australia to tell me she'd had our custody agreement amended to a flexible fifty-fifty.

The generosity of her actions could have knocked me down with a feather.

After the four of us had met up for a surreal and slightly excruciating dinner, I asked Soph what she thought of Elena's new bloke.

She shrugged. 'I mean, some people like that whole *adoring and indecently hot French nerd who speaks five languages and could feasibly model Swiss timepieces* thing. It's overrated, if you ask me.'

I raised an eyebrow then, fairly certain that she was fucking with me, and she planted a kiss on my cheek. 'Girl traded up. Deal with it, Eight. Anyway, you got me.'

I certainly did.

Also, it turned out she and all her friends had been secretly referring to me as Eight the entire time she was working for me. I'm glad I was such an instant open book to her, because I certainly mystified the fuck out of myself for a long time.

TODAY IS the official *family and friends* celebration of Jamie's sixteenth birthday. He turned sixteen in the middle of his GCSE exams, which was pretty shit for him. We found a compromise—he and his mates did an epic day out at Thorpe Park before the exams kicked off, going on all the most terrifying rides over and over, and we agreed that we'd celebrate with our loved ones and some of his friends in slightly classier style once the exams were over, so here we are. He and I also have Centre Court tickets to far too many matches when Wimbledon starts next week.

The contrast between the contented, well-adjusted young man my son is today and the dejected, emotionally closed-off kid he was when I met Soph is pronounced. She'll deny it a million times over, but she saved me. Jamie. Us. Our family. She saw me, and she believed in me, and that belief, that incredible compassion and insight and lack of judgement she demonstrated when I had done little to earn it, transformed my life.

She and Philip have shown me that healing is possible from the darkest and most hopeless circumstances, and they've taught me another secret, too.

Healing yourself has a ripple effect. Being in the orbit of someone like Soph gave me the courage to do the work, meaning I in turn was able to support my son in getting the help he needed to heal from my failings. I rid myself of toxic relationships—namely Richard Kingsley—and I instead invested in the relationships that fed my soul. My son. My wife. Even my *ex*-wife. Mates like Bren and Aide and Miles and, though I hate to admit it, his annoying younger brother. I even consider their father a friend and mentor these days. They're all here today with their other halves. Marlowe can now just about look me in the eye. Saoirse, Lotta and Nora I get on famously with.

We are, in fact, celebrating today on the beautiful terrace of the Montague Knightsbridge, the very same *grande dame* hotel I was once so desperate to get my grubby little mitts on. Miles insisted on making it available for our little shindig, and Saoirse, who is a hugely talented events planner for the Montague and Sorrel Farm joint venture, has made the space look magical without it being a turn-off for teenage boys. She's even procured a wood-fired pizza oven, which is going down a storm with Jamie and his mates.

I adjust my beautiful little girl in my arms and take a step towards my equally gorgeous wife. She's radiant in a long flowing sunshine-yellow dress. Its huge slit shows off her long, tanned legs, and it puts her spectacular tits on a platter. Lola's not the only one who has a thing for them. Far more importantly, she's smiling up at me with more love, more adoration, than I could ever have hoped to elicit in a fellow human.

'Come over here.' I take her hand, steering her over to the north edge of the terrace to where Hyde Park is laid out below us in a heavenly early-summer sprawl of green. Cupping Lola's soft little head for support, I bend and kiss my wife on her plump crimson mouth. Her long dark eyelashes flutter shut, and the familiar awe hits me once again. That I get to spend my life with her. That I make her happy. That, together, we're raising a beautiful little girl and an almost-man, the very sight of whom makes me burst with pride and love.

'I love you,' I whisper. When she opens her eyes, they're filled with so much emotion.

'I love you. So much. I'm a puddle on the floor for you. And this'—she smooths a palm down the front of my new ice-blue shirt—'is making me horny.'

'Feel free to act on that when we get home.'

'Oh, believe me, I will.'

'Home' is unrecognisable now. With hindsight, giving Soph full creative control over the interior overhaul was hasty. She wasted no time in commissioning the Kit Kemp Design Studio to fill every last inch with colour and print and studs and tassels and triple-framed artwork and fuck knows what else.

It's an over-furnished nightmare and a migraine waiting to happen, but I have to admit I love it. It feels warm and friendly and welcoming, just like my wife.

It feels like home, which is a good thing, because I spend most of my time working from there on getting our app off the ground while Soph attempts to finish her doctorate in between popping out humans. In homage to the incredible brain of the woman who inspired it, we furnished it with all sorts of personality profiling tools for both clients and professionals, enabling them to match on a variety of measures before they meet. The Enneagram, naturally, is one of them.

We called it Lynx, and this summer, Jamie will complete two weeks of work experience on the team ahead of kicking off his Computer Science A Level qualification.

My fleeting tryst with my wife is broken in the most raucous way by the Montague brothers descending on us. The middle brother in their trio, Stephen, is a thoroughly nice bloke and not here today. Meanwhile, Miles and I have become fast friends.

We spent a lot of time together once I was done gallivanting around Australia, brainstorming on the future of the new-look Montague Group once he hired me as a consultant. Turns out, he may not have wanted the Kingsleys calling the shots, but he did value my input—greatly so. And I found I enjoyed the strategic aspect of the endless post-takeover planning discussions far more when I wasn't the one having to implement them all.

Spoiler: he didn't cut nearly enough jobs. I called him a spineless cunt and he called me a cutthroat bastard, and then we went merrily on our way together, establishing what is undeniably the premier luxury hotel group in the UK.

I value his friendship enormously. Underneath it all, we're actually quite similar: intense, understated guys who feel the weight of our responsibilities all too much but have a real passion for business. He and Saoirse have been regulars at our colourful home for dinner, and the weekends we've spent at their Cotswolds pad have been some of Jamie's—and our—favourites.

Theo, however is the one who's done the biggest one-eighty, a fact I'm thrilled about, as I came pretty close to avoiding a punch to the nose from him at times. Not one to hold grudges, it appears, he embraced me like a long-lost brother after I handed the Kingsley empire over to his family on a plate. Apparently, it was *the most legendary fucking move* he'd ever seen.

'Here they are,' he sing-songs, ruffling my hair. 'The gold-standard parents. I swear, Jamie is the most pleasant teen I've ever encountered. It makes me really, really hopeful for the twins.'

I grimace. 'I wouldn't be too optimistic.' Theo and Nora's twins are feral.

His face falls. 'Yeah. You might be right. Glad you guys won the teen lottery, though. Hey, gorgeous.'

This to my wife, whom he kisses dangerously close to her lovely mouth. I'd punch him, but this is Theo. I've long since learnt that it's all bluster, that he's as in love with Nora as a man can be.

Out of nowhere, Aide and Bren rock up behind us, and the four of them encircle me and Soph and Lola.

'We were just chatting about godparents.' Bren scoops Lola out of my arms with ease and she goes shamelessly, grabbing at his face with her tiny hands. His and Marlowe's baby boy, Paddy, is about the same age as her. Bren is a great big softie these days. 'Because the pressure is on. There's a lot of money riding on this. You've got to make the call sometime, Kingsley.'

I grin at him. He, Miles, Theo and Aide have been going on about being Lola's godfathers since the day she was born.

'Soph, have we made any decision yet?' I ask my wife, feigning ignorance.

'Hmm.' She pretends to think. 'Don't think so. We'll probably just flip a coin.'

There is immediate outrage.

'I've known you the longest,' Bren says.

'No, that's probably me.' This from Miles. 'I just didn't like him for most of it.'

'I'd be by far the most fun,' Theo says, and Bren glares at him. Those two are far too similar.

'Look, you want your kid to have some proper guidance in life,' Aide points out. 'And I'm by far the most down-to-earth. I'll introduce her to manual labour and show her how to use a hammer. Don't foist some posh twat on her.'

Beside him, Bren's brother Gabe, who's married to Athena, just smiles in quiet amusement. As a former Catholic priest, he's probably the best placed of all of them to offer spiritual guidance to Lola, but he's not the kind of person to throw his hat in the ring like that.

Soph sighs. 'Okay, we did actually make a decision. And it might sound a little OTT, but we'd like all of you to be godparents. And your other halves. May as well share the love, eh?'

Because here's the thing.

You can't choose your family of origin. My parents are notably absent today—my father because I've rightly given up on him, and my mother because she has too much fear and trauma and whatever else to cross my dad. And that's tragic for her, but her reactions aren't my responsibility. Neither are his. I've learnt that much.

You can, however, choose the family you move through life with, and you can choose the humans with whom you surround your children.

Even better, you can choose that one special person who makes it all worthwhile, who decides to love you in all your chaotic, imperfect glory.

I lock eyes with my wife as, around us, our friends celebrate their joint win.

There was a time when I believed that nobody and nothing was perfect up close.

And I was wrong.

Because Soph is.

THE END

Want some spicy flight attendant roleplay on Ethan's private jet? Of course you do! Here you go - enjoy this steamy **bonus scene**:
https://geni.us/vivacity_bonus

SCROLL FOR AN EXCLUSIVE PEEK AT THE <u>FIRST TWO CHAPTERS OF THE HEIR!</u>

And if you'd like to get to know some of the other non-Seraph couples in *Vivacity* better, I've got you:

Miles and Saoirse | A Very London Christmas
Single Dad | Nanny/Boss
https://geni.us/a_very_london_xmas

Nora and Theo | Wilder at Heart
Faking Dating | Reformed Fuckboy
https://geni.us/wilder_at_heart

Lotta and Aide | The Reluctant Billionaire
Billionaire | Grumpy sunshine
https://geni.us/tr_billionaire

Hello!

Firstly, thank you for bearing with me as I stuffed your spicy pasta sauce full of psychoanalytical vegetables!

I'm only half joking. The approach I took in this book was less about ramming self-help down my readers' throats and far more about using the tools I've discovered to depict a human being with raw, messy, real issues and paint a picture of how he might start to heal.

We all love the 'icy billionaire is thawed and healed by true love' trope. I do as much as the next person. And while the entire premise of romance is that we are better together than apart, the healing of trauma doesn't usually work that easily.

I fervently believe that Soph didn't 'save' Ethan. Nor did she heal him. He saved himself. He healed himself. And, in doing so, he was brave enough to mend the relationships with those he loved the most.

Richard Schwarz, the creator of IFS, named his book *No Bad Parts*. It's a compassionate reframe of the idea that people like Ethan are 'broken'. That all of us, to some extent, are 'broken'. I wanted to show that all of Ethan's issues, his very extreme 'baggage' (or unresolved trauma), contributed to the way he showed up in the world. That the fierce protectors he'd created for himself weren't him being an 'alpha-hole' but were a stunningly effective way for his nervous system to protect younger parts of him that had been deeply wounded so that history never had to repeat itself.

I've been working on myself through parts work for the past year or so, and it's changing my life. Only today, I cried when a nasty man cut me off in traffic (I'm extremely premenstrual so forgive me), and at the same time, I marvelled that three-year-old me was allowed to operate my vehicle in heavy traffic. Terrifying!

The biggest shift, I think, has been that I now view all these parts—the immature, the petty, the frantic, the fearful, the exhausting and exhausted—as pieces of me with valid, if ill-founded, concerns. Pieces that are burdened and that only want to be seen and heard rather than shamed or shoved into a corner (and I'm a Three Enneagram who's a recovering Catholic, so Shame is my middle name).

So, next time you see a fully grown adult melting down or behaving like a small child... now you know why!

And as for the Enneagram—this has totally changed how I see the world. Please know that if we meet, I *will* be allocating you a number with irresponsible speed...

Like Athena, Alexander Hamilton, Oprah, Taylor Swift and, let's face it, probably Lin-Manuel Miranda, I'm a raging Three. So now you know why, to paraphrase *Hamilton*, I write like I'm running out of time and I'm never satisfied.

But seriously, it's transformed how I interact with others. With so many of my author friends who've been through Becca Syme's courses and coaching, we use the language of Enneagram and Clifton Strengths and even parts in our everyday discussions. It's given us language to understand what drives us and others, what makes us us.

I'm a better wife because I understand that my Six husband needs to take care of all of us in the same way that I need to blindly achieve, achieve, achieve. I'm a better mother because I understand that when my came-out-of-the-womb-a-One daughter is worried about making a mistake on her homework, that fear is actually existential to her, and that my Five son needs me not to be in his face twenty-four-seven with my aggressive Three-ness. That he also doesn't give a shit what his teachers think of him, a concept I cannot actually fathom.

I'm also a less burnt-out author and healthier human because I've finally (after 47 years) realised that when I have a strong impulse to *do*, it's usually fear-driven and is an excellent sign that I should instead go and regulate.

I could go on for hours, but I've already preached enough. The main thing I would say is that I've enjoyed so very much using these frameworks to turn these characters into the messiest, yummiest humans and give their hearts and their nervous systems exactly what they need. The human experience is so vast, so wild, and I've had a great time playing with that.

If any of the modalities in this book have piqued your interest, then there is a Further Resources section at the end.

Onto my thank yous!

I was extremely nervous about broaching some of these subjects, so I'm beyond grateful for the lovely experts who've held my hand.

My IFS practitioner, Merete, is an incredibly special human, and I'm so lucky to have her help every week in making sense of the world. She read all the IFS chapters and assisted me in moulding Philip to ensure he was spot on. Thanks, Merete!

I'm so grateful to Sam Sellers, AKA Anchored Counselling Services, for lending her compassion and wisdom to a full sensitivity read of the manuscript. Her knowledge of trauma runs deep, and it made the world of difference being able to lean on her.

A massive thank you to my amazing Susie Tate and Rosa Lucas for once again beta reading and workshopping this with me. They were insatiable Labradors when it came to demanding more and more pages, and they really helped me to shape the storyline and the characterisation. (They really, really liked it when Ethan was a shitbag—their favourite word.)

Thank you to Jennifer Brown for beta reading and to my amazing ARC readers for always giving my newborn book babies the warmest welcome!

A big and overdue shoutout to Shane East and Zara Hampton Brown for their extraordinary acting skills on this series. I am amazed and humbled by the way in which they bring my characters to life in the most beautiful way. Thank you, guys!

Finally, the biggest thank you goes to my fourteen-year-old son Paddy, who very much informed Jamie's character. I'd like to apologise for stealing his entire personality and for being the world's clingiest mum as I was writing this book. It was *hard*. I also owe him a big debt of gratitude for explaining CPUs versus GPUs to me as if I was five and helping me work out what would be the most horrifying blunder possible that poor Jamie could make. Paddy built his own PC last Christmas, a process that was awe-inspiring to behold, while my husband Chris supervised uselessly. I'm happy to report that no tears were shed, no graphics cards fried, and no Teslas stolen.

I'm always so grateful to everyone who shows up for me on social media, especially my Nerds Facebook group, and in person.

Thank you all SO much! I couldn't do it without you.

And that brings the Seraph series to a close. I've had a truly fabulous time fucking these good people up and serving them up a whole host of life lessons alongside some amazing sex. I know they'll all live happily ever after, and I'm sure this won't be the last you see of them.

In true Three style, I'm off to get started on *The Heir* now... the first book in my Belvedere series. Not only is Xavier a modern billionaire duke, but he, like our darling Ethan, has a girthy poker rammed up his arse.

Xavier, I'm coming for you.

Love,

Elodie xx

XAVIER

Heavy is the head that wears the crown.

It may be a misquotation, but it's certainly an effective visual—effective enough that it's become ubiquitous when discussing the burdens of leadership.

The original quote, from Shakespeare's *Henry IV Part 2*, actually goes thus: *Uneasy lies the head that wears a crown.*

I, too, would probably feel uneasy if I were a fourteenth-century king who'd seized the crown by deposing my cousin. But as heir to my father's title, the Dukedom of Oxford, I feel no unease. I feel no burden.

I do, however, feel the addictive *heaviness* of it, the weightiness that cossets me like a weighted blanket, that contains me as securely as a swaddle contains a baby, that moulds me into a vessel fit for a singular purpose. I'm a chalice whose form has been carved, worked upon, for the better part of nine hundred years.

If the form takes the shape of my family's centuries of service to our three constant masters—king, country, and this great estate of Belvedere—then the chalice is the perfect metaphor for the moment when I will assume my desperately ill father's title.

Because I know this much:

I will pour forth from my cup for the rest of my life; I will serve and serve until this humble vessel is empty and hollowed out, and I will never regret a single second of this indentured servitude.

'*Arse.*' My brother's voice cuts into my musings with all the subtlety of a bull in a china shop. Given the ominously delicate crash of china shattering on marble tiles that accompanies his schoolboy curse and the knowledge that our estate, Belvedere, is home to the UK's finest collection of Sèvres porcelain, I suspect the analogy is on point.

Let's be clear: Benedict is far from a schoolboy—in biological age, if not in etiquette. Sixteen months may separate our births—our mother took her duties to produce an heir and a spare seriously—but there are aeons between us in terms of the lenses through which we view the world.

I tear myself away from the view of our magnificent aviary

that this conservatory affords us and round on him. 'For fuck's sake, Ben. Why the hell you have to use the Sèvres for your coffee, I have no clue. Use the fucking Royal Doulton.'

He stands, all six-foot-three of him, an ungainly lout surveying the damage with little more than his customary ill-judged amusement.

'The handle gave out. The whole thing broke right off.'

'Because it's old. And delicate. And priceless. We're supposed to *steward* this stuff, not wreck it. There'll be nothing left for my son to inherit at this rate.'

He gives the cleanly broken porcelain handle in his hand a final glance, shrugs, and chucks it into the marble-edged bed of densely clustered ferns that make this room so wonderfully Victorian. 'You do realise that to spawn an heir you'll have to actually bone Slinky at some point, don't you?'

I grimace at the unnecessary vulgarity. My brother did not walk away from his elite education with a soupçon of class. 'Don't call her that. She's Selena to you. And an illegitimate heir is the last thing this family needs. I'll worry about producing an heir when we're married.'

He winks. 'Practice makes perfect, you know.'

'I'm amazed you don't have that tattooed around your dick.'

Dammit. Mere proximity to Ben has me sinking to his level.

'I'm amazed you can even *find* your dick, let alone operate it. You should take it to the shooting range more often.'

'Your concern is touching, but I do alright for myself. I'm just subtle about it, unlike you.'

It's true. I do alright. And it's also the truth that I keep my sex life tightly under wraps. When you've been promised to a high-profile society beauty since birth, it doesn't give you many options to flaunt relationships, but it hasn't hampered my ability to seek release in other ways. In other bodies. It would be the height of disrespect to Selena to advertise that in any way, though.

'Oh, Alchemy is as subtle as it gets. It's very discreet, so don't you worry. You know you just have to say the word, and I'll propose you. You'd be in like a shot, bro.'

Benedict attended Eton and St Andrews, yet speaks like a frat boy. At least, he speaks to *me* like a frat boy, because he knows it gets my back up.

'I don't need to get my end away in some grubby little sex club, thank you.'

I really don't.

He lets out a honk of laughter. He really is extraordinarily self-possessed. I suppose when you fuck as many women as Ben does, it can recalibrate one's sense of one's own worth far beyond what is seemly.

'It's not grubby. Or little. *Au contraire*, it's spacious and elegant and sexy and perfect for my purposes.'

I would never admit it aloud, but I'm not much better than my brother. I get my clandestine fucks when and where I need them. It's just that there's something so depressingly sordid about institutionalising one's sex life, you know?

'I'm thrilled for you. Now, please leave me alone.' I turn away from him towards the great glass doors and survey the view to the aviary and beyond. It's early September, and the lawns are parched from a dry summer, but the vista still inspires awe and delight, which is, naturally, its entire purpose.

Not for the first time, I give silent thanks Walter de Vere, the eighth Duke of Oxford, who acted the most *nouveau riche* of the lot of us—my dear brother aside—and had the original splendid but apparently dark-as-fuck baroque palace razed to the ground three-quarters of the way through the nineteenth century. In the ensuing decade, he hired a French architect and oversaw the construction of the current manor, which is heavily inspired by the great châteaux of the Loire Valley with its dramatically angled roofs and projecting pavilions and dramatic window treatments.

When the miracles of Victorian heating are at your service, you see, you can bear far grander windows than those poor late Stuarts could. And so, instead of poky windows and dreary rooms, we have French doors punctuating all the main reception rooms, allowing our revellers to spill out onto the lawns at every *soirée* we throw.

My brother, disappointingly, has not taken the hint, ignoring the explosion of coffee and china on the marble and stepping right up beside me.

'Speaking of Alchemy.'

'We really weren't.'

'I thought inviting a few of their—shall we say—*hosts* might spice things up a little at the party.'

If I were a cartoon dog, my ears would prick up and my hackles would rise. 'What party?'

'Your thirtieth, of course.'

'I've already celebrated my thirtieth.'

'You had a boring-as-fuck supper at The *Goring,* of all places, for us, Daph, and Ma and Pa, and your delightful fiancée. That's not a party. That's a fucking retirement dinner. I mean, have some self-respect. Nothing says *I had three good decades and now I give up* like supper at The Goring with your parents.'

I remain silent in my disapproval.

'But...' He singsongs it, then trails off.

I sigh. 'But what.' It's barely a question, because God knows, I don't want an answer.

'But when Ma and Pa head off, we have a chance to make it up to you and put this old girl through her paces.' He gesticulates around the conservatory.

'Absolutely not.'

'Absolutely yes.' He sighs and turns to face me, clamping a

hand to my shoulder. I have an inch of height on him, and I intend never to let him forget it. 'Look, mate. I don't want to be a Debbie Downer, but it's far more likely than not that within a year Pa will be dead and you'll be married off to a woman you have no earthly clue how to handle, and—'

I shake off his grip. I have zero issue with his prognosis for our father and for my inheritance, which are both bang-on, despite the last-ditch trip to the Swiss Alps that Pa and Ma have coming up. I do, however, have a major issue with his infuriating and constant belief that he's the only one of us who knows how to use his dick.

'Hang on a sec. Firstly, don't speak about Selena as if she's a dairy cow, and secondly, I will be perfectly capable of "handling" my wife.'

I don't believe that last part for a moment. My fiancée may be a beauty for the ages, but there's no chemistry between us. Zero. I'm not sure it's even feasible to have chemistry with Selena. It would be like having a spark with a glacier: chemically impossible.

Ben rolls his eyes. 'No you won't, mate. You're far too polite to get around that carefully cultivated ice-queen exterior. You two will pussyfoot around each other, and you'll probably have sex precisely twice, through a hole in the sheet, to produce the heir and the spare. It's a shame, because where you see implacability and sky-high walls, I see a hell of a challenge. I bet, once you warmed her up, she'd be fucking fire.'

I press my lips together in abject disapproval of the salacious and objectifying way my brother is speaking about my fiancée, an exceptional woman who is carrying out her duty for her family, just as I am carrying out my duty for mine.

'Why don't you marry her then, if you fancy yourself such a Lothario?'

That makes him laugh. 'Nice try, bro. I'm entirely satisfied with my lifestyle.'

Of course he is. It's feckless and hedonistic and utterly lacking in any sort of duty or purpose, beyond his job as a fund manager. I use the term *job* in the most tenuous way.

It's far more pleasant to turn and look out at the aviary than at his smug, carefree face, so I do.

He sighs behind me. 'I'm sorry. Look—I know you have a lot on your mind. I know you must feel like the weight of the world is on your shoulders.'

'The difference between us is that I bear that weight gladly.' I don't spit the words out. I say them as fact, which they are.

'I know you do, Save.' He puts a hand on my shoulder again, but it's less aggressive this time, more empathetic, even if the old nickname is meant to sting. Xavier. *Saviour. Save.* Always dutiful. Always serving. 'And I'm grateful, honestly. I'm always grateful. I wouldn't be here at all if it wasn't for you. You know that.'

He's alluding to the thing we don't talk about. The thing we never allude to. I make some indeterminate noise of warning, and he sighs.

'Look. I just think a party would do you good. Let your hair down. Get hammered. Remind yourself that you're not an old fart yet, even if you act like it most of the time. I'll sort it out for you. Leave all the details to me.'

While a large part of me suspects this party is far more for Ben's gratification than for mine, I find I have a lump in my throat. It's not often that he expresses his relief, his gratitude, that the buck stops with me. That my sacrifices will ensure his liberty.

Besides, I suspect he's right.

It would be good for me to let my hair down.

I've put this marriage, this dynastic union between two ancient and powerful families, off for as long as I can. But with Pa not long for this world, I can only drag my feet for so much longer. An evening away from it all would do me good.

I trudge over to the bed of ferns, side-stepping the shit-show on the tiles, and fish the broken-off handle out of the lustrous foliage. 'It isn't a fucking bin, and these aren't *just* ferns, you know. Some of them are believed to be the same plants that the eighth Duke planted. Have a little respect, and try to remember that everything in this damned place depends on our careful stewardship for survival. *Everything.*'

Poor Walter de Vere and his wife Annabel would turn in their graves if they could see the dismissively cruel way my brother treats their legacy. They, like many of their peers, were ardently struck down with the same Pteridomania—that's Fern Fever to you and me—as many of their peers, and the beautiful specimens at Belvedere were one of the myriad ways in which their new home became the ultimate status symbol. Their care and cultivation are beautifully documented by Annabel in her leather-bound gardening diaries, all of which are firmly behind glass in the library.

'Got it,' my brother says in a suspiciously agreeable tone. I suspect he'd rip the piss out of me if he wasn't desperate to get me on board with his little social proposal. 'And the party?'

'Fine. But no sex workers, you hear me? And for fuck's sake, make sure the staff have locked up the Sèvres before anyone shows up.'

I'm still twiddling the sharp-edged piece of china when he saunters off, whistling to himself with the lack of fucks that only a second-born son has to give.

*The Heir -
Chapter Two*

IVY

I stoop to pick up the broken-off handle of the china mug with shaking fingers. The crazy thing is that, as it flew straight at me, my first reaction wasn't *oh shit, it's going to hit me in the face.*

No.

It was more like *oh shit, that's Dawn's favourite mug.*

Wills' and Kate's faded, fractured faces smile up at me from the gilded shards on the floor. Even with my cheekbone breaking their journey, they didn't make it. Dawn bought that from the Buckingham Palace gift shop soon after their wedding, along with a commemorative tea towel. It's her pride and joy. She makes her tea in it every day, and it's only a good weekly going-over with bicarb that stops it from being disgustingly stained inside.

Sorry Wills. Sorry Kate. Looks like you won't be part of her morning ritual anymore. I put my spare hand to my smarting cheekbone—that's definitely going to bruise—and flinch at the pain as much as at the thought of how utterly unrecognis-able my lovely stepmother's morning routine will be in a week's time.

And now she'll have one less familiar item around to ground her. To comfort her.

Jesus.

I glance at her as I straighten up. If I'm worried that the smash of china against our tiled kitchen floor would trigger her, I needn't be. She's staring as blankly at the heir to our throne and his bride as if she had never seen them before.

As if she doesn't have piles and piles of *Hello!* with Kate on the cover next to her bed.

As if the bloody mug hasn't had a strict *hand wash only* edict on it for the past decade or more.

'It's okay,' I murmur, as much to myself as to her. 'It's okay—I'll get the dustpan and brush.'

Her brown eyes fix on me, hard and unseeing. The twins have her eyes. Her mouth is pinched, producing wrinkles that belong on a much older woman. She takes a step towards me and then stops, frozen in her cruel prison of immobility.

'Little slut,' she hisses.

The tears spring instantly to the surface, which is ridicu-lous. Right now, my lovely, warm stepmother doesn't know my name, let alone my profession. It can't mean anything.

It *doesn't* mean anything.

Even if she's not wrong.

I am a little slut. I even make a living from it.

I still have the stupid china handle in my hand. I'm rolling it between my fingers like a stress toy. I force myself to set it down on the cabinet where Dawn's treasured collection of porcelain figurines lives and hold out my hands in surrender as I approach her slowly.

'It's me, Dawn.' I lick my lips desperately. 'Ivy. It's all okay.'

Her eyes dart to the floor and then back to me. 'The mug,' she whispers.

I reach her and put my hands oh-so gently on her upper arms. She's skin and bone. 'Yeah. But it's alright. I'll get you another one from the palace gift shop. They always have those commemorative ones in stock. Maybe we can go together.'

All lies. The only tea Dawn Cooper will be drinking in the near future is from a plastic sippy cup with an easy-grip handle, and the only trip she'll be making is the upcoming journey in a community ambulance to a relentlessly average but extortionately expensive care home that is, thank fuck, equipped to manage the various complexities and indignities of her condition.

My stepmother has LBD, or Lewy Body Dementia. Her eventual diagnosis has been a relief, actually, because every health professional on the planet seemed to disagree with what was actually wrong with her for, oh, I dunno, two or three years. At first they thought it was Rheumatoid Arthritis. Then Alzheimer's. Then Rheumatoid Arthritis *and* Alzheimer's. Then Parkinson's. And I probably can't blame them, because the symptoms of LBD are a mind-fuck of epic proportions.

Anyway.

There's no point in dwelling on it, because even if moving Dawn out of her home and away from her family is totally fucking unthinkable, it can't be worse than what we've all— especially Dawn—had to endure these last few years. The twins can't take seeing their mum like this anymore, and I can't take the guilt and worry that eat away at me twenty-four seven because caring for the woman who's been the only parent I've had for the past few years is killing me.

My only comfort is that Dad isn't alive to see her like this. Not his Dawny. Not the woman who put him back together after Mum died, who gave him two more daughters and ensured that he passed away surrounded by love.

'Let's have a sit-down, shall we?' I say in the overly bright voice that I hate even as I hear it come from my lips. The real Dawn would despise the both of us if she could hear me.

With slow steps, I walk her backwards until she's standing in front of her favourite armchair and, gripping her under her armpits like the pop-in carer from a few months ago showed me, I lower her awkwardly back down. One of the many shitty parts of LBD is that your muscles get really stiff, so your limbs go all rigid.

I'm tucking a soft blanket around her legs when she lays a shaky hand on my arm. Her tremors come and go, but they'll get worse now that she's sitting still. 'Thanks, love,' she mumbles. Her speech is growing more and more garbled these days, but I can still understand her. 'My Ivy. Such a good girl.'

I press my hand against hers, holding her palm to my cheek. These moments may be nothing but chinks of light in the dark fog of her terrifying deterioration, but I'll take them. I'll take every single one of them.

With a tight grip on her hand, I turn my mouth so I can kiss her palm.

There are all sorts of legal workarounds at Alchemy, the super exclusive Mayfair club I work at, to prevent them getting into hot water for employing sex workers. And, if I gave enough fucks, I could use the same workarounds to persuade myself that I'm not actually a sex worker—I'm just a fun-loving young woman who works at a swanky members' club as a skimpily clad host and occasionally (read: nightly) bends over for said members in return for a hefty salary and some very decent cash tips.

But we both know I'd be kidding myself.

I'm not ashamed of what I do, exactly. It's honest work

that's kept the lights on at home since Dad died, and the owners look after us all really well. The other hosts are cool, too. There's no competitiveness—everyone's a team. A family. The real beauty of this gig, though, is that I can work late at night and be around to care for Dawn during the day. So no, I'm not ashamed at all. Nor am I under any illusions that I'd get even a fraction of this money working in a shop or a café. I bailed on my A-Levels when Dad died. I'm not exactly a professional hotshot.

It's more that I'm... resigned to it, I suppose. No one wants to believe they'll fuck entitled pricks for money when they grow up. Then again, my dream was always to be a painter, so a cold, hard dose of reality was always going to be in my future, no matter what happened with my A-Levels.

I probably care less about my profession than I should. The truth is that I like sex. I like it a lot. I've never fucked anyone I don't want to fuck in here, and, even if it's not good, I have a whole host of mind tricks that can help me escape in the moment. I can be tied to a cross in reality, while in my head, I'm sitting in Monet's gardens at Giverny, painting water lilies.

If I'm being honest, I feel less guilty about the actual sex-for-money thing than I do about the secret fact that, much as the general level of privilege in this place pisses me off beyond belief, it also galvanises me, I suppose. I don't know if *galvanises* is the right word, but it inspires me.

If I can't have wealth and luxury in my own life, it's nice to have some second-hand exposure to it. It's like going to Harrods—you never want to leave, even if you are secretly judging the customers who make it look like buying three-hundred-pound face cream is the biggest hassle ever. The luxury is infectious. It seeps into your pores and you can't help but think that maybe, just maybe, you'll catch a case of it yourself. Maybe, one day, it'll stick.

That sounds so stupid. I'd like to think that, dreams of painting French waterlilies aside, I'm a practical person. I have too many real-life problems to waste my time mooning over fancy handbags and overpriced food halls. It's more the vibe that gets me than the actual objects, and it's the same at Alchemy. It's not that I want to be any of the patrons, exactly. It's more that I'd like to live here.

The worse things get at home, the sicker Dawn gets, and the scarier our bills grow, and the more trying to keep on top of housework and the twins' homework gets me down, the more of a relief it is to close that heavy front door at Alchemy behind me and know that, for the next few hours, I'm in this fancy place where everyone's biggest concern is how many orgasms they can have.

The really clever thing about this place, you see, is that it doesn't feel slutty. Or if it is, it's a glamorous, powerful kind of sluttiness. Like, intentional boss-bitch sluttiness. It's in this incredible townhouse on a posh street in Mayfair, and the founders have gone to so much trouble to make every detail of the experience feel super luxurious. Nothing about it is seedy or sordid. All the furnishings are gorgeous (even if the ones in The Playroom are all wipe-clean), and it even smells amazing. They spend a fortune on candles from this crazily expensive French brand called Diptyque so that no one has to endure the scent of jizz, which I'm a fan of.

I first came here with this guy I'd been on a couple of dates with. He was a bit of a twat but harmless enough—a finance bro who asked me out when I was working in a coffee shop in the City for a while. It was quite a baller move for him to bring a date to a sex club, but I owe him a lot, because I got talking to a lovely blonde lady at the bar that night, who turned out to be one of the founders, Gen. She was basically the club in human form—expensive and gorgeous—and she offered me a job on the spot. I couldn't say no when I heard what the pay was.

The guy didn't last past that night, but I gave him a pity fuck next time he was in. It seemed like throwing him a spot of commission was the least I could do for helping me land this epic gig.

It feels weird being here in the middle of the afternoon. Rose and Lily have netball after school today, so they'll be home later than usual, and a sweet neighbour is watching Dawn. I asked Gen if I could have a quick chat with her during office hours. The guys who run Alchemy with her—Rafe, Zach and Cal—are lovely too, but I prefer talking to Gen. And, given she's the one who took a leap of faith on me and gave me my big break, I owe it to her to update her directly.

She hands me a lovely cuppa in a chic white mug that I'm sure costs a fortune, and we sit on the huge, modular sofa in the beautiful, airy front room on Alchemy's ground floor. There's barely anything in here apart from this sofa, a big glass coffee table, and a pink stone sculpture of a vulva that lights up, but in a classy way. Apparently it's onyx. Through the double doors, which Gen has tactfully pulled shut, are the founders' desks.

'How are things at home?' she asks, blowing elegantly on her coffee. Everything Gen does is elegant. She totally reminds me of a younger Hannah Waddingham, all platinum hair and spectacular curves and a fuck-tonne of sass. She's married to this hot billionaire tycoon called Anton Wolff, but if I hadn't seen the way he dominates her in The Playroom, I'd assume she wore the trousers in that relationship. I think she does wear the trousers outside of their sex life, to be fair. And today she is literally wearing the trousers—fabulous white wide-legged ones. Her tank top is a metallic beige-coloured knit, and she's dripping in diamonds, and she looks like she should be walking onto a yacht right now. But she's so incredibly kind and so awesome in general that it's impossible to resent her for it.

Anton Wolff is a lucky man.

I blow on my tea, less elegantly, and grimace. 'Not good.'

'Ahh shit, Ivy. I'm sorry.'

She knows all about my home life, and she's been amazingly supportive. Far more supportive than she should ever feel obliged to be for a random member of staff. She's the reason we started getting weekly home visits—she had some high-up friend unleash hellfire on the NHS when she found out Dawn wasn't getting any at-home support.

I shrug, because it is what it is, and we both knew this was coming.

'She's going into a care home the week after next.' I let out a shuddery breath. 'Which is a good thing.'

Gen stands and comes around the huge sofa to sit next to me, plonking her mug down on the table so she can squeeze my hand.

'That *is* a good thing, and not just for your stepmum, but for you. She needs specialist care, and you need to reclaim your life.' She stops abruptly, no doubt remembering that *reclaiming my life* will involve me officially stepping up as the full-time parent to Lily and Rose.

'Yeah. I know. I'll have to quit when it happens, though.'

'I'm so sorry.' She squeezes my hand harder. 'It's all so shite for you. You're such a little rockstar.'

Here's the problem. Deeply uncomfortable though I have been about leaving the girls with Dawn, and leaving Dawn with the girls, these past few months as things have deteriorated, I didn't really have a choice. The money here is just too good. So I've paid carers to watch Dawn during my shifts, which eats into my earnings. But it's the right thing to do, and Alchemy pays well enough to still make financial sense.

I've always said, though, that I wouldn't leave the twins on their own once Dawn was moved to a home. They're barely fifteen. Putting themselves to bed every night, having no parent figure around until I stumble in in the early hours of the morning, is not a proper upbringing. And I won't do it to them, especially after everything they've been through, and especially when school has restarted and they've just begun their GCSE syllabus.

The woman they know as their mother isn't really there anymore. Not often, anyway. Their father is dead. At a decade older than them, I'm the only parent figure they have, and I'm not about to blow my chances of securing official guardianship by working at a sex club and being physically absent most evenings.

Ain't gonna happen.

I just have no bloody clue what we'll do about the money side of things.

'She's being moved a week on Friday,' I tell Gen now, 'so my last night would have to be the Thursday.'

She releases my hand and picks up her coffee. 'You know, you're always welcome to come back on Saturday nights if you want to make a few quid.'

'Thanks,' I say lamely.

'Do you have a job lined up?'

'Not yet. I've applied at the job centre, so let's see. And I've been asking around at local cafés and shops.'

She's silent. We both know the job centre won't come up with anything that pays a fraction of what Alchemy pays.

'I'll have a think,' she says. 'I mean it. I'll see what I can drum up. But actually, I was going to ask you on your next shift if you're interested in working a special party next Wednesday. It's out of London—Oxfordshire, I believe—but they've agreed to bus you all home at the end of the night.'

'Possibly,' I hedge. It would mean a later return home than

usual, probably. Not great for Dawn or the twins. Sounds like a bit of a hassle, to be honest.

She twists and shoots me a mischievous grin. 'Should be a fab event. A *Grosvenor*-themed party.'

'Oooh.' *Grosvenor* is one of my all-time favourite TV shows. It's set in the Regency era and is so sumptuous and glamorous. I rewatch the first season all the time, which is a super spicy story about an arranged marriage between a duke and his new duchess. Sigh. The chemistry between those two was, like, insane, which isn't a surprise, given the actors went on to marry in real life.

'Exactly. One of our members is throwing it for his brother at the family pile—they're a pretty high-profile family. Benedict? Does that ring a bell?'

I think. 'I might recognise him if I saw him,' I say, which is a polite way of saying *I've probably shagged him, but who the hell knows?*

'Well, anyway, it sounds lavish. Benedict tells me the budget is limitless. He wants some of the Alchemy hosts there to help liven things up, essentially. They'll kit you all out in full costume before the party kicks off. Oh, and it pays well.'

She drops a number so fantastical that I gape at her.

'Bloody hell. Seriously?'

'You interested?'

'Yeah,' I mutter. 'Sign me up. I'll make it work.'

Even without any tips on the night, that figure would put a serious dent in Dawn's first month of care home fees.

She gives me a real smile. 'That's the spirit. I know you'll be a fantastic addition. We'll muddle through this. And maybe a day out of London will be just what the doctor ordered. A fabulous swan song for you.'

It will take a lot more than a few hours cosying up to rich fuckers to fix my current ailment, but who cares?

For that much money, they can have whatever they want.

I'll be the life and soul of their posh, boring party for the whole bloody evening.

Even if, behind my Party Ivy persona, I'm dreaming of oil paint and water lilies.

You can preorder The Heir here:

https://geni.us/the_heir

Further Resources

If you'd like to discover more about some of the issues discussed in Vivacity, these may be of interest.

BOOKS

No Bad Parts: Healing Trauma & Restoring Wholeness with the Internal Family Systems Model - Richard Schwartz

Self Help: This Is Your Chance to Change Your Life - Gabrielle Bernstein

Parts Work: An Illustrated Guide to Your Inner Life - Tom Holmes, PhD

The Essential Enneagram - David Daniels, MD

The Journey Towards Wholeness: Enneagram Wisdom for Stress, Balance, and Transformation - Suzanne Stabile

The Path Between Us: An Enneagram Journey to Healthy Relationships - Suzanne Stabile

How To Do the Work - Dr Nicole LePera

It's Not You: How to Identify and Heal from Narcissistic People - Dr Ramani Durvasula

Adult Children of Emotionally Immature Parents - Lindsay C Gibson, PsyD

～

PODCASTS

You Make Sense podcast by Sarah Baldwin:
Parts Work: How Different Parts of Us Show Up in Our Lives (12 Nov 2024)
Getting to Know Your Protector Parts: Perfectionist, Procrastinator & More (3 Dec 2024)

If you want a free 'course', you could do worse than work your way through this podcast from the beginning. It's fantastic.

The One Inside podcast by Tammy Sollenberger - an entire podcast dedicated to IFS

Exploring the Integration of IFS and the Enneagram with Joan Ryan (7 Jan 2022) - the first of 6 episodes on this topic

We Can Do Hard Things podcast: episodes 226 and 227 with Suzanne Stabile on the Enneagram

~

COURSES

Navigating your Nervous System by Sarah Baldwin

This course taught me how my nervous system works and how to regulate myself when I'm dysregulated. It's incredible.

You Make Sense by Sarah Baldwin (not to be confused with her podcast of the same name)

This is a more expanded course and overlaps slightly with NYNS but also covers parts work, boundary work, family systems, attachment styles and a lot more.